Acclaim for Lauren K. Denton

"Reading a Lauren K. Denton book is like spending time with treasured friends. With her warmhearted Southern voice, she expertly guides readers along the achingly emotional path of a marriage in trouble in *The One You're With*. This poignant story touches on how the choices we make can shape a lifetime, for better or for worse, and serves as a reminder to never take love for granted. Fix yourself a tall glass of iced tea and settle in, because you'll have a hard time putting down this lovely, heartfelt novel."

—HEATHER WEBBER, *USA TODAY* BESTSELLING
AUTHOR OF *MIDNIGHT AT THE BLACKBIRD CAFÉ*

"In *The One You're With*, author Lauren K. Denton dives headfirst into a complicated, tangled situation that shakes the foundation of one family's life as they're forced to reckon with both the past and the future. Denton asks the tough questions, and with great sensitivity and intuitiveness, she unfurls an insightful, emotional story of the impact of the decisions a husband and wife in the present day made two decades earlier. A complex, compelling, powerful story about the roads not taken, the seismic shifts that can happen in an instant, and the way that sometimes, the decisions of the past shape the future in ways we couldn't have imagined."

—KRISTIN HARMEL, *NEW YORK TIMES* BESTSELLING AUTHOR OF
THE BOOK OF LOST NAMES AND *THE FOREST OF VANISHING STARS*

"Lauren K. Denton is a master not only of Southern fiction, but at capturing the nuance of complicated, messy relationships. [*The One You're With*] is one of those rare books that I devoured in less than twenty-four hours, yet didn't want to end."

—COLLEEN OAKLEY, *USA TODAY* BESTSELLING
AUTHOR OF *YOU WERE THERE TOO*

"Denton delivers a moving story about the friendship of two women reeling from betrayal and divorce. Rachel Hauck fans will want to take a look."

—*PUBLISHERS WEEKLY*, STARRED REVIEW, FOR *THE SUMMER HOUSE*

"The perfect summer read! *The Summer House* is a beautifully poignant reminder that we are never too young to find a good place to stand or too old to start over."

—KATHERINE REAY, BESTSELLING AUTHOR OF *THE PRINTED
LETTER BOOKSHOP* AND *DEAR MR. KNIGHTLEY*

"This sweet book about family ties exudes so much Southern charm that the scent of magnolias practically wafts from the pages."

—WORLD FOR GLORY ROAD

"*Glory Road* brims with faith and family, second chances and new horizons."

—LISA WINGATE, *NEW YORK TIMES* BESTSELLING
AUTHOR OF *BEFORE WE WERE YOURS*

"Rich, colorful characters capturing my heart, combined with a story that kept me up till the wee hours, *Glory Road* is a perfect read."

—LISA PATTON, BESTSELLING AUTHOR OF *RUSH*

"Once again Lauren Denton brings her lyrical writing and compelling characters to a story that will enthrall readers from page one."

—MARYBETH MAYHEW WHALEN, AUTHOR OF *ONLY EVER
HER* AND COFOUNDER OF SHE READS, FOR *GLORY ROAD*

"Denton crafts a beautiful story with well-drawn, complex characters about the bonds of family, the trials of parenting, and the power of love to soothe the difficulties of daily life. Suggest for readers of Jane Green."

—*LIBRARY JOURNAL*, FOR *HURRICANE SEASON*

"Any reader who values the comfort of family, the possibility of second chances, and the simple truths of love and sisterhood will devour Denton's novel."

—*BOOKPAGE*, FOR *HURRICANE SEASON*

"Readers will devour this story of the hurricanes—both literal and figurative—that shape our lives."

—KRISTY WOODSON HARVEY, NATIONAL BESTSELLING AUTHOR
OF *SLIGHTLY SOUTH OF SIMPLE*, FOR *HURRICANE SEASON*

"Denton's delicious debut [*The Hideaway*] is a treat for the senses and the heart."

—*LIBRARY JOURNAL*, STARRED REVIEW AND DEBUT OF THE MONTH

"*The Hideaway* is the heartwarmingly southern story about the families we are given—and the families we choose."

—KAREN WHITE, *NEW YORK TIMES* BESTSELLING AUTHOR

"Denton has crafted a story both powerful and enchanting: a don't-miss novel in the greatest southern traditions of storytelling."

—PATTI CALLAHAN HENRY, *NEW YORK TIMES*
BESTSELLING AUTHOR, FOR *THE HIDEAWAY*

the
one
you're
with

ALSO BY LAUREN K. DENTON

The Summer House

Glory Road

Hurricane Season

The Hideaway

the
one
you're
with

Lauren K. Denton

THOMAS NELSON
Since 1798

Published in Nashville, Tennessee, by Thomas Nelson. Thomas Nelson is a registered trademark of HarperCollins Christian Publishing, Inc.

Thomas Nelson titles may be purchased in bulk for educational, business, fundraising, or sales promotional use. For information, please email SpecialMarkets@ThomasNelson.com.

Publisher's Note: This novel is a work of fiction. Names, characters, places, and incidents are either products of the author's imagination or used fictitiously. All characters are fictional, and any similarity to people living or dead is purely coincidental.

Library of Congress Cataloging-in-Publication Data

Names: Denton, Lauren K., author.
Title: The one you're with / Lauren K. Denton.
Other titles: One you are with
Description: Nashville, Tennessee : Thomas Nelson, [2021] | Summary: "Written in Lauren Denton's signature Southern style, The One You're With tells a story of marriage, choices, and what a good life really looks like"-- Provided by publisher.
Identifiers: LCCN 2020056046 (print) | LCCN 2020056047 (ebook) | ISBN 9780785232575 (hardcover) | ISBN 9780785232629 (epub) | ISBN 9780785232636 (ebook)
Subjects: GSAFD: Christian fiction.
Classification: LCC PS3604.E5956 O54 2021 (print) | LCC PS3604.E5956 (ebook) | DDC 813/.6--dc23
LC record available at https://lccn.loc.gov/2020056046
LC ebook record available at https://lccn.loc.gov/2020056047

Printed in the United States of America

21 22 23 24 25 LSC 5 4 3 2 1

To Matt. I'd choose you again and again.

CHAPTER 1

MAC

Summer 2000

"Hey, you."

Mac heard the deep voice but was sure it wasn't directed at him. He'd been at Sunset Marina less than three minutes. Only enough time to park his truck and make his way to the dock, where the woman on the phone had said she'd meet him on his first day of work. No one even knew who he was, much less that he was the marina's newest summer employee. At least he was supposed to be a new employee, if he could just find his way to the woman who was supposed to give him the paperwork to fill out.

"Yo, Polo Shirt." It was the same voice, and this time Mac turned. A pale, skinny guy with tattoos stretching from his wrists to his shoulders stood behind the bar of the tiki hut overlooking the marina. He had a shaker in one hand and held out an empty Styrofoam cooler in the other. He tossed the cooler toward Mac, where it landed a few feet shy and rolled to a stop at his tennis shoes.

"I need ice." The guy shook the canister in his hand. It was only seven o'clock. Who would be drinking this early? His black T-shirt was ripped on the sides and bore Alice Cooper's face on the front, complete with black snakes and creepy makeup. "Ice machine's at the back of the dock store," the guy said around the cigarette in his mouth. "Fill it all the way up, if you think you can carry it."

"I'm not . . ." Mac leaned down and picked up the cooler. "You want me to get it for you?"

The guy widened his eyes. "Who else would I be talking to? You work here, right?"

"I think so."

"Carla had to pull Ruiz's boat out of storage." He set the canister down and took a long drag on the cigarette. "El Patron doesn't like to wait, even when he forgets to follow the rules and call ahead. Ah." He gestured with the tip of his cigarette to a tall lift truck rounding the corner of the tiki hut, holding what must have been a thirty-foot boat high in the air. Driving the contraption was a slight woman with brown, leathery skin and brown-gray hair pulled back in a tight ponytail.

"There's the lovely Carla now. Soon as she gets that bad boy in the water, she'll come around with the clipboard. She does it for all the new guys. Wait for her here. After you get the ice, that is." He flicked a glance down the walkway. "Behind the dock store."

Mac nodded. "Got it. Thanks."

"Yep." He squinted at the smoke curling from the corner of his mouth. "What's your name, kid?"

"Mac."

"Mac with the polo shirt. I'm Dave."

Mac shouldered the empty cooler and followed the wooden walkway past the bar and the shop to a large ice machine out back. He set the cooler at his feet and reached for the edge of the lid, but before he could lift it, someone else sidled up next to him and yanked the lid up. A strong tanned arm plunged in elbow-deep and unearthed the scoop.

Mac straightened up and glanced at the girl next to him. "You're cutting in line," he said with half a smile.

"It's not cutting if there's no line. And I'm in a hurry." She kept her head down as she dumped scoop after scoop of ice into the red Igloo of Miller Lite at her feet.

As she leaned forward, Mac's eyes were drawn down by a power much stronger than his self-control. Her cutoff jean shorts were ripped at the bottom and a hole at the corner of the back pocket showed just the briefest glimpse of something red underneath.

"Who says I'm not in a hurry?" Mac tilted his head to try to see her face. "If I don't get ice to Dave with the tattoos, I'm afraid he may add me to his blender the next time he makes a mixed drink."

"Don't worry about Dave. Depending on how many Bloody Marys he's had this morning, he may not even remember he asked you for ice." She let go of the lid and it slammed shut. Finally she turned and thrust the ice scoop at him. "It's all yours."

He grabbed the edge of the scoop and before she let go, their eyes met. It was just a glance, nothing more than a flash of hazel framed by thick black lashes. A flush of pink in her cheeks made his stomach hum with energy.

"Thanks." He tried to appear cool and casual, but her composure rattled him. "I just got here." He hooked his thumb back to the parking lot. "Well, a little while ago. I'm Mac. I'm new."

"I can tell."

At her obvious appraisal of him, his heart sank a little. "Of course you can. Apparently I stick out."

She hoisted the cooler onto her hip and held it there with one arm. Most of her hair was caught back in a thick braid down her back, but a windblown halo of blonde curls had escaped, framing her face. With her free hand she pushed a lock behind her ear, but it sprang right back. "It's not just you. Every year around this time, we get a new crop of guys in to crew for the summer. You're all pretty easy to spot."

He opened the lid of the ice machine again and scooped ice into Dave's cooler. "What makes it so easy?"

"You all have the same look in your eyes. Pure excitement about doing some real blue-collar work for a few months. You figure you'll get a good tan, make some spending money for next semester, maybe have yourself a summer fling. Then you'll go back to wherever it is you came from and later, when you're forty or something, maybe you'll remember this summer as the best one of your life."

He tossed the scoop in the machine and closed the lid, then turned and studied her. What had started as a lighthearted jab now dripped with resentment.

"I . . ." He didn't know what to say. "I'm sorry?"

She lifted a shoulder. "No need to apologize. Just remember this is a real job for the rest of us. We're not here for flings or tans or to find new friends to take us drinking at the Flora-Bama. We're here to work and make money. We're here to get by."

She reached up and pulled her sunglasses down from the top of her head with her free hand, covering up her penetrating gaze with the oversize white plastic frames. "If everyone does their job, we'll all get along just fine." She strode toward the dock.

"Wait," he called. She paused but didn't turn around. "What's your name?"

After a brief hesitation, she glanced back at him. "Kat."

He wanted to say something that would keep her here for even a few seconds longer, but he couldn't come up with anything to grab her attention.

She lifted an eyebrow and when he didn't speak, she flicked her braid back over her shoulder and resumed her walk toward the docks. "See you around."

Leaving Dave's cooler on the ground in front of the ice machine, Mac took a few steps until he could see around the side of the building. He watched Kat as she made her way down the dock to a large fishing boat tied up in the closest slip, its name, *Alabama Reds*, emblazoned along the side in bright-red letters. With the Igloo still propped on her hip, she stepped onto the edge of the boat and down into the hull, then swung the cooler onto a seat. Several men milling around the end of the dock paused their conversation to watch her, but she either didn't notice or pretended not to.

She lifted her head and called up to a man in a wide-brimmed straw hat standing in the crow's nest at the top of the boat. When he nodded, she gestured for the men on the dock to climb aboard. She stood back with her hands on her hips as each one lumbered onto the boat. When the last one boarded, he rested a hand on her arm and leaned down to say something to her. Even from where Mac stood near the dock store, he could see the displeasure on her face. She glared at the man and he laughed, patted her on the lower back, and joined his friends at the back of the boat.

"New kid," called a raspy drawl from behind him. He turned to see the woman from the tractor, Carla, standing by Dave's cooler, staring at him. "I've been looking for you. Dave said you ran off with his cooler." She nudged the now-full cooler with her toe.

"No, I . . ." His words trailed off when Carla cocked a skeptical eyebrow at him. "I'll take it back to him now." He leaned down to pick it up, but Carla stopped him.

"Slow down, bucko. I need you to fill these out first. Birth date, social security number, address." She pointed to a few places on the second page. "And here's your W-9. When you finish, I need to make a copy of your driver's license, then you'll be ready for work." She handed him the clipboard and yanked up the waist of her pants. "I'll be in the store. It's cooler in there. Find me when you're done and I'll show you around."

On her way back to the store, she stopped. "A word of advice. It's not your job to worry about Kat. She can hold her own with those guys and she'll toss 'em overboard if they get too close. She's done it before." And with that, she tightened her ponytail and strode back around the side of the building.

Mac flipped through the papers clamped to the clipboard and sat on the ground next to the ice machine, his back propped against the wall. The top line of the first page asked for *Job Title*. Someone, presumably Carla, had already filled in the words *Dock Crew*. It was the job he'd applied for back in March when he realized if he didn't get away, even for a short time, he'd lose everything he'd worked so hard to put into place.

With only one more year of college ahead of him, tests to score well on, medical school to apply for, a future to plan, two parents to please, a girlfriend to try to keep happy, and a brain that wouldn't stop second-guessing everything at every step, Mac had been on the verge of cracking under the pressure for many months. Telling Edie he needed a break—permanent or temporary, he wasn't sure—had relieved some of the pressure, but it was more like a pinprick, not the flood of relief he longed for.

His best friend, Graham, had already planned to stay at his aunt's beach house for the summer, working a construction job in Gulf Shores for a contractor friend of his dad's. When Mac asked if he could come along, Graham told him to find a job, pack his bag, and head for the little blue house on Old River.

Mac had had friends who'd worked summer jobs at Sunset Marina in high school, and he'd always been jealous of them. While they spent the long summer days working on the docks and in the dock store selling T-shirts, canned drinks, and sunscreen, he'd been working in his father's cardiology office, filing papers, sitting in on patient checkups, and occasionally observing surgeries. He enjoyed it some—he'd always known he was destined for the medical field—but he also wished he'd been allowed to plan his summers, and his life, on his own terms. To make his own way.

Now, at twenty years old and just before his senior year of college, he was finally getting that chance. *"Better late than never,"* Graham had told him as Mac deliberated back in the spring. *"Doctors don't get summer vacations, you know."* Edie, Mac's girlfriend of seven years, wasn't quite as effusive about his decision to go to the beach. But seeing as she'd taken the opportunity to haul herself to the Big Apple for the summer, it seemed they'd both be getting some breathing space.

A breeze off the water ruffled Mac's hair and carried the scent of motor oil and the salty-fresh Gulf of Mexico. He leaned his head against the wall behind him, thankful for the three months ahead of him, days of sunshine and fresh air, time and space to think.

That spring, he and Edie had asked each other big, grown-up questions for the first time. Were they going to stay together after graduation? Was marriage on their horizon? Could they imagine a life apart from each other? When they realized they couldn't answer them, they decided to take some time apart.

Mac loved Edie—of course he still loved her—but he needed this summer to figure out what he really wanted and what they both needed.

Without thinking, Mac cast a glance over to where Kat was now perched on the front of the fishing boat untying a line. As her hands worked the rope with quick, assured skill, her words ran through his mind. *"This is a real job for the rest of us. A way to get by."*

What she didn't know was that this summer could very well prove to be Mac's way of getting by too. Because if he had stayed behind, either back at Southern College taking more premed classes or down in Mobile at his dad's office, he likely would have let go. And the crazy thing was, a part of him wanted to let go of it all—the image of a picture-perfect future he'd clung to for so long. Everyone's lofty expectations that pressed hard on his shoulders. Maybe even the hand of the only girl he'd ever loved.

He hadn't admitted it to anyone—not to Edie, not to Graham, definitely not to his parents—but sometimes he felt that he'd lost his way. He didn't know exactly where things had gone off course, but he was determined that this summer, he'd find his way again. He'd find his true north.

With the papers filled out, Mac stood and inhaled again, coaxing the warm air deep into his lungs, then blowing it out along with the last dredges of tension in his neck. He cast one last glance at the *Alabama Reds*, then grabbed Dave's cooler and walked back toward Carla and his first day of work.

CHAPTER 2

EDIE

Summer 2000

Three days after the end of her junior year at Southern College, Edie Everett sat in Terminal C at the Birmingham International Airport, nursing a lukewarm cup of coffee and trying to tamp down the flutter of nerves in her stomach. She checked the front pocket of her carry-on bag again to make sure the flimsy paper packet holding her tickets was still there. BHM → ATL, ATL → LGA. LaGuardia Airport. New York City.

She slid the packet back into her bag and took another sip of her coffee before leaning back against her seat. She'd kissed her parents goodbye at the glass doors to the airport an hour ago, and for the last twenty minutes, she'd been people watching in the busy terminal, wondering if she'd made the right decision. Wondering if she'd made any right decisions. As for deciding almost on a whim to go to New York City, having snagged a pipe dream of a summer internship, the verdict was still out. She'd never done anything like this before—jumped into any kind of situation or experience blindly, not knowing the people, the plan, or the outcome.

She was being hard on herself—she did know a few things. Like where she'd be working and the type of work she'd be doing. And she knew the likely outcome of the trip itself—returning home with a sketch pad full of street and park scenes, an appreciation for the work of real interior designers, and very likely a new love for a thriving city.

But her outcome? That was the mystery. Instead of planning the wedding she'd assumed she and Mac would inevitably have the summer after graduation, she and Mac weren't even spending the summer together. While she was on her way to her New York City internship, he was headed to the beach for three months of pumping gas into expensive boats and—what? Tying ropes? Selling bait? She honestly had no idea what he'd be doing. Just that he'd gotten a job at Sunset Marina in Orange Beach.

It was a far cry from the previous four summers when he'd worked at Swan Cardiology, learning a very different set of ropes under the scrutiny of his father and packing in the hours he hoped would make his medical school application stand out from the rest. Would *dockhand* make much of an impact on those applications?

Edie stood and stretched her back, then walked a few paces closer to the TV, where a meteorologist wearing suspenders pointed out Birmingham's predicted high temperature for the day. She dropped her cup in the trash can, and it thunked at the empty bottom.

Mac could write whatever he wanted on his applications. He could write *zookeeper* or *ice cream scooper* or *Sunset Marina dockhand*. His grades were enough to get him into any school he wanted, and even if they weren't, Mac himself was enough. He could sell the proverbial ketchup Popsicle, not because of any persuasive manners or sales pitches but because of who he was. Mac was a good one—warm, friendly, humble. Generally the nicest human she knew. Edie had no doubt he'd do whatever he set his mind to—med school, doctor, mayor. Husband. Father.

After their last conversation, would she be there to see any of it?

Edie sat back down next to her bag and checked her camera in the side pocket. She'd packed extra film, but her dad had handed her another pack of three rolls this morning when he and her mom walked her into the terminal.

"Good luck this summer," he'd said as he pulled her into the crook of his shoulder. "And take as many pictures as you can. I've always wanted to see New York City." He winked and smiled, but sadness glimmered in his eyes.

Bud Everett was a hulking bear of a man with arms always ready to hug but a mouth that closed anytime something personal came up. He loved with his presence—with his warm hugs rather than with words. Edie wanted to reassure him that she'd be fine, that she'd be safe and return home in one piece, but as usual her mom had taken over, griping about Mac's absence.

"He should be here to see you off. It's just common decency, especially with the history you two have." She shook her head. "Did he know what time you were leaving?"

"He's already down at the beach, Mom. I told you that."

"Well. Still. He could call, couldn't he? Do you want to call him? Here, Bud, take her suitcase."

It was usually pointless to argue with Dianne Everett, but in a flash of something like defiance, Edie yanked the handle of her huge red rolling suitcase, waved to her parents, and strode down the walkway toward her gate.

In another life she may have been spending the summer in New Orleans, learning under one of the myriad designers in the city, drawing sketches for homes along St. Charles Avenue or Magazine Street. Or she could have been taking the summer to sit in Jackson Square and people watch, painting quick watercolors if a particular scene or person caught her eye, maybe making a few dollars selling her scribbles to souvenir-hungry tourists.

It was just a guess though. Having sent the dean of admissions at the New Orleans School for Design a polite "I'm sorry but my plans have changed" note a scant few months before the start of college, she'd never know what that other life would have looked like. Instead she sat at Gate 4 in Terminal C, thinking of the many paths a life can take and wondering how to choose the right one out of all the possibilities.

A little while later, searching for a piece of gum in her bag, her fingers found something else. A piece of paper, small and folded. She pulled it out and stared at it. It was graph paper, white with light blue lines. A smile tugged at the corners of her mouth—it was just the kind Graham used in his architecture classes.

She let her smile loose as she unfolded the paper, then smoothed it across her knees, running her finger along the creases until they lay flat. His handwriting was loopy and imprecise, unlike his drawings, which were full of sharp angles, straight dark lines, confident and sure strokes. She let her eyes dance across the page, savoring the swirls and dashes that made up the words he'd written to her.

Dear Edie,

You've spent this whole evening sitting on the floor of your dorm planning what you're going to pack for your summer in New York. I know because I tried to drag you out for pizza, but you said you had too much to do. All your lists were spread out next to you—what you plan to bring, what you need to buy, what you need to do before you leave. You seemed nervous. I don't know if that's because you'll be spending the summer in a new place or because you and Mac broke up.

Anytime the two of you hit a rough patch, I try to stay neutral, but it's harder this time. Part of me wants to yell at Mac and shake some sense into him. To do whatever it takes to make him see the good thing in front of him before it's too late. The truth is, as much as I love him, I'd rather lose his friendship than see you be hurt.

And there's my plain truth. You know I love Mac—he's been my best friend since fourth grade—but it's you I hold high in my heart. As high as I can possibly hold someone. And while I'll be sad not to see your face for the entire summer, I'm so glad you're taking this trip. I hope you take the time to figure out what you want and need. Not you and Mac. Just you. Y'all have been together so long you're almost like the same person, but I hope you find the real Edie up there in the big city. I hope you discover so much about yourself that you come home bursting. I fc one can't wait to see it.

Call me if you need to. Or, if it's easier, considering I'll be sper the summer in a tiny beach house with Mac, just send me a postcard. I'll check the mail every day.

Graham

After reading the note a second time, Edie folded it along its original creases and, with shaking hands, pressed the small square into her palm. Graham was her friend, her confidant, her partner in late-night fast-food runs when Mac was busy studying, but she was pretty sure she'd never heard so many words from him at one time in the almost eight years she'd known him. She also wasn't sure she'd ever been on the receiving end of words full of such support, such affection, such validation. And she wasn't sure how that made her feel.

Mac was her person, the one she'd always known she'd marry. They'd been friends since preschool days, and once he'd asked her to be his girl-friend in ninth grade, she—and seemingly everyone else—had known they'd end up together. It was fact, not possibility. Until lately when things had begun to slip. When she'd started to wonder if her life had thus far taken her in the direction she was meant to go. When she wondered if somewhere along the way, she'd confused facts for conveniences.

But reading these words from Graham sent a rejuvenating burst through her, like a zap of lightning or a rush of crisp, cold air in her face. She wasn't just getting away for the summer; she was setting off on a grand adventure. A journey to parts unknown with no one else around to tell her what to do or how to feel. With no one but her and her own desires as her guide.

She tucked the note back into her bag and glanced at her watch. With still a little time left before boarding her flight, she grabbed her bag and headed down the terminal walkway to the newsstand she'd seen on her way in. Next to a display of magazines and newspapers was a spinning rack of postcards featuring picturesque locations around Alabama. She found an oversize one showing the sun setting behind the *Vulcan* statue and took it to the register.

"Can I mail this here?" she asked the man behind the counter.

He nodded and she paid for the card, then sat at a table in front of the newsstand and began to write.

The One You're With

Dear Graham,

I'm waiting to board the plane and I just found your note. After reading your words and soaking them all the way in, I realized I wasn't ready for my trip—I wasn't even all that excited—until now. It's like you've given me permission to go and experience and not look back. At least not for three months. So thank you for that. You're a true friend to me, and I hold you high as well. I know you'll be down south this summer, but I'm tucking you in my heart and bringing you with me to New York.

Mac and I are supposed to call each other this summer and check in, but I'm not sure I'll be able to. Or if I'll want to. So just do me a favor: keep an eye on him. I don't know what he's looking for this summer, and as confused as I am about our direction—our future, even—I hope he finds it.

Keep checking the mail. I'll write soon.

Edie

She wrote out the address, added a stamp, and left the postcard with the cashier, who tossed it into a box labeled Outgoing. Edie smiled as she walked back to Gate 4, thinking of Graham walking down the sandy driveway to the mailbox and peeking inside. He'd laugh when he pulled out her *Vulcan* postcard, as if she couldn't wait until she got to New York before writing to him. Which was the truth.

It wasn't until she sat back down in her seat in the terminal that she realized she hadn't written to Mac. It hadn't even crossed her mind. She leaned forward and pressed her elbows onto her knees and rubbed her hands across her face.

It's fine. It's just fine.

She and Mac weren't together, and it was perfectly okay for her to keep in touch with Graham, one of her very favorite people on earth. Reading such a tender letter from him. Gulping his words like air when she hadn't realized she was suffocating.

She took a deep breath, and when the gate attendant called for boarding to begin, Edie was the first one in line.

CHAPTER 3

EDIE

Present Day

When Edie walked into Southern Stone and Tile, Domingo was waiting with a grin.

"Edie Swan, maybe we should just give you a job here. Your arms look pretty strong—how do you feel about cutting stone instead of designing it?"

Edie laughed and greeted Domingo, her "guy" at Mobile's countertop emporium. It was her third trip out here this week. "I think I'll leave the cutting and hauling to you guys. I'd better stick to what I know."

"You know as much as any of us," he said. "We should probably give you your own desk here."

"Actually that's not a bad idea. I'll take the one in the corner, if that's okay with you."

Domingo laughed. "What brings you out here again?"

"The Donalds."

"What? We have them down for the white Carrara."

"Exactly. And they were excited about it until Laura Lou dropped a bomb on them."

"A bomb?"

"Yep. A bomb in the form of black fossilized limestone."

"She didn't. This late in the game? The marble they already chose—the exact marble they wanted—is scheduled to be cut on Monday."

"I know. I reminded Carol that we found just what she wanted. But once Laura Lou mentioned the fossilized snail shells, Carol was a goner."

"Not me, man." Domingo shuddered. "Knowing all those critters died in that stone—kind of gives me the creeps."

"What'll be harder is the fact that Laura Lou also suggested we make the stone along the wall under the window one long, unbroken piece. Which means I get to play musical chairs with all the appliances now." Edie propped an elbow on the counter and laid her forehead against her arm. "I reworked that wall a dozen different ways and finally got everything to fit. Not that it matters now. When Laura Lou gets a bee in her bonnet about something new she wants to try, the clients go right along with whatever she says. You remember the Barnetts?"

"Of course I do. How could I forget?" Domingo patted Edie's hand. "I'm sorry. I'm happy to show them the limestone though. Even if it is a sad little burial ground." A phone rang from an adjacent desk. "Hey, tonight's your husband's party, isn't it? The big 4–0?"

She'd told Domingo about the surprise party she'd planned for Mac's fortieth birthday when she made her first trip out here earlier in the week for another client. "Yep. Tonight's the night. Come six thirty, the Donalds' limestone and their window elevation will be the furthest thing from my mind."

The front door chimed and they both turned to see perky Carol walking in, her husband, Mike, behind her.

"Hi, Carol," Edie said. "Mike. Y'all remember Domingo. He's going to show us out to the limestone."

"Ooh, I can't wait." Carol clasped her hands together. "I've been thinking about those little fossils since Laura Lou told us about it. She's just a whiz, isn't she? Who else would have thought to add black and white fossils into the mix?"

Edie nodded and pulled her cheeks up into what she hoped passed for a smile. "Yep, that Laura Lou. She is a whiz."

Domingo opened the door and ushered them all outside and toward the large building in the back. The warehouse was loud, with a saw blaring at one end and box fans in each corner swirling the dusty air into a hot breeze. Domingo led them to the far right side where several slabs of striking black-and-white stone were propped against the wall. Lo and behold, the fossils were tiny snail shells.

Carol nearly shrieked with glee. "Look at them, Mike. Aren't they cute?"

Domingo crossed his arms in front of his chest. "This stone was quarried from a seabed in Greece. It's fifty million years old." His implication was clear: it was ancient, not cute.

"Can we have a few minutes?" Carol asked. "I'd like to really take my time."

"Of course." Edie backed up as Carol and Mike scrutinized the stone. "I'll be right over here if you have any questions."

She snagged a seat near the door where a breeze from one of the fans rushed her direction every few seconds, blowing her dark curls around her face. The Donalds' "few minutes" turned into twenty, then thirty. Domingo stood a few rows away from them, and when Edie caught his eye, he tipped his head toward Carol and Mike and tapped his watch.

She nodded and bit her thumbnail. Just as she was about to walk back over to check in with them, her phone dinged with one text, then an email. Both from Laura Lou. Both suggestions for how to make adjustments to the designs Edie had planned for two of her biggest clients.

Laura Lou Davis was the founder of Davis Design Group, one of the most well-known and in-demand firms in Mobile. DDG boasted four designers, including Laura Lou, and three project assistants. They were a small outfit to be so respected, but after working at another design firm for four years before joining DDG—one that had fourteen designers all trying to poach each other's projects—coming to work for Laura Lou had been as much a relief as an honor.

The honor was still there—Edie still got a thrill to be able to say she was a Davis designer—but the relief had long since worn off. At least at Teak & Twill, her first design job after college, once a designer was chosen or assigned to a particular job, it was hers to run with. Any design she worked up was hers alone. With the client's input and approval, of course.

At DDG, any design was subject to Laura Lou's input, and her input generally superseded anything anyone else came up with. With the intrusion of her "helpful" suggestions—"Why don't we try a pocket door here?" or "Did you think about using acrylic drawer pulls here?"—Edie's work often shifted from her own design to Edie and Laura Lou's lopsided collaboration.

Laura Lou had yet to scrap anyone's total design package—yet—but Edie still squirmed with irritation when she thought back to last year's Point Clear disaster. After a requested last-minute "consultation" with Laura Lou regarding the Barnetts' new bay house, Edie's modern farmhouse design, complete with a shiplapped wraparound porch Julie Barnett had specifically asked for, had been reduced to a sleek, industrial nightmare. Laura Lou had been so excited about her stroke of genius that resulted in the overhaul, she practically broke out in hives. Her elation with the final design package must have rubbed off on the Barnetts because, much to Edie's surprise and dismay, they agreed to every last change.

To Edie, it was an eyesore, especially considering the more elegant and traditional homes surrounding it, but *Bay* magazine featured it on their cover for the Christmas issue, and everyone congratulated her on designing such an out-of-the-box stunner.

She dropped her phone back in her bag and approached the Donalds. "I'm sorry to have to run out on you, but Domingo is here if you need anything. And you can call me anytime. If you decide you do want the limestone, we'll need to talk about paint color for the walls and possibly a different finish on the sink faucet. The black and white may not play as well with what you've already chosen."

Carol's face fell. "Oh."

Edie gave her a small smile. "It's a little like dominos. If you make a big change like this, you have to make sure everything still fits. Especially if you decide to move the oven from under the window."

"I see. And will that push our end date back?"

"It may not. It really depends on the different suppliers. I know you have your daughter's engagement party coming up."

"Yes, we do. In December."

"Bottom line, it's your kitchen and your decision. It's a beautiful piece of stone and if you decide on the overhaul, we can work through the plan again and make any necessary adjustments."

Domingo met Edie at the door to the warehouse with a grin on his face. "Laura Lou Davis isn't the only whiz." He kept his voice low. "You're a master. Bringing up their daughter's party? Sneaky. No way will they change their minds now."

"I'm not trying to be sneaky. I just know how convincing Laura Lou can be, and I want them to have all the information before they agree to any big changes. I think our plan from last week is the best arrangement and color scheme, according to what Carol originally told me, but if she decides to go ahead with Laura Lou's changes, I'll do what I can. Even if it does mean I'm back to square one with the drawings."

"That's why they pay you the big bucks, right?"

Edie laughed. "If you say so."

As she walked out of the warehouse and into the bright September sun, she thought about her role as a designer. Edie loved her job, loved designing beautiful spaces for clients, spaces that made them feel at home and at peace when they walked into a room. And she was good at it too. She knew that. But no matter how many kitchens she updated, how many bedrooms she designed, how many houses she renovated, it always felt like something was missing.

Part of it was due to the frustration of having her design packages so often picked apart by Laura Lou. Take the Donalds' kitchen, for example. Edie could have figured out another configuration for the appliances, helped Carol choose another finish for her faucet, tweaked the paint choices, and done anything else necessary to make the kitchen beautiful and functional. But at the end of the day, it was hard to be proud of her work when the heart and soul she'd worked so hard to put into it were chiseled away.

Most of the time, she could call it a fair trade-off. Yes, the micromanaging bothered her, but Laura Lou was, on the whole, a good person to work with and for. She'd been designing houses across the Gulf Coast for thirty years, and Edie had learned more about design in her first year with DDG than she had in her entire design program in school plus the four years she spent with Teak & Twill. She could toss down her pencil and walk away at any time, but that would mean allowing herself to be pushed out of the only career she'd ever wanted. She didn't want to stop doing it, and a move to any other established design house would be a step down.

But it was more than that, wasn't it? There was that quiet, nagging voice embedded deep in her mind that reminded her she could have been doing more. More than just kitchens and bathrooms that, to be honest, were all starting to look the same. More than designing spaces and waiting for Laura Lou's bright-green Post-its bearing the message, "Let's discuss."

The voice reminded her she could have been doing what she loved somewhere else. With someone else. The uncharted path called to her the most when her defenses were down, when she was the most frustrated, the most exhausted. The voice was easy to shut down—she'd been doing it for years—but it called to her nonetheless.

———

With the warm sunshine and gentle breeze swooping in from the bay, Edie lowered her windows as she drove back into town. Oak Hill, where she and Mac had both grown up, was a small community a few miles west of downtown Mobile. It was named Oak Hill by the original settlers of the area who'd followed an old Indian trail to the top of a hill and found grand live oak trees, green-gray moss hanging from the wide-spreading arms, and sweet-smelling air. Those settlers, mainly wealthy downtown residents, poured broken oyster shells over the old trail and built their summer residences on that hill.

Two hundred years later, the area was still a respite of sorts—a small, tightly knit community of stately homes, tree-lined streets, and charming shops and businesses tucked into old renovated cottages.

Edie arrived outside one of those cottages and pulled into the only open spot out front, which happened to be next to Laura Lou's brand-new cherry-red Fiat 500. Not for the first time, Edie wondered about her boss's preference for very small cars. Laura Lou's last car had been a Mini Cooper in the same signature shade of red, which also happened to be her lipstick color of choice.

Edie was constantly hauling things to clients' homes or construction projects: a chair to try at a kitchen island, boxes of backsplash tiles to hold up against cabinets, fruit and flowers for photography shoots after a home was completed. Thankfully for Laura Lou, she had three project assistants who happily did all the heavy lifting for her.

Inside the cool, crisp, spotless lobby, Edie waved to the receptionist and headed down the hallway past the project assistants' offices, each one meticulously decorated with ceramic pots of succulents and felt letter boards with messages like "You Glow Girl" and "Friday: I'm here for it."

Laughter swelled from the kitchen in the back. Edie intended to pass right by and avoid the excitement, but when she heard her name, she paused.

"How'd it go with the Donalds?" one of the assistants, Anne Allen, asked her. The girls were all huddled around a magazine lying on the table.

"It was fine. They're still thinking about—" Edie stopped when she saw the front of the magazine the girls were gawking at. More specifically, who was smiling up from the cover.

"Can I see that for a minute?" She reached for the magazine.

He was sitting in front of a large wooden drafting table in a room lined with overfull bookshelves. One wall was filled with tall windows, and a couple comfortable chairs could be seen at the edges of the photo. Edie remembered that room well. Nothing about it had changed. The man was wearing a faded black tee under a blazer, worn jeans, and black Converse low tops.

Not long ago, Edie had run into an old friend she hadn't seen since her family left Mobile after sixth grade. "You look exactly the same!" her friend gushed, though Edie knew they were empty words. Of course she didn't look the same. Time had marched on, and its movement was visible on her face, in her body. But seeing Graham Yeager on the cover of *Bay* magazine, Edie understood that the concept could be true.

The years had lined his face, of course, but his dark eyes and high cheekbones were the same. His hair was thinner and cropped close, but it was mostly still the dark, almost blue-black it had been when they were younger. And his mouth, tweaked up at one corner as if he were faintly amused by the photographer holding the camera, sent her spinning backward through the years.

"He's so hot," Katie Jo said.

Anne Allen nodded. "Yeah, but he's also a fantastic architect. Winning the McLeod Award is a big deal for architects. Right, Edie?"

"Hmm? Yes. The McLeod is a . . . well, it's a big recognition. And he's . . ."

A quiet moment passed, then the other girls laughed and Maryanne reached for the magazine. Edie reluctantly passed it back. "Even Edie thinks he's cute! And look." She pointed to Graham's hand resting on the arm of the chair. "No wedding ring."

"Maryanne!" Katie Jo laughed. "He's way too old for you. He must be at least fifty."

Only off by a decade.

Laura Lou appeared in the open doorway, her dark hair shining in the overhead lights. Laura Lou's hair was the same every day—a chic, sleek bob that angled down severely in front, the right side tucked behind her ear to show off a large diamond stud. "Did someone forget to invite me to the party?" She noticed the magazine Maryanne held and smiled. "Ah, Graham Yeager. Of course. We've all been hearing a lot about him lately, haven't we?"

She reached out her hand and Maryanne handed over the magazine. Laura Lou thumbed through it and stopped on the full-page spread in the middle. "He's good." She leaned one hip against the doorway. "So good I'm thinking about bringing him on."

"Bringing him on?" Edie asked. "As in hiring him here?"

"Why not? Architecture and design go hand in hand. Maybe with the McLeod under his belt, he'd be interested in partnering." She shrugged.

"It's just a thought. You know him, right, Edie? Didn't you both go to high school at Oak Hill Academy?"

"We did." Edie ignored the strange fluttering in her chest. "College too."

Katie Jo gasped. "You're friends with him?"

"Friends is a bit of a stretch these days."

"But do you think he'd consider partnering up?" Laura Lou asked. "Coming on board as Davis Design's architect in residence?"

"I really don't know. It's been years since we've talked."

"Hmm. Maybe we can track him down. Feel him out."

"It shouldn't be too hard to find him. He lives over the bay." Maryanne tapped the magazine. "Says so in here. His father died and he's planning to renovate his dad's house in Point Clear."

Graham's dad died? How had Edie not heard that?

"I'm sorry to hear about his dad," Laura Lou said. "But I can't say I'm sorry he's moved back." She adjusted the pearl necklace at her neck. "Keep an ear out, Edie. Let me know if you hear anything interesting."

"Oh, I don't think I—"

But Laura Lou was already headed down the hall.

A moment later the girls' chatter picked back up again. "Can you imagine if he worked here? I'd hardly get a thing done."

"I wouldn't be able to focus staring at that face all day."

The girls giggled and Edie took the opportunity to back out and hurry down the hall to her own office, thankfully quiet and still. She tossed her leather backpack down on a chair in the corner and crossed the soft blue-gray rug to her desk.

Edie sat for a minute, her head swirling with fractured memories. In front of her on top of her desk was a fresh sheet of the graph paper Graham had gotten her hooked on back in high school. He'd always used it, not only for his drawings but for English essays, calculus equations, and random song lyrics he was perpetually jotting down in his looping handwriting. He'd given her a sheet of his paper one day and she quickly learned to love it.

Two decades later, Edie still preferred paper over the computer, and she kept sketches, blueprints, and notes on everything from measurements and color choices to dollar amounts and time frames within the bounds of the same predictable squares. The thin blue lines and tiny boxes calmed her now just as they did back then, as if by keeping everything in its right box, she could help life stay on course and in line.

The gossip train in Oak Hill rarely missed a thing, and as such, she'd heard a few months ago that Graham was back in town. The knowledge that he was close by had been like a rock stuck in her shoe—she'd forget about it for a while, but then it would jar her out of nowhere, unsettling her with its presence. And seeing his face on the magazine had yet again jolted her from the present back to the past.

Since Edie had last seen him, Graham had begun to feel like a ghost of that past. They'd shared a different kind of friendship than the one she'd shared with Mac, and for a time, she wondered . . . maybe even wanted?

But then he was gone. For so many years his absence from her life—and not just hers but Mac's too—had felt like an empty, yawning canyon. A blank space that had never filled back up.

CHAPTER 4

EDIE

Present Day

Edie was at her desk, third cup of coffee steaming, the Donalds' window elevation spread out in front of her, when she heard Laura Lou greet someone in the front lobby. Her voice was sugary and chipper, a tone she only used when trying to impress someone or lure in a big-name client.

Surprisingly, the voice that replied belonged to Turner Kennedy. Edie didn't know Turner well, but that didn't mean she didn't know about him. A self-made multimillionaire, he had his hands in everything from shipbuilding and forestry to hotels and restaurants. Turner Kennedy was the quintessential Southern gentleman, with his slow, consonant-dropping drawl, as well as the most prominent businessman in the Mobile area.

Though why he was standing in their lobby, Edie had no idea. Unless it had something to do with his newest acquisition—a prime plot of bayfront property within spitting distance of the Grand Hotel.

It was a rare occurrence for a property like this to go on the market, but Turner had gotten wind of the potential opportunity before it hit the market and offered top dollar for it. He already owned a veritable palace on Ono Island, and rumor had it he also had a spread down on Harbour Island in the Bahamas, but he'd never staked his own claim on Mobile Bay. Until now. The word around town was that he was planning to build his very own Kennedy compound on his new stretch of grass, sand, and gracious oaks, though as far as anyone knew, he hadn't made a move to begin the building process. Everyone in the local architecture and design world had been waiting to see who he'd hire for the job.

"What can I do for you today, Mr. Kennedy?" Laura Lou asked out front.

"I was in the area and thought I'd just pop by for a minute." Edie listened to a few seconds of small talk before her spine froze at his next question. "Is Mrs. Swan here, by any chance?"

"Edie? Sure, sure. She's around here somewhere. I'll show you back."

A moment later, Laura Lou tapped on Edie's door and leaned her head in. "Edie! There you are," she said, as if she'd had to search far and wide to find her. She turned and grasped Turner's elbow, which was all she could reach, considering Turner stood well over six feet tall and Laura Lou was more like five-one in heels. "Mr. Kennedy came by to say hello. He'd like to have a word with you."

Turner laughed. "Now, Ms. Davis, that makes it sound like she's getting sent to the principal's office. There's no need to worry, Mrs. Swan."

Edie smiled and stood. "What can I do for you, Mr. Kennedy?"

"Do you mind if I . . . ?" He gestured to the rattan chair in front of her desk.

"Of course. Come on in. Have a seat."

"Ms. Davis," Turner said as he sat, "would you mind closing that door behind you?"

Laura Lou's eyebrows shot up and she threw Edie a curious glance over Turner's head. Laura Lou Davis was not accustomed to such a dismissal. When Edie gave a small shrug, Laura Lou cleared her throat. "No problem. I need to make some phone calls anyway. Let me know if I can get you anything."

"Will do."

With the door closed Turner crossed one leg over the other, revealing a few inches of blue-and-green polka-dotted sock. His trademark shock of silver hair was brushed back off his forehead. "I hope you don't mind me stopping by unannounced like this. I just wanted a chance to chat with you in private for a moment."

Edie sat and crossed her arms on top of the desk. "It's not a problem at all."

"Thank you. I wanted to talk about the type of work you do at Davis Design Group."

"My work? Okay. Well, I'm an interior designer. Obviously." She laughed a little. "I've worked on a few office spaces and restaurants, but I do mostly residential work." Edie paused, giving him a chance to ask for what he really wanted. When he didn't, she sat back in her chair and crossed her legs. "A lot of kitchens and baths, but also some bigger renovations and new construction." Still no response. "Is there something specific you'd like to know?"

"Yes. Do you have the ability to choose what projects you want to work on?"

"Of course. Sometimes Laura Lou will assign me a project, but most of the time clients contact me directly and ask for what they need."

"That's good." He was quiet a moment, in no hurry. Edie waited. "You designed Ted Barnett's house in Point Clear, didn't you?"

"Yes, sir. I did."

"I don't like it very much."

She raised her eyebrows. "Good to know."

"It's a little . . . austere for my taste."

Edie gave a slow nod and Turner smiled. "You don't agree?"

"It would be unprofessional of me to tell you I agree with you."

He laughed. "Mrs. Swan, I think we'll get along just fine."

"Get along?"

"Yes, I'd like to hire you."

"Hire me?"

"That's right. I just bought some property over the bay and I'd like to put a house on it. I love to fish; Marigold, my wife, loves to sail; and we have a passel of grandkids who need to know the joy of life on the bay." He sat back and grinned. "Anyway, I can do a lot of things, but what I can't do is build a house and make it look good, so that's where you come in."

"But, Mr. Kennedy, all you know of my work is that you don't like the Barnetts' house."

"Please. Call me Turner. And I know the Barnetts' house isn't indicative of your taste. I've seen your website, your past projects. The McDermotts' hunting camp up in Chatom? The Phillips-Whatley house on Primrose? You do excellent work."

"Thank you very much. I know I speak for Laura Lou when I say it's an honor for you to choose Davis Design to—" She stopped when he held up his hand.

"I'm not hiring Davis Design, Edie. I'd just like to hire *you*, if that's okay."

A knock sounded at the door and Laura Lou stuck her head in. "Sorry to interrupt," she said, though she didn't sound sorry at all. "Edie, I forgot to tell you I ran into the structural engineer at the Tuthills' preconstruction meeting Friday. He said to tell you he hasn't forgotten about you, and he's going to touch base about the ceiling joist on Primrose ASAP. He's just been swamped."

Edie had received an email from Greg, the structural engineer, just this morning, and he told her the same thing. She had a hunch Laura Lou was using him as a reason to circle back to her office and get her face in front of Turner. "That's good to know," Edie said. "Thanks for being the go-between."

"No problem at all. Thank you for staying on top of it." She glanced at Turner. "With so many people involved in these big projects, there's always one person who'll drag his feet, but Edie puts those feet to the fire when necessary. She's a go-getter, that's for sure."

"It seems so, yes. I was just telling her I'd like to bring her on as the designer for my new house."

"That's fantastic!" Laura Lou clasped her hands together. "I have to tell you, Turner—it's okay if I call you Turner, right? As soon as I heard about your new property, I started compiling some ideas just in case you decided to talk to us about it. It may be a little forward," she said with a laugh, "but we'll get together and—"

"Sorry, Ms. Davis, but I'll just be needing Edie for this one. I know she'll be a great asset to the team. A go-getter, just like you said." He smiled at Edie. "What do you say?"

"I . . . Yes, I'd love to. Thank you." She tried not to appear as thunderstruck as she felt.

At the door Laura Lou crossed her arms. "But we're . . . You're not . . ." She inhaled slowly. "At Davis Design Group, we typically collaborate on the larger, more important projects. Such as yours. It gives you the benefit of more—"

"Did the Barnetts' bay house benefit from this collaborative effort?" He cut a glance at Edie and winked.

"Oh, of course," Laura Lou gushed. "Ted Barnett is a wonderful client of ours. The house was on the cover of *Bay* magazine, you know."

"Yes, I did see that. Thank you for your offer, Ms. Davis, but I think Mrs. Swan is just the right designer for our house. I can't wait to see what she comes up with."

Laura Lou exhaled through her nose. "May I ask if you're using an architect?"

"You may and we are, though I can't say who it is just yet. He's being a little . . . well, Marigold would say obstinate, but I'm the soft one in our marriage so I'll say indecisive. Maybe knowing Edie has signed on as the designer will push him over the edge."

Edie wasn't one to be wowed by anyone's stature, bank account, or house size, but it was hard to deny that this would be good for her career. Designing a house for the Kennedys was more than a plum assignment—it was the brass ring. The completed house would undoubtedly be featured in magazines for years, with her name attached.

"What does your schedule look like for Monday?" Turner asked, straightening his shirt as he stood. "I'd like to have you both"—he glanced at Laura Lou—"that is, Edie and the architect, out to the site to walk through what we're thinking. Or what Marigold's thinking." He chuckled. "She has a few thoughts—I'll go ahead and let you know."

"I like clients who have opinions. It makes my job easier. And I should be able to make Monday work."

"Great. I'll have my assistant call you later today to set a firm time, but let's tentatively plan for something in the morning. I have a tee time just after lunch. Does that sound okay?"

Edie bobbed her head. "Sounds perfect."

Turner stuck out his hand, and his grip was firm. "Thank you, young lady. I'm looking forward to working with you." He then extended his hand to Laura Lou, who was still waiting by the door. "Always good to see you, Ms. Davis." He grinned, then slipped out and down the hall toward the front door.

The two women stood still and quiet, listening as Turner spoke to the receptionist on his way. When it was clear the entry door had closed, Laura Lou turned to Edie, eyes narrowed. "How did you do that?"

"I didn't do anything. I'm just as surprised as you are."

"Well, I suppose a 'congratulations' is in order." She sighed and smoothed her hands down the front of her red pantsuit. "You just got yourself the Kennedy compound."

As soon as Laura Lou walked out, her high heels tapping quickly on the tile floor, Edie grabbed her phone to call Mac. When he didn't answer, she sent a quick text.

I have some news. Can't wait for dinner!

All Mac knew was that they were going out to dinner for his birthday. For months though, Edie had been planning a surprise, and she worked hard to keep the whole thing under wraps. A lot was riding on it, and she wanted it to be perfect. Mac and Edie had been married for nearly two decades. They'd built a life and a family together. They had good jobs, two kids they adored, a place in the life of their community, and they were lucky. They were happy.

And yet it wasn't like it once was. Where they'd once been two lines winding together, crisscrossing, and circling back on each other, things had changed. Work, obligations, schedules, soccer tournaments, chorus performances, the regular monotony of life—all of it had served to straighten their lines until they were like trains running parallel to each other. Sure, they were headed in the same direction, but they were on wholly separate tracks. Their senses and desires and longings had been dampened and dulled into the mundane—a hello at the coffeepot, a reminder to be at the soccer field at six, a text during the day to please stop at the grocery store on the way home for butter.

And there was that voice, of course. The one that popped up at unexpected moments, the one she always quickly shut down. The one reminding her of paths not explored. Chances not taken.

Just like the tides, marriages waxed and waned. Some days were filled with affection and ease and vitality, while other days they held on by the tips of their fingers as they tried to scrape together a smile or a touch, just to remind each other—and themselves—that they were still in this thing.

That's why Edie planned the party for Mac's fortieth. To show that they were fine. That despite the distance that had crept in, despite the opposing schedules and busyness and half-remembered promises, despite old memories that didn't always stay buried, they were still together. They were going to be okay.

CHAPTER 5

MAC

Present Day

Mac had just started a quick lunch break in his cramped office when someone tapped on his door. Sweet Mrs. Kimble opened the door with a gentle push.

"Hey there, birthday boy."

He smiled. She'd brought a bouquet of a dozen black balloons to work this morning, along with a cookie cake the nurses had been munching on. Those plus the flock of black plastic crows dotting his front yard, courtesy of his family and Flamingo-a-Friend, had started his fortieth birthday off with a bang.

She held out a bag of brightly colored lollipops. "Just wanted to let you know our order of suckers came in." She jiggled the bag. "I've already filled the bowl on my desk, and I'm about to fill up the rest back here in the hallway. Maybe these will keep the screaming to a minimum."

"That's great, Mrs. K. Thanks." He rubbed his eyes with the heels of his hands. "Is the waiting room empty yet?"

"Thank the Lord, yes. I haven't seen a morning like that in a while. I wish it were only the missing lollipops, but I'm thinking this could be an early flu outbreak."

Mrs. Kimble was the best receptionist any doctor could ask for—cheerful with the patients and their parents, organized to a fault, and an ace when it came to convincing insurance companies to cover various procedures and tests—but she had a serious fear of the flu. Anytime a child came in with a sudden fever, Mrs. K. wiped down the front desk with Clorox spray and placed another Amazon order for heavy-duty hand sanitizer.

"We've only had two cases of flu so far this school year. We can't really call that an outbreak, can we?" Mac leaned forward and peeked at his desk calendar. "How's the afternoon look?"

"Just as busy as the morning. Eight checkups on the books, two follow-up appointments, and twelve sick visits. And that's just for you. The other doctors' afternoons are just as packed."

"Well, that's what we're here for. I'd be worried if the phone stopped ringing. I'm going to try to get through some of these charts before my one o'clock gets here."

"You do that. Enjoy your lunch, Dr. Swan. Frank packed me some of his famous tuna salad for my lunch. My stomach's been rumbling for hours. But don't worry—I'll keep the break room door closed while I eat it."

Mac laughed. They'd established long ago that the smell of tuna salad wasn't ideal in a doctor's office full of sick children.

"Oh, and I almost forgot. Vivi Myers had an appointment at two, but her mom called and asked if she could come a little early."

"And you told her no, right? Even the Myerses have to follow the rules."

"Well, I was going to, but she offered to bring a box of glazed doughnuts." Mrs. K. lowered her voice to a whisper. "Krispy Kreme isn't exactly Weight Watchers friendly, but it's my weakness. Even if I did have a skinny slice of your cookie cake this morning."

He sighed. "Tell Mrs. Myers it's fine. And save me a doughnut."

"You got it." Her cheeks dimpled and she backed out of the doorway.

Yes, it was his birthday, and yes, it was a big one, but just as momentous to him was the fact that he'd been the head of his own medical practice for a solid decade. He signed the papers to take over Oak Hill Pediatrics the day he turned thirty, fresh out of his fellowship in pediatric emergency medicine. Dr. McCain, his childhood pediatrician, had called Mac out of the blue and asked if he was interested in taking over his practice, as he'd decided to take an early retirement.

Mac laughed, but after Dr. McCain assured him he was serious and Mac managed a stuttering, "Yes, sir, thank you, sir," he went straight to his parents' house. He didn't so much as send his wife a text before he told his father the news. It still irritated him that his dad was the first one to know. Especially considering his reaction.

"Your own little petri dish of sick kids," his dad had said, holding out his hand to shake Mac's. "Congratulations."

Mac hesitated before reaching out his hand, unsure of his level of sarcasm. In his gut he knew it was a slight, but his foolish heart still hoped for pride. For acceptance. A hearty *atta boy*. "That's what doctors do, right?" Mac said with a smile. "Make sick people well?"

His dad tipped his head. "Sure we do. Though my line of work is a little cleaner. The heart is the crux of everything." He turned and took a bottle of Old Medley Kentucky bourbon from the wood-and-brass bar cart in their living room. Poured a couple fingers into two glasses and added small cubes of ice. "I still say you could have made a fine cardiologist."

Mac didn't take his eyes off his dad as he reached for the glass he offered. "Maybe. Who knows?" He swallowed hard and willed his voice to be firm. "But I'm a good pediatrician, Dad."

"That you are." David Swan raised his glass in the air. "To you and your new business venture. May you do the Swan name proud."

Occasionally Mac allowed himself to think about twenty-year-old Mac Swan, the kid who ran off to the beach to figure out what path he wanted to be on. What would he think of the forty-year-old man he was now? Would he be satisfied? Proud? Would he wonder at the roads Mac had taken?

Of course, it was all worth it. After all, look where he and Edie were now—settled, happy, a good life built from dedication and love. Still though, sometimes he feared they had what they had only because he'd stayed silent. If Edie knew about that summer, would they have such a good life? Would they even be here at all?

———

He'd seen four of his eight checkups, five of the sick patients, and was on his way to see the next one—a toddler with a stomach bug who'd already thrown up in the waiting room, according to the nurse—when Mrs. Kimble called Mac's name. He turned to see her trotting down the hall toward him, her fluffy gray hair like a swirl of meringue.

"Please tell me there's not another cleanup in the waiting room."

"No." Concern was etched in the lines on her face. "There's a young woman here to see you."

"A young woman? A patient?"

"No, it's not—I'm not sure who she is."

"Is she a drug rep?" A cry erupted from exam room three, and he resumed his trek to the next patient. "The new girl from Merck said she'd be by before the end of the week."

"She's not a drug rep, Dr. Swan, and I don't think she's here to be a new patient."

"Well, she'll have to wait a bit. I can't just—"

"I think you should come see her." Her tone was firm.

He stopped and turned around. "Is something wrong? Is she sick?"

Mrs. Kimble sighed. "I'm not exactly sure. But she says she needs to talk to you."

Something wasn't sitting right—namely the fact that Mrs. Kimble kept her gaze somewhere near his left shoulder. Having worked closely with her nearly every day for the last ten years, Mac had come to learn each gesture and facial expression the woman could make, but he couldn't decipher what he saw now.

She turned and headed down the hallway that snaked from Mac's section of exam rooms in the back to the waiting room up front. He exhaled and followed her, pushing his fingers through his hair as he walked.

As he rounded the final corner of the hallway and got his first glimpse of the waiting area, it was the usual cacophony of noise and movement. His was the only pediatric practice in Oak Hill, and with three doctors and a PA, the waiting room was usually full. Today was no different. Children sat with their parents in the red and yellow plastic chairs, some asleep and others focused on a princess movie playing on the waiting room TV screen. Nothing appeared out of place.

Mac glanced back at Mrs. Kimble. "Did she leave?"

She bustled past him and gestured to the far corner of the office, around the edge of the reception desk. A woman sat there alone, but Mac couldn't see her face. Her head was lowered and her hair had fallen forward, hiding her profile. She was older than his typical patients—eighteen or nineteen would probably be a good guess—and no visible injuries that he could see. No bandage-wrapped limbs and nothing was bleeding. She could have been any number of patients there to see a doctor. What had gotten Mrs. Kimble so worked up?

He was just about to ask her that very question when the girl lifted her head and her eyes met his. Without any conscious thought, his heart gave a wild thump and sweat prickled under his arms.

Mac had long grown accustomed to how often people commented on his children's appearances, namely that they both so closely mimicked Edie's. The running joke was that he was the one with weak genes while Edie's were as vigorous as a bull, though it wasn't much of a joke. Both Thomas and Avery had Edie's olive skin and dark curly hair, though Avery straightened hers and Thomas mostly ignored his dark mess of curls. Avery shared Edie's petite frame and Thomas was waiting impatiently for the growth spurt he hoped would catapult him into six-foot range like Mac, though it was looking doubtful that would happen.

If he'd ever wondered what a child would look like who actually resembled him, this was it. She had the same dark blonde hair as him—or at least the same color hair he had before the gray began creeping in—and though she was sitting, Mac could tell she wasn't petite. Her body had a shape and substance he knew Edie always wished she had.

But it was something in her face that caused his chest to tighten. The dimples high up on both cheeks, under her eyes, could have been pulled from Mac's own face, and her nose—strong and a little pointed, with a slight bump along the ridge—was a mirror image of his own. He'd never actually experienced the sensation of time standing still until he saw himself—albeit a much younger version—staring back at him in a stranger's face. And the longer he looked, the more another face bubbled up in his memory, a face he hadn't seen since that one summer so many years ago.

"Tell me I'm not seeing things." Mrs. Kimble stood close enough that Mac could smell the floral scent of her powder mixed with a strong antiseptic. "Is she a niece or a cousin . . . ?"

"I don't have a . . ." Mac's throat was so dry, the words just stopped. He could feel Mrs. Kimble's stare on the back of his neck, but he couldn't turn away.

Finally she moved toward the girl. "Honey, this is Dr. Swan." She looked at him pointedly, then turned back to the girl. "Can you tell us your name?"

The girl's gaze slid past Mrs. Kimble to Mac, then down at her hands. "I'm Riley. Riley Mills." When she looked up again, something else blazed in her eyes. A confidence, or maybe even a defiance. All at once, before the words left her mouth, he knew what was coming next. "I think you knew my mother."

Blood rushed in Mac's ears and he reached out and grabbed the edge of the reception desk for balance as Mrs. Kimble turned and asked him a question. He must have given her an answer, because she helped Riley— Riley *Mills*—gather her things, a purse and a large duffel bag, and ushered her out of the waiting room and toward his office.

Mac followed them, trying to slow the hurricane of images whirling through his mind: dark Gulf waters and sandy feet. The scent of Coppertone mixed with the sweet, metallic tang of boat fuel. Denim cutoffs with a hole in the back pocket. A sly grin. He'd assumed the details were gone, lost to the in-between years, yet in the span of a heartbeat, there they were, bright and blazing in his mind, as if the past had just walked into his office and tapped him on the shoulder.

By the time he made it back to his office, Riley was seated in the chair across from his desk and Mrs. Kimble was flitting around like a nervous hen, straightening the picture frames on his desk and wiping off a speck of dust with her sleeve.

"Thank you, Mrs. Kimble."

"No problem. If I can just have a quick minute with you . . ." She turned to Riley. "He'll be right back, hon." Mrs. K. grabbed his arm and tugged him out into the hallway. When they were several paces away, she turned on him. "That girl is the spitting image of you, Mac Swan," she whispered. She only used his first name when she was upset. "I don't suppose you have any idea who she is?"

He glanced back across the hall to the spot where Riley sat in the chair, her back to them. There was no way he could tell gentle Mrs. Kimble that yes, he had an idea, but that idea was so outlandish—so impossible—he couldn't even think about uttering it out loud. "I'm going to figure this all out."

"Well, get on in there. It may not be smart to leave her alone in your office for long. She could be a thief. Or worse."

His stomach twisted with nerves. "A thief? I doubt she's here to do that kind of damage."

"You never know. My neighbor had his Big Green Egg stolen from a very nice young lady who'd come to his door selling magazines. Sometimes it's the unassuming ones who do the most damage."

Mac made his best effort at a reassuring smile. "Thanks for the advice. I'll be careful."

Mrs. Kimble nodded and he stepped past her and back into his office. Riley turned as he closed the door softly behind him. Then on second thought, he opened it a few inches.

"I didn't mean to make everyone nervous," Riley said as Mac rounded the edge of his desk and sat down.

"I'm not nervous." He leaned back in his chair, then sat forward and rested his arms on the desk.

"Well, that lady was. It was obvious she didn't want to leave me alone in here. As if I'd run off with your"—she gestured to his desk—"files or something."

"I think she just wanted to make sure you were okay."

"You can let her know I'm doing just fine." She winced and shifted in her chair. "But you're probably wondering why I'm here."

"Y-yes. I am, actually. As far as I know, I didn't have any new patients on the schedule for today, so I'm not sure . . ."

Riley tucked her hands under her thighs and sat forward in her chair. Her gaze on him was so intense he had to fight the urge to look away. "Do you have any idea who I am?" Her voice was deep for a young woman, a little raspy, and it reminded Mac of another voice that had an edge, a voice that had once filled his ears and muddied his thoughts. A voice that did not belong to Edie.

With his eyes locked on hers, something in him begged to say, "Yes, yes, I know exactly who you are," but he didn't. He couldn't. Edie's face appeared in his mind, then Avery's and Thomas's. His world. Saying yes would be tantamount to deceiving all of them. Deceiving everyone.

And there was also the possibility that he was wrong. That this girl sitting in his office was in fact a total stranger.

But the longer they held eye contact, the more he realized that was a foolish wish.

Finally she dropped her gaze, and her shoulders slid down too. "Yeah, I didn't think so." She paused for a moment and sniffed, then lifted her head. "My mother was Kat Mills. Katherine, but everyone called her Kat. She worked on a charter fishing boat when she was in her early twenties. She had me when she was twenty-five. We lived in Pensacola, not too far from the marina where she'd worked, though she didn't do the fishing thing anymore once I was born. She waited tables, mostly. Bartended some. Cleaned houses."

She brushed a wisp of hair off her cheek. In the hallway Mac heard the approaching conversation of another doctor and her nurse as they entered the exam room next door.

Across the desk, Riley sat still as stone, then she resumed speaking, as if she were reading from a speech she'd prepared. "Mom didn't talk about my dad much, but I knew he existed somewhere. I mean, everyone has a dad, right? A couple of years ago, she mentioned his name. It just slipped out. It may have even been an accident."

She paused and crossed one leg over the other. "Once the name was in my head, I couldn't stop thinking about it. I finally caved and found him on Facebook. I told myself I wasn't going to check up on him. That his life and his family weren't any of my business. But I couldn't stay away." She closed her eyes. "And your profile was set to public."

It was a moment before Mac realized what she'd said. "My—"

"I mean, you don't post much, but people tag you in a lot of stuff, so I could see where you worked, who you married, what your children look like." She swallowed. "I know I sound like an insane stalker, but I promise I'm not. I was just so curious." She balled her hands into fists. "Like . . . starving for information about you. All Mom said was that you were this great guy who had bigger things to do than bum around the beach with her, but I started wondering. If he was so great, why didn't he help her? Why was he never around when I was young? Or ever? Why did *you* get to have this perfect life while my mom worked so hard and never had anything to show for it?"

He opened his mouth but couldn't formulate a single word.

"Then I realized. You didn't know I existed. She never told you." Riley waited. "I'm right, aren't I? You never knew about me?"

He swallowed hard. Without taking his gaze from her face, he reached over and picked up his desk phone.

"Dr. Swan?" Mrs. Kimble's voice was low when she answered. "Is everything okay?"

He willed his voice to remain strong. "Can you please cancel my appointments for the afternoon?"

"Cancel your appointments? Mac, it's two fifteen. The Myerses are already in the waiting room and you're booked full for the rest of the day."

"Please apologize to Mrs. Myers and let the other patients know I'll fit them in tomorrow. If it's something that can't wait, see if you can fit them into someone else's schedule. Thank you." Her protests rang out as he lowered the phone back into its cradle.

"You're busy." Riley leaned over the side of the chair and reached for her purse sitting on top of the big duffel bag. "I should have called first."

Mac stood when she did, but he held his arm out. "Wait. Please sit. Please don't go anywhere."

She froze, her eyes on him, then lowered herself back into the chair.

"Where's your mom now?"

Her lips drew into a thin line. "I didn't come here to talk about my mom."

"Okay. Okay. I just need to . . ." *Think for a minute.* He just needed a minute to think. He reached both hands up and raked them through his hair. "I'm Mac Swan. Thomas MacDavid Swan. The third if you want to be specific. Is that the name your mom gave you?"

His stomach rolled with nausea. It was so dirty, thinking of himself as just a name, just a guy who passed through Kat's life and left behind . . . well, this child, apparently. But he needed to be sure.

"I don't know about the third business, but yeah." She nodded. "Mac Swan. She said you were the kindest man she'd ever met."

He leaned his elbows on the desk and rested his face in his hands. *Man?* He'd hardly been a man that summer. At least not at the beginning. At twenty years old, he'd been just a kid when he met Kat, when everything he'd worked for had all of a sudden become both too much and not enough.

He pulled his hands from his face. "When were you born?"

"April 6, 2001."

"And your mom is Kat Mills."

Riley nodded.

"Kat Mills. Long blonde hair. Muscles in her arms. She could tie a bowline knot with her eyes closed and she could fillet a whole day's catch in the time it took a group of drunk businessmen to unload off a boat. Does that sound right?"

Riley opened her mouth. "I—I don't know all that about her. She didn't talk about the fishing stuff much. But the blonde hair is right. And she told me she once threw a guy overboard."

"So that means . . ." Mac tried to swallow, but his mouth was too dry. "That would make me your father."

Her eyebrows lifted and she pasted a big smile on her face. "Surprise."

He bit the inside of his cheek until it hurt, hoping the pain would jar him awake. This was uncharted territory. No, it was an alien planet and he was completely alone, with no one to tell him what to do, what to think. No one except this girl sitting in front of him, this girl with a face that looked like his and an attitude cut straight from Kat herself.

His daughter.

At the word *daughter*, Avery automatically popped into Mac's mind. His beautiful, sensitive, hardworking daughter. But this was Riley, a girl he didn't know. His *second* daughter.

No, Mac. Your first daughter.

A bead of sweat ran between his shoulder blades, and the walls of his office seemed closer than they were a minute ago. His breath came quick, as if he were running instead of sitting still. An acute longing to escape crawled from his chest into his throat, and he squeezed his eyes closed.

When he opened them, Riley was watching him with an expression of such pain, such desperation, it pulled him from himself. This wasn't just about him. It was about this girl, too, this girl who'd just met her father for the first time.

What do I do? Of course there was no answer to the question he screamed in his mind. But he owed it to her—he owed it to Kat—to take care of this situation in the best way possible.

Whatever way that was.

"I'm sorry. You just caught me off guard." Mac rubbed his temples. *Understatement of the year.* "But we're here now, and there's a lot we need to . . . to do and talk about. Right?"

The open desperation on her face disappeared, replaced by something cool and flinty. "Look, I didn't come here to have a nice family moment, though I'm sure that's what it seems like. I don't need that and I don't expect anything at all." She broke off. "Well, there is one thing."

"Yeah?"

"I'm on my way to New Orleans. My mom has an aunt there." She studied her hands a moment. "Aunt Mary. Anyway, I'm headed to find her, and I just need a little money. Not much. Buses are cheap and—"

"You're taking a bus? Did you come here on a bus?" At her nod he asked, "From where?"

"Near Panama City."

"With your mom? That's where she lives?"

Riley exhaled hard. "I'm just—I'm not sure how long it'll take me to find my aunt once I get to New Orleans, and I need . . ." She passed a hand over her face and as she did, that desperation reappeared. It was something around her eyes, that delicate, unlined skin pulling taut as if she were willing all emotion away.

"If you could just loan me a little money, I'm good for it. As soon as I get settled, I'll get a job and I'll pay you back. I promise."

Mac drummed his fingers on top of the desk. "What are you going to do in New Orleans?"

"What does it matter? I'm not asking for your permission."

He held up his hand. "Obviously. And I'm in no position to give it."

"Obviously."

"But I can't just hand over money to—"

"To a stranger? Is that what you were going to say?"

Mac laid his hands flat on his desk and leaned toward her. "I'm not going to fight with you. I don't know you well enough to fight with you. But I need to make sure you're okay. Can you blame me for wanting to look out for you a little bit when you've just told me that you're my daughter?"

Moisture rimmed her eyes and her gaze darted away. She shifted in her seat again and rested her hand just above her stomach. Mac missed it before, the swell there beneath her plaid button-down shirt, but with her hand pressed against it, it was as obvious as the sunshine pouring in through his office window. And just as impossible to ignore.

"Is that—are you . . . ?"

She yanked her hand away from her stomach. She flicked a tear away with her thumb and cleared her throat.

"You're pregnant?" he whispered.

"It would appear so. But that doesn't change anything. I'll still be out of your hair soon." She glanced at her watch. "The next bus leaves at 4:40. If

I could just borrow a little money so I can get some food and—" She winced and took a deep breath, then another one.

The rapid breathing, the wrinkled nose, the skin growing paler by the second—Mac recognized the nausea before she did. Just as she put her hand to her mouth, he hopped out of his chair, grabbed the wastebasket from around the side of the desk, and set it on the ground by her feet. Three more seconds and it would have been too late. He turned to give her some privacy as she vomited.

When she finished, he handed her a tissue. "Still itching to get on that bus?"

"I'm fine. It sometimes hits me out of nowhere like that, but it's usually just one and done. I'll be fine for a while." She dropped the tissue into the trash can. "I'm really sorry about that."

"Don't worry about it." Mac set the can by the door, then leaned against the edge of his desk and crossed his arms.

"How'd you know I was about to throw up?"

"Well, I am a doctor. Plus I have two kids." *Three kids.* He sighed. "My wife—Edie—was pretty sick with both of them. I learned the signs well."

Riley nodded. Spots of color had crept back into her cheeks. She rubbed her stomach.

"I'm not taking you to the bus station." Riley opened her mouth to speak, but he beat her to it. "At least not right now. You can't walk into my office and drop this bomb on me and expect me to say, 'Great, nice to meet you, now here's some money so you'll leave.'"

She sniffed out a short laugh. "That's kind of exactly what I expected you to do."

"Well, you underestimated me."

"What am I supposed to do then?" Riley waited for an answer. "Trust me, I don't want to be here asking you for anything. But . . ." She lifted her hands, then let them drop.

If what she was saying was true, if Mac really was her father, he had no option but to help her. He could hardly deny that she was his—the girl had Swan genes practically jumping off her face.

And then there was the small fact that the last time he'd seen Kat—that

September afternoon at the campus apartment he shared with Graham, a month or so after the start of their senior year—he wondered if it was possible. If this exact eventuality might one day happen. The prospect had sparked in a hot flash, then was gone. In the same way that Kat was gone, closing his apartment door behind her.

He squeezed his hands into fists, then released them. This girl—her mere presence in the world—had the potential to ravage Mac's life. It would be so easy to just hand over the money and usher her right out the door and back into anonymity. No one would be the wiser, but he knew himself. Though acknowledging Riley as his daughter would threaten everything—*everything*—he'd never be able to live with himself if he didn't.

He'd figure out the logistics later.

"Look, it's Friday. Stay here for the weekend. Just until I know you're okay and you have somewhere to land in New Orleans." No response. He continued. "Anyway, you can't just go *find* someone in New Orleans. Have you ever been there?"

"No."

"If you don't know where to look, you'll never find this Aunt Mary person. I can give you a place to stay for a couple nights until we sort everything out."

She crossed her arms, her body language mimicking his. "I guess I'm in no position to argue."

"You're not."

"I could get up and leave though. Right now."

He gave a slow nod. "You could. I couldn't stop you."

"You wouldn't stop me?"

"No, Riley. If you get up right now and walk out, I can't stop you. You're eighteen years old. You're an adult. You can do what you want to do." He was hedging his bet, something he'd learned to do with Avery, who was as emotional as she was headstrong. Sometimes giving some slack was just the thing to get them to stick close. But Mac had no way of knowing if it would work with Riley.

She stared into his eyes, much more direct than any teenager who'd come into his office. Most of them would say the words they needed to say, then drop their gaze, as if eye contact was as uncomfortable as staring into a lightbulb. Riley didn't look away though, and her directness was both refreshing and unsettling.

Finally she spoke. "Are you taking me to your house?"

Discomfort wormed its way through Mac's insides. "Not yet. I have a friend . . ." He'd already thought of his mentor, Abraham Fitzgerald, a man who would give his right arm to anyone who needed it, whether he knew them or not. The man who had given Mac the encouragement and stern talks he needed not just to make it through his residency but to thrive in it. The man who'd watched, as proud as any father—prouder than Mac's own—as he established himself in his career and as he and Edie built their lives and their family, one step at a time.

He picked up the phone and dialed. "Do you have a suitcase or anything?"

She glanced down at the dingy duffel bag by her feet.

"That's it?"

She nodded.

"Dr. Swan," the voice on the other end of the line drawled. Mac always loved to hear the man speak, his cadence mixing his early years in Kenya with the decades he'd spent in lower Alabama. It was melodic and honey coated. "You hoping for advice for Thursday's game? I'd say you need to spend a few days practicing your jump shot."

Mac massaged his forehead. "Fitz, I need a favor. A big one."

CHAPTER 6

MAC

Present Day

Twenty minutes later, Mac pulled in front of Fitz's home in the Oakleigh historic district and turned off the ignition. Glancing up at the front porch, Mac could just barely see Fitz standing in his front living room, peering around the curtain. When he saw that he'd been spotted, he ducked his head back.

Riley hadn't noticed. She was staring down at her hands in her lap. "Do you live in this neighborhood?"

"No, I live in Oak Hill. It's up Camellia Avenue."

"You don't want to take me to your house?"

He circled his fingers on his temple. His head had started to pound somewhere on the drive over. "My wife—"

"I get it. No one in your world knows I'm alive."

Mac squeezed the steering wheel until his knuckles protested. "I just need some time to explain a few things. Edie . . ." A small sigh escaped. "I need to talk to her. Alone."

Riley nodded. She passed a hand over her belly.

"If you have any problems tonight, Fitz's wife, Cynthia, should be able to help you."

"Don't worry, I'm not having this baby today. I'm only six months along."

"I just mean she may be a good person to talk to. She's a counselor." Cynthia worked at the Gulf Coast Women's Center, a nonprofit that offered pregnancy services and education to young or underprivileged women, the irony of which was not lost on Mac.

"Oh perfect. Someone to ask me about all my problems."

"She won't do that. She's not that kind of counselor."

"Whatever." Riley's voice was a tired whisper. She sighed as silence filled the car. Mac knew Fitz probably wouldn't be able to keep his curiosity at bay for much longer, but he also didn't want to hurry away from her.

When Riley's phone rang, it startled both of them. It was lying faceup on the seat next to her. *Dex* flashed on the screen, along with a photo of a young man with big, beefy arms wrapped around Riley, who had her eyes closed in laughter.

"Do you need to get that?" Mac asked when she didn't make a move to answer it.

She shook her head and turned the phone off. "Do you have any pictures of your kids?"

"My kids? Yeah. Of course." He pulled out his phone and opened his photos. He scrolled to find a good one of both of them, then held the phone out to Riley. "This was from Easter this year. I took it at our church."

She took the phone out of his hand and held it close to her face.

It was funny how photos didn't always show the whole story. It had been a weird morning that Easter. Both kids had woken up grumpy, despite the jubilation of a resurrection Sunday and the Easter baskets Edie had stuffed with chocolate and trinkets. Thomas hadn't wanted to wear the new shirt Edie had bought him, and Avery had been unhappy with her hair. Stiff fabric and too much humidity were apparently their kids' kryptonite. As a result the four of them had arrived at church cranky and wilted, which, if Mac was honest, was how Sunday mornings often were for them.

Something changed during the service though. Maybe it was the uplifting music or the pastor's sermon, but when it was over, both kids—not to mention he and Edie—were so much lighter. Itchy collars, imperfect hair, and the early morning scuffles were all forgotten. He'd snapped the photo of the kids as they sat together on a bench in the courtyard after the service. They'd been laughing about something, and all around them the cherry trees were bursting with pink blossoms.

It was a beautiful photo, one Mac had opened and looked at many times since then. But now he saw it through Riley's eyes. Such happy, well-loved children. A photo taken by a proud, adoring father. He didn't know much—anything—about Riley's life up until now, but something told him she didn't have many photos like this.

Riley was still staring at the screen. She tapped it when it started to go dark. "How old are they?"

"Thomas is eleven. He's in sixth grade. Avery is fourteen. Ninth grade."

"What about their mom? Can I see her?"

"Sure." He scrolled through the photos and found one of Edie from just last weekend. It had been raining and she was reading on the back porch. She hadn't seen Mac pull out his phone, so he caught her at her most relaxed, with her hair up in a bun, lying back on the pillows, and her feet propped up on the arm of the couch. It reminded him of the early days, before life crept in and they assumed the roles they were to play.

"She doesn't look anything like Mom." Riley handed him the phone and he glanced at the photo again. She was right, of course. Edie's dark hair and slight, almost childlike stature were a stark contrast to what he remembered of Kat—shapely figure, thick blonde braid, and a smattering of freckles across her tanned face.

"How is your mom?" He'd held off asking as long as he could. After almost two decades of forgetting, it had taken only a second to remember it all, and her name now burned in his mind. *Kat.* It was a powerful mixture of past and present. Memory and guilt.

Riley flicked her thumbnails together, her gaze off in the middle distance.

"Riley?"

"She passed away. About a year ago."

"She . . . what?"

"It was a car wreck."

Something hard and fast pulsed through him. Blood thundered in his ears and he turned his head away from her, toward the other side of the street, so she wouldn't see the anguish on his face.

"She wasn't well." Riley's voice seemed to come from far off, like she was on the other side of a thick wall. He turned back to her and leaned forward, pressing his forearms against the steering wheel. "The accident was . . . I don't know. At least no one else was involved. The cops said it seemed like she hadn't slowed at all when her car left the road. No brake marks or anything."

"What do you mean?" He shook his head. "I know what you mean. But what are you saying?"

She shrugged, her face impassive. "All I know is what they told me. That it didn't look like an accident."

In his mind he sat with Kat on the deck of the Flora-Bama—that famed beach bar on the Florida–Alabama border—with a salty breeze in the air, her ominous words about her future, words he'd taken in jest, still ringing in his ears.

"My mom didn't have an easy life, but she loved me." Riley's voice grew defensive, as if Mac had said something to the contrary. "She was a good mom. As good as she could be." Her eyes filled with tears and she rubbed them away. "She loved me."

Mac nodded. "I'm sure she did. I'm so sorry."

The words felt limp, empty, even as they left his mouth. As a pediatrician Mac was used to offering relief and compassion to young people. As a parent it was second nature for him to comfort, to love, to console, and to soothe his children. But in this moment he felt paralyzed and completely ineffective. As if all his go-to remedies were gone.

She leaned down and unzipped a pocket on the side of the duffel bag at her feet. When she sat back, she held an envelope in her hands. She turned it over and over, front to back, back to front. Finally she handed it to him. His name was on the front in blue ballpoint pen, along with his mailing address at Southern College and a thirty-three-cent stamp.

No postmark. The envelope was stiff with age and the seal along the back was open.

She shrugged a shoulder. "You can read it if you want."

Dread coursed through him as he slid a finger into the envelope and pulled out a single sheet of paper. A wallet-size photo slid out with it. One glance at the photo and his eyes blurred. There was Kat, in all her bold beauty, her hair woven into a braid that lay over her bare shoulder. The round, pink cheeks he remembered so well. The freckles splashed across her nose he'd once traced with his fingertip.

But it wasn't Kat who'd brought the hot tears. In Kat's arms was an infant wearing a pink ruffled dress. She couldn't have been more than a couple months old. She had big, shiny eyes and a head covered in blonde peach fuzz, her lips pursed into a perfect tiny heart. *The Swan heart.* Edie had been the one to name it after both Avery and Thomas were born with the same little heart lips Mac had had when he was born.

His fingers fumbled as he shifted the photo so he could read the words on the paper.

Dear Mac,

I'm sending you this photo though I know it's probably going to be a shock. Don't be mad though. At least not until you hear me out. I have a few things to explain, and I have a confession . . .

His eyes blurred all over again as he read the rest of the letter. He stared at the photo again, then turned it over.

Kat and Riley. July 2001.

He held up the letter. "Why . . . ? When did—?"

"I found it after Mom died." Riley smoothed her finger across a string on her shorts. "I was packing up her things. I don't know why she never sent it to you. But it's yours now."

"Riley, if I'd known . . ." What would he have done if he'd known? If Kat had sent him the letter? Or if he'd questioned her further when she'd come to see him?

What would you have done, Mac?

Riley peered at him with a question in her eyes.

Would you have made a different choice?

"I—"

The Fitzgeralds' front door opened then and Fitz appeared in the doorway. Mac sniffed and tucked the letter and photo back into the envelope. "Are you sure you don't want this?"

"Why would I want it? She didn't write me a letter. It's yours." She nodded out the window toward Fitz. "I guess that's him?"

"Dr. Abraham Fitzgerald." He slid the envelope into the center console and nodded toward Fitz as he lumbered down his front steps. "He was my chief when I was a resident. He helped me start my career. He's like my—well, he's more of a father to me than my own father."

Riley took a deep breath and all her bravado, all the swagger, disappeared. Instead she seemed nervous and very young. Mac reached over to her—hesitant, unsure—but when she tensed, he pulled his hand back. Cleared his throat. "He and Cynthia have a garage apartment behind their house. They're known for opening it up to people who need a place to stay for a little while."

Mac opened his door and stood as Fitz approached the car. The man pulled Mac in for a hug—he was as affectionate as he was large—and pounded him on the back. Then he dipped his head to peer into the car and saw Riley sitting in the passenger seat. "Well hello there, young lady." His deep voice rumbled like soft thunder.

"Hello."

Mac stepped away from the car a few paces and turned back to Fitz. "Is your garage apartment open?"

"You know it is. That last resident left practically with his hair on fire. Poor kid, I don't think he was cut out for medicine. Anyway, what are you doing away from the office? Did you take the day off?" He tilted his head, as if the gears in his mind were turning. He glanced toward Riley in the car again, then back at his protégé. "What's going on, Mac?"

Mac opened his mouth, then closed it. Pressed his lips together. "I don't have time to get into it right now. But would it be okay if she—?"

"Stays here—yes. I told you on the phone it was fine."

"Just for a night. Maybe two."

"No problem. Everything okay?" One bushy gray eyebrow tipped up.

Mac cleared his throat. "Not really, no." He glanced at his watch. "But I need to talk to Edie. I'll fill you in later, if that's okay." He glanced up at the house where Cynthia now stood with one slim hip propped against the door frame as she watched them. She wore a flour-smudged turquoise apron over a crisp white shirt and jeans. She held up a hand and smiled.

"Of course. Whatever you need."

"Thanks."

"All right then." Fitz leaned his head down again, peering into the car. "Young lady, are you by any chance hungry?"

Riley's eyes were wide and liquid. "A little."

"Perfect." Fitz rubbed his hands together. "My wife, Cynthia, is in the middle of making a whole mess of fried chicken and we're going to need some help getting rid of it." He walked to her side of the car and opened her door. As she pulled herself out, he stepped back and patted his stomach. "Mind you, I can put away a fair amount, but if I eat too much, she starts going on about my heart health." He gestured toward the house and matched her pace as she made her way to the front steps. Mac grabbed Riley's bag and followed behind. "Sometimes I wonder why she makes such delicious food if I'm not supposed to eat it."

When they arrived at the top of the steps, Cynthia laughed. "I make it so you can eat it, you silly man. You just need to eat the few pieces I give you and not the entire container of leftovers at nine thirty tonight." She held her hand out toward Riley. "Welcome. If you've heard enough of my husband's jokes, I can show you to the apartment so you can freshen up. Would you like that?"

"Thank you," Riley said. Cynthia ducked into the house, but Riley hesitated. She looked back to where Mac stood at the edge of the porch.

"It's okay." He nodded toward the house. "I'll talk to you soon."

She nodded and took a breath, as if steadying herself before walking in. She'd pulled her long hair back into a ponytail, and with it swept back off her face, her soft, young beauty was on full display. Mac still saw features from his own face on hers, but he also saw Kat's high cheekbones, his mother's widow's peak, and curly tendrils at the back of her neck just like Avery. She was a mash-up of so many people he loved. But not all. She looked nothing like Edie.

For one quick, dazed moment, he wondered if she was just a mirage. Some sort of figment that had flashed through his mind, perhaps because of the ad for fishing boats he'd seen on TV the other day. Or the magazine lying on his nurse's desk a few days ago with Graham's face on the front. Or maybe it was the bottle of sunscreen Avery had unearthed from the bottom of an old tote bag that morning and opened in the kitchen, the smell bringing with it summer-strong memories. Maybe it was all a daydream, a flight of imagination. Maybe none of this was real.

But Riley gave him one last glance, and he knew she was real. Heartbreakingly, impossibly alive. Then she walked into the house toward the kitchen with Cynthia.

Fitz whistled low. "I believe you have somewhere you need to be."

"What? Where?"

"Something for your birthday . . . ?"

"Oh, yeah. But how'd you know Edie was taking me out for my birthday?"

He shrugged. "I know a lot of things. Like I know you'd better get on home to Edie and leave this one to us. You call me when you can."

"Yes, sir. And thank you. I'll explain everything."

"Oh, I know you will. And I was serious about those jump shots. They need work." Fitz followed Riley into the house. He smiled back at Mac, then closed the front door behind him.

Standing in his own front yard a short time later, Mac stared up at his house. A white two-story colonial with black shutters, the front porch rails lined with climbing roses. Their orange cat, Ramona, sat on the top step licking a paw, and the yard was still littered with black plastic crows and a gaudy Happy Birthday sign.

His mind whirled. Less than twelve hours ago, he'd been in the kitchen pouring coffee while his family moved around him. Edie sliding a handful of fabrics into her bag, Thomas filling a water bottle, Avery reading up on Reconstruction for her history test. For some reason he'd felt more thankful than usual for the moment together, even if they were all absorbed in their own tasks. It was their life and it was good.

Now he faced the distinct possibility that he was going to turn everything and everyone he loved inside out. This family, these people, this home. His job in the community, their family's reputation. Today's surprise—the mere fact of Riley's existence coupled with the fact that she was ensconced a few miles away in the home of his good friend—had the potential to bring it all crashing down. To bring Mac to his knees and bring everyone else down with him. Everything he'd buried, all he kept from Edie—the hurt he tried to spare her—was about to be laid bare.

He should have known sins never stayed hidden for long.

But this one needed to stay hidden just a little while longer. He wanted to blurt it out, to unload the burden from his shoulders—and savor the relief that would come from finally letting go of the secrets—but he couldn't. Not until things were clearer. Not until he could tell her the truth and then follow it up with a plan of action, a way out of what seemed like a tangled, unthinkable knot.

As Mac took his first heavy step toward the front door, it flew open and Avery burst out.

"Hey, Dad." She trotted down the steps, skipping the last one, Friday freedom evident on her face. "I'm going to Neely's house. We're taking Max for a walk."

"But you and Thomas are staying with Didi tonight, remember?" Mac checked his watch. "She'll be here to pick y'all up soon."

"I won't be long. I already have my bag packed."

"Go straight to Neely's, walk that dog, and come on back. I know Alex lives right next door."

"I got it," she said, already on the sidewalk moving away from him. "Go to Neely's, not Alex's." She glanced back and waved, then kept walking.

Mac's stomach caved. *She's too beautiful.* So smart, so conscientious, so driven, but she had the beauty to go along with the brains, and he remembered all too well what boys in high school thought about.

He sighed a hot stream of anxiety, then crossed the yard, ascended the steps, and opened the front door. Every footstep felt coated in concrete, but he walked with purpose, shoving aside the barely subdued panic that almost choked him. He was prepared to paste on a smile, kiss his wife, and get ready for a nice dinner, but when he saw her upstairs in their bedroom, his courage slipped.

Her phone was pressed to her ear and she was lying back against the pillows on the bed, wearing only her bra and underwear, her legs crossed with one knee propped up. Whoever was on the other end of the line sounded distressed, if the decibel level of the voice was any indication.

Mac dropped his keys on the dresser and sat on the bench at the end of the bed, and when he turned to her, she smiled. Then she pointed to the phone and rolled her eyes.

As she listened to the other person and tried to get a word in when she could, she bounced her foot up and down. Her dark curls were splayed out against the pillow and the room smelled of her delicate perfume. Mac had the sudden urge to bury his face in her neck and breathe her in. Now, while everything was all right.

Instead he pulled off one shoe, then the other, both of them thumping to the ground. He pointed to the bathroom and mouthed, *Shower.*

She nodded and tapped her wrist, the universal sign for "Hurry." He nodded.

A few minutes later, he opened the bathroom door and steam billowed out. Edie was still on the phone, talking about LVL beams and ceiling joists.

After dressing—Edie had helpfully laid out a new pair of charcoal-gray pants and a short-sleeved button-down shirt—Mac brushed his hair and walked back into the bedroom just as Edie hung up the phone.

"I shouldn't have even answered." She tossed her phone on the bed next to her. "She is the most indecisive client I've ever had. And I've had some pretty indecisive clients over the years."

"You're good with that kind of client." He sat at the end of the bed. "You tell them what to do and they're happy for some direction."

"Usually, yes. But this client has asked for so many configurations of the first floor of her house, I think her mind is overloaded. I know mine is." She sat up and reached for her shirt at the end of the bed. "How was your day? Busy?"

"Yeah, it was." He rubbed his hands on the top of his thighs. His muscles felt twitchy, and he had the urge to move and lie down flat at the same time. He stood from the bench.

She paused as she buttoned her shirt. "You okay?"

"I'm fine. I'm hungry though. Where'd you say we have reservations?" He flapped the collar of his shirt away from his skin a few times.

"I didn't. You'll know when we get there." She opened her closet and pulled out a long pink skirt. She slipped it on and tucked her white shirt in, then zipped up the back. With her hair down, part of it pulled back with a jeweled clip, and gold bracelets on her wrists, she looked regal.

"You're beautiful."

She reached down and rustled the skirt around her legs. "You don't think it's too much?"

"No. Not at all."

"Thank you." She took a few steps toward him, then pulled back and stared. "What's wrong?"

An opening. She'd given him an opening and he needed to take it. This minute. Unload it all. Now. He opened his mouth to speak but—

"Oh! I almost forgot." She held up a finger as tension built up in his neck. "Hang on." She grabbed her phone off the bed and tapped out something with her thumbs. "Sorry, I was just supposed to let . . ." She tapped a few more times, then tossed the phone down again. "Okay. Where were we?" She tucked her hair behind her ears and opened the closet door again. "Shoes. I need shoes."

Edie was usually cool and composed, but this evening she seemed scattered. And in more of a hurry than she usually was when getting ready for a date night. Not that they had many of those these days.

She stooped down and pulled a pair of sandals from the floor of her closet. "Thomas is on his way home. Can't remember if I told you that. And Mom's coming soon to pick them up. I told Avery to be back in twenty." She paused. "Do you think Alex is her boyfriend?"

"Her boyfriend?" Mac sat back down again. "I don't know. Is she allowed to have a boyfriend yet?"

"Whether she is or isn't probably doesn't matter all that much. She goes to school with him and he happens to live next door to her best friend."

He exhaled. "You're right. Should we keep her away from Neely's when we're not around?"

Edie fastened the buckle at the side of a sandal. "I don't know. We have to trust her sometime, right? She's a good kid. And she doesn't have a ton of friends. Maybe it's nice that she's connected with someone like him. I mean, he's a total science nerd, which is right up her alley. How much trouble could they get in?"

Mac chuckled. "Do I really need to remind you what all boys think about? Even the ones who are good at science?"

"Hush your mouth. I don't want to be clueless, but I also don't need to know the inner workings of the male brain." She straightened and checked her appearance in the floor-length mirror on the inside of her closet door, then tossed a few things in a small purse—lipstick, keys, cell phone. Mac stood and shoved his hands in his pockets.

Edie stuck her purse under her arm, then stood in front of him and put her hands on either side of his face. "You sure you're okay? You're acting weird. Quiet."

As she watched him, Mac could feel his heart cracking. Like stepping onto a frozen lake and seeing jagged cracks splinter away from the point of contact. Like it could all fall through with just one more step.

He didn't want to take that next step, but he could feel it coming. Ever since that summer, he'd paid for his actions—his choices—in every way he could. He'd worked to be the best husband, father, and provider he could be, and he tried not to keep anything from his wife. Edie was his sounding board, his voice of reason, the person he talked to about everything.

Almost everything.

In their marriage Edie was the cool head, moderate, unflappable. If there was anyone he wanted to talk to about Riley, it was her. But talking to her about Riley would crack that ice wide open.

You made the bed, Mac. Now you've got to sleep in it.

He bit down hard on his lip. "A girl came by my office today." He heard himself say the words before he realized they were out in the open and not just in his head.

"A patient?" Edie's eyebrows lifted just a hair.

"No. Just a girl. Well, not—" He closed his eyes and cleared his throat. When he opened his mouth again, he had no idea what he was going to say. How far back should he go? The incident this afternoon had started almost two decades ago.

"Mac. Where'd you go?"

He blinked and focused on Edie's face. *No. Not now. Not as we're walking out the door. After. Wait until after.*

"Nothing. Don't worry about it." The words just added to his guilt. Because it wasn't nothing. It was the opposite of nothing.

"Don't worry about it? That means it actually is something. If you don't tell me about this girl, I'll worry about her all night. What happened?"

He took a deep breath and exhaled until his stomach clenched. He glanced at the bathroom door, then the floor. Anywhere but at her sweet face. "I have a daughter." He pinched his lips closed. *That came out wrong.*

"Yes, I do too." He heard the smile in her voice.

"No. Another one."

A slight hesitation. A small chuckle. "What are you talking about?"

"The girl who came to see me today." Nausea crept up Mac's throat, ugly and threatening. He swallowed hard. "I met her mom the summer I stayed down at the beach. When I worked at the marina. The girl is eighteen. I—I didn't know." Tears pricked against his eyelids and he let them close. "The math checks out."

"What? What?" The second one was louder than the first, then she let out a small noise, like a tiny sigh or exhalation.

Mac opened his eyes and lifted his head to search her face. He'd lowered his gaze to avoid seeing her face cycle through the emotions, from kind concern to anger or disgust. But instead of one of those tangible, workable emotions, her face was blank. "The summer I was in New York." It wasn't a question. Her voice was as blank as her face. "And you're telling me this now?"

"I didn't know. I didn't know anything about her."

"But just the fact that you met someone that summer. You *really* met someone. And never said anything." She closed her eyes, then opened them, as if trying to blink away reality. "You've never said anything. In all these years." Her tone was incredulous, like she couldn't believe what she was saying—what *he* was saying—but her voice was still so quiet. So soft. It would have been easier if she'd shouted.

"How did . . . ? When . . . ?" She put both hands up to the sides of her face, then let them drop again. "Mac, I don't understand."

"I barely understand it either. She came to my office today. She told me all this stuff about her mom and how she's on her own. She told me her birthday."

"Her birthday?" Edie's eyes were wide and she took a step back from him, then another. "Mac." His name on her lips was a plea, a "please don't let this be true" prayer. He reached for her hand but she pulled it back, away from his touch.

"Edie, please don't. I know this is bad, but it . . . this doesn't change anything with—"

"Doesn't change anything?" If she'd seemed incredulous before, this was pure bewilderment. She held up one hand and her bracelets jangled on her wrist, reminding Mac of their dinner. The reservations they'd no doubt be canceling. "A random girl—what's her name?" He opened his mouth but she shook her head. "No, no. Don't tell me. I don't even want to hear it. A girl comes to see you and tells you all this and you just . . . You're all in? That's it? How do you even know she's telling the truth?"

He closed his eyes. "I just know."

"You just know." The words were slow and deliberate. She stared at him a moment then glanced at her watch. She walked into the bathroom and stood at the counter, her back to him.

Mac's mind raced with all the ways everything would change. Between him and Edie. Him and the kids.

Riley and his children. All of his children together. Until now he hadn't thought about the three of them sharing a space, but suddenly Mac had a mental image of Riley, Avery, and Thomas sitting at a table together, not speaking, just staring.

The front door banged open downstairs. Mac jerked his head toward the bedroom door. *Please don't come upstairs right now.*

"I'm home!" Thomas. A second later the soccer ball thunked against the floor and the door to the fridge opened.

In the bathroom Edie remained still, her hips pressed against the counter, her palms flat on the surface. Then she picked up a stray makeup brush, dropped it in the drawer, and pressed the drawer closed. She lifted her head and her face was clear of any trace of pain or confusion. Any trace of anything. She spoke not to Mac but to his reflection in the mirror. "We have to go."

"Go?"

"Your—dinner. We have reservations."

"Let's just skip dinner. Don't you want to talk about this?"

"Not really, but I know we have to. But we can't cancel dinner. We have to go." She checked her watch again. "Now."

She turned off the bathroom light and breezed past him on her way to the door, but he reached out and grabbed her arm. Not hard, just something to slow her down. "Edie, wait."

She stopped. "We cannot talk about this now." Her jaw pulsed with pressure and Mac could only imagine the words she was keeping inside. Her skin was warm, flushed, and her arm was rigid as iron. He let go and she walked out.

Downstairs, the front door opened again and Edie greeted her mother, Dianne, who always arrived in a whirl of words and excitement. Before Edie could close the door behind her, Dianne had already launched into a story about a rude customer at Firefly, the gift shop she owned with Edie's sister, Blanche.

Edie responded at all the appropriate moments, her voice calm as pond water, with no trace of what had just transpired in this bedroom. Mac needed to go downstairs, but his legs refused to carry him, as if every bit of strength he possessed had drained out. As if he had no life left. Which was exactly how he felt.

He sat on the bench and leaned forward until his elbows pressed into his knees and covered his face with his hands. After a minute he dug his fingers into his hair and squeezed. He wanted to hurt, to bleed, to suffer. It was what he deserved. But instead Edie had been so quiet. So reserved.

Get up. Get up. Get up.

Finally he obeyed. Downstairs, Edie was in the kitchen with her mom and Thomas, who sat at the island with his hand stuffed in a bag of tortilla chips.

"You'll ruin your dinner," Dianne said. "I'm ordering pizza when I get you and your sister back to the house."

"Don't worry, he'll eat that too. He's eating for about three people these days." Edie's voice was cheerful and she looked up when Mac entered the kitchen. "Okay, Mom. We're going to head out. Can you lock the door behind you? Avery should be back here in a few minutes. She's coming from Neely's."

Edie leaned down and kissed Thomas on the head. "I'll see you tomorrow, okay? And use your manners."

"Got it."

Mac crossed the room and hugged Dianne, then squeezed Thomas's shoulder. "Be good."

"Yep. Oh, Dad." Thomas looked up at Mac. "How does it feel to be over the hill?"

Mac ruffled his hair. "Feels great, buddy."

On their way out of the kitchen, Mac heard Thomas ask Dianne, "Do you know why they call it over the hill? What hill are they talking about?"

Mac followed Edie out the front door and closed it behind him. The air outside was warm, and he shaded his eyes from the last sharp rays of sun that streamed through the tree canopy on their street. A few houses away, the Tanners' kids played on a swing hanging from a low limb in their front yard. The ice cream truck was nearby, its familiar music jangly and off pitch. Scents abounded from every direction—jasmine on the side fence, new cedar mulch in the flower beds, and wisps of Edie's perfume.

She was already down the steps and waiting for him on the walkway to the driveway, her slim hips sheathed in that radiant pink, her shoulders sharp and proud, her hair dark and wavy. Mac drank her in, every curve and angle, and his heart surged with hope and the beauty of this moment.

Maybe, just maybe . . .

As he approached her, she held out her hand toward him and relief flooded through him with such force, he wanted to cry. He reached out to take her hand, but she shook her head in irritation and pulled her hand away.

"The keys," she said, her voice monotone. "I'm driving."

CHAPTER 7

EDIE

Present Day

Mac had always been the thoughtful one in their marriage, the one who sent Edie unexpected bouquets of flowers, who planned impromptu trips to the beach or weekends in New Orleans, who stuck funny notes in their kids' backpacks. And he always knew just the right gift for anyone, whether it was his highbrow mother, his office manager Flo Kimble, or Edie's "don't spend any money on me" father.

Not having that same gift-giving knack, she'd booked The Back Alley, an Oak Hill favorite with a hidden outdoor courtyard, for Mac's fortieth birthday, hoping the surprise would cover up for her lack of creativity in this area.

Plus it would be a way for everyone who loved him—and in their small community, that was a lot of people—to be able to celebrate him. He'd touched many lives, and not just because of his thriving pediatric practice. She was constantly running into people at the grocery store or in their neighborhood who stopped her just to say how much Mac had helped them in some way, whether it was offering to contribute to a charity fund-raiser, finding a window in his packed schedule to see an old friend's child with the flu, or even just taking the time to have a real, honest conversation with someone who desperately needed it. He was bighearted and lavish, always willing, always dependable.

Which made the news Edie had just heard all the more unbelievable. She was tempted to shake it off. To brush it aside and force herself to believe it wasn't true. How could it be? Mac fathered another child? There was just no way.

But she couldn't shake the antsy, nervous feeling in her stomach. She could still remember that long-ago day when she and Mac broke up. The fragrant late-spring warmth, the dogwood trees in full bloom outside her dorm on the Southern College campus. How he put his head in his hands and she stared at his fingers as they came to their decision. It was such a strange feeling, after being linked to him for so long, to consider that maybe they weren't actually going to be together forever.

"Edie?"

Taking the job at the marina was an uncharacteristic move for studious, deliberate Mac Swan, but then again, so was her taking an internship in New York City practically sight unseen. They said good-bye after her last exam and didn't see each other again until a few days after class had started for their senior year.

"Edie, please say something."

It was the longest they'd ever gone without seeing each other. And when they returned to school, they didn't talk much about the previous summer. "It was fine. I had fun. New York was busy. The beach was hot." And they'd jumped back into their relationship as if nothing had changed. It had changed, of course. The summer had happened. But they clung to each other with more fervor than before, perhaps both of them determined to push past the *almosts* and *not quites* and *what-ifs* of those intoxicating summer months.

Edie turned left on Camellia Avenue and made a quick right into a parking space in front of The Back Alley. She'd asked all the guests to park down the street, so there were only a couple other cars out front. Nothing to spoil the surprise of the sixty or so guests waiting in the back courtyard. Seven minutes until they expected the Swans to walk in.

She put the car in park, but neither of them moved.

"Are we just going to walk in there without saying anything?" Mac asked. "That'll make for a very interesting dinner."

"What do you want me to say? There's too much. There's not a single question I can ask that won't lead to a hundred more. And we don't have time."

"We have plenty of time. I don't see what the big deal is. People break dinner reservations all the time. The kids are with your mom—we can take all night if we want. Let's talk, say everything we need to say, figure this out."

She shook her head slowly. She was the queen of figuring things out, of finding a solution that before seemed impossible, of unearthing the key that unlocked something previously hidden. She did it all the time, both with her clients and with the kids. But this was different.

She smoothed her hands across the fabric of her skirt. She'd felt so pretty before. She'd bought the skirt and top specifically for the party because they made her feel festive and energetic, and she wanted everything to be perfect for Mac's party.

Now all she could think was, *What else do I not know?*

She checked her face in the rearview mirror, opened the door, and stood. From inside she heard Mac groan. "Edie. Please."

She waited by the car until he opened his door and shut it behind him. With her clutch tucked under her arm, she took his hand and they walked inside.

"Dr. and Mrs. Swan," the hostess said, a little too loudly, prompting a waiter to disappear around the corner of the desk. "We're so happy to have you tonight. Your table will be ready in just a moment."

Edie whispered her thanks and willed the smile to stay in place. She thought of all the people who'd be there. The Tidwells would be front and center—Todd Tidwell had gone to medical school with Mac, and Edie had recently designed the new addition on their home. The Jacobses, Logans, and Maurys would be there, all ready to buy Mac a beer and rehash old memories from school and the basketball court. Friends from church, from Mac's office, from the neighborhood. Dianne was bringing Thomas and

Avery by for a bit, and Edie's sister, Blanche, would probably make an appearance at some point. That is, if she could fit it into her busy Friday night social schedule. Even Mac's parents were coming, having driven down from their new home in North Carolina for their only child's fortieth birthday.

So many people who loved and respected Mac Swan. So many people who needed to think everything was just fine in the Swan household.

The waiter reappeared, a smile on his face. "Right this way."

They followed behind him as he wound through the tables, and when they approached the door to the courtyard, Edie stepped to the side so Mac could go first. He hesitated but she kept her gaze just past his shoulder. Finally he stepped past her. The waiter opened the door to music, happy cheers, and the jubilant blaring of party blowers.

Everyone was in high spirits. Wineglasses emptied and were refilled, beer bottles clinked, laughter and conversation poured from every nook and cranny of the courtyard. A table set up on the far end offered a bounty of Mac's favorite foods—fried shrimp, hush puppies, coleslaw, and barbecue ribs. A friend sat on a stool in one corner with his guitar and a harmonica around his neck, singing everything from James Taylor and Sturgill Simpson to the Grateful Dead and John Mayer. Small wrought-iron tables were scattered throughout the courtyard, which dipped and meandered, creating little pockets of privacy where smaller, more intimate conversations were taking place. Pots overflowed with late-summer blooms and trailing ivy. Candles and white twinkle lights gave just the right amount of illumination.

It should have been a perfect night. One of those no-responsibility nights when they could eat and drink as they wished, laugh with their friends, enjoy good conversations, maybe dance a few slow songs together, then go home and, if they weren't too tired, see where the night led.

Instead they faked it. Or at least Edie did. She couldn't say exactly what was going on in Mac's head or heart, but every time she glanced at him from across the courtyard, she could see his tension. He always held stress in his neck and shoulders, causing him to roll his head side to side or rub the back of his neck. It wasn't so obvious that anyone else would notice it—or if they did, they'd probably just assume he was sore from the gym or maybe a more-energetic-than-usual basketball game—but Edie saw it. And where he felt it in his neck, she felt it in her stomach, a prickly ball of anxiety sitting heavy and preventing her from eating anything more than a single fried shrimp.

Edie's mom brought the kids by early, as they'd planned ahead of time, and they headed straight for Mac with hugs and exclamations of "I can't believe you didn't know!" and "I can't believe Thomas didn't spill the beans!" They ate their fill of ribs and shrimp and smiled politely as the adults gasped over how much they'd grown.

Her dad came by too, having made the trek from his little house up in the country. He kissed Edie's cheek, shook Mac's hand, and hugged Thomas and Avery. Edie's heart hurt even worse when she saw him gaze around for her mom. When he finally spotted her, his shoulders dropped, though he didn't go to her. She was too absorbed in a conversation with one of Mac's nurses to notice him watching her.

Or at least she pretended to be. When he made his way through the crowd to the door a short time later—he'd never been one for parties—her mom paused her conversation to watch him walk out. Her face held a mix of sadness and irritation. It had been a year since Edie's parents had separated, and it was still as weird as it was the day they'd told her it was happening.

After an hour or so, her mom left with the kids and Edie breathed a little easier. Being in their presence—seeing their faces and knowing their lives were about to be upended—made Mac's revelation sting even more.

At some point during the evening, as Edie gathered the handful of birthday cards and small gift bags that had accumulated on the tabletops, someone patted her on the back. It was Mac's mentor, Dr. Fitzgerald.

He reached around her with both arms and squeezed. He smelled of cinnamon and something else smoky and faintly exotic. "Edie. You've put on quite a party for your husband."

She smiled. "Thanks. I wanted to . . . Well, I'm glad it's a good party."

Fitz turned around so he could see the rest of the party. "I saw Thomas and Avery earlier. It's amazing how fast children grow. Though I'm sure you know that, seeing it happen day by day."

"I do. It seems like they should still be running around in diapers with pacifiers in their mouths."

Across the courtyard, Mac's parents approached him. His mother, Louise, in her prim cream sweater and pearls, air kissed near his cheek. David, his father, shook Mac's hand stiffly. It amazed her, every time she saw the three of them together, that someone as loose and friendly as Mac could have come from two such formal, stoic people.

"How's work going for you?" Fitz asked. "Any interesting new clients?"

"Oh, it's fine. Nothing too crazy. Though I do have one man who's asked me to design his master bathroom around a piano."

Fitz's eyes widened. "A piano? In a bathroom?"

She nodded. "A baby grand. Granted, it is a large bathroom, and he said the acoustics were perfect. But still."

"But still," he agreed.

"Is Cynthia here? I haven't seen her tonight."

He hesitated just a hair longer than he should have, which gave Edie a second longer to study him. His mouth was open, as if he'd forgotten what he wanted to say.

"Is she okay?"

"Oh yes. Yes. She's fine. She just needed to stay home tonight. Needed to take care of some things." He paused a moment. "Everything else going okay with you?"

Abraham Fitzgerald was as kind as they came, soft-spoken, a gentle giant. She usually loved how he always asked just the right question or said just the right thing. But tonight, his gentle prod felt intrusive.

"Everything's fine." She tapped the edges of the birthday cards in her palm. "Thanks for coming tonight. It's good to see so many people here for Mac. I need to stick these with my purse."

"Sure, sure. I came over here for a couple more hush puppies anyway. Just don't tell Cynthia."

She smiled. "Your secret is safe."

As she set the cards and bags on an empty table by the door, Mac appeared at her elbow. "Hey," he said quietly. "I've been trying to get back to you all night, but people keep grabbing me to talk."

"It's fine. It's your party. That's what's supposed to happen."

"I know, but—"

"Edie! Mac!"

At the squeal they both turned their heads. Leesa—wife to Carlton, both of whom they'd known forever—was trotting toward them, heels tottering over the cobblestones, a full martini glass in her hand. Her blonde hair was a cascade of sculpted waves, and she wore a white off-the-shoulder jumpsuit that showed off her equally sculpted arms.

Leesa hugged Edie, sloshing a little bit of her drink—thankfully on the ground and not on Edie—then reached for Mac. "Happy birthday, big guy. How does it feel to be the first one of the group to hit the big 4–0?"

"Oh, you know," Mac said with a wry smile. "I feel much wiser."

Carlton joined them. He shook Mac's hand and kissed Edie's cheek. "The Swans sure know how to put on a good party."

"Thank Edie," Mac said. "She did it all."

Leesa and Carlton looked at her expectantly. She just smiled.

"It seems the gang's all here," Carlton said after the awkward pause. "We could pretty much recreate an Oak Hill class photo. But you know who I haven't seen? Graham. Where is that guy? He just kind of dropped off the map, didn't he?"

"Oh, that's right!" Leesa said. "Graham Yeager." His name came out as a sigh. "I always thought he was kind of sexy."

Carlton stared at her, then laughed. "Not your first martini, is it?"

"Nope. That's why the car key is in your pocket, not mine." She turned back to Mac and Edie. "Whatever happened to Graham? Y'all were inseparable in high school. You too, Edie. All three of you. Like two pods in a pea."

"Okay," Carlton said. "I think that's our cue." He clapped Mac on the back. "Happy birthday, man. Let's meet up sometime soon."

"Yeah, yeah. That'd be great."

As soon as they left, Mac leaned his head toward Edie's. "Can we talk for a second?" He put his hand on her lower back and guided her a little ways away, where a wrought-iron trellis covered in vines blocked the view from the rest of the party.

He glanced around—maybe to make sure they were alone or maybe to stall—but she spoke first. "It's not true, is it?"

He shoved his hands in his pockets. Gazed down at his feet. Somewhere in a tree above them, a bird chirped despite the absence of sun, its melody cheerful and free of care.

"It's the only thing I can come up with that makes sense," she whispered. "You were at the beach for three months, maybe not even that long. There's no way you—"

A sudden burst of laughter came from the other side of the trellis. When it died down she continued. "You wouldn't have had time to even meet someone unless you knew her before or . . ." She felt her face go slack. "Or it was a one-night stand. Tell me this wasn't a Flora-Bama fling—"

"Edie, stop." His voice was suddenly sharp, the voice he used when he wanted to get the kids' attention if they were ignoring him. The voice he used when his patience was growing thin. At the sound of it all her words dissipated. They stared at each other in the silence that slipped between them, then she nodded.

"It wasn't like that. I told you, I knew her from the marina. She worked on a boat. A charter fishing boat." The creases between his eyes deepened.

It was a moment before she spoke. "She worked on a boat?"

He cocked an eyebrow at her and pressed his lips together. She shut her mouth. "Yes. She worked hard. It wasn't a summer job for her like it was for me. It was her living."

Everything in her wanted to recoil as he defended this mystery woman.

"We got to be friends, and . . ." He sighed. "I didn't mean for it to happen."

She covered her face with her hands. How could this be true? This was *Mac*. He was supposed to be the good one.

She pulled her hands away. "This is not happening."

"What happened happened—it shouldn't have, but it did—and I realized as soon as I saw you back at school after that summer that it was you I wanted to be with. No one else." He put his hands on her arms and leaned down to meet her gaze. "*No one else.* And I haven't wanted to be with anyone else since then."

"Well, that's comforting, seeing as how that's what a marriage is. Not wanting someone other than your own spouse." Graham's face swam in her mind, but she pushed the image away. This was an entirely different situation.

Mac exhaled and blinked hard.

"You've never mentioned her. Not once in all these years."

"There's never been a reason to."

Edie laughed, incredulous. "Being truthful with the woman you planned to marry wasn't reason enough for you?"

"No, I—"

"I get it. No, really, I get it. Because now there is a reason. Honesty in a marriage clearly wasn't enough, but a living, breathing human being—who you conceived with another woman—is definitely a good reason to tell the truth."

Her words dripped with ugliness and sarcasm, but she didn't care. She dragged warm air into her lungs in an attempt to calm her racing heart. "You're sure this girl, the one who came to see you, you're sure she's yours? What about a paternity test?"

It was a trashy daytime talk show question, as if they belonged on opposite ends of a stage, the audience roaring and pointing.

"It's not necessary."

"Why not? Why would you not want to make sure?"

He raised his hands, then let them fall. "We can do one if it makes you feel better. Okay? But you'll see why when you meet her." He shook his head and gave a small laugh. "Edie, she looks just like me."

"You've got to be kidding me." This wasn't her real life. It couldn't be. She clenched her teeth together so hard her jaw ached. She waited for him to say more, but he just stood there with an unbearably sad expression on his face. "Mac, it feels like you're just expecting me to take this—to accept it—and not ask questions."

A couple walked by them headed for a small table at the back of the courtyard. When the husband saw Mac, he called out a hearty, "Happy birthday, buddy! And Edie, great party."

"Thanks, man," Mac called. "Thanks for coming."

Edie forced a smile and waved, then turned back to Mac.

"I'm not expecting anything," he said quietly. "I don't know what to expect. There's no rule book for this. I have no idea how to explain to my wife, the woman I love, that I have a child—another child—waiting for me at Fitz's house."

"She's at Fitz's house?" Edie blurted. Her heart sank. The too-long pause. That was why Fitz was here alone. Cynthia was home with the girl. An ache crept through Edie's chest at the realization that other people had known about this before her. "I can't talk about this anymore."

From the other side of the trellis, someone called Mac's name. "Where is that guy? It's his party!"

"Go on and see them." She gathered a handful of her skirt in her hand so she could more easily negotiate her way across the old cobblestone bricks in her heels. "It's your party."

His eyes were weary, his mouth open and pained. "Please don't—"

She turned and headed back toward the remaining crowd.

———

They were silent on the way home. Edie's feet ached, her cheeks hurt from holding a smile, and they were both talked out. It should have been a perfect night, capped off by the manager of the restaurant sending them home with a box containing the remaining slices of Mac's red velvet birthday cake. Under other circumstances, they might have gone home, quietly kicked their shoes off, grabbed two forks, and eaten the cake in bed. Their world had changed though, and there was no way to make it go back to the way it was, no matter how fervently she wished they could.

But if they really could rewind time and make it all go away, would that mean Mac hung on to his secret while she remained in the dark? If given the choice, would she choose blissful ignorance or gut-wrenching awareness?

And just like that, her mind was back in New York City, sitting across the table from Judith, deciding between truth and ignorance. The red pill or the blue. If only she'd known all those years ago what kind of truth she was actually dealing with.

At the moment she wasn't sure which one was better.

"It must have been significant—what you had with . . ." She paused. "I don't even know her name." She'd parked in the driveway, but neither of them had moved to open their doors. The light from the front porch bathed one side of his face in light, but it didn't reach his eyes.

"What was the girl's name?" She shook her head. "The girl's mother?"

"Kat." His voice was quiet. "Her name was Kat."

"Kat." Edie tasted the word on her tongue. She tried to imagine what the woman may have looked like, but she couldn't bring up any kind of mental image. "Do you still talk to her?" If he'd kept her a secret from Edie once, what was keeping him from keeping her a secret again?

"I haven't talked to her in almost twenty years."

"But does she know . . . that you know?" She had so many questions, they came out rapid fire. "Are you going to call her? Don't you think a mom would want to know if her daughter has gone off to find her father? Who did this girl think her father was? How could—?"

"Edie, I'm exhausted. I know we still have a lot to discuss, but—"

She snorted out an ugly laugh. "You could say that."

"Can we please just stop here? Let's get some sleep, then we can get back to it tomorrow."

Eyes wide, she stared at him. "Sleep? How in the world am I going to sleep? How are you going to sleep? You need to call . . . Kat." She inhaled and blew the air out slowly. "You need to tell her what's going on. She needs to come get her daughter. The girl can't stay with Fitz and Cynthia, and she sure can't—"

"Edie, Kat is dead." Mac leaned his head back against his seat and closed his eyes.

"What?"

"She died a year ago."

Through the closed windows, a siren wailed in the distance. Edie's stomach rolled.

"Not only does Riley have a father who's essentially been a deadbeat her whole life, but she's motherless too." He reached down to unbuckle his seat belt, and the latch clanged against the raised window.

Riley. Mac's daughter's name was Riley. Edie took a moment to digest that. And the fact that if all this was true, Mac was right. He had been, essentially, a deadbeat father.

She breathed in and let it out in a slow stream. "You and I have been building this life together, but her memory has been seared in the back of your mind. Our whole marriage."

"Edie. No." His voice was almost a growl. She knew she was pushing him to his limit—and it took him a lot to reach that limit. "That's not what it's been like. I told you, I haven't spoken to her since that summer." He paused. "Not once."

She bit down hard on her lower lip. What was happening? Her husband had never once given her the slightest hint of unfaithfulness, but this earthquake of news rattled everything loose. All of a sudden, the building blocks of their marriage felt as flimsy as paper.

"Can we go in?"

She nodded.

Once inside their house—the familiar scent of the candle by the door, the cool air, Thomas's history binder on the foyer table, one of Avery's shoes on the bottom step— Edie felt exhaustion hit her like a physical force. Mac headed straight for the stairs, trudging up each one like his feet weighed a hundred pounds each. She followed him, but she stopped in the doorway to their bedroom. Mac collapsed onto the bed, toed his shoes off, and began to unbutton his shirt. He turned to where she stood at the door, a question in his eyes.

The idea of that lost perfect evening still shimmered at the edges of her mind, just far enough that she couldn't grasp it. Their firm mattress and soft white duvet that enveloped, cocooned. Mac, with his thick hair end-of-the-day messy and his sweet, weary face.

Life in their house, in their world, was busy, and they were usually exhausted at the end of each day. She supposed it was no surprise it had been a while. It was easy to find reasons not to connect when they often felt more like business partners in life and parenting. But tonight, climbing in next to him in their quiet, empty house, pressing her leg to his, his arm snaking around her body . . . It would all be so easy. So effortless.

If everything wasn't so different now. If they weren't living an altered reality.

"I can't. I'm going downstairs." She took a step back and retraced her path down the stairs.

Behind her, Mac called, "Edie, please come back."

She left her shoes on the bottom step and moved toward the back of the house, quiet as air. The rooms were dark but she could have navigated them in her sleep, so familiar was this house to her. She trailed her fingers across tabletops and chair backs on her way to the den. She'd designed and redesigned the interior of their home over the years, moving pieces around, changing color schemes, painting walls, not following trends of the design world so much as the urgings she felt sometimes when she studied a room and discerned something wasn't right. She'd reorder and shuffle and fluff until the room offered life again. A new welcome. She loved doing it in their own home as much as she loved doing it for her clients.

She and Mac still had a couple pieces of furniture from the early days of their marriage. Most of it she'd painted or reupholstered, but the one piece that hadn't changed from the day they bought it was the oversize blue-and-white couch in the den, the one calling her name now.

She tapped Thomas's soccer ball out of the way and moved a couple of magazines off the foot of the couch before she crumpled. Sinking onto the down-filled pillows was heavenly, despite the throbbing in her head. She took off her earrings and dropped her bracelets to the floor, then stretched out her legs, savoring the tug and release on her tired muscles.

When she finally found a comfortable position and lay still, all she could think about was the woman from the boat. Kat. He said he hadn't talked to her, but had he thought about her over the years? Did he wonder about her? The fact that she was no longer alive did nothing to take away the sting that Mac had wanted someone other than her. It was selfish, considering all she'd questioned and wondered that summer, but wanting and acting were two vastly different things. He'd acted; she hadn't.

But what if she had? The question crept in from somewhere and gently brushed up against her. What if she and Mac hadn't gotten back together and instead it had been Graham and her together, charting their path back up to New York after graduation, to a job, a partnership, a life? Why didn't she choose that path? What had stopped her?

The answer, of course, was Mac. His constancy and his honesty. His devotion to her and her own trust in that devotion. Their mutual desire for family, warmth, and stability.

Regardless of what should or shouldn't have happened in the past, she and Mac had built a life together and had two beautiful children. Never in a million years would she have thought they'd be dealing with the fallout of that summer so many years later.

Their bedroom was directly above her, and several minutes later the bed creaked, then the floor. Her breath stopped as she tracked Mac's footsteps on the creaky hardwood floor. It was quiet a moment. Could he be gathering his nerve, preparing to come downstairs? Was he nervous? Repentant? She imagined his warm hands reaching to take her, his kind eyes spilling over as he unburdened and explained and tried to make right. She pushed herself up onto her elbow, her heart leaping in her chest.

He moved again, another creak on the floor, then his footsteps tracked back to the bed. Edie waited until the bed squeaked as he crawled back in alone before she closed her eyes.

CHAPTER 8

MAC

Summer 2000

After that first day, Mac didn't see Kat again for a while. Which was probably a good thing, considering how bushed he was at the end of every day. Two of the guys who were supposed to start as dockhands the same time as Mac failed to show up, and in her frustration, Carla worked him extra hard.

"What's the matter with you kids these days?" she'd ask in her raspy voice anytime her path crossed his. "Always expecting things to be handed to you. And when you do get something—a paying job where people expect you to show up and work—you blow it off for the next best thing."

Finally one hot afternoon, after pressure washing the bottom of a twenty-eight-foot Robalo only to find out he'd washed the wrong one, Mac snapped. Well, he snapped as much as someone can snap who'd been raised to be respectful and polite. "Hey." Mac cut his eyes toward Carla. "I'm not the one who didn't show up."

She pretended not to hear him as she ripped open a pack of Marlboro Reds, her second of the day. They stood outside the dock store, in the slim strip of shade next to the building. One of the boat captains lumbered by,

77

a mess of fishing poles under his arm and a net over his shoulder. Carla lifted her chin in greeting.

"Carla." Mac got her attention again. "I'm here. See me?" He held his hands out to his sides. She squinted at him through the haze of smoke that hung in front of her face. "You hired me and I showed up. I want to work. I *am* working. I just spent two hours power washing the wrong boat—because you wrote it on the wash sheet—but I'm not complaining. In fact, I'm about to walk over there and start all over again. On the right boat."

She took another drag off her cigarette and blew the smoke halfheartedly over her shoulder. Her brown-gray hair was pulled tight to her head, as usual, but today she'd wrapped a skinny white ribbon around her short ponytail. "I didn't tell you the wrong boat. I'd say someone pulled a fast one on you." She dragged on her cigarette. "But you're right. You're a good kid. Unlike the rest. Maybe you'll make it 'til the end of the summer. Usually I have to send them packing by the time the Fourth of July rolls around. I got no time for slackers."

She stuck her half-smoked cigarette in the sand-filled butt bucket outside the dock store, then opened the door. "The owner of that Robalo likes to wash his boat himself. He never allows temporary hands to wash his baby. You did a good job on it though." She shrugged. "Maybe he won't be too mad this time." She held the door and stepped to the side as a customer walked past before she stepped into the crisp, cool air of the store. The glass door whooshed closed behind her.

Mac sighed and wiped his forehead on his shirtsleeve. When he turned around, Kat stood directly behind him—bright-blonde hair in a long braid, white sunglasses propped on top of her head, denim shorts, arms crossed.

"D'you get on Carla's bad side or something?"

"What? No, I—" When she grinned, Mac realized she was kidding. "Well, maybe I did a little. I didn't mean to."

"Don't worry too much about it. Happens every summer. She likes to throw her weight around, especially with the new guys."

"Yeah. I'm figuring that out."

Kat hooked her thumb back toward the boat storage facility. "You headed this way?"

He nodded and fell into step beside her. The last time they'd spoken, she lit into him about being a college kid hoping for a responsibility-free summer. She seemed looser today, not wound so tight, but she still made him nervous. And that alone should have been reason enough for him to keep his distance.

"Carla mentioned you're from Mobile," she said. "Are you driving back and forth every day?"

"No, I'm staying with a friend. His aunt has a house on Old River."

"Must be nice. How's your first week been?"

He hesitated, trying to gauge her attitude. "It's been good, I guess. Hard. But good."

"A little hard work's never a bad thing."

He let that sit for a minute, trying to see her words from a different angle. Her voice was nonchalant, but the slim knife-edge of sarcasm was apparent. Was she mocking him?

"I know how to work hard." Mac couldn't keep it in any longer. "At school, at home, everywhere. I've been doing it every day my whole life. Don't talk to me about hard work like I know nothing about it."

He kept his eyes straight ahead, on the rough wooden boards under his feet, the palm trees that lined the walkway, the boat storage building that loomed at the back of the parking lot, but he felt her stare. He set his jaw to make himself appear harder, stronger.

"Didn't mean to set you off," she said. "I was just making conversation." He heard her smile without having to see it.

"No, you weren't. You took one look at me when I arrived and decided I was lazy. Some goof-off here to get a tan. I'm right, aren't I? But that's not why I'm here."

"Then why are you here?"

The sarcasm was gone, and her voice was sharp. Direct. She stopped where she was on the walkway and after a couple more paces, he stopped, too, and turned back to face her. She pushed a flyaway hair behind her ear and propped her hands on her hips. He tried not to notice the taut muscles in her arms.

"I get it. You're not here for fun. But you're here for something. So what is it?" She'd dropped her sunglasses back onto her face, but he saw an eyebrow dart up behind the frames.

A flood of words threatened to pour out. He hadn't been able to properly explain to Edie, or even to Graham, why he needed the time away, but maybe the fact that Kat was a stranger would allow him to put it into coherent words.

Then a loud catcall erupted from somewhere to his left. A guy in Carhartt overalls and a yellow tank top waved from the entrance to the boat barn.

Kat groaned.

"You know him?"

"Do I know him? I know them all. Come on." She took off for the barn and Mac followed.

"Hey, good lookin'," the guy called as she approached. "I figured you'd still be out on the water."

"We had to head in early. It was a bachelor party, and the guys couldn't handle the swells out in the Gulf." She put a hand up to shade her eyes.

"You don't usually come in early for things like that."

"True, but we got paid whether we stayed out the whole day or not, and they begged us to bring them in. They puked all morning."

"Lucky you, then. You get an afternoon off."

Kat tipped her head to where Mac stood a few steps behind her. "This is Jeff. He likes his overalls." To Jeff, she called, "Say hey to Mac. He's on the dock crew."

"Hey, Mac on the dock crew. I saw you washing Jimbo's Robalo. You're a brave soul." Jeff ran his thumbs underneath the straps of his overalls.

"Not brave. Just following orders. It was on the wash sheet, so I washed it."

"That Carla, man. She can make mistakes when she's writing down orders."

"That's funny. She said she didn't do it." His voice sounded bolder than he felt.

The guy shrugged, a hard glint in his eyes. "Maybe the heat got to her." He tipped his chin. "Hey, Kat, want to hit the Bama with us tonight? Mudbugs play at ten."

"Don't tell me you've forgotten what happened the last time I went out with you."

"Oh no, ma'am, I have not forgotten that."

"Sure you want to go down that road again?"

He laughed. "Know what? I think I'll rescind my invitation."

"Smart move." She turned to go but stopped and took a few steps closer to him. "Can I see Carla's clipboard for a minute?"

"Sure." He grabbed the clipboard—the one where Carla listed all the boats that needed to be prepped and readied for a day on the water, and the ones that needed to be flushed, washed, and prepped for storage—and handed it to Kat.

She ran a finger down the page and stopped halfway down. "How long have you been working here, Jeff?"

"Three years. Why?"

"Just curious. I've been here for six, and I've worked with Carla that whole time. I'm pretty familiar with her handwriting."

"That so?"

"Yeah. And this?" She held the board out to him, her finger pointing to a line. "Where it says Jimbo Everly? This isn't hers." She shoved the clipboard at him. "But it sure does look like your chicken scratch."

Jeff laughed. "You caught me." He nodded at Mac. "It's all in good fun, kid."

"I can take it."

"Well, I'm glad someone can. Because Miss Mills here sure can't."

"I can take a lot of crap. I'm just really tired of yours. Everybody's got a job around here, Jeff. Let Mac take care of his."

Without waiting for his answer she headed toward the docks. Jeff turned back for the barn, shaking his head. Mac stood still a moment, then jogged to catch up with Kat. She'd stopped next to *Alabama Reds*.

"Hey," he called. "Thanks."

"For what?" She hopped down into the boat's hull, her feet landing quietly.

"For helping me out with Overalls back there."

"No problem. I don't pass up any chance to put Jeff in his place."

The sun beat down hard, casting diamonds onto the water around the boats. A lone seagull sat on a tall piling and ruffled its wings as music from Dave's tiki hut breezed by.

"What happened when you went with him to the Bama?"

Kat snorted. "He kept shaking his scrawny hips and trying to pull me out on the dance floor. Didn't listen when I said no." She shrugged. "He got a little handsy so I gave him the knee. Changed his tune pretty quick."

"I bet he did."

She gazed off into the distance a moment, then turned back to him.

"I'd better go and wash the right boat," he said.

"Get to it then."

His Reef flip-flops squeaked as he headed back up the walkway.

"I'm not letting you off the hook, by the way," Kat called.

He stopped. "What do you mean?"

"I want to know why you came here. Why you left your cushy life to work on a dock for the summer."

"It's a long story."

"We've all got long stories. But suit yourself. Keep your secrets." She busied herself with the dials on the boat's wide dash. "See ya 'round, kid."

CHAPTER 9

EDIE

Summer 2000

"Edie, were you able to snag the swatch book?"

Kaye's voice floated from her windowed office facing Fifth Avenue. Edie set her mug of black coffee on her cubicle desk, grabbed the book, and walked it down to the lead designer at Kaye Snyder Interiors.

"I knew you could do it." Kaye smiled when Edie tapped on the door and held up the thick book full of fabric swatches from Village Fabrics. "It just takes the right amount of charm and humility to get them to loosen their grip."

"It was nothing to do with me," Edie said. "All I did was mention your name and they practically shoved it at me. The guy at the front desk said if you don't see exactly what you want, they'll go into the vault and pull some of their discontinued lines."

Kaye beamed. "The design muses are smiling down on us today. I think we'll be able to find something Reese will like. Have you had a chance to peruse the book?" Kaye flipped through the pages as strips of linen, cotton, silk, brocade, and damask slid past.

"I did see one I thought had some potential."

Kaye sat back in her chair. "Show me."

Edie turned a few more pages and stopped at the swatch of scarlet-and-cobalt silk.

"Interesting combination." Kaye nodded.

"I know it's a little bold. But when, um . . ." She swallowed hard. It was difficult to get used to using celebrities' names as if she actually knew them. "When Reese was here the other day, I noticed her purse."

"I did too!" Kaye said with a gleam in her eye. "That red was stunning, wasn't it?"

"It was. This scarlet here is pretty close to the shade of her purse, and, I don't know, I think the cobalt is a great contrast. Plus, her heels were blue." Edie smiled. "It was such a fresh look. I thought, why not mimic that on her pillows?"

Kaye rubbed the silk between her fingers a moment, considering. When the moment stretched, Edie spoke again. "If you think the red and blue is too punchy, look what happens if you add this peach and sky blue with it." She grabbed a couple more strips of silk and held them next to the red and blue.

Kaye tilted her head. "Well now, that's a whole palette, isn't it? It's unexpected. And very fresh." She gazed at it a moment longer. "I like it. Let's get her approval and if she's game, we can build the whole living area around these colors."

She closed the book and set it to the side of her desk, then pressed a button on her desk phone. "Candace. Call Reese and schedule our next meeting. Edie has a color palette to present to her." She hung up and smiled. "Good work, Edie. You have a great eye. And that's hard to teach."

Edie pressed her lips together and nodded. "Thank you."

———

When Edie first heard about the internship with New York City interior designer Kaye Snyder, she discarded the opportunity as impossible. But then she and Mac broke up, and before she could overthink it, she marched to her professor's office and filled out the application. Two weeks later, she got the call that the internship was hers.

Which brought Edie here, unlocking the door to the skinny stairwell that led from the street up to the tiny fourth-floor walk-up that was her home for the summer. She'd spent the rest of that afternoon ferrying elevation drawings and swatches to clients all over the city with Kaye, getting lost on the subway, and pausing at small, tucked-away parks and courtyards to draw anything that caught her eye. Which, in this city, was just about everything.

Her ankle throbbed from missing the last step going down into the subway station earlier in the day, and she was sure her sore feet would never recover from the amount of walking this city required, but she didn't care. She loved it and still couldn't believe she was lucky enough to be here.

Bypassing the door to her apartment, Edie kept going until she reached the seventh floor and the door to the rooftop. She opened it and let the cool night air soothe her as she caught her breath. She'd discovered the rooftop patio by accident her first week here, and most nights, as long as the weather was good, Edie ate her dinner sitting at a metal table overlooking the bustle of Lexington Avenue. Tonight she propped her feet on the rail and savored the scene. A horn sounded far below, followed by a yell and a burst of laughter. As the lights of the city glowed and flickered, she thought of Graham.

Since the day she'd arrived, she'd been buying postcards to remind her of the nooks and crannies of the city. She pulled one from her bag now, tapped her pen against her bottom lip, then began to write.

Dear Graham,

I'm sorry to say I won't be returning to Alabama. It was great knowing you, but I've decided to stay here in the Big Apple. The excitement and pace of life is something I didn't know I needed, but now I don't think I can do without it. Please pack my things and send them to my apartment on East 86th, care of Kaye Snyder, my boss, benefactor, and pretty much my favorite person in the entire world.

I'm kidding, of course, though I am head over heels in love with this city and my job. You know who else would love it here? You. It seems every time I turn around, I see something else that makes me wish you were here, seeing all this and soaking it all up. In fact, I can't believe you don't already live here. The place screams your name.

I know you're working hard and all, but if you decide to skip town and head to the city for a quick trip this summer, I know a gal who'd be happy to serve as your tour guide. She may get you lost, but she'll buy you a bagel to make up for it.

Edie

CHAPTER 10

Mac

Present Day

When Mac woke, the light through the window told him it was later than it should be. He knew he'd overslept, but caught in that stupefying place between awake and asleep, he could barely pinpoint what day it was, much less the specific time. He slid his leg to the side to see if Edie was still sleeping, and when it touched only cool emptiness, everything from the day before rushed back:

Riley in his office. *I have another child.*

Edie's face as she tried to comprehend.

Her stiff smile as he stepped into the courtyard to wild shouts and cheers.

And later, the sound of her walking downstairs, away from their bedroom. Away from him.

He sat up and strained to hear. It was so quiet in the house, he could hear a lawn mower whining from down the road. A car passing by their house. Faint voices from the Millers' house next door.

Then he heard the *ding* of the microwave downstairs. Assuming the kids were not up and back home at—he checked the clock on his phone—7:40 in the morning, Edie was awake and in the kitchen.

With his stomach twisting he pulled on a pair of shorts and a T-shirt, ran a hand through his hair, and headed downstairs. At the bottom step he paused, willing himself to be all the things he needed to be to get through this day. This week. And for however long everything was different. He'd created it all—everything in him that felt wrong and guilty and sick, and everything that was hurting Edie. It was all his fault. The load on his shoulders was huge and unwieldy. A mountain range. A universe.

The closing of a cabinet door dislodged him from his daze. He turned and passed through the short hallway that held the years of their marriage and family life on the wall in wooden frames. Snapshots, flashes of time, both formal and fun. Grins and laughter, hidden moments and meaningful occasions. He directed his gaze to the floor as he walked toward the kitchen.

Edie stood at the counter buttering a piece of toast, wearing a pair of shorts and a long-sleeved blue shirt with *Oak Hill Patriots* emblazoned on the front pocket. Avery's shirt. The long pink skirt from last night was nowhere to be seen. She must have found the change of clothes in the laundry room.

"Toast?" She held a slice of bread over the toaster. He managed a nod, and she dropped the slice in and pressed the lever down. "The coffee's stronger than usual." She carried her mug and plate to the table and sat facing the window, with her back to the kitchen. "I figured we could use the extra shot of energy."

Her normalcy—or at least a version of it—surprised him. He'd expected nothing but coldness and anger. And it might be coming, but for the moment, the seemingly normal conversation was a grace he wanted to bathe in.

When he sat across from her with his toast and coffee, she wrapped both hands around her mug and sat back in her chair. "So how are we going to do this?"

"Do . . . what exactly?"

She lifted an eyebrow. "Figure out Riley. What to do with her. We've got to do it quickly. I've already texted Mom and she said the kids can stay with her at the shop until later this afternoon. I told her we had a few things to take care of on our own. But they'll come home eventually. We have to have her squared away by then."

The Edie of last night had been dejected, bitter, and ultimately deflated. All valid and expected feelings considering all he'd dropped on her. But what sleep she managed to get on the couch must have rejuvenated her, because this Edie was pert. Direct. Resolute. This was brass-tacks Edie.

She set her mug down and pinched a piece of crust from her toast, then popped it in her mouth. "The first thing we have to do is get her from Fitz's house. Do you think it's too early to call him?"

"I don't think so, but he said it'd be okay if she stayed with them for a little bit. They have the apartment in the back and—"

"No. She's not their problem and Fitz and Cynthia shouldn't have to take the brunt of it." She shook her head. "We'll have to go get her, but then where to take her, I'm not sure."

"Where to take her?"

"Yeah. I mean, she can't stay here. Obviously."

She said it so plainly, so confidently. He wanted to agree. *Of course, you're right. It'd be ludicrous to have her here.*

But he hesitated.

"Mac. You don't seriously think we can bring her to our house. What about our kids?" She opened her eyes wide. "How would we explain her? And how she's connected to you?"

"We can't tell them anything but the truth."

She stared at him a moment, then exhaled a humorless laugh through her nose. "Of course. Nothing but the truth." Angry tears brimmed in her eyes, but she rubbed them away before they could fall. "We could always give her some money and let her leave."

Riley's words rang in his mind. *"All I need is a little money . . ."*

"Babe, I—I'm sorry, but I can't do that. I can't push her away. She's . . . my daughter. She's a part of me, whether I knew it or not. Would you be able to do that? Turn your back on your own child?"

"Of course not. I could never be in this situation."

"Biologically, you couldn't. But if by some chance you found out you had a child you didn't know about, could you leave her on her own?"

Her jaw was set firm, her gaze icy, but Mac saw the small shake of her head.

"Well, neither can I. She's here in our world, and I can't just get rid of her. I won't." He surprised himself with his own resolution.

Edie took a deep, shaky breath. Pinched her lips together. Then whispered, "I can't believe you never told me this."

He sighed and tipped his head back, closed his eyes briefly. "I told you—I haven't kept Riley from you our whole marriage. I didn't know of her existence until yesterday. Trust me, I'm reeling just as much as you are."

She stood quickly and walked a few steps away. "But *Kat*, Mac. What about Kat? Why did you never tell me you had a *thing* that summer? You told me about the guy in the overalls and the one who made cocktails in the little hut. And that woman who rode the tractor all over the place, carrying the boats. But of all the people you told me about that summer, you never mentioned a Kat."

"In hindsight I know I should have, but back then I guess I didn't think there was a reason to tell you. I mean, Edie, we were broken up. Don't you remember? Meeting someone should have been okay. It shouldn't have been something I needed to run home and tell you about."

"Yes. Meeting someone should have been fine," she said, her words low but pointed. "But you more than *met* the girl, Mac."

"Was I supposed to come back and tell you that?" He was losing his control but he couldn't help himself. It felt so good, like letting air out of an overfull balloon. "Is that what you would have wanted? For me to come back to school and greet you with, 'Hey, babe, guess what? I slipped up and slept with someone this summer. How was New York?'"

It may have felt good to get the words out, but now he wished he could reel them back in. Across the room, Edie's mouth went thin. "No," she said quietly. "I would not have wanted to hear that."

He stood and walked toward her. She took a step back, but he caught her by the shoulders and forced her to remain there with him. "Edie, I

90

know I've messed up. But I will do anything to make this better for you. And for us." When her image blurred, he blinked the tears away. "I'll do whatever I need to do to fix it. I just need you. I need you with me."

Her gaze held his for a long moment. Her eyes were red but her tears were gone. Then she used her thumbs to brush the dampness from his cheeks. "I have to take a shower. You call Fitz. Tell him we're on our way."

A little while later, they stood on the old wooden boards of Fitz and Cynthia's front porch. September wasn't doing them any favors; the barest hint of fall they'd felt days before had evaporated in the face of another wave of thick humidity and temps near ninety. Mac's heart thrashed in his chest and sweat beaded on his back.

Next to him, Edie appeared cool and fresh. If she felt anything like what he was feeling inside, she sure didn't show it. Mac raised his hand to knock, but before he could do it, the door whooshed open and Cynthia stood in the doorway.

"Edie." She pulled Edie into a hug. "I'm glad to see you." Over Edie's shoulder Cynthia caught Mac's eye and her smile fell. Disappointment—or maybe disapproval—flowed from her short twists of gray hair down to her red-and-white Nikes.

Cynthia pulled back from the hug and patted Edie's arm. "I have a pan of banana bread cooling on the stove. Go ahead and cut yourself a big slice."

Edie walked into the house, leaving Mac with Cynthia. He waited, and when she didn't say anything, he made a move to step forward into the house, but she held her arm up. He thought she was going to stop him, but she wrapped her arm around his neck and hugged instead. "I can't stay mad at you, young man. But you're sure in a pickle, aren't you?"

He pulled back and stared at her.

She looked at him deadpan. "You think I don't know who Riley is to you? She's cut from your very same cloth, Mac Swan."

He hung his head. "Cynthia, I can—"

She held up her hand. "I know you want to explain, but now's not the time. And anyway, you don't owe me an explanation. Now, my husband, he may want it. But me? I just want to know everyone's going to be okay. You and Edie, *and* that young girl you dropped off here."

She gave him a measured stare, then motioned for him to pass into the house. "He's not here, you know," she said over her shoulder on her way to the kitchen. "He's teaching a Saturday class."

Fitz hadn't been retired from the medical profession six months before he decided he was bored. Luckily for him, the medical community still had a spot for him. He'd been teaching CME courses at the University of South Alabama for years now.

"I know," Mac said. "We were hoping to talk to Riley."

In the kitchen Cynthia opened the fridge and pulled out a pitcher. Edie stood at the window overlooking the Fitzgeralds' manicured back-yard and the green clapboard garage that housed a small apartment above. "Good luck," Cynthia said. "I went out there a little while ago to see if I could get some banana bread in her—she didn't eat dinner last night—but she was still asleep. I tried talking to her last night. I had her in here helping me make dinner. She seemed to enjoy it—gathering ingredients, chopping vegetables. But she stayed shut tight as a clamshell. Except for that blasted phone. Y'all want some tea?"

Mac nodded, and when Cynthia glanced at Edie, she nodded too. Cynthia pulled down two glasses and filled them.

"What do you mean about the phone?"

Cynthia handed him a glass and he took a long, cool sip, then pulled out a stool and sat at the counter. Edie moved to a spot next to him, but she didn't sit.

"The whole time she was in here with me last night, that phone kept ringing. A few times she didn't answer it, but the one time she did, she ended up in tears. She took the phone into the backyard, and I watched her from in here. She paced back and forth, talking with her hands, the whole nine yards." Cynthia crossed her arms and leaned her hip against the counter. "Whoever it was sure gave her an earful."

Mac remembered Riley's phone ringing yesterday. The dude with the big arms and Riley turning the phone off.

"I don't know what's going on with her," Cynthia continued, "but she just seems so tender. Raw, you know? But at the same time, something's made her hard. It's an uneasy combination, and I see it a lot in my line of work." She rested her hands on the surface of the counter. "Look, Mac, I don't want to meddle—"

"You're not meddling. I brought her to your house, so you can say anything you want. I'm really sorry. I just . . . I didn't know what else to do in the moment."

"Hush, now." She patted his hand. "You know I don't mind her staying here. I just want to make sure we get her what she needs. Especially with the baby coming."

The realization hit him like a punch to his solar plexus. In the horror of having to tell Edie about Riley and Kat, then the party and working so hard to pretend all was well, he'd completely forgotten to tell her about the pregnancy. More than that, he'd forgotten about it at all. He could only imagine what Edie felt.

A moment later Edie's mouth gaped, as if it had taken a minute for Cynthia's words to sink in.

"Edie—"

The back door opened and Riley stood in the doorway. When she saw Mac, she froze. Then her eyes darted to Edie.

"Riley." Cynthia grabbed another glass and filled it with tea. "Here you go, honey."

"Thanks." Riley crossed the floor and took the glass, then took a few steps back again. She wore the same denim shorts from yesterday and an oversize white shirt. She'd knotted it on the side, which only served to accentuate the bump in front.

Edie's eyes roved over Riley's body, from her head down to her feet. Riley glanced toward the back door as if judging the quickest escape route.

"Now that everyone's here," Cynthia said, "I'm going to scoot out. I missed my walk yesterday, so I need to get it in today. Can't let up on the exercise at my age."

Mac stood and set his glass in the sink.

"If y'all head out before I get back, it's fine to just leave the front door unlocked." She motioned for Mac to lean down. "You do what you need to do," she whispered. "If you need to leave her here another night, or however long, it's fine by us."

"Thanks, Cynthia," he whispered back. "Not many people would have been okay with a situation like this."

"Well, what can I say? We love you." She patted his cheek. "And something tells me things will turn out all right."

Then she walked out the back door, leaving the kitchen a silent tomb of discomfort. Mac glanced back and forth between Edie and Riley. His wife and his daughter. His other daughter. Neither of them looked at each other. Riley was staring at him, but Edie had gone back to the window, her back to the room, one hand on her hip, the other on her cheek.

"Edie?"

She turned at the sound of her name. Her face was no longer angry—it was worse. Her cheeks were damp, her eyes red. She blotted her cheeks with the heels of her hands. Mac thought she'd say something to Riley—a hello, or at least some kind of acknowledgment—but it didn't come.

Riley glanced at him as if waiting for some direction.

"How about we go sit down?" He gestured through the side door into the living room.

Riley moved first, walking through the door and sitting on the couch, but Edie shook her head. "I can't, Mac." She turned and stared out the window again, toward the sun-dappled patio and backyard beyond. "I can't go in there with you." Then she was walking away from him. Again.

He watched her on the patio until a phone rang and the sound pulled him back to the kitchen. Through the doorway into the living room, he saw Riley sit forward and decline the call. After one last glance out toward Edie, he walked to the living room.

Riley had crammed herself as far into the corner of the couch as she could, so Mac sat on the opposite end. He propped his elbow on the back of the couch cushion and rubbed his forehead.

She winced, then tucked one leg underneath her, resettling herself against the arm of the couch.

"You okay?"

"I'm fine. The baby just moves a lot. Feels like she's trying to stick her feet up into my chest."

"She?"

She glanced down and sighed. "Yeah. It's a girl. That's what they tell me anyway."

"So you have a doctor? You've had checkups?"

She swallowed. "Of course I have."

"Okay. Just with you away from home, I wanted to make sure, you know . . . that things are going well." He didn't want to admit that he'd wondered if she'd been to an OB at all. She seemed so on the verge of flight, like maybe pinning herself down to a doctor, to a place to have a baby, would have been too much.

"Things are fine."

"Do you have a boyfriend or . . . ?" He waited but she didn't say anything. "Is there someone else who has an interest in this child? Someone waiting for you at home?"

She picked at a string on her shorts and shook her head.

"Are you sure?"

She pulled her head up. "There's no one." Her voice was firm. "I'm doing this on my own."

"But all those phone calls . . ."

"You can't ask me about that. And what do you know about any phone calls?"

"You mean the handful of times your phone has rung and you've silenced it instead of answering?"

She didn't respond.

"Plus Cynthia mentioned someone's been calling you. And whoever it was seemed to upset you."

"Good to know y'all have been discussing me and my phone calls." The words would have dripped in snark if her voice hadn't been so weak. So tired.

"It's not like that. We haven't been discussing it. She just told me today before you came in. She was concerned. I'm concerned."

"Well, that's nice." She exhaled, a frustrated little puff of air from her mouth, and turned her head toward the window. Mac was struck again by her resemblance to him. It was almost like looking at a star in the night sky. If you steadied your gaze just next to it instead of right at it, its brightness was piercing. In the same way, when he looked right at Riley, he saw the obvious differences—she was feminine, decades younger—but catching a bit of her profile like this caused such a fire of tenderness inside him. The way her cheek dipped in just under her eye, her strong nose, the way her eyes tugged down slightly at the outside corners—it made him want to both move toward her and pull away. A craving—a *need*—to wrap her in a hug eighteen years in the making, and another one, equally as strong, to stand up, walk out of the house, and pretend none of this was happening. That none of it had ever happened.

Can't do that, Mac, a voice in his mind said. *She's here. She's yours.*

A clock ticked somewhere in another room. Next door a dog barked. Then Riley's phone rang again. When she didn't make a move to get it, he glanced at it, lying faceup on the table. Same dude, same arms, same laughter. Possession. Happiness. Or at least something resembling it.

"You going to answer it this time?"

She shook her head.

The ringing stopped, then started again. He watched her watching the phone. Finally he reached down and pressed the button on the side, silencing the ringing.

"Thanks," she said quietly.

"And he has nothing to do with the baby?"

When she didn't answer, he sighed. "I want to help you. You came to me for help, remember?"

"If *you* remember, I came to you for money. Not to have people breathing down my neck, poking their heads into my business, trying to figure me out."

"Riley, what did you think would happen? Really? Did you think I'd hand you a wad of cash and send you on your way? Just let you appear and disappear with no concern for . . . for anything?"

She shrugged.

"Is that what you wanted?"

"It's what I asked for, isn't it?" Her words were brash now, but her eyes—bare, thick lashed, and weary as hell—told a different story.

"Yes, you did. You asked for bus fare to New Orleans so you could go find your aunt whoever. But Riley, there are a whole bunch of ways to come up with a few dollars, and none of them involve tracking down the father you've never met and strolling into his office."

He felt like he was standing at the edge of something big, the deepest canyon on earth, with his toes right up against the drop-off. The next step, whatever it was, would be irreversible.

The thing was, he couldn't help thinking he could still get out of all this. He and Edie both could. He could give Riley the money, which was all she'd specifically asked for. It was all she wanted, right? He'd watch her take it and call a cab and disappear. It would be fairly easy. They'd never have to tell the kids—or anyone else—anything, and Riley would be on to whatever came next in her life.

But with that thought came a painful clenching in his stomach. Watching her walk out, carrying her child—his *grandchild*—into the unknown of a busy city, so young and so alone.

He clamped his lips together until it hurt. "The thing is, Riley, I have this hunch that you didn't come to me just for money. That there's something else you want. Something more. And I want to give it to you. Whatever you need. Your mom . . ." He hesitated, remembering sandy feet against hard wooden planks, the warm Gulf water at night, phosphorescence winking in the dark. That letter she wrote but never sent.

He clenched his jaw. "She said she was fine but I don't think she was. I think she needed my help. I think she needed me. But she didn't ask and I was an idiot and too ignorant to see what was going on." He leaned toward her, angling his head into her sight line until she met his gaze. "I'm not that young kid anymore, and I won't make the same mistake. You're here, I'm here, and I'm not going anywhere. And neither are you. At least not until you tell me what you need."

"What about your wife? I'm sure she'd be fine if I just disappeared."

"You don't know Edie. She's good in a crisis. And she's got a big heart." He swallowed hard, hoping his words were true. "She'll want to help you too."

Then they both heard a noise and there was Edie standing in the doorway to the living room. How long had she been standing there? How much had she heard?

Riley rested her elbow on the arm of the couch and briefly covered her eyes with her hand. "I don't know what I need."

"Okay. That's fine. But will you let us help you figure it out?"

She sighed and pulled her hand away. Shook her head. Then he heard it, a muttered whisper. "Fine."

He exhaled and looked at Edie, his face asking all the questions he couldn't say out loud—*Are you okay? Is any of this okay? Are we doing this? And by this, what do I even mean, exactly?*

Edie gave her head a small shake, anger rolling off her in waves. When she turned back, he realized it wasn't anger, it wasn't exasperation, it was resignation. She crossed her arms and shrugged as if to say, "Do it. Fine. I don't care."

He rolled his head side to side, his neck aching with tension, and turned back to Riley. "Will you come with us?"

"Come with you where?"

"To our house." His stomach plummeted as he said the words. It was the only answer, the only solution, even if it was a temporary one. Avery. Thomas. Their home. Their world, all threaded together. All of Edie's fears were his too.

The Swans plus Riley. He tried to imagine it, but his brain was dark, the screen empty.

"Okay," Riley finally said, her voice nearly a whisper.

"Okay." He rubbed the tops of his knees, then stood from the couch. "I can grab your things from the apartment. If that's all right."

She nodded. "My bag's on the bed."

He headed for the back door, pausing next to Edie in the kitchen doorway. He laid his hand on her arm and squeezed gently, but she didn't meet his gaze.

Outside, he crossed the patio and opened the white gate to get to the garage and the staircase that led upstairs to the apartment. On top of the bed sat Riley's duffel bag, packed and ready to go. Had Cynthia told her they were coming? No, Riley was asleep when they'd arrived. But from the looks of it, she'd been planning to go somewhere today.

Mac held the back door as it closed and entered the kitchen quietly. When Edie saw him her shoulders dropped, and Riley stood from the couch, one hand on her belly.

"We're ready," Edie said.

He glanced at Riley. She nodded.

"Okay then."

As they descended the front porch steps, the sun ducked behind a cloud, shading the yard and street beyond. When they reached the car, Riley opened the back door and slid in. Mac closed the door behind her and looked at Edie. "Home?"

"Where else would we go?"

"I—I don't know. I just want to make sure you're okay."

"Okay?" Her chuckle was empty of any humor. "None of this is okay."

He swallowed hard. "The kids."

Edie tucked a strand of hair behind her ear and shrugged. "I know. The kids."

The thought of them knowing about their father's mistake, his indiscretion, was a horror he hadn't fully let himself think about.

A memory crashed into him like a wave—Kat in her Jeep, her blonde hair tangled in the wind, white sunglasses on her face, her arms bare and tanned. Mac turning his face toward the blue Gulf waters to the south, ten million shards of light playing on the gentle swells, his heart surging with possibility and desire.

Thinking of Kat as just an indiscretion, as nothing more than a screwup, felt wrong. Unkind. Even more than that, it felt like an insult. Like she was something unfortunate that had happened to him when he was younger, instead of what it actually was—him purposely, resolutely straying from the path laid out in front of him. Taking one step after another, away from all that was assumed and familiar, and moving into unknown territory. A land as thrilling as it was forbidden.

She'd been a mistake and not a mistake. How was he supposed to reckon with that? He thought he'd laid that summer to rest a long time ago, and now here he was reliving it in his mind all over again. Not to mention facing the consequences.

Once in the car, the three of them sat silent. In the backseat Riley stared out the window. Next to Mac, Edie's face was impassive. She squeezed her hands together in her lap, her lips moving in silent conversation.

CHAPTER 11

EDIE

Present Day

It's not her fault.

It's not her fault.

It's not her fault.

Edie repeated the words to herself like a mantra, or a prayer. No matter what had happened between Mac and Riley's mother all those years ago, no matter what happened the rest of today, or tomorrow, or in the days to come, Riley wasn't at fault. She hadn't willed herself into existence, she'd had no choice who her parents were, and she definitely didn't have a choice in her mother dying. She was young, she was pregnant, and from what Edie could tell, she was entirely on her own.

And there was no denying that she was Edie's husband's child. Forget the paternity tests, the double-checking, the questions. If Mac were an eighteen-year-old girl, he'd probably look just like Riley. It was heartbreaking.

As much as it pained her to admit it, the whole ugly situation tugged on her heart, deep down in her core. Riley was barely older than Avery.

If somehow, in some wild turn of events, the same thing had happened to Edie's baby girl, she'd want someone to reach out and help her. To see her. To take her in. So regardless of her convoluted feelings toward her husband at the moment, and despite the fact that this girl could very well be the thing that shattered Mac and her, she would take the role.

And so here she was, taking her in. Literally. Inside their house.

It didn't mean she had to be happy about it though.

Riley stood in the foyer and took everything in—the wide staircase, the framed family photos on the wall just ahead, their cat who sat curled into a tight orange ball on a chair in the living room.

Edie tried to feel something for her—anything—but she felt nothing. Only a sober acceptance that she was now empty. She could only go through the correct motions: make a plan, check it off one by one, make it all tidy.

"Your house is nice." Riley stood with her duffel bag in one hand and her other hand on her hip.

"Thank you." Edie walked past her on the way to the stairs, her arm brushing against Riley's. She probably imagined the jolt, but the hairs on her arm stood up and her heartbeat thundered in her ears, her rational brain saying, "This is all fine," while everything else said, "Get out while you still can."

She slid her hand along the wooden banister as she climbed the steps, Riley lagging behind. At the top she stopped in front of the room that technically was a guest room but was used more as office, overflow clothes storage, and repository for all the kid things she'd been unable to part with over the years—board books they'd teethed on, smocked Jon-Jons and seersucker bubbles, a Calico Critters dollhouse. An old Amazon box sat on the bed, full of too-small winter coats Edie had been meaning to take to Goodwill, along with Avery's dress for the homecoming dance Edie needed to have altered.

Edie moved the box to the floor and laid the dress across it. "It's kind of a mess in here. It's been a while since we've had a guest."

"It's fine. I won't be here long. I'm going to see my aunt Mary in New Orleans."

"Really? Mac didn't say anything about that."

"Yeah, she's my mom's . . . aunt. So my great-aunt."

"Okay." Edie swiped her hand across the desktop next to her. Gray dust coated her fingers. She wiped them against her skirt. Riley put a hand up to her mouth and stifled a yawn, but not very well. Edie tried to imagine going through a pregnancy on her own—no husband, not even a mother to answer questions. Edie and her mom had never been super close, but she'd still leaned on her mom heavily during her pregnancies and in the early months afterward.

"I'm sorry about your mom." Riley didn't respond, and Edie slid her gaze down to the bump under the young woman's shirt. "How far along are you?"

Riley hesitated, then smoothed her hands down her stomach. "About six months."

About. When Edie was pregnant with Thomas, she often forgot exactly how far along she was, but with her first pregnancy, with Avery, she knew down to the day. Most moms she knew were the same way. That first time you remember all the details, all the measurements. Every distinct sensation.

She counted through the months in her mind. "So you're due around the end of the year?"

"Yeah, sometime around then. Is it okay if I take a nap?" Riley sat on the edge of the bed and stretched her back. "I'm just really tired."

Edie nodded and moved to the door. "Sure. The kids will be home a little later." She didn't know why she said it. Why she felt the need to let her know more was coming.

"That'll be nice and awkward, I'm sure."

Edie backed out of the room as Riley slid off her shoes. Just before closing the door, she saw Riley lay back against the pillows and close her eyes.

Downstairs Mac was standing in front of the open fridge with his arms crossed. He closed the doors when she came in. "I thought I was hungry, but I don't think I could eat a bite if I tried. Does she want food?"

"She's napping." Edie crossed the kitchen to the basket of shoes by the back door, then unearthed her tennis shoes from under Thomas's muddy cleats.

"Where are you going?" Mac asked as she leaned down to tie her laces.

"On a walk. I can't . . ." She glanced back at him as her fingers worked. *I can't stay here.*

"Hold on, can we talk for a minute?"

She straightened up and pulled her hair into a ponytail with the elastic band around her wrist. "What should we talk about?"

"Edie. Please. Sit down."

"I can't do that. I can't sit across from you like everything's fine. Like we've just had an argument we need to work through. Mac, you're about to have a grandchild. What am I supposed to do with that?"

He covered his face with his hands and rubbed hard. When he pulled them away, his eyes were red, the crease between them more pronounced than usual.

"I always thought . . ." A quiver crept into her voice, but she swallowed it. "Having grandchildren is something we should be doing together. Experiencing *together.* But you're doing it now. You're the one having a grandchild. Not me."

"I'm sor—"

"Don't. It's too late for an apology." She turned for the door but he stood, his chair scratching against the floor.

"Wait. Don't go. We have to . . . Edie, we can't *not* talk about all this."

She whirled around and faced him. "Okay, talk. Tell me how it happened." She held up a hand. "Not how *it* happened. Just . . . how did the two of you happen?"

Mac sat back down in his chair, hands clasped over his knees. "She was working on one of the charter boats, like I told you. We got to be friends." He paused, and when he began again, the words came easier, like he'd been waiting for someone to take out the plug so he could talk about that summer. About her.

"It was good to have a friend there. Most of the guys who worked at the marina were pretty rough. Not the kind of people I normally hung out with. There was something, I don't know, refreshing about it though. To be around these people who knew nothing about me. Didn't know I was premed, didn't know my grades or my past or my parents or . . . anything."

They didn't know about her. That's what he wasn't saying.

"We just started hanging out a little. Casual. On the rare occasions when neither of us was working."

"Casual. Right up until it wasn't."

He raised his hands, then let them drop. "At some point, I guess, yeah." He rubbed his temples. "It was so long ago. I don't remember everything in detail."

"It's okay. I don't want details."

They were both quiet. Was Riley awake? Could she hear their conversation? What must it be like for her to be with two total strangers, one of whom was her father, and the other . . . Well, Edie wasn't anything to her.

She reached for the doorknob, but his next words stopped her.

"Why didn't you ever call me that summer?"

She jerked her head in his direction. "What?"

"No postcards, no phone calls. Nothing for three months."

Edie opened her mouth, but words didn't follow. Then, "Are you saying you slept with Kat because I didn't send you a postcard?"

"Of course not."

"Are you sure? Because that's what it sounded like."

"No, that's not what I meant." He clamped his hands behind his head, then pulled them down forcefully. "I know we broke up, but still—there was nothing. For three months."

"Communication goes both ways, Mac. You didn't call me either. You didn't write." She hated the pettiness in her voice. The bite. The dragging out of decades-old hurts and giving them air and space to breathe.

He sat back in his chair and exhaled. "You're right. I didn't call; you didn't write. I did my thing; you did yours. My thing was . . ." He glanced up at the ceiling and rolled his neck. "I made my choices and I have to deal with them, but what about you? I know we never talked much about that summer, but did you not stretch your wings at all? Test any waters?"

The way he eyed her, as if he knew everything. She swallowed hard as her stomach tightened with nerves.

"What about the letters, Edie? To Graham?"

All those words back and forth. The wild impossibilities she'd considered. The pie-in-the-sky plans they'd made, even if they both knew they were impractical. Had Graham told Mac about the letters? Not that it mattered anymore.

"What about them?" she asked, much more casual than she felt. "They were nothing more than pieces of paper. That's the difference between our summers. I wrote; you acted."

"What if that was just because you and Graham were a thousand miles apart? What if you'd been in the same place?"

"It doesn't matter. We weren't."

"I think it does matter. It wasn't just me thinking of other possibilities, was it?"

She reached behind her and opened the door, letting in a whoosh of warm air, then mentally pushed aside the monstrous mess they were in. They needed to figure out logistics. "Riley said she has an aunt in New Orleans. She told you about this?"

"Yeah. Though it seems unlikely that someone would take off from Panama City on a bus headed for New Orleans to find someone."

"Regardless, this Mary may be the perfect person for Riley to be with." The wet blanket of heartache lifted a little as Edie shifted from the past into the present. *Make the list, check the boxes.* "All we have to do is figure out how to get her to New Orleans, agreed?"

"I guess so."

She stared at him.

"I don't know. I just want to make sure it's a good situation for her. A good place for her to be. I mean, with the pregnancy and . . . I just don't know what she needs. And we don't know who this Mary is."

"Mac, we don't even know who Riley is."

"I know that. But what if I want a chance to figure that out? If she's my daughter . . ." He was whispering now. "I owe it to her. I owe her so much."

Edie absorbed the words like a punch to her stomach. It was like he'd drawn a line in the sand—he and Riley on one side, she on the other.

Edie was sitting on the back porch steps, cooling down from her walk that turned into a run, when she heard a car stop in front of their house. Voices filled the quiet afternoon. A door opened, then another one slammed closed. One voice carried over the other two. *Mom.*

Edie had spent the day wanting the kids home so badly, she could almost feel them with her fingers. Thomas's still-thin shoulders. Avery's soft dark hair. She wanted them here, in their house, so she knew they weren't going anywhere. In this place where everything felt like it was slipping, she wanted to draw them close to her.

Her mom's peal of bright laughter brought her back to herself. She stood and headed around the side of the house.

Mac was already there, marveling over the gleaming white convertible at the curb. "Dianne, is this yours?"

"Sure is. I got tired of my Honda. Decided to make a change."

"It's quite a change." He reached into the backseat to grab the kids' bags. Edie pulled Thomas and Avery in for a hug before Mac ushered them straight to his car with the promise of Moon Pies from Cuppa Café.

"But you always say those have too much sugar in them," Thomas said, crawling into Mac's backseat.

"They do." Mac cranked the engine. "But I'm feeling generous."

As much as the kids loved sugary, highly caffeinated drinks, Edie had a feeling a Moon Pie Macchiato wasn't going to help soften the news Mac had to deliver. They weren't little kids anymore, and it almost took her breath away to know that the next time she saw her children, they'd be changed. They'd know for sure that their parents—or at least their father—had had a life before they came along. That he'd lived and learned and loved. And that there were consequences for everything.

She followed the car with her eyes, then turned to her mom, still sitting in the driver's seat with the engine running.

"It's a great car, Mom. What does Dad think?"

"Oh, you know your dad. He's nothing but a stick in the mud. He thinks my Honda was just fine. But I have to tell you, Marilyn's a lot more fun."

"Marilyn?"

Mom ran her hand along the top of the dashboard. "She's so pretty I figured she needed a name."

"She is pretty," Edie said quietly. Inside was all cream leather and chrome accents. A water bottle sat in the cup holder, the words *Drink Up, Buttercup* in swirly pink letters along the side. "I told you earlier you didn't have to bring them home. Mac was going to swing by—"

"Oh, I know. I needed to stop at the pharmacy up on Camellia so I figured I'd bring them on home. And anyway, I wanted to surprise you." She patted the dash again. "I'd stay and chat, but I need to get cleaned up." She adjusted her glasses that hung from a beaded chain around her neck. She wore a cream silk top with two buttons undone, allowing her freckled cleavage to peek out. An armful of bangle bracelets and a gold and pearl necklace completed her look. Her always-perfect hair was blonder than usual and smoothed into a new style—a long fringe of bangs swooped to the side of her face, the other side tucked behind her ear.

"You look pretty cleaned up to me."

She *pshh*'ed and flipped her hand. "These are work clothes. I'm meeting the girls for drinks and tapas at that new place near the river."

"The girls" were her golf buddies, a quartet who'd been meeting together for years over eighteen holes and gossip afterward. And the Five and Dime was the newest downtown Mobile restaurant. Ultratrendy and superchic was what Edie had heard.

"Ooh," Mom squealed. "If Mac's going to be with the kids, why don't you come with us? It'll be fun. Once they see Blanche, we'll probably get some special treatment."

Edie's younger sister had worked her way up the ladder of Instagram influencers and now held court to thousands of faithful Your Daily Blanche readers. She covered everything from the hippest summer dresses and skincare lines to the hottest new restaurants and vacation spots. If she was having drinks at Five and Dime, it was guaranteed they'd be on the house.

"Thanks, but I'm going to stick around here." Edie glanced back at the house, thinking of Riley inside. A slight movement caught her eye, and she spotted Riley at the window upstairs, peeking through the plantation shutters.

"Everything okay?" Mom asked, one hand on the gearshift.

"Of course. Everything's fine."

"Okay then." Edie took a step back as her mom wiggled her fingers in a wave and put the car in drive. "Talk soon."

When Mac's car pulled up the driveway, Edie was in the kitchen making tacos. She wasn't hungry, but she figured everyone else would be. Plus, she desperately needed something to do to keep from going completely mad.

The sun had already dropped in the sky, the road cast in a golden hue. From her spot in the kitchen, she could see Avery open her door first, then Thomas. Mac followed behind them. The three of them filed in the back door one by one. Avery's eyes were red but Thomas seemed strangely unaffected, though his eyes darted around the room as soon as he entered the kitchen.

"Where is she?" he asked.

Mac looked at Edie and she nodded toward the ceiling. After Riley came out of the guest room briefly for a bite to eat while Mac and the kids were gone, Edie hadn't seen her again. It was frustrating to say the least. She wanted to know so much—if Riley had talked to her aunt, if she'd made plans, why in the world she'd burst into their world and changed everything—but she didn't know how to ask.

At one point Edie had marched upstairs to demand some answers but stopped. She must have stood outside the door for three full minutes, her mind tearing through possibilities and memories, before she headed back downstairs, pulled the ground beef out of the freezer, and dropped the hard brick onto the counter.

"I think she's resting, buddy," Mac said.

"I'm going to my room." Avery skirted past Thomas and headed for the stairs.

"Avery." Edie set the spatula down and climbed to the landing in time to see Avery glance toward the guest room door, then enter her room across the hall. She closed the door firmly behind her.

Downstairs, Thomas ducked back out through the door. "I'm going to kick the ball around. Call me when dinner's ready." A moment later they heard his soccer ball slamming up against the side of the garage as he practiced shooting.

Taking her spot at the stove, Edie stirred the ground beef and taco seasoning. "How did it go?" She might as well have been asking about a patient's checkup. Or one of his weekly basketball games.

Mac slumped into a chair. "As well as it could, I guess." He rubbed his hand over his face. "They just took it. Avery hardly asked any questions, but Thomas hammered me. Not like he was mad, just curious. He wanted to know when I'd found out, where she'd been all this time, what she was like. Whether you knew, what you thought about her."

"What'd you say?"

"I told him it was all really new and that we were learning about each other." He sat forward and leaned his elbows on his knees. "He asked how long she was going to stay, if you were mad. What her middle name is." He shook his head. "But it took a minute to sink in with Avery. She just sat there for a while, then she said, 'I have a sister.' Just that. Nothing else. 'I have a sister.'"

Later that night Edie was surprised to hear Thomas call, "Come in," when she knocked on Avery's door. Avery was propped against the pillows on her bed, her hair piled on top of her head, and Thomas lay on his back with his legs up against the wall. He slid his legs down and turned around when Edie walked in.

"What's going on in here?" she asked softly. She pulled out Avery's desk chair and sat, swiveling it around to face them.

"Just talking," Thomas said. "About Riley." He bent his fingers into air quotes, as if that wasn't her real name.

"Mom." Avery's voice was a plea. "What is happening? Who is this girl and why is she here?"

Edie tucked her hair behind her ears and sat forward. "Did Dad tell you—?"

"Yes, he told us she's our *sister*. Or half sister or whatever. But—Mom." Her face slackened as she stared at Edie. "What are we supposed to do with this? Does anyone else know?"

"No. None of us knew until yesterday."

"Not even Didi?"

Her stomach squirmed with discomfort at the thought of her mom finding out. "No. She doesn't. Not yet."

Avery exhaled. "What am I supposed to tell people? It's mortifying to know my dad . . . *ugh*." She covered her eyes with her hands. "He had a baby."

"Duh." Thomas pointed back and forth between Avery and himself. "He had two."

"Three," Avery corrected. "But only one before he was married. Which isn't supposed to happen, right?" She looked at Edie pointedly.

"That's not what Parker said," Thomas blurted. "He said his sister—"

"Guys," Edie interrupted. "You don't need to tell anyone anything. At least not right now."

"But won't everyone know?" Thomas asked.

"Not necessarily. And there's no need to bring it up with anyone. She has an aunt in New Orleans who she's hoping to stay with, so it may be that she's only here for a little bit—maybe just a couple days—until she finds her aunt and heads that way."

"Then what? Everything just goes back to normal?" Avery's eyes were wide.

Edie hesitated. "I don't know, honey."

Tears filled Avery's eyes and she flew up off the bed and ran to Edie, wrapping her arms around her neck. Edie cupped the back of Avery's head with her hand, savoring the feel of her daughter's warm skin against her own. It had been a while since Avery had turned to her like this for comfort. "It's going to be okay."

"But how?" Avery sobbed. "How is it going to be okay?" She pulled back, a smudge of mascara under one eye and her nose runny. "How are you okay with this? Don't you feel betrayed?"

The word undid her. *Betrayal.* That's what this was. It was a betrayal, not just to Edie but to their kids, their marriage. Their family. Where did they go from here? Even if Riley left on the first bus to New Orleans, how were they supposed to pick up the pieces and continue? Nothing was what it was—or seemed—two days ago.

Thomas sat watching her carefully. It was normal for sensitive, dramatic Avery to jump to worst-case scenarios, while Thomas was generally unbothered by situations that would rattle most people. He acted nonchalant, but Edie couldn't tell how he really felt.

She turned back to her daughter, brushed the tears off her cheeks and chin, and smoothed her hands up and down her arms.

"I wish this would all just go away," Avery said. "Go back to the way it was."

"I know, baby. I do too. Sometimes families go through things that are hard, things we wish we didn't have to go through, but we're a family and that will never change. I promise."

Thomas slid off Avery's bed, dragging her comforter down with him. He moved to stand close to Edie, and she hugged both of them tight, one in each arm, and kissed their warm cheeks.

"Your daddy and I both love you so much. Nothing changes that."

"That's what parents say when they're getting a divorce," Avery said.

It felt like the earth shifted, knocking everything inside her off balance. *Divorce.* The word had been tapping her on the head since Mac uttered the words, "I have a daughter," just before his party. She couldn't deny it had crossed her mind, no matter how forcefully she batted it away.

She'd been with Mac so long, she hardly knew what a life without him would be like. It'd be like losing a part of herself.

Was it a part she could do without?

When Edie finally spoke, she was as honest as she could be. "Honey, your dad and I are trying to figure this out, one step at a time. We'll fill you in as much as we can, but this is big stuff. Adult stuff. I don't want you to worry."

"Easy for you to say."

"I know. It's easy to say, harder to do. Dad and I don't have a plan yet. We don't know what's going to happen. But hopefully we will soon. And we'll tell you as soon as we do."

Avery nodded and wiped under her eyes. Thomas stretched his arms over his head and shook his hair off his forehead. "I'm going to bed." At the door he paused. "It's still strange that Pop's not at home with Didi."

Edie sighed and wiped a hand over her face. "I know. It's strange for me too."

"I wish I could have stayed at the hunting camp with him. I hate going to Didi and Aunt Blanche's shop. I always leave smelling like a girl."

"I bet Pop would have loved to have you out there. Maybe next time. I'll talk to him about it, okay?"

Thomas nodded, then retreated into the hallway. A moment later his door closed softly.

"Are we going to church tomorrow?" Avery asked quietly.

"I don't know." Edie hadn't thought about church. They obviously couldn't go with Riley, right? How would they explain the extra person with them? A friend of Avery's? A cousin? The tangled knot just kept growing. "Let's see how things are going when we get up."

She nodded and Edie kissed her cheek again.

With both kids somewhat settled, she walked to their bedroom and found Mac sitting on the bed. "Is she—?"

"Riley's really anxious," he said quickly. "Just feels unsettled and out of place. And I don't think she feels good. Physically, I mean."

Edie pulled out her pajamas, then closed the drawer a little firmer than necessary. "I wasn't asking how she feels. I was just wondering if she was asleep."

"Edie—"

"If you want to be concerned about someone's feelings, you should probably start with Thomas's and Avery's." It was a struggle to keep her voice under control.

Mac took a deep breath. "How are they?"

"Worried. Confused. Scared. Things they can't even name." She squeezed the small pile of clothing in her hand, her fingers aching with the pressure. "She can't stay here, Mac. You know that, right? It'll tear them apart. It'll tear everything apart."

"We don't know that."

She stared at him, not comprehending his blatant lack of regard for their family, their kids, their entire life. "We do know that. I know that. We can't just . . . She can't . . ." Edie raised her eyes to the ceiling, as if it held the answers. "How can you not see this?"

"I do see it. I know it would be difficult. And I don't even think she wants to stay here. I don't know what she wants."

How about what I want? What we *need?*

He sighed and pulled off his shirt, then leaned back against his pillow, one arm slung up over his head. The only light in the room came from the lamp on her side of the bed.

After changing clothes in the bathroom, she climbed into bed next to him. Flat on her back, arms crossed over her chest, she stared at the ceiling fan whirling on high. Her mind tumbled with worries and questions—Riley and Kat. Mac's past and her own. All the things they knew, and everything they didn't.

Mac shifted and turned onto his side toward her. She could feel his eyes on her, coaxing her to turn to him. She considered. Weighed what she wanted to say against all she needed to hold close. Then she reached up, clicked off her lamp, and rolled onto her side, away from him.

CHAPTER 12

MAC

Present Day

In the middle of the night, Mac was awoken by a noise. Not one of the regular nighttime noises he was accustomed to—trains blowing their whistles down by the river, eighteen-wheelers cruising through Mobile on I-10, the fish tank bubbling in Thomas's bedroom. This was different. This was teary. Sniffly.

Sure it was Avery unable to sleep, he walked through the dim hallway darkness to her room and put his ear to her door, but it was quiet. Then he heard it again, coming from the other side of the hall. He repeated the motion, standing outside Thomas's room, then outside the bathroom door, leaning his ear toward it. There. It was in the bathroom. A soft moan and another sniff.

He knocked lightly, then heard Riley's voice. It was pitched higher than usual. "Don't come in."

"Riley?" he asked softly. "What's going on?"

"Nothing." Another sniff. "I don't know, but I—you can't come in."

Something in her voice made his heart rate kick up. He tapped again on the door with the pads of his fingers. "Are you dressed?"

"Kind of."

"I need you to cover up. I'm going to come in."

Her sniffles turned into crying then. At her soft sob, a flock of birds took flight in his chest. He turned the doorknob and eased open the door, unsure of what he'd find. He checked the floor, expecting her to be there, but instead she sat on the toilet. He could just barely make out her outline in the glow from the streetlight outside the window.

He averted his eyes and took a step toward her, closing the door behind him. "Are you sick?" He flipped the switch to turn on the light over the shower. Not as bright as the overhead light but at least he could see a little.

She squinted and sniffed, then grabbed at her stomach. "I don't know." Her breathing accelerated.

He crossed the space quickly and knelt next to her. Thankfully his medical instincts and gut reaction to seeing a young person in obvious pain took center stage, casting aside the awkwardness and inappropriateness of the moment.

"You've got to tell me what's going on." He pressed a hand to her forehead, then her ears. No fever.

"It hurts." She dropped her voice to a whisper. "It keeps coming, like it's squeezing really hard. And there's . . . some blood."

He glanced in the general direction of her knees, which were clamped together, then back to her face. "You're bleeding?"

"Mm-hmm." She sat for a moment, then sucked in a breath and blew it out slowly.

A curse tumbled from his lips. "You're having contractions. When did they start?"

She pushed her hair back from her face. "I don't know. They've been off and on for a long time. They've picked up in the last few days though."

"Days?" He sat back on his heels. "Why didn't you say anything?"

"They haven't been hurting like this. This is new."

"Okay, how bad is the bleeding?"

"It's not much." She leaned down and put her face in her hands. "Can you go away? This is humiliating."

"Riley. I'm a doctor. This is what I do."

"You sit by half-naked girls on the toilet?"

"No, of course not. But do you really want to be alone right now?"

She shook her head, her face still covered by her hands. "Can you get Edie?"

He thought of the last visual he'd had of Edie. Her jaw set, lines of her body rigid, then turning away from him. He swallowed hard. Edie was a good one to have in a crisis, but something told him she'd probably prefer to skip this crisis.

"You sure?"

She nodded miserably.

Okay.

He put his hand on Riley's shoulder and squeezed. He realized as he walked out of the bathroom that it was the first time he'd touched her. He'd bumped into her earlier at the bottom of the stairs, but this was the first intentional touch. A touch to give care, comfort. He had a hunch if she wasn't doubled over in pain, she would have shrugged his hand away. As it was, she didn't acknowledge it at all.

In their bedroom he crept to Edie's side of the bed. She was still on her side with her back to his side of the bed. He knelt and said her name. She was a heavy sleeper, and a mere whisper would do nothing to rouse her. Her hand twitched but nothing more.

"Edie. I need you to wake up, babe."

She groaned and turned her face into the pillow, then up to him. One eye cracked open. "What is it?"

"Riley's in the bathroom and she needs your help."

"What?" She pushed herself up onto her elbow and rubbed her eye. "Why does she need help in the bathroom?"

He swallowed. "I think she's having contractions. And she says she's bleeding."

Edie gave no reaction at first, then she jolted into action so quickly, he had to put a hand on the floor to keep from falling over. She flung off the covers, swung her legs over the edge of the bed, and bolted out of the bedroom before he'd even stood up.

He followed her to the bathroom and waited outside for a moment, unsure of his place but feeling pretty certain time was of the essence. He was a pediatrician, not an OB, but he knew bleeding and contractions at six months weren't a good thing. He waited another moment, then followed Edie in.

Edie sat on the side of the bathtub, elbows on her knees, her body leaning forward toward Riley. Her voice was surprisingly gentle, and as it mixed with Riley's whimpers, it reminded Mac of years past when Edie would get up with a sick Avery or Thomas in the middle of the night. He hadn't thought of those nights in a long while—the seemingly endless hours of sitting up with a croupy toddler or a vomiting child or someone scared after a nightmare. And through it all, Edie's gentle voice was an ocean of calm in an otherwise chaotic night.

Her voice was that ocean now, and it seemed to have calmed Riley. Or maybe the contractions had just lessened.

"Riley, you'll have to stand up," Edie said. "I need you off the toilet so we can go to the hospital."

"The hospital? I can't—I don't have—I can't go to the hospital."

"What? Why not?"

Riley grabbed a wad of toilet paper and blew her nose, then flung it into the trash can. "I don't have any money, okay?"

"You don't need money to go to the ER. They'll treat you no matter what." She glanced at Mac and he nodded.

"They will?"

"Yes," he said. "And the sooner we get you there, the sooner we can figure out what's going on."

Edie stood and took both of Riley's hands. "Stand up. I'll help you."

Riley obeyed and began to stand but then paused and looked at Mac standing by the door. "Can you . . . ?"

"Mac, I've got it." Edie was gently pulling on Riley's hands, trying to coax her up. He ducked out and closed the door behind him.

In their bedroom he threw on a pair of shorts and a T-shirt and slapped a hat on his head. He grabbed his keys and shoved his wallet and phone in his back pocket, trying to think of who might be on call tonight, when Edie's soft voice sounded in the hallway.

She had one arm around Riley's back and was holding her other hand. "She's ready."

He reached out a hand to take Edie's place as Riley's crutch, but Riley looked at Edie with wide eyes. "You're not coming with me?"

"Oh, I . . ." Edie glanced at Mac. "We can't leave Thomas and Avery here. I need to stay with them."

"I'll take you, Riley. We can leave now. I may even know the doctor who's on call tonight, so maybe we can get you in a little quicker."

Riley flicked a glance his way, then back at Edie. "You can't come?"

Embarrassment, though he knew it was misplaced, burned his face, but the crushing disappointment hurt worse. His daughter had chosen Edie instead of her flesh-and-blood parent standing right here. It was foolish to think he could possibly make up for a lifetime of absence in one fear-filled night, but he couldn't help it. He was thankful the hallway was mostly dark, hiding whatever expression betrayed his emotion.

Edie glanced at him again, then to Riley. Finally Edie's shoulders dropped and she pushed her hair back behind her ears. "I'll take her."

There was no arguing. He was the one already dressed, he had his keys, his arm was out ready to take Riley, but he knew the tone of Edie's voice. He wouldn't get anywhere. She was sure.

"Hang on just a second," she said to Riley, then darted into their bedroom.

Riley leaned over and braced her hands against her knees. Mac leaned down next to her. "Does it hurt?"

She nodded. He wanted to say something helpful—to tell her everything would be okay, that Edie would take care of her, that things would be brighter tomorrow—but the truth was, he didn't know. Where Riley would be tomorrow, whether she'd still be pregnant when she left the hospital, whether he'd see her again or meet his grandchild—he knew none of it.

His heart was pounding, but then Edie returned in a pair of leggings and a shirt, her dark hair gathered into a messy ponytail. Before he could transform his worries and questions into coherent words, Edie was walking Riley downstairs, one hand on her elbow, the other around her back.

At the bottom of the stairs, Edie opened the front door and ushered Riley through the doorway. Just before she closed the door, Mac saw Riley's profile in the glare of the streetlight at the end of their driveway—the plane of her forehead, the angle of her cheekbone, the swell of her belly.

Three days ago he didn't know she existed, and now he might lose her all over again.

Please don't take her from me.

CHAPTER 13

EDIE

Present Day

Edie had lived in Oak Hill her entire life, but zipping out of Oak Hill down Camellia Avenue with Riley next to her, everything felt different. Foreign. The trees were ghostly in the moonlight, and the streets were deserted, though considering the hour, it wasn't surprising. They passed through the still and empty town, her car the only hive of activity.

"How fast are the contractions coming?" she asked Riley.

Riley kept a firm grip on the seat belt that stretched across her chest. "I don't know. They just come and go. But they hurt now. They weren't hurting before."

"Before? You mean when you were in the bathroom?"

"No, before tonight. I've been feeling, whatever this is, for a long time. I thought it was just the baby rolling over. It never hurt though. My stomach would just get really tight for a minute, then it would pass."

Edie remembered the sensation well. "But you never had any bleeding before tonight?"

She turned her head toward the window. "No."

When Edie was eighteen, her biggest concern was what she was going to wear to Mac's Thursday night basketball game. What the subject would be for her next painting in art class. What college she'd be going to in the fall. What felt monumental in her life at the time was nothing compared to the facts of Riley's life.

Edie tried not to think about all she didn't know. Even if, by some miracle, Riley left tomorrow, safe in the care of someone else, what would happen with her and Mac? How could she move past the shock, the betrayal, the mortifying fact that her husband fathered a child in the few months they'd lived in two different places and she was just now finding out? How could they possibly move past this?

And what if she decided not to? What if it was just too much?

She pulled into the brightly lit parking lot of Mobile Memorial Hospital at 3:40 a.m. At other hospitals in larger cities, ERs were likely filled this time of night with the sick and hurting. At their small hospital, Edie had no trouble finding a parking spot right outside the ER's glass doors. She swung in, put the car in park, and helped Riley out of the car.

Inside, a fluorescent light pulsed over the waiting area where a few people sat. A nurse, an older woman wearing pink scrubs and red-framed glasses, looked up from a computer screen and smiled as they approached. When she saw Riley—thick blonde hair twisted into a disheveled braid, splotchy face, the swelling in her belly obvious under her shirt—her smile faltered.

At the counter Edie put a hand on Riley's back. "She needs to see a doctor. She's six months pregnant and having contractions. And some bleeding."

The nurse stood and pointed to a clipboard. "Sign in here, then have a seat. I'll call Dr. Abad now."

The form asked for name, address, and doctor's name. All Edie knew was "Riley."

"Can you fill this out?" She handed Riley the clipboard with pen attached. Riley accepted it and they took a seat on a hard plastic bench next to the desk.

Less than a minute later, another nurse opened a side door and pushed a wheelchair through. She called them and motioned for Riley to sit in the chair.

Riley looked at Edie. "I can walk."

"Maybe, but you're not going to. Come on." Edie tugged her hand and led her across the room to the nurse with the chair. Finally Riley sat and the nurse wheeled her down a few hallways and through a set of double doors with the words *Labor and Delivery* in bold black letters over them. Edie's stomach tightened.

I can't do this.

The nurse opened the door to a room that contained a stark, sterile bed, a computer with multiple screens and tools, and various bits of machinery hooked to the wall behind the bed. Riley whirled around in her chair. "I can't do this." Her voice was high and panicked. "I'm not having this baby tonight. I'm not ready. I can't—"

Edie had nothing to offer, because Riley's thoughts echoed her thoughts. Thankfully the nurse stepped in.

"Honey, that's why we're here. To hopefully keep you from having the baby just yet. Let's see what's going on before anyone jumps to conclusions."

As she situated Riley in the bed and took her vitals—blood pressure, temperature, oxygen levels—she asked when the bleeding had started and how heavy it was. When the contractions began and how far apart they were.

"The bleeding was just a couple spots." Riley's gaze flicked to Edie as the nurse held a thermometer to her forehead. "And the pain has slowed down some. It's not as bad as it was."

The nurse eyed her. "Are you just saying that because you want to get out of here quickly, or is it the truth?"

Riley eyed her back. "Truth."

"Good. Can you feel the baby moving?"

She nodded. "A little."

The nurse jotted down a note on her clipboard and pulled a folded gown from a slim closet in the corner. "We're going to do an ultrasound, see how the baby's doing, then Dr. Abad will come in and do a physical exam. Is that okay?"

"Yes." Riley's voice was soft.

She handed Riley the gown. "Bottoms off, gown open in the back. I'll be back in just a moment."

———

They'd been in the exam room for hours, with an assortment of nurses, residents, and PAs coming in and out—checking vitals again, starting an IV line of fluids, adjusting the monitors—when their initial nurse tapped on the door and walked in. They'd hardly had a moment alone for Edie to ask Riley some questions. To get the answers she needed so she could carve a path forward. Riley had already given blood and urine samples, had her physical exam, and was now lying back on the bed with the head raised, her gown pulled up, and her belly wrapped in the soft straps of a fetal monitor, which recorded her baby's—her daughter's—heart rate and any distress.

The nurse crossed the small room toward the white paper trailing out of the computer next to Riley. "This is looking good," she murmured, then turned to Riley and unstrapped her belly. "We can turn this off now. I think we have enough information."

"Do you know yet what's going on?"

"Looks to me like just a flare-up of Braxton-Hicks, but let's wait for the doctor. It shouldn't be much longer."

She grabbed her clipboard from the counter next to the sink. "I noticed there's some missing information here. I need a home address and your OB." She set her pen over the page. "Miss Mills?" she prompted when Riley didn't give an answer.

Riley peered up at Edie with anxious eyes, and Edie made a quick decision. "Can you give us a few minutes?" she asked the nurse.

She clicked her tongue against her teeth. "Yeah, okay. I'll be back in a few."

As soon as she closed the door, Edie crossed her arms over her chest and turned to Riley. "Out with it."

"Out with what?"

"All of it. I need you to tell me everything. You show up here un-announced, pregnant, and you haven't told us a thing. Why you came, what you're looking for, what you left behind. And who the father of this baby is. What your plan is. I've kept myself from asking too many questions, but I'm done with that."

Edie hadn't intended the anger, but it oozed out from the gashed place deep inside her. It registered on Riley's face but instead of returning it, she just seemed smaller. Diminished. "I . . . I can't answer all that."

Edie sighed and pressed the heels of her hands to her temples. "I'm sorry. That was harsh." She leaned her hip against the side of the bed. "If you need my help—if you need my husband's help—I need you to tell me the truth now. I can help more if I know what's really going on."

Lying there pressing her fingertips gently against the sides of her belly, Riley seemed so young. So vulnerable. To think that a mere three days ago, they'd been completely unaware of her existence. But she was here now. Real and undeniably alive.

She nodded at Edie. "Okay. I'll tell you what you need to know."

"Do you know who the father is?"

"Of course I do." Riley didn't say anything for a moment, then she ex-haled, her cheeks filling with air then collapsing. "His name is Dex. Dexter Mahoney."

"Is he your boyfriend?"

A shoulder shrug. "Not really. He's just a guy I know."

"How well do you know him?"

"Enough to know he doesn't want the baby."

"But he does know about the baby?"

She rubbed her eye and nodded. "He actually was a little excited at first. Or he seemed like it anyway. But when he found out I needed a place to live—"

"Why'd you need a place to live?"

"Because Tammy couldn't foot the bill for both of us."

"Tammy?"

"My mom's best friend."

"Okay." Edie pulled the rolling stool up to the edge of the bed. "Can we go back? Let's start with your mom." She hesitated. "Mac said she passed away a year ago. Is that right?"

A nod.

"Where did you live after she died?"

"With Tammy, like I said. Mom and I had been living there since we moved out of Steve's house."

"Steve?"

"Steve was this guy my mom married. But he was . . . Well, he wasn't all that nice. To either of us. When Mom finally had enough, Tammy said we could move in with her. I was, like, fifteen. We were living there when Mom had her wreck."

"And Tammy made you move out?"

"No, she didn't make me move out. Tammy's great. She said I could stay there as long as I could support myself. And I was doing okay at first. I started working at the Winn-Dixie after school and on the weekends. That's where I met Dex."

"He worked at the Winn-Dixie?"

"No, he just shopped there."

"How old is he?"

"Twenty-two, maybe. Twenty-three."

Edie sucked in a breath. "Okay, let's keep going. How'd you keep up with school if you were working so much?"

Riley shrugged. "School was always pretty easy for me. I graduated in May with straight As. Well . . ." She rolled her eyes. "Except for one B, but that's just because the teacher didn't like me. I threw up in her classroom. The first couple months, I threw up a lot." She pulled at the hem of the blue flowered gown. "It's why I lost my job. Turns out, they don't want sick people working in a grocery store. I told them I wasn't sick, just pregnant, but for a while there, I couldn't get through a shift without running to the bathroom. Tammy told me she was barely scraping by and needed a roommate who could pull her own weight."

Edie ran her hands over her face. Fatigue was pulling hard and made her mind fuzzy. And it was hard to comprehend the sadness of Riley's story.

"Then she decided to move to Apalachicola to be closer to her new boyfriend. She paid some extra rent so I could stay while I was figuring out what to do. Which was basically either get a roommate or move out. Of course, she didn't understand why I didn't just move in with Dex. That's what she was doing with her boyfriend, and she wasn't even pregnant."

A knock sounded at the door and the nurse poked her head in again. "Can I—?"

"We need a few more minutes," Edie said with a pointed look. "Thanks."

The nurse sighed and closed the door again.

"So you didn't want to move in with Dex." Edie tried to get her back on track.

Riley shook her head. "I know Tammy meant well, but that's what got my mom in trouble. At least that's how I see it."

"Your mom? What do you mean?"

"My mom was pregnant. That's why she married Steve. She had a miscarriage though." She was quiet for a moment. "You must be thinking terrible things about her. And it would make sense considering . . . everything."

"No, I don't—"

"Pregnant twice, all those years apart, two different men." She looked up at Edie. "And one of them your husband."

Nausea burned in Edie's throat. The fact that he wasn't her husband then did little to keep it down. She clamped her lips between her teeth and breathed through her nose.

"I know what they call that kind of woman. But she wasn't like that. Things just never worked out well for my mom. It was always one bad thing after another." She focused on Edie again. "Steve was a bad thing. And I'm not saying Dex is necessarily a bad thing—he never hit me. He didn't even come close."

That was this child's definition of "not a bad thing"? Not hitting her? Edie closed her eyes as she let that statement wash over her.

"I just . . . I couldn't believe Tammy expected me to move in with him. I mean, he lives in an apartment above a bike shop. Motorcycles. There's a tattoo parlor up front and a big garage in the back. Did she expect me to move in with my belly and my bags of diapers and my crying baby?"

The expression on her face—as if she were the one expecting Riley to move in with him—sent a wave of guilt through Edie's entire body, head to toe, and her selfishness shriveled into a hard knot in the middle of her stomach. Her own childhood had been relatively easy, her parents generous, her life comfortable. And Mac had been home with them all these years when this girl and her mother had nothing but struggle. Edie had two beautiful, well-loved children whose life appeared nothing like Riley's.

And perhaps the worst part? It occurred to her—just for a blink—that if Riley had moved in with Dex, she wouldn't have brought any of this chaos into their lives.

"I told myself a long time ago I wouldn't go down my mom's path. I loved her—I still love her—but I wouldn't make the same mistakes." She held her hands up. "And here I am."

They sat in silence for a moment, Riley's words ringing in the air like an echo.

Edie had moved her chair in front of the door earlier, so when the nurse opened it again, it bumped into the chair leg and jostled her. The nurse slid her head in the crack. "I'm very sorry, but I have to—"

"It's okay." Edie stood and moved the chair. "You can come in. Sorry I blocked the door."

The nurse sniffed, clearly peeved and wanting to wash her hands of them. "So." She held the clipboard in one hand and a pen in the other, ready to jot down the missing details. "Address?" She peered over the edge of the clipboard at Riley. Riley looked at Edie.

"Three thirty-four Linden Avenue," Edie said.

The nurse wrote carefully. "Doctor?"

She answered again. "Dr. Abrams, at Abrams and Wolfe."

She tapped her pen on the page. "That wasn't so hard, was it?" When she opened the door to leave, the on-call doctor was standing on the other side, his hand raised to knock. "Good timing." The nurse thrust the white paper from the fetal monitor toward him. "They're all yours. Oh, and Abrams is the OB."

Dr. Abad pulled the stool out from under the sink and sat down. "Sounds like you've had a rough night." He kicked one long leg out in front of him and propped his iPad on his knee. "Your blood and urine tests didn't show anything except that you were dehydrated, but we took care of that with the fluids. Dehydration can definitely cause Braxton-Hicks contractions to increase."

"But they don't usually hurt that bad, do they?" Edie glanced at Riley. "She seemed to be in a lot of pain."

"Everyone feels them differently. You're right in that they don't usually hurt too bad, but if you throw in some round ligament pain, which is common at this stage of a pregnancy, plus fear and anxiety about what's happening, I'd say increased pain wouldn't be out of the picture. You were right to bring her in though. Any contractions that don't go away or that increase in frequency need to be checked out." He tapped his pen on his knee. "In your case though, the fluids made the contractions subside, the light spotting you mentioned earlier has stopped, and you're not dilated or effaced."

"That's good, right?" Riley asked.

He smiled. "Yes, it's good." He glanced at the white spiral of paper the nurse had handed him. "Fetal monitor shows the baby looks good. No distress. All this tells me you're not about to have this baby." He crossed his arms. "Are you ready to get out of here?" He caught Riley midyawn and laughed. "I'll take that as a yes. Make an appointment with Abrams as soon as you can. I'll send this information over to her so she'll have it on hand. I'm sure she'll tell you this, too, but take care of yourself. Eat when you're hungry, and drink as much water as you can. That'll help keep the contractions from getting out of hand." He rubbed his hands over the top of his knees. "And you two are free to go."

He stood and reached out to shake Riley's hand. "Good luck to you, Miss Mills." He swung his gaze to Edie. "And to you too. Is this your first grandchild?"

Rattled, she uttered a stammering, "Um . . . I—yeah. Yes. I don't have any grandchildren."

He glanced down to his iPad again. "I'm estimating the due date to be mid-December. Looks like it'll be an extra-special Christmas this year."

Edie had been telling herself that Riley's presence in their lives would be brief. Then she'd be gone, a candle snuffed out, with only a wisp of smoke left behind. As Edie drove through Oak Hill's Sunday morning traffic—people making their way to church, to brunch, maybe the grocery store—she knew she was wrong. Riley wasn't going anywhere. She was here—in their world, in their lives, in their guest room—for a time. A season. Perhaps even longer. Her brain struggled to wrap itself around this fact.

"Tell me about Aunt Mary." Edie took a right onto Camellia Avenue.

She hadn't noticed, but Riley's head had lolled to the side and she'd been dozing on the short trip back to the house. At Edie's words she jerked her head up and rubbed one eye. "Hmm?"

"There's no Aunt Mary. Am I right?"

Her loose bun of blonde hair drooped to one side. Riley didn't answer, only heaved a big sigh. Edie took it as a no.

"You stopped at Mac's office on your way somewhere, but if you weren't going to New Orleans, then where were you trying to go?"

Riley chewed on her bottom lip, then propped her elbow on the window ledge.

"This was your end point, wasn't it?" She knew the answer but she needed to hear Riley say it. "You were coming to Mac. To us."

Exasperated, Riley pulled her hand down and turned away from Edie. "I've been on my own for a long time. Even when my mom was still here, it felt like I was the adult. The one with the straight head. But I did what I needed to do. I made it work." Her words were decisive. Sure. The voice of someone with a history behind her and a long road ahead. But then she closed her eyes and wrapped her arms around herself, and all that aged maturity slipped away. "I hate asking for help. I *hate* it. But I didn't know what else to do."

Edie took slow, deep breaths as she swallowed the bitter pill of her own arrogance. Her own ignorance. Mac had realized before Edie had that they couldn't turn Riley out. They couldn't dump her, couldn't ignore her, couldn't leave her on her own. But Edie knew it now. Everything would have to be adjusted, from work schedules and meetings to family expectations and grocery lists. The kids would be hit hard. Sharing your home with a sister you didn't know about before yesterday? Unthinkable. Making a place at the table and on the couch for your husband's daughter, a girl you had no hand in conceiving? It went beyond words.

She didn't know what would happen with her and Mac, whether they'd be able to survive this storm, but for right now, Riley was a child having a child of her own, and she needed a place to be. She needed a home. How heartless would Edie be if she were to follow her initial urges and pretend Riley didn't exist? She'd wanted her gone. Lord help her, but she had. Right up until this moment, when Riley admitted—however hard it was for her to do so—that she had nowhere else to go.

Edie was a mother, and mothers had certain codes, just like doctors. Do no harm. Put others first. Help when needed. And always love—even when it's hard. Even when it flies in the face of everything you feel.

"You can stay with us. For the rest of your pregnancy. After that—"

"After that, I'll be on my way."

"Where will you go?"

"I don't know. But I have a few months to figure it out."

She and Riley couldn't have been more different, but her words sparked the realization that they were in the same place: in limbo, waiting while they figured out what to do next.

"Once the baby is here, we'll see how things are going and what you both need," Edie said. "We'll just . . . We'll see where we all stand. How does that sound?"

"Do I have a choice?"

Edie met Riley's gaze. "Yes. You do."

Riley lifted her hands, then let them drop. "Okay. Fine. I'll stay." Then, quieter, she said, "Thank you."

"You're welcome. Is there anyone you need to talk to about staying here? Maybe Tammy? Dex? They'll want to know where you are, right?"

She gave a slow nod. "I'll call Tammy and let her know I'm okay. And Dex." She sighed. "I don't know. I don't really want to call him."

"That's up to you. You're eighteen, which means you can do most things without anyone else's permission. Being the father, Dex probably has some rights, but being the mother, I'm pretty sure your wants supersede his."

Edie took a left off Camellia onto Linden Avenue and relished, as she always did, the cool tunnel of shade down the center of the road. Proud historic homes on each side. Wide, century-old trees. Small yard signs proclaiming everything from the recent Boy Scout pancake breakfast to various school athletes and their jersey numbers. The late-morning sun shone its dappled light onto the sidewalks, and a breeze stirred the leaves overhead.

She pulled into their driveway and they sat in silence. Next door, the Miller boys threw a football back and forth in the front yard, still in their church clothes, while nearby a friend sang the Auburn fight song at the top of his lungs. A few houses down, Mr. Gregg stood in the middle of his front walk untangling strands of twinkle lights in preparation for his annual Christmas lights show that began every year the day after Halloween.

All around them signs of a changing season abounded, including the swollen belly of the young woman next to her. Edie couldn't fight the coming changes in their lives any more than she could fight the constant forward motion of the calendar.

Riley sat still with her gaze straight ahead, her face both young and worn at the same time. When she finally turned to Edie, her eyebrows were knitted together, causing just the smallest of creases between her eyes.

"You ready?" Edie asked.

After a moment Riley nodded.

Together they crossed the yard, ascended the steps, and walked to the front door. Edie shoved down her nerves and opened the door. Mac sat on the couch in the front room. Thomas sat next to him, his soccer ball in his hands. Down the short hallway, Avery sat at the kitchen island, her school notebooks spread out on the surface in front of her, though she was staring and chewing on the end of her pencil instead of working.

As soon as they walked in, everyone's head swiveled in their direction, though the rest of their bodies seemed frozen in the moment. Get up or stay still? Speak or remain silent?

Edie made the decision for them.

"Back porch, five minutes. We need to have a family meeting."

CHAPTER 14

MAC

Present Day

"So everything's okay?" Avery asked, after Edie filled them in on the last several hours at the hospital.

Edie glanced at Riley, who was picking at her thumbnail. "Well, she was pretty dehydrated, which made the Braxton-Hicks increase."

"What does a contraction feel like?" Avery's face was a mixture of awe and disgust.

Until now it had seemed like Riley wasn't paying any attention, but her answer came quickly. "It's like two fists clenching together inside your stomach." She put her hands together and squeezed. Avery's eyes were wide.

Thomas scrubbed his face with his hands and leaned forward with his elbows on his knees. Mac could only imagine how badly he wanted to escape the conversation. Almost as badly as Mac did, and he was a doctor.

"So how much longer 'til the baby comes?" Avery asked.

"Close to three months."

No one spoke for a moment, then Avery asked the thing they all wanted

133

to know, the thing they were least able to answer. "What about after that? After she has the baby?"

"We don't know," Edie said, her eyes on Mac. He tried to read her, to tell what she was feeling, the things in her mind she couldn't say, but she looked away. "We'll just see how things go."

Riley spoke again, glancing between Avery and Thomas. "I know it must be so weird to have a random stranger staying in your house." She changed positions and uncrossed her legs. "More than that, a random stranger who's about to have a baby."

"You're not that random." Thomas tapped his soccer ball between his feet. "You're our half sister." Avery's eyes grew round and she glared at him. He gave a half shrug. "What? It's true, isn't it? And anyway, it's not a big deal. You gotta live somewhere. Might as well be with us."

"It is a big deal," Riley said. "I guess I just want to say I'm sorry. And if you hate me, I understand. I'd hate me too." She moved her gaze from the kids to Edie, then to Mac.

"Riley, no one hates you," he said.

"Are you feeling better?" Avery asked Riley. "Your baby . . . Is it okay?"

Riley's hand went to her belly—an unconscious movement—and she nodded. "I think she's fine. Except for a bunch of kicks to my ribs."

"It's a girl?"

Riley nodded.

"But your fingernail polish is blue."

Riley peered at her nails covered in sparkly blue polish. "Yeah. I guess I should change it to pink, huh?"

Avery shrugged. "I like the blue."

"Thanks."

Mac watched Avery as she asked Riley more stammering, stilted questions. Such a small age difference between the two girls, yet there were worlds between them. He thought of Avery and her friend Alex down the street. Avery and other boyfriends she might have in the coming years. And he was hit again by how much he'd missed in Riley's life. Would she be eighteen and pregnant if he'd been around for her through the years?

The image of Kat walking out of his apartment early that fall, after he'd returned to school, swam through his mind. As a college senior, hardly an adult, should he have been able to parse out the truth from a woman's subtle hints? Now, with hindsight, he saw the glaring signs.

I should have seen. I should have known.

But he didn't. Sure, maybe there had been a tiny twinge—a question—in his gut, but he ignored it because of Edie. Because of his choice and their future. Because of all that was laid out in front of them.

———

That night, after tucking the kids into bed—though at these ages, there wasn't much tucking-in happening—he followed Edie into their bedroom. She pulled a pair of pajamas out of her dresser and retreated into the bathroom. When she came out a couple minutes later wearing the thin white top and blue pajama bottoms, he smiled at her. "You must be exhausted."

She sat on the edge of the bed with her back to him, and her shoulders dropped in an exhale. "I am."

"Thank you for taking Riley to the hospital. For taking care of her."

She nodded. "I couldn't *not* do it. She needed someone. She needed a woman."

"She did."

Edie shifted and pulled one knee up on the bed. "She's had such a hard life, Mac."

He'd assumed things had been hard for her, but to hear it confirmed was a blow. "What'd you find out?"

She closed her eyes and massaged the bridge of her nose, then told him all she'd learned about Riley from their early morning conversation. Kat's bad husband, moving in with a friend, Kat's death. Riley getting pregnant, losing her job, having to find a new place to live.

"And to make matters worse, she had straight As in school. Underneath all the rebellion and bitterness, I think she's actually a pretty smart kid. She's worked, she's taken care of herself. It's like . . ."

"It's like what?"

"It just seems like none of this is her fault. It's crazy because I've been repeating that to myself to keep from wanting to throw her out of the house, but I think it's actually true. She was handed this crappy life that threw her one bad thing after another. And she has nowhere else to go. That's why she came to you. She's literally out of options."

"What about her aunt Mary?"

"You were right to be suspicious. There's no Aunt Mary. There's no one." She shifted again so she could look at him directly. "No one but you."

He held her gaze. "Well, not just me. She has *us*." A muscle in the base of his jaw pulsed, which would eventually send a shot of pain directly to his neck. "Right? She has both of us."

Edie rubbed her forehead with the tips of her fingers. "She has us until the baby comes, but beyond that . . ." She lifted her shoulders. "I don't know, Mac."

"Edie." Mac sat up and leaned toward her. When he tried to take her hand, she pulled it away. "Edie, what does that mean?"

"I don't know, okay?" She stood and moved away from the bed. "I don't know what I mean or what I want." She groaned, as if making the words come out was painful. "I'm just so mad at you. I don't want to be mad—I hate being mad at you—but it's not going away. I can't stop thinking about you and . . ." She paused when her voice wavered. "Everything's just so messed up and I don't know what to do about it."

Tears burned behind his eyes as he stood from the bed and moved toward her. He stopped when she shook her head. "I know. It is a mess. But, Edie, we can work through this. We have to work through it. I can't do anything without you. You are my world." His voice broke on the last word. "I would never do anything to hurt you. You have to believe me."

Her eyes were red, her face beyond tired. "But you have. Every day that you've kept this secret, you've lied to me. It doesn't matter that we weren't together that summer. It's still a lie. And it hurts."

They held each other's gaze from opposite sides of the bed. Finally she sighed and grabbed her pillow off the bed. "I can't stay in here tonight," she said, her voice empty of all emotion, as she moved toward the door.

"Please don't go."

She hesitated in the doorway, and everything froze as he waited for her to turn back around, but she didn't. A moment later she moved silently down the stairs.

CHAPTER 15

MAC

Summer 2000

Mac was used to hard work, but not like this. Working summers in his dad's office, he was always tired at the end of the day, but it was more mental exhaustion than physical. Even days on the high school basketball court were nothing compared to the work he did at the marina, eight or nine hours a day, most of it in the blazing heat.

He was sunburned at the end of every day—no matter how much Coppertone he slathered on his pale skin—and drained, his muscles limp from carrying ice chests, docking boats, loading coolers, and washing hulls.

The crazy thing was how good he could feel despite his total depletion. He'd never known that physical exhaustion could be a relief. Instead of the sensation of his dad's constant eye on him, it was Carla's roaming eye he had to watch out for. Instead of his parents' expectations weighing him down, it was the ice chest he hauled for the men heading out on a 5:00 a.m. fishing trip to the oil rigs. And instead of his blindingly bright future spooling out in front of him like a yellow brick road, it was the wooden walkway of the marina, the paths that led him from the store to the dock to the boatyard.

He wasn't naive. He couldn't work at a marina for the rest of his life, like Dave with the tattoos, who apparently had no bigger aspirations than to make the best Bloody Mary on the Gulf Coast. Mac would need more than that, but he also had a hunch he needed less than what everyone else said he needed. What everyone else assumed he wanted. He didn't know exactly what he wanted, but he relished the fact that for once, he was the one making his decisions. He was his own man, and the freedom was delicious.

And tonight, at the conclusion of a long shift that ended at nine, he was headed home. Or at least to Graham's aunt's little blue house on stilts—their home for the summer. He'd heard several of the other dockworkers talking about going to the Flora-Bama, but he couldn't imagine pressing through the crowds and dealing with all the drunk dancers crowding against him. He'd gotten into the habit of sitting on the end of the dock when he got home from work, enjoying the quietness of Old River at night, the dark water calm and still after a day full of boats, WaveRunners, and skiers churning up its surface. Sometimes Graham sat with him, but more often than not, Mac was alone. But he was okay with that. It seemed the water kept calling to him, even after his work for the day was done.

Mac was headed back home to that dock when someone called his name. He turned to see Jeff from the boat barn walking toward him, one strap from his overalls unhooked and falling forward over his chest.

"What you got planned for the night?" Jeff wiped his hands on a dirty rag and stuffed it in his pocket.

"Nothing but getting off my feet. And maybe putting some aloe on my neck." Mac pulled his shirt collar away from his tender pink skin.

"Poor baby. Did you get a sunburn?" Jeff smirked and Mac pulled his hand away from his neck. Resumed his walk to the parking lot.

"Just kidding, man. Listen, I need a favor."

Mac paused.

"A bunch of us are going out, and we want Kat to come. She'll listen to you. She's had a hard time lately, and we want to cheer her up. Will you see if you can get her out?"

"She doesn't listen to me. I don't think she listens to anyone."

"I'm telling you, man. She likes you. If you ask her to come, chances are she'll say yes. Give it a shot."

Mac played it off, but the words lit something inside him. He sighed and rolled his neck side to side to work out the tension, then winced at the stretch on his pink skin. "Is she even still around? I haven't seen her in a while."

The truth was, he had a hard time not keeping tabs on her, and at the moment he knew she was in the dock store talking with Carla. He'd only been at the marina for a month, but it felt like an invisible thread connected him to Kat, making him hyperaware of her every movement.

"She's here. She's inside. Who knows?" Jeff shrugged. "Maybe she's waiting on you." He winked at Mac. Mac rolled his eyes and exhaled. "Do it for us, man. It's more fun when she's around, trust me."

"Yeah, I heard it was fun when she gave you the knee."

"I'm not saying I didn't enjoy it." Jeff's laugh turned into a leer, making Mac's stomach crawl. "But hey, if you want to go on home and ice your burned neck, I understand."

Without another word Mac headed back to the dock store. When he opened the door, a welcome rush of cold air met him, along with the sight of Kat. She sat on the stool behind the desk as Carla closed out the register.

"Too late, kid," Carla croaked. "No more purchases tonight."

Ignoring Carla, Mac focused on Kat. "I don't want to go out tonight."

"That makes two of us."

Mac sighed long and loud. "But I have to go."

"Who says?"

"It's kind of a guy thing. But here's the catch—I need you to come with me."

Carla snickered, then covered her mouth when the laughter turned into a cough. "He's bold, you gotta give him that."

Kat glanced at Carla, then back at Mac. The glaring overhead light shone on her cheekbones, her chin, the curve of her neck. "You *need* me to come with you? How's that?"

He shrugged. "Strength in numbers. They'll skewer the new kid. You're good at shutting Jeff down though." He held his breath. This girl made him feel as squirmy as a worm on a fishing line, but Carla was right. Something was making him bold.

She stared at him, then slid off the stool. "I'll give you an hour. Then I'm going home."

"Sounds perfect."

———

They made their way through the tangle of bodies and disjointed rooms within the legendary roadside dive bar, passed the crowded pool tables, skirted around the people dancing to two different bands, and found a relatively quiet spot on the top level. Not many people came to the Flora-Bama to find peace and quiet, but when everyone else crowded onto the dance floors and packed the establishment's many different bars, that's exactly what they'd found in this out-of-the-way corner.

Their single hour passed quickly. Now that they were approaching the two-hour mark and closing in on 11:00 p.m., Mac's fatigue had mysteriously disappeared. Earlier, he'd thought about calling Graham and getting him to come meet them so he could meet Kat, but he thought better of it. Mac hadn't yet mentioned Kat to his best friend, and something held his tongue each time he started to talk about her. Because there wasn't anything to say, really. Kat was just a girl who worked on a boat. A girl who was probably taking pity on him, coming out tonight solely to protect him from the guys who liked to have a little fun at his expense. So he forgot about Graham and enjoyed his time with Kat.

"Jeff said something about you going through a rough time."

A breeze from the Gulf a hundred yards in front of them lifted their hair and tickled their skin. A strand of Kat's hair blew up and caught on her eyelashes. Without thinking, Mac reached out and brushed it away.

Kat watched him a moment longer, then turned her gaze back to the water. "He doesn't know anything about me."

"So you're not going through a rough time?"

"And if I was? What would you do about it?"

He shrugged. "Listen to you talk about it."

"What if I don't want to talk about it?"

"You don't have to."

"Good." She took a long sip of her drink, then shook the ice at the bottom of the cup.

For a little while Jeff and Dave and a few other guys had flitted around them, trying to goad Kat into dancing or doing shots or some other inane activity she clearly didn't want to do. But when a group of girls had sauntered in, all clad in cutoffs and bikini tops and seeking the company of anyone who'd buy them drinks, they forgot about Mac and Kat, leaving the two of them blessedly alone.

"You know I'm still waiting to hear why you came to the beach for the summer." She set her cup on the floor by her feet.

"Oh, so we can talk about me, but not you?"

"Yep. That's usually the way I like it."

"I tell you what. I'll tell you something about me if you'll tell me something about you."

"That's fair." She tilted her head. "You first."

"Okay." Mac said the first thing that came to his mind. "I'm not sure I want to be a doctor."

Kat's eyes widened. "You sure went deep fast."

He shrugged a shoulder. "Your turn."

She was quiet a moment. "I don't want to work on a boat my whole life."

"What else do you want to do?"

"Nope. Your turn."

He bit his lip. "I'll disappoint both my parents if I don't go to med school."

"You mean like if you decide you want to work at a marina for the rest of your life?" She grinned.

"Trust me, I've already considered that."

"Trust me, you don't want to do that. You're not cut out for it."

"Thanks."

"It's not a bad thing. Take Jeff—you do not want to be Jeff. He's cut out for it. Even Carla. Can you imagine her doing anything but smoking packs of cigarettes all day, riding the boat lift and bossing everyone around?"

Mac laughed. "Yeah, it seems pretty perfect for her."

"That's why she's been doing this for decades. It's why Jeff will still be here in twenty years, working on boat engines and chasing girls at the Flora-Bama."

"But you don't want to be here in twenty years?"

"If I'm still doing this in twenty years, I think I'd kill myself." Kat shook her head. "I don't know what I want to be doing, but it isn't this." She tipped her head back and stared at the stars.

"I feel the same way." He felt her turn her head toward him. "It's not that I don't want to be a doctor. I do, but it feels like someone else has been pulling the strings, making my body go this way and that. Take the classes, get the grades, keep the girlfriend, follow the path." He rolled his neck. "What if I want to choose my own path? Decide for myself what I want?"

"So don't follow the path. Why's it so hard?"

He scoffed, then ran his hands through his hair. "I have no idea. In twenty years, I don't want to look back and realize I never took the chance to do something different. To make my own choice about what I want my life to be like. To have it not look like my parents' life."

"What does their life look like?"

"Perfect. It looks perfect. He's the respected cardiologist, she's city council president. They've covered almost an entire wall in our house with their awards and recognitions. Framed articles from magazines and newspapers. No pressure there, right? Our house is on the spring home tour, my mom is an adjunct English professor, and my dad plays golf with the mayor every Saturday. They give and give and give to all these people and all these causes, but to each other, I think they're strangers. When they manage to be home at night at the same time, they don't even hang out in the same room, and then they go to sleep and wake up and do it all over again."

His heart beat rapidly at the exertion, at the admission of the fault lines in his family's home life.

"That doesn't sound perfect to me," Kat said quietly.

"Me either. It's what everyone else sees though."

Laughter and carousing from a lower bar wound its way up the wooden staircase to where they sat in silence, the waves crashing invisibly down the beach. A headache was just beginning to throb in the space behind Mac's eyes.

"So that's why you're here," Kat said after a moment.

"What?" His voice was gravelly, as if his body had just now realized the late hour. His muscles ached and his skin was tight, his throat parched.

"Why you came here. You came to choose your next step. Whatever that is."

"I guess so. I just wish I knew how to figure out what that step is."

"It'll come. When the time is right, you'll know what you need to do."

He glanced at her, surprised by her softness. The gentleness in her words. "I hope you're right."

"Trust me." She slid her hand onto his and squeezed before she stood. "It's way past my bedtime. If I stay any longer, I'll turn into a pumpkin."

Mac stood next to her and turned around, staring back and down toward the crush of people around the dance floor. "We have to get through all that if we want to reach the door."

She grinned and held out her hand. "Come on. I'll show you the way."

CHAPTER 16

EDIE

Summer 2000

Dear Edie,

I'm glad to know the mail actually works here. Your letter this evening shows me that our mailman does more than just hang out at Lost Key Diner, which is where he is every time I go in the place. There's this whole crew that hangs out there—the mailman, a couple of police officers, a guy in a McDonald's uniform, though there's no McDonald's for miles, and a guy who's always wearing flowered swim shorts and a straw hat with a whistle around his neck. I wonder what he does all day, and who's on the receiving end of his whistle.

I'm also glad you're enjoying New York City. I have been to the city once—I don't think I told you that. Years ago, my dad was hired to build a house for an old friend of his on Long Island, and he took me with him on one of his trips. I hung out at the job site during the day, but at night we went into the city. We didn't go anywhere specific; we just walked— from the World Trade Center all the way to Central Park. I fell in love with it, just as it sounds like you have.

You asked me to keep an eye on Mac for you, and I am. He's fine, other than the fact that he comes home most nights smelling like fish and boat fuel. He says hi. (Just kidding. Not that he wouldn't say hi, but I haven't mentioned that we're writing to each other. I'm assuming you'd like me to keep our secret love letters under wraps. Although if my assumption is wrong, say the word and I'll tell him all about it.)

Write back soon,

Graham

Dear Graham,

How could I not quickly return a secret love letter? By all means, please keep it under wraps. No need to make anyone uncomfortable with our fierce love and devotion.

Look again at the photo on the front of this postcard. Go ahead—I'll wait.

That little green bench just to the left of center is one of my favorite places I've found so far in this city. It's so out of the way, buried in this hidden corner of Central Park, I can hardly believe someone else saw it worthy of remembering just like I did. Though in a city like this, I guess it's crazy to think you can be the very first person to see or do anything. It's all been seen and done before.

Anyway, I sat on this bench the other day with a notebook and mapped out my next few years. It's just a guess (because who knows what will happen), but being here alone yet among all these smart, creative people, I'm thinking a lot about what life could look like and where I'll be. Maybe I'll be here. Wouldn't that be something?

Love,

Edie

CHAPTER 17

EDIE

Present Day

It was a Monday morning like any other—no one could find anything, everyone was running a few minutes behind, and the cat yakked on the living room seagrass rug. Edie scurried around as she usually did, gulping coffee, trying to find everyone's required items, and cleaning up Ramona's hair ball without gagging herself, but inside she was empty. It was like the weekend's events had burned away all her emotions, and she was left with a desolate landscape.

She tried to shove it all away as much as she could though, because today was about the Kennedys. The job and their meeting. She still hadn't told Mac about being hired for the project. She needed to tell him—he'd be excited for her—but sharing job news and talking about the upcoming day felt too normal for all that had recently transpired between them.

She left Avery scarfing down a yogurt smoothie and Thomas searching for his cleats, and found Mac upstairs brushing his teeth, dressed except for his socks and shoes. He leaned his head out of the bathroom and smiled around his toothbrush, his eyes wary. "You look nice. Do you have anything big going on today?" He leaned down to spit, then rinsed his brush and palmed water into his mouth.

"I do, actually." She picked up a chunky coral necklace from her jewelry tray and held it up to her neck.

He pulled a length of floss in his hands. "Really?" Winding it expertly around two fingers, he began flossing. Mac Swan was nothing if not diligent about dental hygiene, regardless of the emotional temperature in the room.

"Yeah. I have a pretty big meeting this morning."

"So that's why you're dressed up. Who's the meeting with?"

"Turner Kennedy."

He lowered his hands. "Kennedy? The new house?"

She nodded.

"He hired Davis Design to do the work?"

"Not us. Just me. He hired me to be the designer."

"Are you serious?"

"Yeah." Her cheeks tugged up into a smile. "I don't know why he hired me and not one of the other designers. Or even Laura Lou herself."

"That's easy. It's because you're good. Everyone knows it. Obviously Turner Kennedy knows it."

She shrugged.

"Babe. This is a huge deal. I'm so proud of you." He moved toward her with his arms wide for a hug. Normally she'd savor the chance to burrow deep into his broad chest and warm arms—to soak in his affection—but her body felt as frozen as her heart. In the end he patted her awkwardly on the arm and kissed her cheek.

"Thanks," she said quietly. "I'm meeting him and the architect over the bay at nine thirty. I don't know who he's hired, but he wants us both to see the actual property."

"Over the bay." He turned toward the door. Just across the hall was the door to the guest room, where Riley was in bed with a stack of Avery's hardcover Harry Potter books.

"How long will you be gone?" he asked.

"I don't know. Turner's playing golf around lunchtime, so it should end sometime before then."

"Okay. I just don't . . ."

"You don't what?"

"I don't want to leave Riley alone too long. You know?"

Something hot sparked inside her. "Sure. But you don't expect me to cancel my meeting, do you?"

"No." Mac gazed down at his hands. "Of course not. It's a big deal. I know that." He bit down on his lip and nodded slowly.

"She's not a little girl, Mac. She'll be fine. I'll check on her when I'm back in town."

"I'd stay with her, but after canceling Friday afternoon, I'm doubling up on patients today to try to fit everyone in."

The spark transformed into a streak of fire that flared in her body. She was almost grateful—the fire was better than the emptiness. "The fact that your day involves sick kids doesn't diminish the work I have to do. You can't dump Riley on me, like she's my responsibility." Edie tried to tamp down the flames.

Mac's eyes widened at her tone. "No, Edie—that's not what I meant." His shoulders dropped. "It was a jerk thing to say. I'm sorry."

She bit down hard on her lip as she rummaged through her earrings, searching for her favorite gold hoops.

"I'm not expecting you to forget anything," he said. "I know you can't do that. I just need to know you're—"

"That I'm what? That I'm okay? That I'm feeling fine? I can't give you that assurance."

"Okay. You're right." He searched her eyes. "I love you, Edie. I love you and our family."

"I know," she said after a moment.

"Nothing will ever change that. And I'll do whatever I need to do to earn back your trust."

She nodded, then slipped her earrings in place, grabbed her bag from the bed, and with one last glance back at him left the room.

Just a couple nights ago, Mac had felt like a stranger. Like his confession—of Kat, of Riley, of that summer—had whisked the old Mac away and replaced him with a new Mac who looked exactly the same but felt entirely different.

But that hadn't happened. No one had taken the real Mac from her. This was the real Mac. And maybe that was the kicker. This Mac—the one she'd married—was also Mac Swan, Riley's father. And she was having a hard time reconciling that both Macs were the same person.

"I love you and our family. Nothing will ever change that." His words were hauntingly similar to what she'd said to the kids earlier in the weekend. *"We're a family and that will never change."* Why did they feel such a need to remind themselves of these immutable facts? Who were they trying to convince?

The drive over the bay rarely failed to soothe her, but today even the sight of Mobile Bay, stretching out flat and silver to the south, couldn't touch the mile-a-minute thoughts racing through Edie's mind. When she rolled into Fairhope, she lowered her windows to try to flush some anxiety out with the breeze. At a red light on Section Street, she slowed her breathing, then checked again the address Turner's assistant had given her.

By the time she reached the curve in the road that took her past the entrance to the Grand Hotel, she'd managed to shove the morning—the entire weekend, really—into a back pocket of her mind. It wasn't gone, but it was hidden for a while, and she felt clear. Full of purpose. Excitement bubbled to the surface as she made a right onto the gravel driveway that would take her to the Kennedys' new property.

Turner stood in the scrubby grass about halfway between the driveway and the boardwalk that ran alongside the bay. With his silver hair shining in the sunlight, he was pointing out toward the water. His wife, Marigold, stood next to him wearing a blaze-orange shift dress and a wide-brimmed straw hat over her honey-blonde hair. Edie's heart thumped as they watched her roll to a stop next to their cars.

"Edie!" Turner boomed as she exited her car. "Come on over."

When she reached them, he gave her a quick, friendly embrace, then motioned her toward his wife.

"Good to be working with you," Marigold said, her voice Katharine Hepburn–deep and her handshake firm.

They chatted a minute about the location and the soon-to-be neighbors before Turner gestured toward a grassy spot on the other side of the property. "There's a table back up this way where we can talk. Maybe bounce some ideas around and get your feel for the space. And the architect's, too, of course."

Edie followed the two of them, picking her way carefully through the soft, sandy dirt underfoot. "Speaking of the architect, do you expect him soon?"

"Oh, he's here. He's out on the wharf. Said he wanted to get a view of the property from the water." Turner pointed toward the ramshackle dock that appeared to be held together more by memories than actual wood and nails. "It'll come down, of course," he said, as if reading Edie's mind. "That one won't quite work for Marigold's Catalina."

As they came out from under the shade of the trees, Edie noticed the man who sat at the end of the wharf. He was leaning against a piling, and it looked like he was drawing or jotting down notes. Maybe making early sketches of ideas.

Edie raised her sunglasses to get a better look. Something about him was familiar. It was the way he was so casually leaned back, drawing with his knee propped up in front of him. She ignored the quiver in her chest.

When they reached the table, Turner and Marigold took seats next to each other on one side, and Edie took a spot on one end of the other long bench, leaving space next to her for the architect.

Once they were settled, Turner craned his head around toward the dock. "I hate to get started before—oh, good. He's heading this way."

A heated awareness slid over her as Edie watched the man walking down the wharf. In a rush she realized why he'd seemed familiar. She grabbed her bag off the seat next to her and rummaged inside it, searching for anything to keep from having to meet his gaze. Finally she set her jaw and lifted her head.

Graham was looking right at her, one cheek tweaked up into a smile. "Hello, stranger."

"Hi," Edie said, her voice overbright. "Good to see you."

His eyebrows lifted and he cleared his throat. "Yeah, you too."

"Graham mentioned that you two know each other." Turner gestured to the empty space next to her, and Graham stepped over the bench and sat down. "Hopefully that'll make this whole process even better."

"We do know each other," Edie said, her gaze skittering sideways at Graham. "It's been a while though."

"Well, what better reason to get reacquainted than a big project to dive into? Now, Edie, we saw your original plans for Ted Barnett's house, before Ms. Davis got her hands on them. Regardless of how the house ended up, we loved your vision." Turner clasped his hands together on the table. "And as for our architect, we knew we wanted to work with Mr. Yeager. Problem was, he didn't live here."

Graham held his hands out and shrugged. "Yet here I am."

"As soon as I heard he was back down south, I called him up and asked him to build me a house."

"I appreciate the confidence. And I may not have worked with Edie previously, but I'm well aware of the scope of her work. I think our methods will mesh well."

Graham was aware of her work? She was taken aback, but maybe she shouldn't have been. Of course, she was aware of his, too, having kept tabs on his career over the years. Over the last decade and a half, he'd designed homes across the country, from Texas all the way up to New York. She was proud of him every time she saw another of his houses in a magazine or online. Proud and a little sad.

Marigold's cell rang and she answered it, pausing their conversation. Edie let her gaze slide from Graham's drawings up to his face. After seeing him in *Bay* magazine, then all the upheaval that stemmed from Riley's appearance and her mind spinning backward to memories from that summer, of course Graham would be the architect of Turner's house. She probably should have seen it coming.

Graham. Her old friend, the biggest question mark in her life, and the one person she'd be working most closely with over the next however many months it took to complete this massive undertaking.

They'd even talked about this very thing once, or at least written about it. Them working together, architect and designer, hashing out ideas and making a name for themselves. It seemed like they'd finally be doing it, but not exactly in the way—or the place—they'd planned.

Marigold hung up and dropped the phone in her bag as Turner turned to Graham and Edie. "So what do you say? Can we make this official?"

Edie glanced at Graham, then back to Turner. "I'm on board. I'm looking forward to getting started," she said, her tone crisp and professional.

Graham gave that half-tweaked smile again. "As am I."

Turner tapped his knuckles against the wood table. "Great. We want you two to get to work and knock our socks off. Speaking of, Graham, I noticed you making some notes out there on the dock. How long will you keep us in suspense?"

Graham opened the notepad of paper in front of him—the same graph paper he'd always used—and turned it around so Turner and Marigold could see it. "They're quick sketches, nothing concrete. I just wanted to get a feel for the way the land sits and the angles to the water."

As Turner and Marigold studied the sketches, she felt Graham watching her. His gaze lingered and her stomach fluttered. Startled by her body's subconscious response, she sat up straight and uncapped her pen, then capped it again and set it on top of her notebook.

"Do you have any particular style or color palette you'd like to use?" She struggled to maintain her focus. "I could go ahead and start pulling some colors and finishes to give you an idea of the spaces together."

Marigold looked at her husband, then back at Edie. "Aside from a few family heirlooms I'd like to incorporate, I'm open to your suggestions. Just nothing fussy. We like to entertain, but we also don't want to be worried the grandkids will ruin a priceless rug."

"I promise nothing will be fussy. I see lots of open spaces. Natural colors. Hardworking fabrics that won't stain easily, but not so casual that it loses its dignity." She glanced at Graham. "When you open the front door, it'd be great to be able to see straight through to the bay out back. Lots of windows, of course, but super energy efficient to keep out the heat."

Turner grinned and put a hand on his wife's back. "I'd say we're in good hands."

———

By the time they said their good-byes and the Kennedys walked back to their cars, a breeze was blowing in from the south. Dark clouds had gathered along the horizon, though the warm sun was still bright. She and Graham watched them drive slowly down the driveway and turn into the curve between the trees.

Next to her, he exhaled. "That went better than I expected."

"What were you expecting?"

"I'm not sure, honestly. I hadn't seen Turner Kennedy in years. I wasn't planning to take on any jobs for a while, but he's hard to say no to."

"I saw you in *Bay* magazine. It was a good article."

He scoffed. "I hated that interview."

"Why? It was impressive. The McLeod Award? That's a big deal for an architect."

He shrugged. "It is. And I appreciated it. I just don't like the fanfare. I thought the article would just be about my work, but the woman kept asking me all about my family, how I spent my time when I wasn't working. Why I'd come home."

"Understood," she said with a smile. "No personal questions."

"I didn't mean you."

"It's okay. I promise I won't poke my head in any more than what's necessary to do the job. Except how long have you been back here? I heard you were home, but . . ." She shook her head. "I don't know any details. Then again, maybe that's exactly what you want."

"I moved back in July. Dad died in March, and it took me that long to finish up my projects, tie up loose ends." He stuck his hands in his pockets, his gaze unfocused. "I sold my house, drove the U-Haul here, and moved into Dad's place." He tipped his head to the north, in the direction opposite the Grand Hotel.

The house appeared in her mind as if she'd just been there yesterday. Pale yellow paint, screened porches on the front and back, the inside crammed full of antique sideboards and hutches, heirloom silver, and baskets of every size. Mr. Yeager had been a hoarder of sorts, but a hoarder of beautiful things. The three of them—Mac, Graham, and Edie—had spent plenty of time on the porch and the dock of his dad's house. In the boat, in the water, on the beach.

"I'm really sorry about your dad. I had no idea until I read it in the article."

"Thanks." He toed the gravel with his shoe. "Do you have time to walk out to the dock with me for a minute? I'd like your opinion on something."

"Yeah. Sure." She dropped her notebook on the table, then followed him out toward the rickety wooden dock. The breeze picked up again, blowing heady air into their faces and hair. She turned her face up to the sun as she walked, savoring the warmth that thawed some of the icy places in her chest.

"You still love the water, don't you?" he asked.

She opened her eyes to find him watching her. "I do. I always love being over here. It—I don't know. It opens up something inside me. If anything's tight, the water loosens it."

"I know what you mean." When they got to the boathouse about halfway down the dock, he stopped. Shoved his hands back into his pockets. "It's really good to see you, Edie. It's been a long time."

"It has."

"How's Mac doing?"

"He's fine," she said quickly.

"Good. And your kids? You have two?"

She swallowed. "Yep. Avery and Thomas. How about you? How've you been all this time?"

"Pretty good. Working hard. It's nice to be back though. There's not much water in Austin."

"But you lived near the water in other places. Weren't you in Sea Island for a while? And Charleston? Even up in New York?"

He cocked an eyebrow. "You've been keeping tabs."

"No, I just read about you. It's hard not to when you grace the pages of just about every trade magazine that crosses my desk."

"You haven't done so bad for yourself. I see your name here and there too. You've done some beautiful work."

"Thanks." She tucked her hair behind her ear, but the breeze tugged it out of place again. "So what'd you want to ask me?"

"Right. Well, you see how the shoreline cuts out a little here?"

He pointed to the line where the water met the sandy beach, explaining his thoughts regarding the presentation of the house, but as she listened to him, all she could think about was that phone call. It had been long distance, a New York City pay phone all the way to Orange Beach, Alabama. She thought about the question she'd asked him, the one he never actually answered. The curious subject they avoided when they returned to school. The emails she sent him later that were never answered or even acknowledged.

She and Graham had never dated—it was always Edie and Mac—but there had been *something*. There had to have been or else she never would have asked him that loaded question, even if it was prompted by a second glass of wine at a café on Delancey Street the night of her twenty-first birthday.

Something or nothing, it still felt like she and Graham had broken up all those years ago. And now, standing next to him after almost two decades, a cloudy pool—of hesitation, of something incomplete—filled the space between them instead of the clear waters of good and true friendship it could have been.

There were a lot of things it could have been.

Graham's arm was extended, tracing an invisible roofline. "Don't you think?"

"Yeah, I . . ." She bit her lip. "I'm sorry. I got distracted."

"The angle. And the roof. If we bring it low, it'll help keep rain off the porch, and they can use it more for parties."

"Yes, that's a smart idea."

Graham pulled out his pen and a scratch piece of paper from his pocket and made a quick note.

Thunder rolled on the other side of the bay, and a line of seagulls landed on a dock a few hundred yards away, one on each piling. Graham and Edie remained quiet on the walk back up the dock toward the property, then as they gathered their things from the wooden table under the trees.

"You don't have a car," she said when she peered around the trees and saw the driveway sitting empty except for her own car.

"Nah. I walked."

The weather had turned quickly, as it often did on the water, and the breeze was tinged with the coolness that came with rain. "You want a ride back home?"

"Home." He seemed to roll the word around in his mind. "It hasn't been home in a long time. But it's starting to feel that way. Or at least like it could be that way again."

"Are you planning on staying in your dad's house?"

He shrugged. "I'm not sure. There's a lot to go through. A lot to keep and a lot to get rid of, but at the moment, I'm not sure what belongs in which category."

"I loved that house and all the things he crammed inside it. He was such a sweet man."

"Of course he was sweet to you. He adored you."

"That's true. He did."

"He asked about you, you know. From time to time. He'd ask what you were up to, how you were doing." He shifted and kicked a pinecone near his foot. "It would have made him really happy to know you and I were working together."

"Did you know I was going to be the designer before today?"

"I did. Turner told me he was going to ask you."

"That explains why you didn't seem nearly as surprised as I felt when I saw you walking down the wharf."

He just smiled. "I'm glad to be working with you. I know how interior designers can be sometimes. I prefer to work with people I like."

"Well, I'm just glad to know you like me." She bit her lips together. "I mean, I wasn't sure how it'd be. The first time we saw each other after so many years."

He looked over her head, as if he couldn't wait to escape.

"Anyway." She cleared her throat. "I'll let you get on back home. Unless you'd like that ride."

"I don't mind the walk. I'll start getting some of these ideas down on paper. Why don't you check your calendar and let me know when we can meet again."

"Sounds good."

He headed toward the boardwalk that cruised in front of the property, and she turned toward her car and climbed inside. After waiting a moment, her eyes found Graham on the walkway as he passed in and out of sight through the trees. His hands were in his pockets, and his gaze was directly ahead of him, not veering to the side or back over his shoulder.

———————

Edie was in eighth grade, sitting alone in the Oak Hill Academy cafeteria, when she met Graham for the first time. Content with her sketch pad and pencils, she hardly noticed the scurry of activity all around her until someone sat across the table from her. She didn't look up from her drawing, expecting it to be someone who'd accidentally sat at the wrong table. But the person didn't move.

Finally she lifted her eyes. It was the new kid. Most everyone at Oak Hill Academy had been in school together since their diaper days, so new people kind of stuck out. Though with his blue-black hair and the ever-changing tattoos he drew on his arms under the sleeves of his uniform shirts, this boy stuck out more than usual. Word was he'd already gotten in trouble with the principal for his hair touching the top of his collar in the back, but he didn't seem to care.

Edie froze, waiting for this mirage of a boy to disappear, but he didn't. He just sat there studying her drawings.

"What are you working on?" He gestured to her pad with his chin.

"Oh, um, nothing, really." She tried to cover the paper with her arm, but he reached out and pulled the pad toward him.

"Is this a blueprint?" He traced her drawing with his finger—the black lines that delineated the different rooms of her house and the blue lines where she'd suggested moving walls and opening up spaces. "It's really good. I figured you were over here drawing a still life or something."

She stared at him. Had he been watching her?

"You know, a still life? Like a bowl of fruit or something?"

She huffed. "I know what a still life is. But I don't have a bowl of fruit."

He smiled, a lazy half grin. "I know. It was just a guess. So what's the blueprint for?"

"It's just something I'm doing for my dad. He's renovating our kitchen and asked me to draw out the plans."

"Seriously? He asked you to do it? No offense." He held his hands up. "'Cause this is really good."

She shrugged. "He's a builder. And he knows I like to draw."

The bell rang and they both stood. She set her pencils back in their case and shoved her sketch pad in her bag. The boy grabbed her lunch tray before she could get it.

"Thanks," she said.

"No problem. I draw a little too. I want to be an architect like my dad."

"Really? I've thought about that too." *I have?* She'd never told anyone that—wasn't even sure if it was true—but saying it out loud to this strange boy felt good.

"Makes sense." He tossed her trash in the garbage can and dropped her tray in the pile on top. "You're already drawing blueprints."

They headed for the double doors, but before they could push them open, Mac strode through.

"Oh hey," he said to her. "I was just coming to find you." He noticed who she was with and grinned. "I see you two already met. This is great."

She glanced back and forth between them. "Y'all know each other?"

"Yeah. He's Graham." Mac shrugged, as if that explained everything. "My friend from camp. I told you about him."

Mac had told her a friend of his from Camp Woodpine was moving to Mobile from Mississippi, but she'd expected someone just like Mac—with his floppy hair, freckles, and general *aw-shucks*-ness. He was pretty much the best-loved kid in Oak Hill. Graham didn't seem like that kind of guy.

"So you're Mac's Edie," Graham said slowly, as if seeing her with new eyes.

"I'm just Edie." She glanced at Mac, who was still smiling. "And you're Mac's friend."

"Just Graham." He bumped his fist against Mac's shoulder. "But yeah. We met, what, four or five years ago?"

Mac nodded. "I had to sleep in the bunk above him. Kept me up all night with his snoring."

It wasn't like she and Mac were dating—they were thirteen years old. No one actually dated then. But everyone knew they were close. Their friendship had solidified years before, dancing around the maypole in preparation for the school spring festival. Other friends had come and gone, but their friendship remained steadfast and had only recently begun to test the waters of something more than friendship.

Even still, the way her heart pounded when Graham stood next to her felt strangely unkind to Mac. Like she was betraying him, even though there was nothing concrete to betray.

Graham hooked his thumbs under the straps at his shoulders, his fingers clasped across his chest. Blue ink snaked down from his shirtsleeve toward his elbow in the form of a rope and anchor.

"I like your tattoo," she said.

There was that lazy smile again. "Thanks." He shoved the cafeteria door open with his hip. "Shall we?" He held the door open as she and Mac walked through it.

Even now, Edie could still remember with striking clarity how different everything felt—how different *she* felt—after the three of them became friends. It was like everything around her had a zip of strangeness, of newness, like the sun had traveled backward or the sky had flashed to purple. In the span of a lunch period, something had changed in her world.

From that day on the three of them were truly inseparable. They weren't always in the same classes—especially as Mac took more advanced sciences and math, and she and Graham leaned more toward English and art—but as soon as they sat together in the cafeteria for lunch or outside on the front steps during a free period, their easy banter began, their words climbing all over themselves like puppies. They were an odd trio, but they worked.

Even after Mac had asked her to be his girlfriend at the end of ninth grade, she'd walk home from school every day and wonder what would become of the three of them. What would become of her, the girl who had come to love two boys equally? In very different ways but in equal amounts.

She and Graham were close, but he'd never let on that he thought of her as anything but a friend, so it was easy to fall for Mac in more of a romantic way. Especially when he never shied away from letting her know exactly how he felt about her, a tenderness she appreciated.

Still, if someone had asked her to pick between them—to choose only one of them to spend her time with—she'd have been hard-pressed to make the choice. In fact, if Mac hadn't made the choice for her, asking her out on her first real date and giving her her first kiss, she may never have been able to choose between them.

And with that, her path was set. She had been fifteen years old. The path was confirmed at age twenty-two when Mac asked her to marry him, and she looked forward, not back, and said yes.

For one wild moment on her drive back across the Bayway, she gave herself over to the luxury of considering how differently her life could have turned out if she'd looked the other way. If she'd given another answer.

Then her phone sitting on the passenger seat buzzed, and her husband's name and face lit up the screen, startling her out of her memories and pulling her back into the real world around her.

CHAPTER 18

MAC

Present Day

For the last five years Mac had played basketball once a week with a ragtag group of doctors of varying specialties and skill levels. Some played ball in high school, a couple in college, and one had never played anything more than Horse in his childhood driveway, but they all appreciated the chance to blow off a little steam every Tuesday night and generally let their teenage selves run free.

Fitz had started off playing with them, but after blowing out a knee, Cynthia had put her foot down. He was now forbidden from doing much more than some low-key refereeing and shouting encouragement—and occasional good-natured ridicule—from the sidelines.

Having played in high school, Mac could usually handle himself on the court, especially against a bunch of doctors, most of whom were creeping up in age just like he was. But this evening, the first game after Riley moved in, he was a mess. He dropped balls, missed shots, tripped over his own feet, and double dribbled. He was a forty-year-old playing rec league ball. With his mind all over the place, his feet and arms seemed to follow, though never in any direction that helped his team.

Serving as coach to everyone, regardless of which team they were on, Fitz ran around trying to help, but when Mac's playing went from bad to worse, Fitz went from "Let's go, Mac!" to "Mac, what are you doing?" all the way to "Son, you are embarrassing yourself. Get your butt in gear."

When the game finally ended—Mac's team lost by twenty-seven points, largely due to his mistakes—his teammates gave him halfhearted high fives and trudged off to the parking lot to return to their homes and lives. Instead of going with them, Mac stayed where he was on the metal bench, nursing his squeeze bottle of cold water, the court in front of him bathed in a yellow glow from tall lights posted at each of the four corners.

They played at the public courts off Camellia Avenue, the long thoroughfare that stretched from the middle of Oak Hill all the way through Mobile to the river downtown. Most nights they had the place to themselves, but tonight, a group of teenagers was playing scrappy ball a court away. Mac kept his gaze on them, remembering how good it used to feel to be able to dart around the court like that as a limber-legged sixteen-year-old.

Fitz lumbered back to the court after the rest of the guys left. "Now that we've got that out of the way, why don't we have ourselves a little chat." He sat on the bench next to Mac. "You ready to tell me about that young lady you have staying with you?"

"According to Cynthia, you both already know who she is."

"I have an idea, but I'd rather hear it from you."

Mac leaned forward onto his elbows. Ran a hand through his sweaty hair. The air temperature wasn't all that high, but the humidity had sky-rocketed, thanks to an afternoon rain shower.

"I've got all night, Mac." Fitz settled back into his seat and clasped his hands across his lap. "I have nowhere to be."

Mac set his bottle down and reached for the basketball by his feet. Passed it back and forth between his hands a few times, then he told Fitz everything about Kat and Riley. When he finished, he sat silently, watching as the other boys packed up their balls and water bottles, hopped on their bicycles, and pedaled away.

"Did you stay in contact with this woman, Kat, after you and Edie had moved on together?"

Mac knew what Fitz was asking. "No. You know me, Fitz. I'm not that kind of guy."

"No, you're not." Fitz rubbed his chin absently. "But it doesn't always take 'that kind of guy' to make a mistake."

There it was, that word again. The word that kept tripping him up. *Mistake.* Every time he wanted to pull Edie to him and tell her Kat had been nothing more than a mistake, something stopped his words. He couldn't utter it. Because all these years later, he could still remember how it felt in those days he spent with Kat, and she hadn't felt like a mistake.

"What happens next?"

Mac dragged his hand across his face, then stood and dribbled the ball back onto the court. "I think she may leave me, Fitz." He positioned his feet at the three-point line, shot, missed.

"You're serious?"

He jogged to the ball and scooped it up. Dribbled slowly back to midcourt. "I don't know if she'll be able to get past this. And I understand—it's a lot to get past." He bounced the ball once, twice.

"Well, if I know Edie, she won't do anything hasty. Maybe you'll have time to convince her there are clearer roads ahead."

Mac blew out a laugh. "I'm not sure how clear those roads will be. I have another child, Fitz. And a grandchild on the way. Not to mention a wife and two kids to try to hang on to."

Fitz stretched his leg out in front of him and massaged the area just above his knee. "No matter how you look at it, it's a lot to deal with. A lot for you, for Edie and the kids. Even a lot for Riley."

"Yeah. And on top of that, Edie was just hired for this big project at work. She's designing a house for Turner Kennedy." A cicada buzzed against one of the tall lights overhead. He had to speak loudly to be heard over it. "The architect is a friend of hers. Of ours."

"Oh yeah?"

"The three of us were friends in school. Then we went to college together. We were pretty close."

The understatement was so enormous, it was almost laughable. Graham and Mac hadn't been "pretty close." Graham had been Mac's best friend.

Then he withdrew. Pulled away from Mac and from Edie. The fact that he did it without an explanation had always bothered Edie, but Mac didn't need Graham to explain why he'd ended his friendship with him. Mac knew.

"So it's a good thing that she'll be working with him?"

"I don't know." Mac jumped and released the ball from his fingertips. Missed again. "It's kind of complicated."

The evening after her meeting with the Kennedys over the bay, Edie had mentioned that Turner had hired Graham as the architect for his house, but it had almost been an afterthought. As if the reentrance of Graham into her life wasn't anything noteworthy.

"Graham Yeager?" Mac had questioned.

"What other Graham do we know?"

The letter he'd seen that night at the beach. The *Dear Graham* in her neat, slanted handwriting. The realization that maybe he hadn't been the only one who'd kept a secret that summer. "Wow. You and Graham working together."

"Yep. It should be interesting."

He grabbed the ball just before it rolled onto the other court and ran back to the alley.

"What makes it complicated?" Fitz asked.

Mac bounced the ball. "I think Edie and Graham had a thing for each other once. That same summer I was at the beach."

Fitz chuckled. "And here I thought you two kids had everything figured out. Just shows you can never judge a book by its cover."

"You're right about that." He shot and missed again.

"Boy, have you forgotten how to shoot the ball?" Fitz walked toward Mac and held his hands out. Mac passed the ball to him. "Tell me this. How are you and Riley?" Fitz shot, and the ball sank cozily into the basket. He grinned and Mac rolled his eyes.

"I don't know. It's this weird limbo. I want to get to know her, but I don't know how long she'll be here, and I don't even know what she wants from me. Or if she wants anything at all." He walked toward the ball, but Fitz beat him to it. "You're not allowed to play, remember?"

"Psshh." He bounced the ball behind his back. "I'm not allowed to jump. Cynthia can't say a thing if all I'm doing is shooting." He shot again. The ball bounced off the rim. He grabbed the rebound and passed it to Mac. "You say you don't know if she wants anything from you. I'd say the mere fact that she chose to go to you—her father—when she had nowhere else to turn means she's looking for something."

"And what's that?" Mac asked, both wanting his mentor's wisdom and fearing it at the same time. He held the ball with one hand against his hip.

"Attention. Care." Fitz shrugged. "Love. I don't know a lot about women—even at my ripe old age—but something tells me an eighteen-year-old girl chasing after her father instead of some random fella who may not have her best interests at heart is something to celebrate."

Mac swallowed and let the ball slip to the ground. He bounced it a few times, then caught it again. "But what if I'm giving everything I've got to Edie and the kids? To work, my patients? What if I don't have anything left for Riley?"

"You will. You have three children, Mac. You may not have known it before, but now you do. And we already know you're a good dad. I have no doubt you'll figure out how to love this one too. It won't be the same as it is with Avery and Thomas, I'll give you that. But you'll love her nonetheless. Maybe you already do."

Mac took a deep breath and let it out slowly.

"You're a good man, Mac."

"I can give you a whole bunch of reasons why that's not true."

"You are. I know it. And deep down Edie knows it too. You just may have to figure out some new ways to show her."

Mac bounced the ball twice, bent his knees, and sent the ball arcing through the air toward the basket. It finally went in.

Mac made it home after work the next night just as everyone was convening back at the house after a makeup soccer practice, an intense homework session at Cuppa Café, and a last-minute run to the grocery store. Edie was in the kitchen attempting to clear the debris of exploded backpacks off the island and start dinner, Avery and Thomas were arguing over whose turn it was to unload the dishwasher, and Ramona sauntered through the open front door and deposited a dead mole in the middle of the floor just to show she could do what she wanted.

After taking care of the mole and shooing Ramona outside, Mac found Riley sitting alone on the back porch.

"How are you doing?" He sat across from her and massaged the back of his neck.

"Pretty good." She appeared freshly showered, with pink cheeks and her hair damp around her face. "I told Edie I could help with dinner, but she told me to sit and relax." Riley pulled her hair up off her neck, then let it fall again. "Problem is, that's what I've been doing all day. A whole lot of nothing."

The noise level rose inside as Edie called to Thomas to come get his cleats out of the kitchen, and he yelled back that he was getting in the shower. Avery's voice carried outside to them through the open back porch door. "Ugh, I can still smell that dead mole in here."

Mac smiled to himself, relieved to hear the sound of life in their house. "I think we still have some time before dinner. Would you like to take a walk with me?"

"A walk? Like, outside?"

"Sure. We can get out and you can stretch your legs."

Just when it seemed like she wasn't going to answer, she nodded. "I'll go get my shoes."

Five minutes later, they were on the sidewalk in front of the house.

"Which way?" she asked.

He glanced right, then left, and he noticed Thomas standing at the edge of the driveway watching them. Mac waved, but as soon as he did, Thomas darted away. No smile, no wave.

"Which way should we go?" Riley repeated.

"Your choice." She pointed left, and after one more glance back to where Thomas had been standing, they headed left toward the entrance to the neighborhood. Almost without realizing what he was doing, Mac scanned each yard and driveway for neighbors, and his eyes bored into the drivers of each car that passed, searching for a familiar face.

They hadn't yet told anyone about Riley's presence in their lives, in their home. As far as he knew, no one had even seen her; therefore, no one knew the significance of the young woman walking next to him. Though if anyone saw them together, he imagined they'd immediately know the truth. He wasn't ready for the explanations, though they'd eventually be inevitable.

At the end of their street, instead of turning left and continuing around their block, he steered them across Azalea Street and into the newer part of the neighborhood, where he knew fewer people. Instead of the scraggly limbed oak trees and homes with historic plaques, the streets here were lined with fresh new crepe myrtles, decorative streetlights, and Craftsman houses with white picket fences.

For a while they walked mostly in silence, only commenting here and there about the cacophony of cicadas in the trees and the smell of cut grass as they passed a man pushing a lawn mower. Mac watched her though, taking in as many details as he could. Like how she walked purposefully, her stride long and brisk. And the way she slowed and stared at a small knot of kids playing with a dog on the other side of the street. One little girl separated from the bunch and chased a ball that had rolled into the driveway. Riley's eyes were glued to the little girl as she picked up the ball and ran back toward her friends.

At one point, she paused and put her hand on her belly.

"You okay?"

"Mm-hmm," she murmured. "It just takes a second for it to go away."

Edie had taken Riley to see Dr. Abrams on Tuesday. The report was that Riley could resume her normal activity as long as the contractions didn't grow stronger or more frequent, just like the labor and delivery doc had said. In fact, she said the baby looked perfectly healthy and she didn't foresee any issues.

"Edie dealt with contractions like that," Mac said. "More with Thomas, but with Avery too."

Riley resumed walking. "I was just glad nothing was wrong. After deciding to keep the baby, I actually don't . . . well, I don't want anything bad to happen."

Such casual words—*"deciding to keep the baby"*—but they held magnitudes. He swallowed. "You considered not keeping the baby?"

"I considered a lot of things." She pointed to her belly. "This was not my plan. No one would actually plan for something like this unless they're crazy."

He had so many questions, it felt like they were competing for space in his mouth, but most of them were of the overly personal variety: *Who is this Dex person and why did you sleep with him? Were you using contraception?*

And less personal but no less intrusive: *What in the world are you going to do after you have this baby?*

And there were others, ones he knew he could never ask. Questions that went straight to the heart of everything: *Out of all the choices you could have made, why'd you decide to knock on my door? And what took you so long?*

But he had a hunch that for most of these questions, Riley would have no answer. So instead he went for easy. "What's your favorite food?"

"What?" He'd caught her off guard, asking her something that had nothing to do with the baby. "Why do you want to know that?"

He shrugged. "I don't know you. But I want to. I want to know what you like to eat."

She pressed her lips together, and for a moment he thought she would ignore the question. Then her cheeks tugged up at the corners. "I like sushi."

"Sushi?"

She nodded. "I've only had it once. At this little place in Pensacola. Tammy was trying to cheer me up after Mom's wreck. We went to a movie, then she took me to dinner."

"She tried to cheer you up with raw fish?"

Riley scuffed her feet along the ground. "I liked it."

"Okay. Two points for an unexpected answer. How about this—what's your earliest memory?"

"That's easy. My mom braiding my hair." She was quiet a moment and Mac remembered Kat's hair, the long braid that snaked down her back every day that summer. The memory of it blowing out from her head like a pale halo when she unwound it on the beach.

"Mom worked really hard and always seemed older than she was. Older than other moms at school. And she looked a little . . . rough. Like someone you wouldn't want to mess with. But her hands were so soft." Riley tilted her head a little, as if trying to better see the memory. "My hair was really long when I was a kid, and she'd work her fingers through it so carefully to get the tangles out. It never hurt."

How his soul ached for Kat and for this child. His child. *"It never hurt."* So much in her life had hurt, but her mother's hands were soft and gentle. Her mother was gone. *Kat* was gone. There was so much he wanted to know about Kat, so many questions he wished he could ask her. Had she felt abandoned? Hurt? Did she hate him?

No, Mac. Your head cannot go there. This *is the here and now.* This *is your life.*

He cleared his throat. "What do you want to be when you grow up?"

"Um, I think that's already pretty much laid out for me."

"You mean being a mom?"

"Yeah. I've made my choices, and here I am." She put her hands on each side of her belly and sighed. "Can't change things now."

"No, but you know you can be more than one thing."

"Sure. Like Edie's a mom and works on houses. You're a dad and a doctor. But that kind of stuff doesn't happen to girls like me."

"What about when you were younger? What'd you want to be then?" She shrugged.

"Come on. Every kid has an idea of what they want to be."

"Did you?"

"Sure. I wanted to be an astronaut."

"An astronaut. Really?"

"Really. I was obsessed with Buzz Aldrin and Neil Armstrong. Jim Lovell. I wanted to go to the moon and Mars and Saturn. In that order."

"Guess your life is pretty much a failure then, isn't it? I don't see you going to any of those places."

The edge of resentment, or maybe anger, in her voice jolted him. He slowed and turned toward her. "It's not a failure to change your mind. Or to make adjustments when your original plan doesn't work out. Like the fact that I get sick on airplanes." He resumed walking. "Not ideal for someone hurtling through the atmosphere at 3 Gs."

"What about someone who wanted to be a doctor but got pregnant instead? I'd say that's a big fat failure." Her voice was quiet despite the negative words, and she kept her gaze straight ahead.

"You want to be a doctor?"

"Wanted. As in used to. And I know it's stupid. It sounds like I'm trying to suck up to you or something."

"It doesn't sound stupid. What made you want to be a doctor?"

She tucked her hair behind her ear, a faint smile on her face. "So I could help people. I fell off the swing set in our backyard when I was eight. Landed right on my elbow. Mom was at work so I called 911."

"You were home alone at eight years old?"

She lifted a shoulder. "What else were we going to do?"

Again, he was hit by the magnitude of the burden he'd unknowingly heaped onto Kat's shoulders. It was staggering.

"Anyway, I was terrified, obviously. I'd never been to a hospital or even seen an ambulance up close. But the paramedics were so nice and funny. They made it a lot less scary." She kicked a rock and it skittered ahead of them. "And the doctor who set my arm told me everything he was doing. He was so calm, he made me feel calmer. After that, I decided I wanted to be a doctor." She let out a rough laugh. "But here I am and things have changed."

"You don't want to help people anymore?"

She scoffed. "It's not like I want to hurt people. But I'm not exactly in a position to help anyone. I can barely help myself. I mean, look at me." The quietness was gone and some of that initial spunk, the snark, was back. "I'm living in your house solely because I couldn't help myself. How in the world could I possibly help anyone else?" She held her hands out, then exhaled and let them drop. "I'll probably just be a waitress or . . . I don't know. Clean houses. Just something to pay the bills."

Not on my watch. The words came from somewhere deep inside him, fully formed and as true as anything else he knew.

For years he'd been telling Thomas and Avery that they could shoot for the moon. No matter how far-fetched a desire, they could aim for it and work hard to try to achieve it. Even if they didn't make it all the way, the work, he told them, was what would make them stronger. The *working for it* was what would shape them into better people.

And why should it be any different for Riley? Yes, she'd have a baby, which made everything infinitely harder, especially without a partner to help, but why shouldn't she aim high and set that goal of becoming a doctor? Or a lawyer or a nurse or a teacher or anything else she wanted? Mac wanted the moon for her, just like he wanted it for Avery and Thomas. Regardless of how hard the road may be for her, it didn't mean she couldn't set her course and it didn't mean she wouldn't hit her target.

"I have a feeling you don't want to hear the rousing speech that I really want to give you right now."

"If it's along the lines of 'You can do anything you set your mind to,' then you're right."

"Then I'll just say this one thing." He stepped off the curb and gestured for Riley to follow as he headed them back the way they'd come. "A baby doesn't have to mean your life stops for good." She snorted, but he continued. "Hear me out. A lifetime is long—assuming all goes well—and having a baby is just one small part of it. An important part, of course. One of the most important, I'd say. But it's not all."

"That's pretty easy for you to say. You're not the one having the baby." Her words were devoid of optimism, but her face was a fraction lighter. A little less pinched.

A few minutes later they stood on the sidewalk in front of the house. She squared her shoulders, as if trying to summon even a small bit of courage. He wanted so badly to hug her, to wrap his arms around her and infuse her with strength for whatever was coming ahead, but they weren't there yet.

"Have you ever been on a roller coaster?" he asked instead.

"You ask the most random questions."

"I'm getting to know you, remember? Roller coaster, yes or no?"

"Just once. I threw up all over the person in front of me."

He hung his head and laughed. "Same thing happened to me."

"Really?"

"Yep. I was nine. Haven't been on one since."

A purple dusk had fallen around them and fireflies winked in the bushes. "Thanks for walking with me."

"Yeah. Thanks for asking. I kinda liked it."

"Good. Let's do it again tomorrow."

She nodded and Mac led her up the steps to the front door. When he opened it and stepped back, she hesitated only briefly before walking inside.

———

That night, Mac stayed downstairs long after everyone else had gone up. His body felt restless, like his legs wanted to take him on another walk—or better yet, a run—but his mind was exhausted from the mental strain of keeping all the various people and emotions separated into their appropriate compartments. Finally he gave up.

After turning off the lights, he climbed the stairs, slow and quiet. Riley's light was off, but the lights in both Thomas's and Avery's rooms were on. He carefully opened Avery's door first. She was asleep with her science notebook lying open on her chest, her glasses askew on her face. He tiptoed into the room, careful to sidestep the squeaky spot in the hardwood floor, gently lifted the glasses from her face, then set them on her bedside table.

In Thomas's bedroom Mac found his son sprawled across his bed, sheets tangled around his knees, his dark, curly hair damp on his forehead. Mac pulled the string to turn on the ceiling fan before he walked out.

In their room Edie was asleep on her side, the blankets pulled up, revealing only the dainty curve of her neck. It was good to have her back in their bedroom, though the emotional temperature between them was still chilly.

Her dark hair was splayed out against her pillow, her eyelashes a dark swipe of color against her cheeks. With Riley and Kat filling his mind,

Mac was struck again by their physical differences—Edie's fine dark hair and olive skin. Riley's hair was thick and blonde, her pale skin dotted by a constellation of freckles. Just like Kat. Just like him.

He sat on the floor by his side of the bed, where the light from Edie's lamp cast just enough glow to be able to see. He kept such a tangle of receipts, reminders, old calendars he couldn't toss out, and other useless debris in the drawer of his bedside table that Edie said it was a land unto him alone. As a result he knew she'd never find the envelope he'd hidden under his 2013–2014 calendar.

He pulled both the letter and photo out of their hiding place and sat with his back against the bed, his knees bent in front of him. After checking to be sure Edie was still asleep, he read the letter again, start to finish. Studied the tiny photo. Having stared at it so many times in the last handful of days, he felt he knew the details of Riley's infant face as well as he knew his own. And Kat's face . . . Well, he didn't need to memorize that. Kat's face was still etched in his mind, even after all these years.

He thought he'd forgotten her. Thought he'd left her behind along with the busted flip-flops he'd worn for much of that summer. But she'd been stubbornly persistent, lingering in occasional dreams, wisps of memories, the scent of boat fuel and the sound of seagulls. He tried hard to forget, telling himself he was with the woman he'd been meant to be with all along. Edie was his bride, his very lifeblood, and he'd wished many times he could dig around in his brain and pick out the parts that clung to Kat, like she was a drug his body or mind still craved.

But what if it wasn't Kat those errant brain cells craved? What if it was something else? *Someone* else? Maybe all this time it wasn't the memories of Kat clinging to him, but the presence of Riley. His child. Even though he'd been unaware of her.

CHAPTER 19

MAC

Summer 2000

Mac was working a late shift, helping to haul boats out of the water and cleaning them before loading them onto the lift to be taken back to dry storage. He actually preferred the late shifts—the temps were a little cooler, plus it was always fun to see the big boats idling back into the pass, their holds full of red snapper, grouper, and amberjack they'd caught during their day on the Gulf.

The real reason he liked working late shifts, though, was that he got to see Kat. He wouldn't admit it to anyone else—he barely even let himself think it—but as the boats came in soon after sunset, his gaze flitted around the marina, searching for that windswept shock of blonde hair, the white sunglasses perched up top, the mile of tanned legs and sculpted arms.

One evening, not long after the Fourth of July, he was driving the lift back toward the boat barn from the marina when he saw her. She stood at the fish cleaning station with her back to the boats, wearing her trademark cutoff shorts and a white T-shirt knotted on the side. Her hair was swept into a ponytail, exposing the scoop of soft skin along the side of her neck. His heartbeat quickened as he parked the lift, tossed the keys to Jeff, and hopped down onto the hot asphalt. He hurried toward her, his mind scrambling for just the right thing to say—something funny but not childish, something to give her some relief at the end of what was probably an exhausting day.

Just as he thought of a perfectly witty comment, a man approached her from the parking lot. His build was slight and he wore a tight black tank top, a silver chain snaking out of one pocket of his jeans and into another. Black boots, dark sunglasses despite the dusk. With everyone else in the vicinity wearing brightly colored fishing shirts, sunglasses on Croakies around their necks, flip-flops, and baseball caps, this guy more than stood out—he loomed.

Mac was still fixated on the stranger's appearance. Why would some-one like him be hanging around a marina when it seemed like fishing would be the last thing on his priority list?

The guy grabbed Kat roughly and pulled her in for a kiss.

A low growl, a sound more animal-like than anything he'd ever uttered, escaped from Mac's throat. He broke into a run, determined to get her away from this punk who was clearly trying to hurt her and force her against her will.

Unsurprisingly, Kat took care of herself. She yanked her arms out of his grasp and swatted his arm. Then she lifted her hair off the back of her neck and said something to him that made him smile. When she took a step toward him, he casually leaned in and kissed her cheek. And she let him do it.

Something in Mac's chest clenched, and dread filled his arms and legs, making him slow to a stop in the middle of the walkway. He watched as the guy spoke again. Kat nodded and he sauntered off toward a black car parked under a tree along the side of the parking lot. The car rode low to the ground, its windows darkened to a likely illegal shade. The guy opened the door and closed it behind him. A moment later a deep bass beat pumped out, the sound making its way to the marina despite the buzz and chatter all around him.

Unsure of what to make of both the guy and the crushing sensation in his chest, Mac veered off the walkway and toward the dock store, where Carla was ringing up a man with bare sandy feet and a towel wrapped around his waist. Mac stood at the side window, next to a display of shell-encrusted keepsake boxes and tubes of sunscreen and aloe, watching Kat as she rinsed out an ice chest and hoisted it onto her hip for the walk back to the boat.

"Looking for your pot of gold out there?" Carla asked from the register.

Mac turned. "Me?"

"Yeah, you. Is there a reason you're not out there working? We have eight boats unloading fish and passengers, which means we have—you guessed it—eight boats to wash and put away. And instead of doing it, you're in here lollygagging."

"Sorry." He turned back to the window. "I was just . . ." He leaned forward to peer around the edge of the building to where *Alabama Reds* was docked. He couldn't see her.

Behind him Carla snorted. "You got it bad. Anyone with eyes can tell who you're searching for."

"What? No. What are you talking about?"

"Your poker face is terrible, kid. And I have to tell you, Kat's a tricky one. You might want to steer clear."

Mac shoved his hands through his hair, then crossed his arms. He wanted to deny her, but he was also curious. "Tricky?"

"Yeah. Tough. And apparently taken." She tilted her head toward the opposite window, through which Mac could see the black car by the fence.

"You know who he is?"

"Unfortunately. Marco worked here for a little while, but I didn't like his attitude. The way he carried himself. He acted like we should all be thankful anytime he decided to show up for work." She clicked her tongue against her teeth. "He comes back around now and then to see Kat. I don't like it."

Mac clenched his teeth together, then yanked open the glass door. He bypassed the dock and headed for the lift to finish his job of hauling the boats out and washing their hulls. Afterward, his legs wet and his shoulders burning, Mac strode down the dock toward Kat's boat. He glanced at the parking lot only to see the black car still there, its parking lights illuminated.

As Mac approached the *Alabama Reds*, Reggie, the captain, was handing supplies down to Kat from the upper deck. Mac hung back on the dock until Reggie climbed out of the boat. "No need to haul her out of the water tonight. We'll be out again early tomorrow."

"Yes, sir." Mac stepped out of his way.

At the sound of Mac's voice, Kat smiled. "I'm almost done."

"No hurry."

"Maybe not for you, but I'm in a hurry." She grabbed a long-handled stiff brush and began to scrub the floor of the boat.

Mac thought of the guy. *Marco.* "Why? You got a date?"

Kat paused her scrubbing. Her brow furrowed, then she grinned. "Yeah. A date with my bathtub and a whole lot of hot water. Maybe a glass of wine to go with it."

"That sounds nice." Mac's cheeks burned. "I didn't mean . . ."

Kat laughed. "I know what you meant. And yeah, it does sound nice. Which is why I'm in a hurry to get out of here."

She worked the brush around the edge of the seats and back toward the engines, then gestured to the water hose looped on a hook on one of the pilings. Mac unwound the hose, turned on the water, and handed the nozzle down to her. She aimed the spray at the soapy floor and rinsed the water down toward the drains at the back. When she finished, she pulled herself out of the boat and sat on the edge of the dock with a loud exhale.

After winding the hose back onto the hook, Mac sat next to her. Their legs dangled toward the water, and she gently kicked hers back and forth. Lights on the sides and end of each dock shone down on the water, and faint strains of Bob Marley flowed from a boat several slips away.

"I think someone's waiting for you in the parking lot."

"He can wait a little longer."

"I thought you said your date was with the bathtub." He sneaked a glance at her. She'd propped her hands on the dock behind her, her head back, her eyes closed.

"It is," she said without opening her eyes.

"Why's he here then?" He couldn't have been so bold if her eyes had been open. Not if those hazel eyes had been trained on him, making his insides quiver and weakening his resolve.

"He's giving me a ride home. My car's in the shop."

Mac nodded. What a nice guy. Driving her home. No ulterior motive at all. "I could have given you a ride home." He felt rather than saw her turn toward him, but he didn't meet her gaze. "How long have y'all been dating?"

"I'm not dating Marco."

"Does he know that?" he shot back.

"Wow. Something under your skin?" This time he did look at her, only to find a smile playing on her lips. "Go ahead," she said. "Get it off your chest. What do you want to say about him?"

Mac shrugged. "I—nothing. I don't have anything to say about him. I don't know the guy. He just seemed . . . possessive."

"Possessive," she repeated quietly. "You actually may be on to something there. But it's nothing to worry about. I can take care of myself."

They sat in silence a moment longer, Bob singing about the three little birds and a group of seagulls cackling from somewhere farther away. Mac couldn't stop thinking about the way Marco had grabbed her so roughly, kissing her like he could do exactly what he wanted.

"Marco and I just hang out from time to time," she said, as if she'd heard his thoughts. "He's probably not . . . Well, he's not like you. Let's just say that."

"What's that supposed to mean?"

She shifted her position, taking the weight off her arms and sitting forward. Her shoulder slid against his arm, her skin warm against his. "I don't know." When she turned toward him, their faces weren't far apart. Close enough that he could see flecks of gold in her eyes, illuminated by the dock light a few feet away.

He fought the urge to look away, to lessen the intensity. Her boldness was invigorating. Captivating. So different from most girls he knew, with their polite Southern manners, their social graces, their silly mind games.

"New kid!" Carla's voice rasped out a yell that sent her into a coughing spell. "I need you to punch out."

"You'd better get up there before she yells again." Kat held in a laugh.

179

They stood and walked to the dock store. Mac paused by the door as Kat kept walking toward the parking lot.

"Hey," he called. When she turned back around, Mac realized he had no idea what to say. He just wanted to stop her, to give her one last image to think of as she sat in that low-slung car with Marco, the guy who got to drive her home. "Do you . . . ?" Without warning Edie's face flashed in his mind. Her soft brown hair, her playful smile, her dark eyes he'd gotten lost in so many times.

She smiled. "Do I what?"

"I . . . ," he managed, then stopped. "I don't know what I was going to say." He rubbed his forehead and cursed under his breath.

"Think about it. Let me know what you come up with." Kat walked toward the car. She opened the door, which turned on the interior light. Marco's arm was draped across the passenger seat. She sat and closed the door as he leaned toward her.

———————

When Mac got home that night, he trudged up the stairs to the front door and let himself in. He expected to see Graham sitting in the small den, but the room was empty. One of the Jaws movies—the one at SeaWorld—was on the TV, the volume low.

Mac dropped his keys on the kitchen counter and, with one eye on the TV, pulled a box of cereal from the cabinet and a spoon from the drawer. As he passed Graham's bedroom on the way to the couch, he heard the sound of the shower. Mac sat and took a bite, then relaxed back into the cushions, relishing the release of his muscles.

A few sheets of paper sat on the coffee table. Mac nudged them out of the way as he propped his feet on the table. He closed his eyes a moment, then focused on the TV, where a robotic-looking shark was swimming purposefully toward the underwater tunnel full of people.

A moment later the AC clicked on and one of the papers floated to the ground. Mac reached down and grabbed it, and as he did, he noticed the handwriting. Small, slanted to the right, and very familiar.

He and Edie hadn't spoken since they left school at the end of May. They'd both said they'd check in with each other, because what else was there to say when you were parting ways with the person you'd been with for practically your whole life? But he hadn't heard a thing from her. No phone call, no postcard, and no email. Then again, he hadn't contacted her either. It had been radio silence both ways.

And this letter wasn't addressed to him.

Mac set his bowl on the coffee table and picked up the papers. With a pounding heart he let his eyes skim the pages, realizing in an instant this could very well be only one of many letters sent from New York to Alabama. And that maybe some had been sent the other way too.

He pressed his elbows into his knees, thinking of Kat and how weak-kneed he'd become around her. Everything she stirred in him, ranging from confusion to restraint to flat-out desire. He'd so far tamped those emotions down, knowing it would be unfair to Edie, or at least unkind. Competing emotions warred inside him now—hot and ugly jealousy next to a new awareness, an alertness.

With a glance toward his best friend's door, where the sound of the shower still swelled, he sat back again and began to read.

Dear Graham,

Today's walk home from work was pretty miserable. It had just rained, which in New York City means the sidewalks get really slick and all the cars splash dirty water everywhere. I was soaked because I'd forgotten my umbrella, I was hungry, and my feet hurt because I'd walked twelve blocks in wet shoes. Then I looked up, and in this little sliver of sky between two tall buildings, I saw a rainbow. Someone bumped into me from behind because I'd stopped in the middle of the sidewalk, just staring at it.

In a split second my mind carried me back to that day you and I went fishing. Mac was supposed to be there, too, but instead he was at home, sick with food poisoning from bad barbecue. So it was you and me sitting in your green aluminum boat, inside that quiet little cove down the bay from your house. We fished and talked and laughed a lot.

Then it started to rain, but the sun was still shining, and we saw that rainbow, remember?

When I turned to see if you'd noticed it, you were already watching me. I wanted so badly to know what you were thinking, but before I could ask (though I'm not sure I would have had the nerve), you cranked the engine and motored us out of the cove and back toward your house. By the time we got back, it felt like something had changed between us. Something was different.

Mac was at the door when we walked in. He'd started to feel better and didn't want to miss out on the fun. And everything went right back to the way it always was. Me and Mac. And you. I've wondered this before but I've never asked—why did you stick around? Why did you put up with us? We must have been so annoying together. I'm glad you stuck with us, but it must have been awkward for you. I'm sorry for—

"Hey."

Mac's head jerked up at the sound of Graham's voice. Graham stood in his bedroom doorway in a pair of shorts, toweling his hair. "I didn't hear you come in." He glanced at the papers in Mac's hands.

Mac set them back on the coffee table and picked up his cereal bowl. "I just got here a little while ago," he said around a bite of now-soggy cereal.

Graham stared a fraction too long, then ducked back into his room. He came out a moment later, pulling a shirt over his head. He sat on the other end of the couch. "Work okay today?"

"Yeah," Mac said quickly. "It was fine. How was yours?"

Graham shrugged. "It was good. Hot."

"What's with the letter?" The words were out, though he hadn't made the conscious decision to ask the question.

Graham shook his damp black hair off his forehead. "We're just keeping up. She's been filling me in on her job. Her apartment." He shrugged again. "Life."

Life, Mac thought. Nothing in that letter had been about her job or her apartment. Her words to Graham were heated. Sincere. They were full of emotion and they hadn't been directed to him.

Maybe she's moving on. Maybe I should too.

Their words died off as the shark on-screen tore into an unsuspecting water-skier. Graham stared at Edie's letter on the coffee table and Mac worked his jaw, preparing to either ask a question or answer one, but Graham spoke first. "This is a terrible movie."

Mac exhaled through his nose. "Yeah. It really is."

They watched the rest of the movie in silence, as Mac's cereal disintegrated in his bowl and Edie's letter fluttered on the coffee table in front of them. Mac wanted to say something—about the perceptible change between the two of them, his fear that their friendship was fading—but confusion and defeat drowned his words.

CHAPTER 20

EDIE

Summer 2000

Up on the rooftop patio, Edie had just finished a letter to Graham, her mind ablaze with old memories and the thought of working with him in this pulsing, electric city, when the door to the stairwell clanged behind her. She turned in her chair to see a girl walking toward her, a brown paper bag in one hand and the other hand holding a leash that led to a shaggy brown dog.

"Hello." Edie smiled.

"Hi. Do you mind if I sit with you?" The girl gestured to the other seat at the table, where Edie was eating her takeout.

"Sure I mean no, I don't mind."

The girl sat and the dog crouched at her feet, panting and whining. "This is not for you," she said, then turned her head and sneezed. "I already fed you." She sniffed, then pulled two white Mama Yu boxes from the bag and set them on the table in front of her.

When Edie chuckled, the girl smiled. "What is it?"

Edie pointed to her own small white box, the words *Mama Yu* printed in bold red type.

"Great minds," the girl said. "Either that, or the convenience of a Chinese restaurant right downstairs is too easy for both of us to pass up."

"Maybe it's a little of both. I'm Edie."

"Judith," she said with another wide smile and a sniff. "And this is Fletcher."

"He's cute." Edie reached down and rubbed his soft head.

"Thanks. He's my brother's. I'm staying in his apartment this summer while he's in DC. He's letting me stay for free on the condition that I take care of Fletch." She took a bite of her sesame chicken. "Which would be totally perfect except that I'm allergic to dogs."

Edie laughed. "You're allergic to dogs? And you have to stay with him all summer?"

Judith nodded. "Basically I look like I have a really bad cold all the time. Which is why we spend as much time out in the fresh air as we can. Well"—she shrugged—"relatively fresh. It is New York City, after all."

Edie ate the last few bites of her lo mein and dropped the box back into her brown bag.

"Where's your postcard going?" Judith pointed with her chin to the postcard sitting in front of Edie.

"Oh. To Alabama. Orange Beach, specifically."

"The beach. That sounds nice. Is that where you're from?"

"No. Well, I live in Alabama, but my . . . a friend is living there for the summer."

"A boy?" Judith comically wagged her eyebrows up and down. Judith's hair—deep, fiery orange and springing out from her head in coils and ringlets—bounced as she tilted her head.

Edie laughed and Fletcher barked, as if he wanted to join in the fun. Edie reached down and petted him again. "Yes, he's a boy. But he's not my boyfriend." She didn't mention that her boyfriend was staying there too.

Ex-boyfriend.

"How old are you?"

"I'm twenty," Edie said. "At least for another few weeks. How old are you?"

"Twenty-two. I'm just asking because it seems like at a certain point, it gets hard to have boy *friends*, don't you think?"

"I don't know. I hadn't thought about it."

"For me, if I like a guy enough to want to spend my time with him, I start wondering why I'm not considering him as a boyfriend. Long term, you know? Like your guy there." Judith pointed with her chopsticks to Edie's postcard. "You obviously care enough about him to keep in touch while you're here. What's stopping you from dating him?"

Edie opened her mouth, but she had no response. Judith laughed. "I'm sorry. I've been told I can be a little too blunt sometimes."

They kept chatting while Judith finished her dinner, exchanging much easier information about hometowns, schools, jobs. Edie was pleased to discover she liked Judith—she found her honesty and genuineness refreshing, if a little blunt like she'd said.

Later, when they descended the stairwell to their respective apartments, they made plans to meet on the roof again the next night for dinner. Edie went to bed that night with a new lightness in her heart, happy to have made a friend in the bustle of summer in New York City. With her window raised a few inches to let in the night air, Edie lay on her back and pondered Judith's words. *"At a certain point, it gets hard to have boy* friends."

Was that true? She'd had guy friends over the years, and she'd never had a hard time with their friendships. They were friends, cut and dried. More Mac's friends than hers, sure, but they were plenty friendly and it had never been an issue.

Then there was Graham. They'd been friends, too, and on almost all levels there had been no issues. The three of them—she, Mac, and Graham—had developed the strongest of friendships, almost without trying. But then there were those random, infrequent occasions when she'd find herself alone with Graham—listening to music while Mac was otherwise occupied, riding with him in his little Honda Civic to get fast food at midnight, walking out of Brewster Hall together after an art lecture—when her nerves would tingle and she'd stumble over her words and she'd wonder why and how Graham made her feel so stirred up.

Then the guilt would come for feeling those things when sweet Mac was waiting for her in the cafeteria or the hallway outside her dorm room or on the quad. She'd shake off the confusing feelings about Graham and go back to enjoying the sure thing in front of her.

But now in the wake of their breakup, Mac was no longer that sure thing, and almost without realizing it, her mind had conjured two very different futures for herself. She just wished her mind would tell her where she fit.

CHAPTER 21

EDIE

Present Day

Edie opened the creaky wooden door to Cuppa Café in the heart of Oak Hill at the beginning of the week, her computer bag slung over her arm. She often brought her work here when she thought a change of scenery might jar something loose in her mind and give her the spark she needed to get an awkward kitchen corner just right or figure out where to fit a claw-foot tub in a bathroom that didn't seem to have room for it. Something about the way the light streamed in the back windows of the one-hundred-year-old cottage or the way the hardwood floor squeaked and strained underfoot made her feel like she could absorb the wisdom from all the life that had taken place here and use it to fuel her imagination.

Though today it wasn't fuel of imagination she needed; it was determination and resolve. This morning she'd received an email from Laura Lou that told her—not in actual words but in tone and insinuation—that the project wouldn't be hers alone. She'd already known it would be difficult for Laura Lou to sit on the sidelines while she did the work, and the email only confirmed it.

Edie,

I've been thinking about the Kennedys. It's so exciting to think of Davis Design Group attached to a project of such magnitude. Congrats again on snagging the job. I'd like to make sure we're all on the same page before you get too far into the details, so why don't we discuss this week? How does Wednesday morning work for you?

In the meantime check out the link below to an article from *New Orleans* magazine regarding Turner's grandmother's house on St. Charles Avenue. I think a suggestion about adding some Creole touches to the new house as a nod to his forebears would be wise.

LLD

Edie propped her chin on her hand and stared at the words. She could practically feel Laura Lou breathing down her neck. Edie sat up straighter in her seat and tried to corral her resolve, her fire, her determination to stand firm and hold tight to her design choices.

She hated that she still felt the need to prove herself to Laura Lou when she'd been a DDG designer for eight years and had a long list of satisfied and repeat clients, but maybe that was about to change. If she could make it work, this job could be her chance to show Laura Lou she was capable of seeing a project through, start to finish, solidly on her own.

I never would have had to prove myself to Graham.

The thought was there, blazing bright in her mind, without her awareness of its existence. But it was true, wasn't it? If she'd chosen that path, if they'd made that future happen, no way would she have to be proving herself to him. Her choices would be her own, and he'd support them. End of story.

She straightened in her seat and focused on what was in front of her—her work, her here and now.

An hour and a half later, she closed her laptop and reached her arms up to stretch her sore back. The table surface in front of her was covered in various drawer pulls, bits of tile, and paint chips in a wide array of blues and greens that she'd pulled from her bag of samples, and she had four pages of notes plus some room layouts sketched on graph paper.

When someone called her name, she heard it as if through a fog. She turned and was surprised to see her mother. Dianne juggled three to-go cups of coffee in her hands and jostled her way toward Edie's table in the back. She kissed her daughter on the cheek, then perched on the edge of the seat across from Edie. Her powdery perfume mixed with the aroma of roasting beans, creating a dizzying blend.

"I'm just grabbing some coffee for the girls and heading in to the shop."

"The girls? Did you hire someone else?"

"We did! Didn't I tell you? She's a student at South Alabama and just the cutest thing you've ever seen. Blanche has already featured her on her Instagram page. Oh, and did I tell you? Firefly now has its own page. And of course Blanche has told her people about it. We already have two thousand followers, and it hasn't been up a week yet. Can you believe it?" She blew on her cup of coffee and took a sip. "*Bay* magazine called last week and said they want to do a feature."

Edie watched her mom as she talked. It was so strange to see this new Dianne, though the change had hardly been sudden. At one time in her life, Dianne Everett had been the reigning queen of ladies' bunco at Oak Hill Country Club. She'd worn pearls to the grocery store, donned tasteful heels to run errands, and never appeared in public without her lipstick.

These days instead of pearls, heels, and crisp white button-downs, it was chunky-heeled sandals, skinny jeans, and tops in curve-hugging fabrics. Firefly had become the trendiest shopping destination in Oak Hill, and Dianne was taking regular trips to the casinos in Biloxi with "the girls."

If you hadn't known the old Dianne, you might be tempted to call this one exciting—an older woman racing into the coming years with gusto and pizzazz. To Edie—and she knew to her dad too—it was just jarring.

". . . but then we moved the rack to the side of the shop and it fixed everything," her mom said. "So the entire back wall is mirrored now and the effect is perfect."

"That's great, Mom. I'll have to stop by and see it."

"You really should. And while you're there, I can show you the new wraps we just got in. Adorable."

"How are things going with you and Dad?"

Mom waved her hand and all but rolled her eyes. "Oh, you know. Same old, same old."

"Have you talked to him in a while?"

"We stay in contact, yes. After all, someone has to make sure he has groceries up there. Knowing Bud, he'd forget to stop at the store and have nothing to eat in the entire house except beef jerky."

Her words were terse, but her eyes held a wistfulness Edie couldn't ignore.

"The kids were talking about how strange it felt to spend the night with you and not have Dad there."

"Well, good thing kids are adaptable. They'll get used to it eventually. You did."

"I'm not used to it, Mom. I hate it. It feels terrible knowing you're both on your own."

"I'm not on my own. I have Blanche and the shop. I have my friends. You. My life is just fine."

"What about Dad then? You were his world. He would have done anything for you."

"Oh, honey, we've been over this. I'm doing all these new things, trying to enjoy life as much as possible, and he's just . . . he's just Bud. Bud who whittles his sticks. Bud who likes his old flannel shirts and his routines and his Folgers coffee. We're not the same people we once were." She shrugged. "We've changed."

As much as her mom tried to convince everyone of that fact, Edie couldn't help but wonder if it was really her talking or just some late midlife crisis.

"You were married for forty-seven years."

"Don't I know it."

Edie reached up to rub her forehead and found her hands were shaking. "Mom—"

But her mom's phone buzzed, and she held up a finger as she peered at the screen. "Oh, it's Blanche. She's waiting on her coffee. I have to run, honey." Mom stood and shouldered her bag. "Please try not to worry. I'm doing just fine. Better than fine, actually. But . . . maybe call your father. You know how he is."

"Yes, I do."

Then in a flurry of coffee cups, perfume, and promises to "talk soon!" she was gone.

———

An hour and a half later, Edie pulled up in front of her dad's hunting camp. In the South the term "hunting camp" had all manner of connotations. For some, it meant a primitive cabin, with beef jerky, cowboy coffee, and tree stands. For others, it meant polished wood, a full kitchen, and a featured spread in *Garden & Gun*.

Bud Everett's hunting camp was neither of these two extremes. It was a small one-bedroom cabin with daisy-printed curtains on the windows, an easy chair in front of a large fireplace, and a well-worn table made out of an old wagon wheel. The screened-in porch was almost as big as the space inside, and from it you could see through the trees to the stream-fed lake full of trout, bass, and catfish, depending on the time of year.

It's possible her mother might have spent a night or two at the camp over the years, but she quickly deemed it Bud's domain—too far from civilization for her taste—and he was fine with that. Especially after Mom announced she wanted the separation and he had to find a new place to live. Edie knew her dad wasn't happy about the situation, but she also knew he probably didn't mind the extra time in the woods.

She found her father down at the lake sitting in an aluminum chair, his fishing pole propped into a large Folgers can next to him. He heard her stepping through the crunchy leaves and turned. A slow smile crossed his weathered face. "Well, hey there, missy." He stood for a hug.

"Hey, Dad."

"What are you doing all the way out here? Shouldn't you be at work?"

"I should. I moved a couple of meetings though. I wanted to see you."

"I'm glad you came. Hang on just a minute and I'll get you a chair."

"No, it's okay. I don't—"

"Just watch my pole."

Dad traipsed back up the hill she'd just come down, then returned a moment later with a second folding chair. He set it down next to his and settled back into his own. On the ground next to his chair was a long, smooth piece of wood. He picked it up and set it in his lap. "I think this one's going to be a dolphin. See the beginnings of the tail here?" He pointed to the end of the stick.

"It'll look good."

They sat in silence for several minutes, no sounds around them but the rustle of the leaves overhead in a gentle breeze and the birds flitting in the trees. A single fish jumped in the middle of the pond and slapped back down on its side.

"Have you caught anything today?"

"Not a one. They're out there; they're just not hungry." He turned to her. "But fishing is just as much about the sitting and waiting as it is about the catch."

"The journey, not the destination, right?"

"Exactly."

She thought of what her mom had said in the coffee shop. *We're not the same people we once were.* But she was wrong. Bud Everett was the same as he'd ever been. Her mom was the one who'd changed.

"How are you doing, Dad?"

"Oh, you know. Pretty good."

"Do you have enough food?"

"I have plenty. I stopped on my way in."

"I still don't like the idea of you being out here by yourself all the time."

"What are you talking about? I love this place." He stretched his arm out toward the water, then back toward the house. "Nothing but peace here. Nothing but calm." He lowered his arm. "Though the nights do get a little long. Without your mother's running commentary on everything from TV shows to politics, it can get . . . well, it can be pretty quiet."

She waited for him to say more, but he was still, his gaze focused on the end of his line in the water.

"It's been almost a year, Dad," she said softly. "Are y'all going to be able to fix this?"

He lifted a shoulder. "I can't say. I'm just waiting until your mom figures out what she wants."

"Mom? What about what you want? Do you want a divorce?"

"I do not. But it seems your mom needs something different than what I can give her." He held his hands out. "This is me. And I'm not sure this is what she wants anymore."

Silence wrapped around them again. A fish nibbled on Dad's hook, pulling the orange bobber under the water, but no catch.

"Everything going okay with you?" he asked after a few minutes. His voice was break-Edie's-heart kind. Not intrusive but available.

Words crowded in her mouth. *Actually, Dad, Mac has another child and I'm afraid we're broken. On top of that Avery's growing up, Thomas only wants the company of his soccer ball, and my work doesn't feel right anymore. Basically my world has upended.*

But she held the words in. She didn't want to add to her dad's problems with her own.

"I'm doing okay, Dad."

He reached down and adjusted his pole in the can, then rested his hand on her knee. He squeezed gently, warmth from his hand seeping into her skin. Tears burned at the back of her eyes, and when one threatened to fall, she turned away so he wouldn't see.

CHAPTER 22

EDIE

Present Day

As in any small community, the gossip train in Oak Hill was a busy one. Edie had no idea how it started, who'd uttered the first "Have you heard?" but it didn't take long for heads to begin quickly turning away at her glance, hands to fly to mouths to block covert whispers, smiles to appear forced.

Instead of feeling relieved that the secret was out and she didn't have to broach the subject cold, she felt lonelier than ever. So many things bounced around in her head—Riley, Avery and Thomas, Mac and her—but instead of talking to her husband about it, she kept it inside. She wasn't always a big talker, but when it came to matters of their family, their children, or their marriage, she knew it was important to go beyond her comfort level and discuss important things with him. But he no longer felt like the easygoing, easy to talk to, easy to laugh with Mac she'd always known. Instead he felt like a stranger.

So she kept the deepest part of her, her biggest concerns, to herself. She didn't tell him how bruising it felt to see him and Riley head off on another of their evening walks, leaving the three of them behind. She knew he was essentially trying to make up for lost time, but adding weight to one side of the scale meant taking it from the other side, and she worried the kids—their two kids—would feel the shift.

She didn't tell Mac how she worried about Thomas and how he'd started taking long walks around the neighborhood by himself, doing nothing but walking and occasionally kicking his soccer ball in front of him. She didn't share with Mac her worries about Avery and how lately she'd been studying longer hours than seemed necessary for her ninth-grade classes. She'd always been studious and hardworking, but her frustration with herself over anything less than a perfect grade was out of character.

Then there were her parents—her mom's casual dismissal of an almost five-decade marriage and her dad's equally casual attitude about his displacement to the woods—and her job. Her partnership with Graham in designing a house for her biggest client yet.

Her heart and mind felt full to the point of overflowing, and the task of keeping it all together occupied nearly all her energy. She just didn't have anything left to give.

Firefly had originally occupied a teeny space between two other, larger commercial spaces in a strip in midtown Mobile. Barely larger than a walk-in closet, the shop had been stuffed to the gills with all manner of candles and diffusers, wooden cutting boards and coasters, pewter trays and mint julep cups, and monogrammed wineglasses.

When the space next door became available, Edie's mother and sister snatched it up and expanded, offering stylishly distressed skinny jeans, chic wraps, and leather gloves in the winter, and Turkish towels, hip platform wedges, and huge straw hats for summer. In a handful of years Firefly had made a name for itself, and the fact that Your Daily Blanche usually set up camp on the art deco couch at the back of the store didn't hurt the shop's popularity.

When Edie climbed out of her car in the parking lot of Firefly, she saw Needa Van Camp striding across the small lot toward her car. Needa, whose daughter had graduated high school with Edie, was one of the shop's most faithful customers. Edie waved and headed toward Needa to say hello, but the woman quickly pointed at her watch and called out a cheery, "So sorry, hon, but I have to run!" She sat in her car, cranked the engine, and was gone before Edie could say a word.

Inside Firefly Edie found Blanche stretched out on the pink couch holding her phone, her slim legs propped up on one end, her head on a yellow fringed pillow. As usual her thumbs were going a mile a minute.

She turned when Edie walked in, and in a flash she swung her legs to the floor and dropped her phone on the couch next to her. "Edie—" she began, but stopped when their mother walked in from the back room, her phone in one hand, her other hand fumbling for the glasses hanging from a dainty chain around her neck. As soon as Mom saw Edie, she tossed the phone on the counter and strode toward her.

"Edie Swan." She pulled her into a flowery hug. "I talked to you two days ago and you told me nothing. I had to hear it from Needa Van Camp." She pushed back and held Edie at arm's length, one eyebrow raised. "Let me tell you, she was pleased as punch to be the one to tell me about my very own daughter's marital strife."

Edie glanced at Blanche. "I tried to warn you," her sister said quietly.

"Mac has a *daughter*? What in heaven's name—?"

"Mom, if you'll just—"

"Why didn't you say anything when I saw you at Cuppa? It was humiliating, Needa prancing in here talking about you and Mac as if you'd called her yourself and personally told her the news."

"I assure you that did not happen."

"Well, regardless, honey, why didn't you tell me right away? I can't believe I didn't know something so important when apparently everyone else in town already knows. Even your sister knew."

Edie glared at Blanche, who frowned then picked up her phone and began to swipe.

Edie exhaled. "Mom. First of all, I'm sorry you were so humiliated. Trust me, I know the feeling. And second, I wasn't the one to start the word spreading. If it were up to me, no one else would know at all."

"Well, that's nonsense. You know this town runs on gossip and king cake. No way would they leave this juicy morsel alone."

"Juicy morsel? Thanks."

"You know what I mean. Now, Edie, what in the world is going on? Did Mac cheat on you?"

"Lord, I hope not," Blanche muttered. Edie and Mom both turned to her, but she just shrugged. "Once a cheater, always a cheater. Everyone knows that."

"Blanche. You're not helping." When Mom turned back to Edie, her eyes were soft. "Please tell me."

"It's a long story." Edie sat on one of the chairs next to the couch. Her mom sat across from her, hands clasped in her lap, waiting for the rest. "In a nutshell, Mac met a woman the summer he stayed down at the beach."

"And when was that?"

"When I was in New York. Remember?"

"Oh, for Pete's sake. That was forever ago. You weren't even married then."

"I know. Anyway, they got close. He didn't know she was pregnant. Didn't know, in fact, until Riley walked into his office."

Mom's mouth hung open, her lips a dusky pink. "Riley," she said after a moment. "And she's staying with you? Are you adopting her or something?"

The word sucked the air out of Edie's chest. *Adopting?* The thought hadn't even entered her mind. Had it entered Mac's? He wouldn't need to adopt her though, since she was already his.

But none of this mattered if Riley was going to be gone as soon as she had the baby.

"Yes. She's staying with us for now. We're just holding on until she has the baby, then we'll figure out what happens next."

"The baby?" Blanche and her mother's voices rang out in tandem. They glanced at each other, then back to Edie. "She's having a baby?" Mom managed. "When?"

So there was one thing the gossip mill had missed.

Edie swallowed and rubbed the top of her knees. "In a few months."

They sat in silence a moment—when you say the unthinkable, what else is there to say?—until the bell on the door jangled and two women walked in. Mom hesitated, then stood and walked toward them. "Hi there. Anything I can help you ladies with today?"

Blanche remained on the couch, her thumbs in overdrive.

"Blanche, don't you work here?"

"Of course," she murmured. "Why would you ask that?"

"I'm just wondering what you do during your shifts."

"I bring in customers." She held her phone up and shook it. "Anytime I mention a new item, we sell out."

"I guess I shouldn't be surprised to know you knew about Mac and me already."

"Of course I knew. Kayla told me about it."

"Kayla?" How in the world had . . . ? *Stop, Edie.* It was pointless to try to dissect it, to figure out who'd thrown the match that had started the flames jumping. And it didn't matter, really. The important thing was, the fire had been lit.

"I'm sorry, Edie."

For the moment Blanche sat still, her hands at rest, her eyes on Edie. If her forehead hadn't been dosed with Botox, she probably would've had a line of concern between her eyes.

"Thanks." Edie was touched, and she thought of all the things she could say, the load she longed to lighten. "It's pretty overwhelming."

"I'd imagine so. It's so sad." Her eyes were wide. "I always assumed the two of you would make it."

Edie swallowed the lump in her throat. "We haven't . . . not made it yet."

"Oh, I know, but I just can't see how any marriage would make it through something like this. I mean, take Mom and Dad. They broke up over much less."

Edie wanted to come back with something that would put Blanche in her place. That would make her see she was clueless about the intricacies of a marriage. But she had nothing.

The bell jangled again, this time ushering in her parents' next-door neighbor. "Brenda!" She and Mom hugged and chatted a moment about neighborhood news. You never would have known that only moments ago, her mother had been shocked, dismayed, and highly humiliated.

"Edie, dear, good to see you." Brenda hesitated, then stepped closer. "You look great. So well rested. Is the family doing okay?"

"I'm . . . We're fine. Just fine."

"Well, that's good to hear." She made a dainty fist and thrust it toward Edie. "You keep on with that brave face."

Several minutes later, Brenda walked out with a pair of feathery earrings and the other two ladies left with wrapped hostess gifts. In the ensuing calm Mom gave Edie a tight hug. "I hate this for you," she said, her voice cracking at the end. "You and Mac have always been the perfect couple. You've been together forever, have two great children—" She pulled back. "Three. Three children now, right?"

"I have two kids, Mom."

"Yes, but—"

"Avery and Thomas."

"Don't sass me. I'm still your mother."

"I'm not sassing you. I only have two children. And yes, Mac has three." She heaved a big breath and blew it out. "I'll fill you in on more details as I know them, but for now, that's all I have. Have you . . . Does Dad know?" She thought of her sweet dad sitting all alone by the lake with his fishing pole and his whittling stick.

"No, I haven't told him. But I will if you don't."

"I'll tell him. I just need to figure out how."

"Well, you'd better tell him quick before Needa Van Camp runs up there to his hidey-hole to tell him first."

"Got it. Now I need to get back to work," Edie said. "I just wanted to stop in and say hi."

"I'm glad you did. You don't come by here often enough. And it was good to hear the news from the horse's mouth."

"Edie's not a horse, Mom," Blanche said from the couch.

"Talk about sass—that girl sasses me all day long," Mom whispered to Edie.

She smiled and whispered back, "You chose to work with her, remember?"

Mom rolled her eyes. "Don't remind me."

Blanche thumb-typed one last thing, then stood abruptly. "We need a picture before you leave."

Edie groaned. "Blanche, no. I need to go."

"It'll just take a sec." She moved them toward the window and positioned herself between them. With her platform wedges, she towered over both Edie and their mom, and as she leaned down so their faces would be together, Edie had to maneuver around her waterfall of blonde balayage waves. She held her phone out in front. "Smile big. Now hang on," she said after snapping the pic. "Let me get the filter on there." A few taps, then she slid her phone into the sequined fanny pack at her hip. "All done. And don't worry," she said to Edie. "You look fine."

"Thanks, B." Edie leaned in and gave her a quick hug, then hugged their mom.

"Call me if you need anything," Mom said. "I'm serious."

"I will."

"You know, you may want to consider talking to someone about this. A professional, I mean."

"Ooh, I know a great therapist," Blanche said. "She's this self-care goddess in Fairhope and she's fabulous. Look for Talk to Tina on Instagram. If you go see her, ask her about her jade roller. It may help your . . ." She tapped her fingertips against her cheeks.

"I'll keep that in mind, thanks."

"Bye, hon. Call if you need me."

"Oh, I have reservations at Citron Saturday night if you want to come."

Edie finally squeezed out the door in a flurry of air kisses and gulped the fresh air. She needed to swing back by the house on Primrose to check the status of the ceiling joist before meeting Carol Donald at Southern Stone and Tile yet again to see another slab of fossilized limestone, but in her car, Edie took a moment to check the photo Blanche had posted to Instagram.

Three smiles—though Edie's was a little forced—three heads of shiny hair, three faces with nary a line, fine or otherwise, thanks to Blanche's Wrinkle Remover filter. They looked like three happy young women enjoying a breezy day of shopping and fun. Maybe they'd just had lunch or a latte, or maybe they were on their way to get mani-pedis. Maybe they had no cares in the world beyond their Saturday night dinner reservation.

Edie was stunned by the ability of a single photo to erase all semblance of actual reality. For all the people who talked about authenticity, embracing imperfection, and #nofilter self-acceptance, the online world on the whole was still a highly curated view of the good side of life. And gazing at that photo, Edie had a sinking realization that her life was not that much different. On the surface what she and Mac had created together looked really good. *"So well rested,"* according to Brenda. It was only underneath that the cracks had begun to deepen.

CHAPTER 23

MAC

Present Day

Mac was enjoying the last few minutes of his lunch break when his office phone rang.

"Good afternoon, Dr. Swan." Fitz's voice was a baritone rumble. "I just wanted to check up on you and that young lady."

Mac balled up his napkin and arced it toward the trash can by the door. Missed by a foot. "When you say it like that, it sounds pretty seedy."

"How's she doing?"

"She's . . . pregnant. She's dealing with some uncomfortable early contractions. And honestly, I think she's a little bored. Which I understand. A girl her age should be doing more than just sitting around being pregnant."

"Then she should get a job."

Mac ran a hand over his head. Hearing it from Fitz was another nudge. He'd been thinking about Riley's words to him on their walk. That she'd need to get a job to pay the bills. Not that she was paying bills at the moment, but if she was going to be staying with them at least for the next few months, a little of her own money might feel good to her. Plus a job would give her something purposeful to do. From what he'd gathered about Riley's past few years, it sounded like she'd already been working a lot more than any other teenagers he knew, and the fact that she wasn't working might have been feeding some of her angst.

Then again, maybe the *not working* was exactly what she needed after several hard years.

"Mac?"

"Yeah. Sorry. I'm just not sure what would work best for her."

"Maybe she's the one who should figure that out."

"Maybe. Though her track record of deciding what's good for her might not be the best."

"Because of the pregnancy, you mean."

"Well, yeah. I'm sure she thought this Dex guy was the best thing for her, and look where that got her." He jammed his thumbs against his eyes, hating the words as they came out of his mouth.

Fitz was quiet a moment, and Mac waited for his gentle rebuke. "Let off your steam with me or with Edie. Even on the basketball court. But I'd advise against saying anything like that to her."

"I know. I won't. I just . . . Fitz, I'm in so far over my head. I don't know what to do." He braced his elbows on his desk and leaned his forehead against a fist. In the hallway outside his office, he heard a burst of conversation, letting him know his break was almost over.

"Do you remember what I told you when you were a brand-spanking-new resident? You were so nervous you'd accidentally kill someone, give them the wrong dose, or miss signs of a heart attack. Remember?"

"I remember feeling that way, but I don't remember what you said. Probably something along the lines of 'Buck up and do your job.'"

"Not quite, although that's not bad advice. What I told you was to take it one step at a time. Start with something small, then take the next step. Don't worry about big leaps. Now's not the time."

"Small steps."

"That's right. They tend to be easier."

"What's the first small step?"

His laugh was a deep rumble in his chest. "You'll have to figure that out on your own. I can't take your steps for you, Dr. Swan."

———————

After his last patient of the day walked out the door at five thirty with a lime-green lollipop in her hand, Mac closed his office door and prepared to call his father. He didn't want to do it. The day had been long, with late appointments, crying children, and exasperated parents, and all he wanted was to go home and see his family. He wanted to wrap his arms around his wife, which hadn't happened in a while. To kiss Avery's cheek and kick the ball around with Thomas. Maybe go for a walk with Riley. He wanted to pretend for a minute that everything was normal. He craved normalcy.

But he couldn't go any longer without telling his parents about Riley. She was their grandchild, after all. It was only fair, although his dread at his dad's reaction already felt like chalk in his mouth. Had his parents not moved several years ago when they retired, they undoubtedly would have heard about Riley already and demanded answers from him. But their home in Cashiers, North Carolina, was far enough away from the shady streets of Oak Hill that they were able to stay pleasantly removed from all that happened back home.

He stood and walked to the bookshelf on the opposite wall where he kept his old med school textbooks and AAP reference books. A cabinet door at the bottom concealed a shelf behind it, and he reached in and pulled out a bottle of bourbon. Old Medley, his dad's longtime favorite. Mac rarely pulled it out. He did it on the first anniversary of taking over the practice. And again when he changed the name to Swan Pediatrics. The last time he'd pulled the bottle out, Swan Pediatrics had been voted Favorite Pediatrician in Oak Hill.

So far, the bottle had only been used as a way to celebrate, but this evening, he used it for courage. Or maybe it wasn't the bottle he hoped would give him courage, because as he pressed his dad's name on his cell phone, a silent prayer ran on a loop in his mind.

"Hey, Dad."

"Mac. Hi."

"Do you have a minute? I just wanted to check in."

His hesitation was brief, but Mac caught it. "Oh sure. It's fine."

Mac swirled the bourbon in the little cubes of ice he'd pulled from the office kitchen, trying to quickly cool it down.

"I'm glad you called now," his dad said. "A few minutes later and you would have missed us. Your mom and I are having dinner with friends at Canyon Kitchen."

"That sounds nice."

"It is. You should come up sometime and see the place. You can bring the family."

Mac pulled his lips in and bit down. His parents had said something to that effect almost every time he talked to them, but the few times he and Edie had actually tried to set a date to visit them, there was always some reason why it wasn't a good time for them to come up.

"Maybe we'll do that."

"How's work going? Have you started to see cases of the flu yet?"

"No, it's not too bad yet. We've already started our flu clinic though, so our nurses have been pretty busy with that."

"I'd imagine so. And the family? Is everyone okay? How are the kids?"

"Fine. They're fine. Avery's joined some kind of science team at school, and Thomas is playing soccer, as usual."

"Avery's going to be your smart one, you know. Maybe she'll be the one to follow the Swans into the medical world."

Smart one? "You're right. Avery is smart. Very. But Thomas is smart too. He's bright, he's athletic, he's—"

"Of course he is. Of course. But Avery's your go-getter. She's always been that way, even from a young age."

And how would you know that? Mac wanted to ask. His dad was many things, but an involved grandparent was not one of them. His dad was Riley's grandparent too. How would he describe her? Mac tilted his head side to side, anxiety worming its way around his chest and up his throat.

"Dad, I've got—" He stopped when he heard his mom's voice in the background.

"What's that, dear?" his dad asked. The sound grew muffled a moment and when he came back, he apologized. "Your mom says hi. She's going to head on up to dinner." He took a sip of his drink, then cleared his throat. "You were saying something, before your mom walked in?"

"Right. Yes." Mac stood and walked to his window. Outside, the early evening sky had taken on an orange tinge, and cars zoomed by on Camellia Avenue, drivers headed home from work or out to dinner with their families. He took a sip of the now-cooled bourbon. "I need to tell you something, Dad," he managed. He closed his eyes, waiting for the heat to subside, silently praying the courage wouldn't.

"I'm all ears, Son."

Mac forced the words he'd been practicing all day past the boulder in his throat. "Do you remember the summer I spent in Orange Beach before my senior year of college?"

"Of course I remember. You worked at a marina."

"That's right. I met a young woman while I was there, and we got to be friends." The words sounded so stilted, as if they were lines in a poorly written stage drama, but he kept going. "At the end of the summer, we went our separate ways. She stayed there, and I went back to school. Edie and I got back together, we graduated, got married—"

"Mac, I know all this."

"I know you do. I just needed to . . . Anyway, my point is . . ."

I cannot say this. I can't do it. I can't tell him.

"Yes?"

"She had a daughter. The woman—her name was Kat—she had a daughter, and that daughter . . . is mine. I'm—she's my daughter."

Dad was silent, much like Edie was when Mac told her. Waiting on his dad's response was only marginally easier. When he finally spoke, his voice was cold. "You got her pregnant?"

"I did. I didn't know it. But I did."

His dad was silent. Mac could almost see him staring straight ahead, his jaw set, his eyes surging with disappointment. "I assume you know this now because the mother came to you for help. Child support? Is that what she wants?"

"No, no. The mother—Kat died last year. So she doesn't need anything. And the child is eighteen. Her name is Riley. She's living with us at the moment."

"What? Why?"

"She was alone. And she's pregnant."

He scoffed. "Like mother, like daughter, I guess."

"That's not fair. You don't know a thing about either of them."

"You're right, Mac. I don't. Do you? How long have you known about this child of yours?"

"Just a couple weeks."

"A couple weeks." He barked out a laugh. "Mac, I'm . . . I'm . . ." He sputtered. "I am speechless. I am finding myself with no words to offer you. Is there anything else you plan to tell me?"

"I guess not. I just wanted you to know what's going on. She's . . . well, she's your granddaughter."

"She's no granddaughter of mine."

"She is, Dad. She's my child, I am your son, therefore she's your grandchild."

"She's an illegitimate child, that's what she is. And how do you even know she's yours? Have you done a paternity test?"

Mac cleared his throat. "I haven't. I don't need to. She looks just like me."

"Do the test," he boomed. "I don't care if she's your mirror image. The very first thing you should have done is a paternity test. Any doctor worth his salt would know that. And any man worth his would do that."

It was all Mac could do to ignore the intentional slight. "Dad, she's my child. I can't ask her to submit a vial of blood so I can have a lab confirm it. That's like saying the only way I'll help her—or . . . or love her—is if she gets a stamp of approval."

"Yes. That's exactly what you're saying."

He sighed and blew his air out slowly. "I assume you'll want to tell Mom. Maybe she'll be interested in meeting her grandchild."

Dad huffed, exasperated. Then, "I will tell her. But I'll wait until after our dinner. No need to make a scene at the restaurant." Mac heard the rustle of his dad standing and the rattle of ice in a glass. "How is Edie taking all this?"

Mac hesitated. He'd rather his dad think he and Edie were on solid ground, that he was the one being insensitive, but downplaying Edie's anger felt cruel. "She's getting to know Riley. We all are."

They were both quiet. If they'd been in the room together, it would have been a standoff. Mac was determined not to break first. Thankfully his dad did. "I'll talk to you later then. I need to go meet your mother."

"Okay. Good-bye, Dad."

On the other side of the window, traffic on Camellia Avenue had slowed, and the sky was now slashed with deep purple. An ounce of bourbon remained in the bottom of his glass. He swirled it, then tipped his head back and drained the glass.

CHAPTER 24

EDIE

Present Day

On Wednesday morning, Laura Lou burst into Edie's office just as she was pulling out a new paint selection book. Carol Donald had decided to go with a different hue for her walls but, in keeping with her shifting preferences, wasn't sure if she wanted to go for a warmer cream tone or a cooler blue tone. Edie told her she'd come up with some options that would work with the new limestone counter surface, and she'd set aside this morning to do it.

When Laura Lou swung herself into the chair opposite Edie's desk, Edie could see her plans being brushed aside.

"The architect, Edie. I can't not know any longer."

"It's Graham." Edie lifted her shoulders and sighed.

"Of course it is. The one person I wanted to add to our workforce has been—" Laura Lou sat up quickly. "You know what though? This could be a very good thing. He'll get to see what it's like to work with a DDG designer, and maybe it'll help swing him in our direction when we offer him a job."

Edie started to laugh but stopped quickly when Laura Lou eyed her. "Sorry. I just—I'm not sure he's the type to join a group. He's been on his own for a long time."

"That is true." She picked at the end of her perfectly manicured thumbnail. "Let's just see how it goes. I'd like you to keep me in the loop as the project progresses, okay? Were you able to talk to Graham about the Creole details I mentioned?"

"Well, no, I—"

"I really think it would set the house apart. Elevate it above even the grandest houses already on the bay. Let me know what he says about it. Or if you want, I can call Graham and—"

"Oh no, it's fine, Laura Lou. I'll take care of it. And I'll let you know what he says." She'd been doing this long enough to know placation was usually the best route.

Over the next half hour Laura Lou went through the file folder she'd brought with her, one she'd filled with Pinterest images and magazine pages to show exactly what she had in mind for those Creole details, as well as the massive shell-encrusted light fixtures she had a hunch Marigold would rave about.

Edie, on the other hand, had a hunch the ten-foot brass contraption covered in pink and white coquina shells would fall right into Marigold's dreaded "fussy" category, but Edie held her tongue.

When Laura Lou finally left as breezily as she'd burst in, Edie stared down at her desk covered in papers, paint chips, and drawings and felt completely rattled. So much for her morning.

Her phone rang and Cynthia Fitzgerald's name lit up on her screen. She said a quiet "thank you" for the reprieve.

"Edie, dear, how are you?"

"I'm good."

"I'd say I'm glad to hear it, though I have a feeling you're lying through your teeth."

Edie leaned back in her chair. "And I'd say you're probably right."

"Well, I wish I was calling with an offer to help you, but what I'm really calling about is Riley."

Just hearing Riley's name made her stomach jump with nerves. "Okay."

"How do you think she'd feel about coming in and chatting with me for a bit? I'd imagine she has all kinds of questions about the baby and what to do when she comes. I may be able to help her sort through some things going on in her mind."

"To be perfectly honest I think she'd hate the idea. She'd probably say she doesn't need to talk to anyone. But I think it's a great idea. I can't imagine what she's going through. Dealing with a pregnancy alone like this."

"She's not alone though, is she?"

"No. I guess she's not."

"Edie, I know this is hard for you."

Her vision blurred as her eyes filled, but she tipped her head back and gazed at the ceiling until they subsided. "I'm doing okay."

"Well, you just remember it's okay not to be okay. It's okay to feel however you feel. And it wouldn't be the worst thing for you to have someone to talk to about all this as well."

She swallowed the lump in her throat. "I know."

Cynthia was quiet a moment. "Well, it's last minute, but I have some time open this morning if you'd like to go ahead and bring Riley in."

Edie's desk was covered in all manner of design details, all specifically chosen to add a veneer of beauty and luxury to a home. To hide all possible imperfections and mask anything offensive.

What am I doing?

She stood and grabbed her bag from the chair. "I'll run home now and see if I can get her to come with me."

"Great," Cynthia said, a smile in her voice. "I'll see you soon."

On her way home, Edie practiced her lines.

"Cynthia's known for helping people in situations just like yours. There's no need to be nervous."

"She's been doing this for thirty years. Countless young women have sat in her office and walked through the months ahead of them, as scary as they may have seemed at the time."

And if she needed them, Edie had the big guns ready: "If you're going to stay here with us, you have to talk to Cynthia."

But as it turned out, she didn't need any of them. She found Riley in the kitchen, organizing items in the pantry. All the cereal boxes were out on the counter, but the canned goods were stacked neatly, and jarred sauces, boxes of pasta, and extra peanut butter and baking goods were lined up according to height and food type. It only took one glance around the kitchen to see that everything was significantly cleaner than it had been when Edie left for work that morning. The counters gleamed, the sink was empty, and the dishwasher hummed.

"I can put it all back if you want," Riley said when she noticed Edie standing in the doorway. "I just thought it made more sense this way. Everything was all mixed up in here."

"No, it's great. Thank you."

Riley kept working, her back to Edie, turning the cans a little to the right or to the left, ensuring all the labels were facing squarely out.

"Do you want to go somewhere with me?" It wasn't one of her pre-planned lines, but seeing Riley in her kitchen, working so diligently, had thrown her off.

Riley paused. "Go where?"

"The Gulf Coast Women's Center. It's where Cynthia works. You met her—"

"I remember. I liked her." She turned one more can, then backed out of the pantry and closed the door. "If it'll get me out of this house, I'll go anywhere you want."

A few minutes later they were headed downtown. It was an Indian summer afternoon, the sky turquoise blue, with a few brown-edged leaves falling over the street as they drove. Fall in lower Alabama was more thought or hope than an actual season, but as they crept closer to Halloween and Thanksgiving, even those this far south would begin to see the signs of coming cooler weather.

"What's the Gulf Coast . . . What'd you call it?"

"Gulf Coast Women's Center. It's a place for women with unplanned pregnancies. They offer counseling and education. I think they even have some parenting classes."

"So it's where you go to learn how to be a mom?" Her head was turned toward the window, her belly a round swell, one that seemed to be growing by the day.

"It takes more than one day to learn how to be a mom. I've been one for fourteen years and I'm still learning every day."

She snorted. "Yeah, right."

"I'm serious."

Riley turned, skepticism plain on her face. "You really feel that way?"

"Absolutely. I don't know if you ever reach a point where you feel like you know exactly what you're doing. Or if you do, I'm definitely not there yet."

"I don't know if that's comforting or terrifying."

"That pretty much sums up parenting in general. Some days you feel comfortable in your role as a mom; other days, it's pure terror."

"Oh, well, thanks for that."

Edie glanced at her. One hand had crept up to her belly and she rubbed it absently. "You'll learn. It's what we all do."

The GCWC occupied a cheery yellow building on an otherwise drab downtown street. Many of the other establishments had broken windows or plywood covered in graffiti, but the women's center was a bright spot of life. Several cars dotted the parking lot, and flowerpots around the front door were bursting with late-summer lantana, trailing petunias, and leggy impatiens.

In the waiting room a few women sat in chairs along the wall. One child played at a messy table covered in crayons and coloring books. A TV mounted to the wall played a *Friends* rerun with the sound turned down. The front desk was empty, and the clipboard bore a sign-in sheet dated two days ago, with all the lines filled.

Edie was about to pull out her cell to call Cynthia when a man zoomed by in the carpeted hallway behind the desk. He was obviously in a hurry, even jogging to get wherever he was trying to go, but he turned his head as he passed. When he saw them standing at the desk, he stopped and backtracked but must have slipped on something, because in a rush, he disappeared from sight.

Riley laughed, then put a hand over her mouth.

The man shot up from the floor, snatching a piece of paper from the carpet as he did so. "Sorry about that. I slipped. Would have been funnier if it had been a banana peel." He balled up the paper and dropped it in a small blue recycling box before he set both hands on the desk. "Sorry for the wait. We're a little short-staffed today." He smiled at Riley. "I'm Charlie. I mean, Dr. Pine." He stuck out his hand and she shook it. "Well, sort of doctor." He scratched the back of his head. "I mean, I *am* a doctor, but I'm a resident. A medical resident." He cleared his throat. "Do you have an appointment?"

Edie stifled another laugh. "Sort of. We're friends with Cynthia and she asked us to come by. Is she in?"

"Mrs. Fitzgerald? Sure. Let me get her for you." He walked back the way he'd come, obviously having forgotten his earlier important errand.

While they waited, another woman walked in the door behind them. She bypassed the front desk altogether and went straight to a waiting room chair. She braced herself against the arms of the chair as she sat, her belly stretching beyond what seemed possible.

"Whoa," Riley whispered.

"Twins." The woman pointed to her belly when she noticed Riley watching her. "Didn't plan for one, much less two."

It was a few more minutes before Cynthia met them in the waiting room, and in that time two more women came through the doors.

"This is a happening place today," Edie said to Cynthia, who waved them around the desk.

"You're not kidding. Y'all come on back here where we can talk."

As they followed Cynthia down the hallway, she turned and spoke over her shoulder. "I have to apologize. It's not usually so crazy around here. Our office manager had to start her maternity leave earlier than we expected, and I'm just now realizing how much she actually did around here. We're stretched so thin, I promised Dr. Pine dinner if he'd come over from the children's clinic next door to help out. But don't you worry. I have all the time in the world for you." She glanced back at Riley and smiled.

They turned right at the end of the hallway and headed down another until they reached her office in the back. Just outside her door was a small couch and a table with a lamp.

"Edie, if you want to sit here, maybe Riley and I can have a few minutes to chat on our own?"

"Sure." Edie looked at Riley. "You good with that?" She swung her heavy bag onto the couch and opened it.

Riley's eyes grew wide. She cast a furtive glance into Cynthia's office.

"If you want me to come in, I can—"

Riley exhaled in a short, hard burst. "It's fine. Let's go chat." She strode into Cynthia's office, sat in a chair, and crossed her arms over her chest.

Like coldness rippling in her veins, Edie had the distinct sensation that she'd let Riley down. She'd felt it before with Avery, on those unpredictable occasions where it seemed she'd broken some pact they'd had between them, one Avery was acutely aware of but that Edie didn't know existed until she'd broken it.

Cynthia winked at Edie. "We'll be fine. If you need anything while you're out here, just knock." She closed the door softly behind her and greeted Riley again in her straightforward but kind manner. Riley's voice in answer was clipped.

Edie sat on the couch for a moment without moving. *How did I get here?* It was hard enough navigating life with one sensitive teenager and an overly mellow preteen. Throw a second teenager into the mix—and a pregnant one at that—and Edie was in so far over her head, she wasn't sure which direction was the surface and which led further into the depths.

As she massaged her temples, a nurse walked by with the woman expecting twins. They paused outside an exam room down the hall, and the nurse laid her hand on the other woman's arm. The woman nodded and wiped her eye before walking into the room.

As they disappeared inside it, a young couple with a toddler entered the hall from the other direction. Edie tried not to stare as they walked by.

Their clothes were well worn, and the little boy's shoes had holes at the ends, with one toe threatening to poke through one of the shoes. But as the family walked down the hall, the man took the woman's hand, lifted it to his mouth, and kissed it.

A moment later someone cleared his throat and ventured, "Um, Mrs. . . . Um . . . is everything okay?"

Edie lifted her head. Dr. Pine was peering at her. A long purple Mardi Gras necklace now adorned his neck, along with the stethoscope. He was a nice-looking kid, short dark hair, glasses, a faded blue T-shirt showing under his lab coat. When he smiled, his cheeks dimpled in a way that made Edie want to smile too.

"Just checking. You looked like you might have been in some pain."

"No. I'm fine."

"Okay. Because I'm about to head out, and I didn't want to leave if you needed anything."

She smiled. "I'm good. Really."

He gestured toward Cynthia's closed door. "Is this your daughter's first time at the center?"

"My—? Oh, she's not . . . I'm not her mom."

"Oh. I'm sorry. I just assumed . . ."

"It's okay. I'm just a friend. And yes, it's our first time here."

"Well, hopefully by the time she has her baby, we'll have the children's clinic back up and running at top speed."

"What's wrong with the clinic? Has it closed?"

"Did Mrs. Fitzgerald not tell you? Dr. Richman left, and without a practicing physician on board, they can't keep it open. I mean, I'm technically a physician, but not when it comes to operating a clinic like that on my own." He adjusted the necklace around his neck. "If they don't find someone, Mrs. Fitzgerald will have to close it down."

"That'd be a shame for all these families."

"It would. But at least we have the women's center. It's such a good thing for girls like your . . . your friend."

He nodded good-bye and Edie opened her bag, pulled out her Sherwin-Williams fan deck, and searched again for just the right complement for the Donalds' black-and-white counters. In Cynthia's office behind her, Riley's voice filtered through the thin wall. Edie couldn't make out words, just the tone behind them. Riley seemed softer now, less perturbed than when she'd entered.

Edie dropped the fan deck back into her bag and pulled out the elevation drawings for the Primrose house, checking to make sure the window measurements had been changed to reflect the new ceiling height. As she reviewed the numbers, her cell rang with an unfamiliar number.

"I know you said you'd call when you're ready to discuss the Kennedys," Graham said, "but I literally have nothing else going on. I've already done preliminary floor plan sketches and I'd love for you to see them."

"I'm sorry, who is this?" She pinched her lips together before they betrayed her joke.

"Edie?"

She laughed. "Graham. I'm kidding. I'd recognize your voice anywhere."

He was quiet for just a second too long. "I don't know what else you have going on. For all I know you have three dozen projects in the works. I could have been anyone."

"I'm glad you called." She lowered her voice as a nurse walked by with another pregnant woman. This one looked younger than Riley. "I can't wait to see your sketches."

"It's all really early, of course. And I haven't put it into AutoCAD because I want to get your input first. What's tomorrow look like for you?"

"Tomorrow." She closed her eyes and envisioned her big desk calendar back at her office. "You know what? I can make it work. Where and what time?"

"How do you feel about The Blue Fin on the Causeway?"

"I love it."

"Eleven thirty?"

"I'll see you then."

When Cynthia's door opened and Riley walked through, she wasn't smiling but she didn't seem upset either. Cynthia crossed the hall to a slim desk and reached into the top drawer, pulling out an assortment of brochures. One by one she handed them to Riley. "This is the one on Lamaze

I told you about. Here's the nutrition one for you and your baby, and this one's about rest and exercise. Oh, and this one has the most up-to-date car seat regulations."

Riley smirked. "Don't need that one. I don't even have a car."

A car. Edie was so used to driving her own kids around, it hadn't fully registered that Riley wasn't driving, even though she was eighteen. "Did you have a car back home?"

She nodded. "It was a beater though. It's in the shop with a busted transmission or something. I didn't have the money to fix it, so it's been there a while."

"How'd you get to work?" Cynthia asked.

Riley shrugged. "I found rides."

"Well, at some point you'll need a way to cart your daughter around," Cynthia said. "So read up on car seats. And those health classes I told you about? Remember you get points that you can redeem for necessities like car seats. And other things too—baby clothes, diapers. Just something to keep in mind." She patted Riley on the back. "I'll walk you out."

When they made it back up to the waiting room, a nurse stopped Cynthia. "Mrs. Fitzgerald, can you sign this, please?"

"Y'all hang on just a second." Cynthia turned to the binder the nurse held.

As they waited, another woman walked in the front door and glanced at the clipboard on the desk. When she trudged off to find a seat, Riley walked to the desk and grabbed the clipboard. She turned the piece of paper over, wrote today's date at the top, and handed it to the woman. "There. Now you can sign in."

The woman took it from her and jotted down her name on the top line. "Thanks."

Cynthia noticed Riley's quick action. She planted her hands on her hips. "You trying to get yourself hired around here or something?"

"Maybe," came Riley's quick retort. "Why? Are you hiring?"

Cynthia studied Riley a moment. "What's your experience?"

"My experience?" Where her shoulders had been squared, even a little defiant before, now they slumped forward ever so slightly, like all her air had fizzled out. "I've never worked in an office before."

Cynthia seemed disappointed too. "Hmm," she murmured. When someone else walked up to get her attention, she gave Riley a gentle hug and squeezed Edie's arm. "Bring her back next week?"

"I think Riley needs a job," Edie said as she and Mac cleaned the kitchen after dinner, all three kids having scattered to various parts of the house. While he scrubbed a pot in the sink, she ran a damp cloth over the island, cleaning away all the crumbs and water rings. It was their normal end-of-night routine, though these days the normalcy was a façade.

Mac's hands paused and he reached up and turned off the water.

"She organized our pantry and cleaned the entire kitchen this morning," she said. "Out of pure boredom. I think she needs something to take her mind off waiting for this baby to come."

"I've been thinking the same thing."

"You have?"

"Yeah." He seemed relieved, like the tiny fact that they both felt the same way about something was a victory. "What'd you have in mind?"

"Well, I took her to see Cynthia this morning and—"

"Why didn't you tell me? You took her to talk to Cynthia?"

"Yeah. Is that a problem?"

"No, I'm just surprised you didn't tell me earlier."

"There hasn't been much of a chance. Anyway, I'm telling you now."

"How'd it go? Did it seem to help?"

"It's hard to tell. She seemed okay when we left. And I think they're going to talk again next week. But things just felt a little chaotic there. They don't have anyone answering phones or checking people in at the front desk. People were coming in and out of there too fast for them to keep up." Edie stopped, thinking again of how confident Riley seemed when she asked Cynthia if she was hiring, then how completely and quickly she deflated, discounting her experience and usefulness.

"What if she got a job there at the center?" Edie asked. "She said she's never worked in an office, but I have a feeling she's a hard worker. Maybe she could get in there and be an extra set of hands around the place."

"Hmm." Mac wiped his hands on a dish towel. "And we have Tancy's car in the garage."

"Avery's car?"

"It's not Avery's yet."

Tancy was Mac's great-aunt who'd died last year. His dad had asked him if they wanted her car for Avery to use when she turned sixteen, and it seemed foolish to turn it down, even if Avery cringed in embarrassment at the prospect of driving a twenty-year-old Buick Skylark around town.

"It'll be sitting in our garage for two more years," Mac said. "With Riley driving it, at least we wouldn't have to pull it out and crank the engine every week."

Logistically, it seemed like a smart move, though it might not seem that way to Avery. It wasn't like she or Mac could stick around to drive Riley back and forth to the women's center for either work or the classes Cynthia had mentioned. And she definitely couldn't stay in their house doing nothing but reading and organizing canned goods for three months. That would be like prison.

"I'll talk to Cynthia about it," Edie said. "See if she thinks it would even be possible."

"Thanks for doing that. And for taking Riley to see Cynthia. I think that was a good call. It's good for her to talk to someone who knows more about all this than we do."

Edie nodded.

"How about work for you? How are things going with the Kennedys?"

"It's okay so far." She thought about telling him she was meeting Graham to see his drawings but thought better of it. It was late, she was tired, and bringing up Graham's name had the potential to send them down a road better taken not so late at night.

She swept the broom under the stools at the island and dumped the debris in the garbage. "I don't think Laura Lou trusts me with this project, even though I'm the one Turner hired. She keeps pulling tighter on the reins when what I really want to do is throw them off completely."

She stopped short. Was that what she really wanted? To throw off her reins? To head off on her own? It had crossed her mind over the years, at small moments and in subtle ways, but Davis Design Group was the top of the food chain as far as design firms in the area. It was the group so many clients turned to as soon as they realized they needed a designer's input and guidance. She'd always assumed she'd be shortchanging herself by leaving.

She waited for Mac's usual encouragement, or maybe even a suggestion to follow her gut, but neither of those came. Instead he picked at his fingernail. "I kind of get where she's coming from. Even if you're doing the work, her name will be attached to it, and it's a big job. I can see how it would be difficult to let go when the outcome reflects on you."

She opened her mouth in retort, but shock had stolen her words. In some deep-down place, she knew there was some truth in his words, but the fact that he was essentially siding with Laura Lou settled in her like sand between bedsheets.

"But I'm sure the house will be great," he said quickly. "Turner's hired a . . . a good architect, and I know he's got a great designer. I can't wait to see how it turns out."

When they climbed into bed a little later, Mac slid easily into sleep, as if their few minutes of relatively peaceful conversation had assured him that all was okay. She turned off her lamp and rolled onto her back, then watched the ceiling fan until it made her head spin.

CHAPTER 25

MAC

Summer 2000

From the beginning of their friendship, Mac and Graham had been an odd pairing. Mac was hardworking, dependable, and adored by kids, teachers, and camp counselors, while Graham was pensive, artistic, and unafraid to break the occasional rule.

They became fast friends after being paired as bunk mates at Camp Woodpine the summer after fourth grade, and for the next three summers, they requested to be in the same cabin for their month-long camp session. Even in those young years, Mac was everything Graham wasn't—and vice versa—but they hit it off anyway.

Once Graham and his dad moved to Point Clear just before eighth grade, the boys' friendship was solidified and they began making plans for all the school years and all the summers. Which was why Mac assumed the summer at the beach would be just one more long stretch of bonding over fishing, arguments about music, and impromptu midnight Waffle House runs.

Instead Mac found himself increasingly unable to share his life with his friend, and he missed that. He missed their easy conversations, their jokes, the way almost anything could remind them of something in their shared history. He missed his friend.

Graham wasn't sharing much with Mac either. He was obviously keeping up some kind of communication with Edie—and right under Mac's nose. And Mac hadn't said a thing to Graham about all he was supposed to be figuring out this summer. Honestly, Mac felt foolish admitting to anyone that he'd lost his way.

But the biggest thing Mac hadn't mentioned was Kat. Not once. At first it was because there was nothing to mention. People met other people every day, and it didn't always warrant a conversation. But over the course of the summer, something had changed, and Mac found himself sliding toward Kat despite his best intentions to slow it down or stop it completely. Maybe it was seeing Edie's letter to Graham or something in his own heart, but finally he allowed those intentions to drift away.

Everything about Kat was a contrast to Mac's familiar, composed, steady life. She refused to be put in any kind of box, and she lived by her own rules. Yet for some reason, she was letting down her steely walls for Mac. And on top of that, he'd discovered she was older than him by several years. Not that age mattered, but it was just one more way she was teaching him this summer, showing him how to stand on his own two feet.

She was an enigma, a mystery he couldn't get enough of.

One night after they both got off work—Kat from a trip out into the Gulf that lasted an extra two hours because of a storm that had blown up off the coast, and he from a late shift that went even later because the boat lift broke down—she called to him from the top deck of her boat.

"Hey, wait for me before you leave. I'll be up there in a minute."

Mac had been on his way to punch out in the dock store, his shirt damp with sweat and fish scales and his stomach aching with hunger, but her voice made him forget his discomfort. Their schedules had been out of sync, and he hadn't seen her in several days.

By the time she made it to the store, he'd already clocked out and was sitting on the bench outside the door. "Do you have plans tonight?" she asked.

"No, I'm done. Spent."

"Not yet. You're coming with me. I want to show you something."

"You might want to think twice about that." He stretched his legs out in front of him. "I stink."

"No worse than me. And we can rinse off where we're going."

He popped a questioning eyebrow her way, but she just kicked lightly at his outstretched foot and waved him toward the parking lot. "Come on."

Minutes later they were in Kat's white Jeep on Highway 292 headed toward Florida. With the top down the wind made conversation difficult, so they traveled in silence. Instead of worrying about where she was taking him, what she meant by rinsing off, and how he should act or speak, Mac let himself relax. He tipped his head back against the seat and closed his eyes as the warm night air whipped around them.

They passed the Flora-Bama, and a few miles later, Kat turned right on Johnson Beach Road. A few more miles and she slowed at the guardhouse and nodded a smile at the man on duty. He nodded back and pressed a button to raise the gate.

"I didn't know you could come out here at night," Mac said as the road curved to the left past a pavilion, then straightened out. With no moon in the sky, the way ahead was dark, and he could just barely make out the dunes rising on each side of the road.

"Usually you can't. The guard's on duty to keep people away this late. But Steve and I have an understanding."

"You come out here a lot?"

She shrugged. "Sometimes. It's a nice place to be alone."

She kept driving until she reached a post near a streetlight. A sign on the post read, *Keep off the dunes.* She kicked off her shoes, grabbed a quilt from behind the front seat, and motioned for him to follow her between the dunes to a wide-open stretch of sand. Before them was the Gulf, ebony-dark under a sky covered in a thin scrape of clouds.

Mac paused in the near darkness, then headed for the water's edge where Kat already stood. A few feet away gentle waves slowly lapped the shore. Once his eyes adjusted, the water and landscape around him were a ghostly murky gray instead of black.

The air was salty and fresh, and he felt his shoulders drop an inch. "I've been out here, but never at night. Thanks for showing it to me."

"You're welcome, but I haven't shown you anything yet."

Kat took a step forward, and with one leg outstretched she dug her bare toe into the wet sand and dragged it across the ground. In the wake the sand lit up with tiny, glowing green dots.

He sucked in a breath.

She did it again, this time dragging her other foot through the sand and stirring up more of the alien green glow. Mac let out a goofy, confused sound.

"It's called bioluminescence," she said.

"I know about it, but I've never actually seen it. It's plankton or something, right?"

"Phytoplankton. Sometimes tiny bits of jellyfish. But it doesn't hurt."

"Is it always out here?"

"Not all the time. Or at least you can't always see it. It's better when there's not much of a moon. I had a feeling tonight would be a good night to see it."

Mac tried for himself, digging his heel into the sand and pulling it to the side. The sand glowed green. "That's so cool."

"When I was a kid, my dad used to take me out on the beach at night. We'd pretend we were astronauts on a new planet. We'd be out on this deserted stretch of beach with no houses for miles, so it wasn't hard to imagine." She skimmed her foot across the sand again, setting it alight. "I'd pretend the green was fairy dust we had to bring back to earth. I filled bucket after bucket of sand to take home, and I was always mad when I couldn't get it to glow again the next night. Whatever it was, it probably died on the way home."

The sound of merriment, of conversation and happy shrieks, filtered across the water from a large boat several hundred yards offshore, rocking gently over the swells. Lights along the sides illuminated groups of people milling about on both decks.

Mac and Kat watched the boat as it passed them, probably heading for the pass that would lead them back into the lagoon and into Old River.

"You were right," Kat said when the boat was not much more than a smudge on the water. "What you said earlier, I mean."

Mac turned to her. "What did I say?"

"That you stink." In the faint moonlight she wrinkled her nose a little and smiled, then pressed her lips together to stifle a laugh.

"Oh yeah? Well, like you said, you don't smell much better." He bumped his shoulder against hers, and she winced. Reached up and covered the upper part of her arm with her hand. "I'm sorry, did I—?"

"No, it's okay. It's not you." She pressed her fingers against her arm and rubbed a little.

"You okay?"

"I'm great." She took a few steps forward—an incoming wave flowed over her feet—but kept her gaze on him. "Remember what I said about us being able to rinse off?" She watched him a second longer, then pulled her shirt over her head. Her bra underneath wasn't skimpy—it was white, with straps that crisscrossed in the back—but still his heart pounded in his chest.

Mac looked away, and when he dared to glance back, she was flinging both her shorts and shirt back toward shore before she ran headlong into the water and dove under the waves.

Mac stared helplessly at her clothes in a pile at his feet, as if the discarded items could tell him what to do.

"Hey," she called. "Come on in. It's warm."

He hesitated and she laughed. "Come on," she teased. "You need a shower, right?"

He exhaled hard and before he could second-guess himself, he pulled off his shirt and shorts and followed her into the water, only his boxers sticking wet against his skin.

"Watch this," she said when he reached her. The water came up to the middle of Kat's chest, and Mac forced his eyes to remain on her hands as they slid smoothly in the water. In the wake was the same bright green.

He tried it a few times, swishing his hands through the water and watching the contrails of phosphorescence, trying to ignore the phantom sensation of millions of microscopic jellyfish and phytoplankton clinging to his skin.

When he turned to Kat, she was floating on her back. Her blonde hair had fanned out around her head, shining in the weak moonlight, and her arms moved back and forth, lighting the water green all around her. Nerves twitched low in his stomach and he turned, afraid his face would reveal the strange sensations bursting in his body.

When her fingertips grazed the side of his leg, he jumped. She lowered her legs and stood. "Easy there," she said, standing close now. "It's just me."

They moved through the water side by side, watching the green glow as it fanned behind them. Mac was hyperaware of her body so close to his, occasionally bumping into him and setting his skin ablaze.

A moment later Kat dove under the water and surfaced a few feet away. "So is there someone who wouldn't be happy to know you're swimming half-clothed with a strange girl?"

He lifted a shoulder. "You're not that strange."

"Thanks." She reached out and flicked water in his direction. "There is someone waiting back home though, right?"

A bolt of longing and frustration shot through him and he closed his eyes, pushing away thoughts of Edie's full-faced grin and the feel of her small, warm hand in his, then feeling guilty for pushing them away. "She's not exactly waiting. And I don't really want to talk about her."

"Why not?"

He thought of all kinds of easy answers, answers that would move them quickly onto safer topics, but for reasons he didn't understand beyond the fact that it was dark and he was loose and relaxed and this girl made him feel like he was on fire, he chose honesty.

"Because even saying her name while I'm next to you feels like a betrayal. It feels out of place. Like she doesn't belong here, even though . . ."

"Even though what?"

"Well, she's not my girlfriend, for one."

"But you said—"

"She was my girlfriend. She'd been my girlfriend for a long time. But we broke up a few months ago."

"Ah." A single loaded word.

Mac tilted his head. "*Ah* what?"

"Another reason why you're here this summer. To get over her."

"No, it's not that. I can see how it appears that way, but I'm not trying to get over her."

"If you say so."

He flicked a drop of water off his cheek. "More than all that, it's because of you, okay? Because I'm here with you and . . ." He hesitated, determined to make the words come out right. "You make me feel alive in a way I haven't felt in a really long time. It's like everything inside of me is moving. Or shifting. You make me . . ."

Somehow they'd moved through the water toward each other without him realizing it, and her face was so close he could hardly breathe. In the weak light he could see the freckles across her nose, the baby-fine hairs at her hairline.

"I make you what?" she whispered.

"You make me feel strong. Like a real man." He closed his eyes a second. "That was stupid. Sorry."

"It's not stupid. And the way you look at me . . . You see me in a way others don't." She held his gaze, then glanced down at his mouth and sighed. "But I can't be with you, Mac."

His chest tightened. "Why not? Is it Marco?"

Kat set her jaw. "Marco doesn't dictate what I do."

"What *does* he do? Did he do this?" He lifted his hand from the water and grazed the barely visible bruise on her shoulder with his fingertips.

She shrugged away from his touch, then sank until the dark water covered her shoulders. "It's nothing. Marco has nothing to do with me and you." She tipped her chin toward him. "Anyway, you're the one with the girl you can't even talk about."

"She's not . . . It's not . . ." He groaned and pushed his hand through his hair. "Why are you talking like this? You keep trying to push me away."

Kat stared up at him. "I know the kind of world you come from, Mac. It's a dreamland where all the girls are nice and all the boys are Prince Charming. But that's not how it is in real life. In real life the girls aren't perfect and the guys are like Marco. Sweet and kind one minute and the complete opposite the next."

"But why put up with that? With someone who's only good to you half the time? Don't you want someone who treats you right all the time?"

"And who's that going to be?" She stood to her full height and faced him squarely, water streaming from her hair and down her arms. "You?"

He took a step even closer, energy pulsing through his limbs. "What if it was me? Huh? Who says I shouldn't be the one to get to treat you right?"

"You don't want me like that, Mac. I'm a summer fling." She hurled the words at him, as if she knew they'd hurt him.

"Stop. I wouldn't be here like this if that's all you were to me. Quit telling yourself you're less than what you are."

He was breathing hard now, but he pulled himself together when he saw the expression on Kat's face.

"I don't deserve someone like you."

When he placed his hand against her cheek, she leaned into it. "Why not?" he whispered against her lips.

"I—"

Then he kissed her answer away and all their words vanished.

CHAPTER 26

EDIE

Summer 2000

Dear Edie,

You say it like it couldn't happen—you in New York City after college, working, establishing your career you enjoy in a city that sets you on fire. I say, why not? Hear me out.

You're there already, your foot more than firmly in the door, and just down the hall from the boss herself. An internship like this will open doors to almost anything you could possibly want after graduation. You'll show them who you are—talented, hardworking, creative—basically indispensable. Then, just when everyone is thinking you're comfortable and settled, you'll shock them all and strike out on your own. You find that perfect street corner, hang your sign, and fling open your doors to your very own clients. Edie Everett Design. Has a nice ring to it, doesn't it?

Now, imagine an architect in the space right next door. Maybe there's even a door between the offices, allowing the two of you to walk back and forth whenever you want. Bounce ideas off each other. Argue over who should pick up the takeout. Maybe even collaborate on some projects. And what if this architect is someone you totally trust and know well, someone who shares your taste in music and black coffee?

Now, I ask you, wouldn't that be something?

Dear Graham,

It would, but why stop there? Why not call it Everett Yeager Designs? Or what about—the Everett Yeager Group? There. I think I just nailed it.

And while we're in this imaginary future, let's talk about our office. If we're going in together, we should ditch the separate but connected offices and combine forces altogether. We'll need two large desks, comfortable chairs and couches for clients, maybe one of those fancy Italian espresso makers so we can get our fixes there in the office rather than having to navigate the foot traffic outside. Big windows overlooking the street. Oh, and a doorman and an elevator. Why not aim high, right?

Back to the real world now. How are things at the beach? How's your job? How are you and Mac doing together? I know you got along great in that dingy campus apartment, but are things still going okay? I just ask because you haven't mentioned him. He and I haven't talked at all, so for all I know, his dad could have called and demanded he come back and work in his office for the summer. That actually doesn't seem too far-fetched now that I'm writing it. I hope for Mac's sake he's able to stick it out at the beach. Hopefully the time away will be good for him. I know it is for me.

Dear Edie,

All is well at the beach. I'm at the job site every morning before six, and we work until five in the afternoon, sometimes later if afternoon thunderstorms slow us down. You know I've worked on construction job sites since I was fourteen, but I've never worked hours like this. I think it's good for me though. If I'm going to be designing houses, I need to know what's required of the guys who'll actually execute my drawings.

Earlier in the summer, Mac and I hung out most nights. We fished some. Talked some. But we're doing less of both now. After a day of hauling beams or concrete blocks, sometimes I can barely lift my arms enough to hold a fishing pole. Also he's been working more late shifts, so we're not seeing as much of each other. I think it's a good thing. Sometimes even friends need to take a break.

As for my proposition, I'm sensing that you're mocking it. The Everett Yeager Group is no joke, I assure you. Designer and architect, two for the price of one. You called it an "imaginary future" but I'm in, Edie. You say the word and I'd build this future with you in a heartbeat. And before you laugh, I'm as serious as I've ever been. I'd plan a future with you. A real one. (Though I have to point out that a fancy espresso maker would be great, but you do know we'd have an assistant to get our coffee for us, right?)

Love,
Graham

P.S. Can I call you?

Edie's new friend Judith was spending the summer working at a coffee shop in the theater district and going to as many Broadway casting calls as she could. Considering Judith's expressive face and enthusiastic personality, Edie thought she'd be a shoo-in as an actress, but Judith had yet to land a role in any show.

"I'm not even trying out for the big Broadway shows." Judith munched on a wilted salad she'd brought home from the coffee shop. "Off-Broadway is fine with me. Heck, off-off-Broadway would be great. Just something to get my foot in the door."

"Didn't you serve one of the actresses the other day?"

"I handed her a coffee and a blueberry muffin. She barely noticed me." Judith propped her chin in her hand. "You're so lucky you're getting to work in the actual industry you want to be in. You haven't even graduated and you're already working as an interior designer."

"I'm not, really. I'm still very much an assistant, but I don't know. Maybe one day."

Try as she might, Edie hadn't been able to get her mind off Graham's letter since she read it on the subway a few days ago. She'd reread it at work and again on her long walk home at the end of the day when the subway broke down.

Why does it have to be imaginary?

I'd build a future with you.

What did he mean? Was he only talking about business? Or something more?

The truth was, her friendship with Graham had taken a turn this summer she hadn't seen coming. Instead of seeing him face-to-face—and risking that frequent sensation when she was alone with him, the lightning that made her words stumble over each other and her face redden with heat—she was able to say the words almost in secret, as if they were in a dark room together, where the shadows hid fears and banished inhibitions. She was bolder in her letters than she ever was in person, and it was all she could do not to run to the mailbox every evening after work to see if he'd sent a response—his looping handwriting on the blue-and-white graph paper.

So far it had felt like they were teetering on a high wire, daring each other, prompting and teasing each other with words full of delicious abandon and freedom, but those last few words—*"I'd build this future with you"*—had struck her almost mute. No way would she be able to talk to him on the phone.

But they'd also made her think of Mac. What about the future she'd always thought she'd build with him? Whether she was willing to admit it or not, she'd begun to miss him. His lopsided grin. The feel of his arm around her shoulders. That sense of safety, of shelter, she felt with him.

Fletcher barked, startling Edie so badly she knocked her drink over. As she wiped the dampness from her legs and lap, Judith stared. "What's going on with you? You're a million miles away."

"It's nothing. I'm just all wet now."

"I don't mean the drink. I mean your head. What's going on up there?"

Edie balled up the damp napkins and tossed them on the table. She sat back in the metal chair and sighed. "That postcard you saw me writing the first time we had dinner out here?"

"The one you were sending to your *friend.*" She wiggled her fingers in air quotes.

"Right." Edie smiled. "My friend. Graham." She sighed again and bit her thumbnail, prompting Judith to set her fork down and lean forward.

"I knew it. Graham's not a friend. Okay, spill it."

"There's not much to spill. He really is my friend. But lately it feels different."

Judith grinned and pulled her hair up into a ponytail.

"But there's a lot more to it." Edie lifted her hair off the back of her neck and sat up straighter in her chair. "I had a boyfriend. Mac. We dated a long time and it was . . ." She shook her head. *Too much to explain.* "Well, we broke up this past spring. And the three of us are best friends, so the breakup makes things a little weird."

"Wait—you, your ex-boyfriend, and the guy you're writing are all best friends?"

"Yes."

"That sounds terribly awkward."

"It was never awkward until now. It just always worked. We worked. But now Graham and I have been sending each other these letters and postcards . . ."

"Are you writing to Mac too?"

"No. I've thought about it but I haven't done it. He hasn't written me either."

"Do you think the two of you will get back together?"

"I really don't know. Part of me can't imagine *not* being with him—forever—but I don't know if that's just because we've been together for so long or if we really do belong together."

"And then there's Graham."

"Right. Graham. He and I have never dated. We've never even talked in person about the two of us. But sometimes there'd be this, I don't know, this random thought or question that would pop into my head sometimes.

And now that I'm away from school, away from regular life—away from Mac—that thought is stronger and stronger."

"Well, don't keep me hanging. What's the thought?"

"What if it's Graham? What if he's the one I'm really supposed to be with?"

Judith sat quietly a moment, her face betraying the gears clicking and shifting in her mind. "Has he said anything that makes you think he's feeling the same difference you feel? Or is it just you living in rebound world?"

Edie laughed. "It's not about Graham being a rebound. That makes it sound like he'd be just a fling. An impulse. But he'd never be that. He's important. He's significant." She gave a slow nod. "And yes. He's said a few things. Or written them, at least. But I don't know what he's really thinking."

"Then you need to talk to him about it. If he's as good a friend as you say he is, you owe it to yourselves to figure out what's going on. Either you leave your friendship the way it is—hands off—or you decide to take a step forward together."

Edie pressed her lips together.

"Now, enough about boys." Judith grinned and rubbed her hands together. "You have a birthday coming up, don't you? A big one?"

"I guess so. August fifth, I'll be twenty-one."

"And we'll be celebrating in all the best ways." Judith squealed. "You don't have anything else planned, do you? Can I be the one to take you out?"

"Sure. You're pretty much my only friend here, other than my boss. But something tells me Kaye Snyder won't be offering to take me out for my birthday."

"Well, good. It's my job and it's going to be great."

Dear Edie,

Every time I've sent you a letter this summer, I've gotten a response from you exactly five days later. I don't know much about the postal service, but my best guess is that it's taking two days for my letters to make it to your mailbox. You mail your response the next day, and then two days later it lands in my mailbox. We're going on nine days here though, which means my last letter made you nervous. And I'm sorry if that's the case. I just thought it was time for me to be up-front with you and tell you where my head is these days.

Well, that's not exactly accurate. These aren't new feelings, Edie, but I can see now how my words probably made you feel. Don't worry—I'll tuck them back in where they belong, and you won't hear a thing about it from me again. Though I will ask you not to throw out the idea of an Everett-Yeager business venture one day. I don't care where we're located or how long it takes to make it a reality. I think it could be great. I think we could be great.

Graham

CHAPTER 27

EDIE

Present Day

When Edie first saw the letter, she assumed it was just another stray piece of paper that had fallen out of the drawer in Mac's bedside table. It wasn't the first time it had happened. He was always shoving random things in that drawer—notes from the kids and his patients, odds and ends he collected in his pockets during the day, bits of paper and receipts. Once in a blue moon, he'd go through the drawer, separating the wheat from the chaff, but more often, it was chock-full, with things sometimes falling out and littering the floor underneath the table.

This morning she did her usual quick sweep of the upstairs, grabbing stray items and putting them where they belonged. She grabbed the letter from the floor under his table along with a pair of dirty socks, chucked the socks in the hamper, and shoved the letter in the pocket of her bathrobe. She didn't think about it again until she took off her robe to get dressed and heard the rustle of paper in the pocket. After pulling her favorite easy black dress over her head and stepping into a pair of slides, she pulled out the paper and headed to the bathroom to toss it in the trash.

She didn't know what made her take a second look as she reached down toward the trash can, but when she saw the distinctly feminine handwriting, she paused. It wasn't her writing, and it was a lot of words, covering both sides of the page.

She flattened the letter on the bathroom counter and scanned the page quickly. Her mind was on the upcoming lunch meeting with Graham, the floor plans he'd show her, and the still surprising fact that he was back in her life at all. When she read the first line though, all her thoughts evaporated.

Dear Mac,

I'm sending you this photo though I know it's probably going to be a shock. Don't be mad though. At least not until you hear me out. I have a few things to explain, and I have a confession.

First, I'm asking for your forgiveness. When I came to see you in Birmingham last fall, my intention was to tell you I was pregnant. Not to get anything from you, but because it felt wrong to keep it from you. I couldn't get the words out, and I'm sorry. I think a part of me hoped you'd somehow be able to tell. That you'd take one look at me and see past the wall I always feel like I have to keep up, and you'd know my truth—that I was carrying your child, and that somehow, despite that wall, I'd fallen for you. I fell for you just as hard as you fell for me, though I didn't have the courage to tell you. I wanted you to see past all my defenses and my stubbornness and take me in your arms and accept me and somehow make a life for us. For the three of us.

It's ridiculous, I know. Nothing more than a fantasy. The truth is, you have your own life. I saw it when I stood in your apartment and saw all your things—your textbooks and notebooks, your bulletin board filled with Post-its and test dates. The mug with the lipstick stain on the rim that I knew belonged to Edie.

I don't fit in your world, Mac. I know it now, and I knew it at the end of the summer when I bailed on you instead of meeting you like you asked me to. The faint and naive hope that I was wrong was what made me go find you in Birmingham, but it only took a few minutes to realize

I wasn't wrong at all. You were on a path, and that path didn't include me. And that's okay. It really is okay.

Believe me when I say I'm not telling you about Riley now so you'll do anything. Consider yourself off the hook. I just wanted you to know about her. But please know that I'm fine. Riley and I are just fine. Look at the photo. Look at us. See for yourself.

With shaking hands Edie pulled her hands away from the paper as if it were fire, or poison. Everything that happened that summer and in the first few months after they returned to school ping-ponged in her mind.

"*Look at us*," Kat had written. Taking the letter with her, Edie opened the drawer of Mac's bedside table and rummaged around until her fingers felt the slick surface of a wallet-size photo. With a rock-hard knot of agony in her chest, she knew what the photo would show before she even withdrew it from the drawer.

There she was. Kat. Blonde hair, tan skin, beautiful. And baby Riley. Pink, happy, picture perfect. *July 2001* was printed on the back in careful letters. Edie slid to the floor, her head on her knees, the letter on the floor in front of her.

This woman had been a mystery to her—less than that, a nonentity—and yet she'd known all about Edie. She'd gone to see Mac that fall, which meant Edie and Mac had already gotten back together. They'd stood in his apartment together, looked at each other. She saw Edie's cup on the counter, stared around at all his things. What else had happened? What else did Edie not know?

By the time Edie made it to The Blue Fin for lunch, her nerves were scraped raw. Her heart rate hadn't slowed since she walked on shaky legs down the stairs of her house and got in her car to drive to the meeting. She'd intended to go to the office first to check a few items off her to-do list, but she sat on her bedroom floor for so long, brain and body numb, she'd missed her chance to do anything productive before meeting Graham at eleven thirty.

The hostess at The Blue Fin led her out onto the patio overlooking the Delta. The air was warm but not hot, and the round table in the corner, where Graham sat with his back to them, was covered by a large blue umbrella.

"There you go." The waitress gestured to the empty seat next to Graham. "Can I bring you something to drink?"

"Just water, please."

She nodded and retreated, and before Graham could turn around and say anything, Edie leaned over the table to study the papers he'd spread out in front of him. "Okay, show me what you got."

"Hello to you too."

She nodded briskly, then pointed at the drawing on top. "This is the front exterior? I like this roofline." She kept her eyes on the drawing and away from his face.

He hesitated, then shifted in his seat and moved the drawings so they were in order. "I drew the roofline like we talked about at that first meeting. I angled it a bit more, but it's still the same idea. I'm thinking cedar shake roof too. It looks better and it'll last longer, though it is more expensive."

"I doubt Turner will be checking receipts."

"That's what I was thinking too."

The waitress appeared and set down her glass of water and refilled Graham's. "Y'all ready to order?"

Graham looked up at Edie where she was still standing at the side of the table. "You ready?"

"You go ahead. I'm not going to eat."

Graham hung his head. "I thought you said you loved this place."

"I do." She kept her eyes on the waitress. "I'm just not that hungry."

He sighed. "I'll have the fish sandwich. And can we have some crab claws too, please?"

"Sure thing." The waitress slid her notebook in her apron pocket. "Hon, if you change your mind about eating, just let me know. I'll have your crab claws out in a few."

"What's going on with you?" Graham asked as soon as the waitress was gone.

"Nothing. I'm fine."

He reached in front of her and scooted out the chair next to his. "Then can you please sit? You're making me nervous."

She dropped her bag and sat, then propped her elbows on the table. "What else?"

He kept his eyes on her a moment, then began pointing out various details and measurements on the pages in front of them, his gaze occasionally darting up to her face. She started off well, following along as he moved from page to page, but the words in Kat's letter kept bubbling up in her mind, flooding her all over again with confusion, shock, and anger. Edie tried to wall off the compartments in her brain that had anything to do with Mac, Riley, and Kat, but it was useless. Her brain didn't have compartments—it was one vast ocean, with everything swirling together in a potent tide.

When Graham finished talking, she gathered the drawings together and tapped the edges on the table. She studied each drawing, forcing herself to see past disparate lines and angles to the beautiful plans he had drawn.

"What do you think?"

"I think they're great. You did a great job."

He waited, clearly allowing her time to say more, to say anything helpful, to show that she was going to be an equally involved partner in this endeavor, but her words were gone.

When her eyes began to burn, she pulled her sunglasses down from the top of her head and settled them on her face. She felt a little better with the world around her darkened.

He gently pulled the drawings from her hands and set them to the side. "I can keep asking you what's wrong and you can keep saying you're fine, but why don't you just make it easy for us both and tell me what's going on."

"What's going on," she repeated quietly, then for no discernible reason, she began to laugh. Next to her, Graham chuckled. "Okay, we're laughing. That's good, I guess."

Apparently something in her, the part going crazy, thought his words made the whole situation funnier because she had to cover her mouth to keep it all in, but it kept coming, bursts of laughter that rocked her head and shook her shoulders.

When her eyes began to tear, Graham sat forward and put his hand on her back. "Edie? Please talk to me."

Caught somewhere between humor and grief, tears streamed down her face. She reached for a napkin and dabbed it under her eyes and her nose. She sniffed, trying to regain what little bit of dignity she might have left, but it had all leaked away. After a minute though, the sobs passed and her nose stopped running, though her eyes refused to quit tearing.

"I'm sorry." Finally her breathing returned to normal and she no longer felt like she was hyperventilating. One kind word from him though—too gentle, too soft—and she'd crumble. Her gathered composure was fragile at best.

She glanced back to the other tables on the deck. Behind them, a few feet away, three ladies sat with their heads together. One was looking Edie's way but she quickly turned back to her friends.

"Don't worry about them," Graham said. "They're just upset we're not making the eavesdropping any easier for them." He scooted his chair closer to hers to block their view, then handed her his napkin. "Here. For your . . ." He gestured to her face. She sniffed again and wiped her eyes. Smears of mascara stained the napkin.

"Okay." He folded his hands together and rested them on the table. He leaned his head toward her and spoke quietly. "I think after all that, I deserve some sort of explanation."

"You deserve it?"

"Yes. It's in the code of friendship that if one person has a come-apart in the presence of another, an explanation is required."

One side of her mouth lifted of its own accord. "A come-apart? Is that the technical term?"

"More or less. Regardless, what just happened here was a complete come-apart."

She smiled even as her mind stumbled over that phrase "code of friendship." "It's been a long time since we've actually had a friendship."

"That's true." A breeze ruffled the edges of the umbrella over them and he turned his face toward the water. "I don't like seeing you so upset, Edie. Even if it's been a while since our friendship has been . . . well, what it was."

"It's been almost twenty years, I'd say."

Something began rattling around in her brain just then, like a butterfly trapped in a jar, its wings tapping against the sides as it searched frantically for fresh air. All over again she felt the sting of Graham's sudden withdrawal from their lives all those years ago. The day was still etched so clearly in her mind.

He'd been striding across the quad, two cardboard boxes in his arms, the flaps bouncing under his chin. It was early October, the sky a swath of cloudless cerulean. Edie and a friend had just returned from seeing Matchbox 20 in Atlanta, and she was eager to regale him with all the concert details. He liked to pretend he hated the band, but she knew he secretly listened to them.

"Hey!" She ran to meet him in the middle of the grass. "I've been looking everywhere for you. What's with the boxes?"

"Oh, I'm, uh . . . I'm moving. Actually."

"Moving?" She stared at him. "Where are you going?"

"There's an empty dorm room in Paxton Hall." He shrugged. "No one was taking it, so the RA said I could have it."

"What? Does Mac know?" They'd lived together since sophomore year. Plus, Graham hated the dorm rooms.

He nodded. "He knows." Graham turned and began heading toward the dorm on the other side of the quad.

"Graham, wait—"

"Edie, it can't go on like this," he exploded. "You, me, Mac. I can't be your third anymore." She felt the force of his words like a blow to her chest. She actually took a step back. "What'd you think would happen? That we'd just go on forever, like the Three Musketeers? No. I'm out. I can't do this anymore. If I stay . . ." He kept his eyes on her, then glanced up. "Mac knows why I had to leave. You can ask him if you want."

Then he walked away from her and didn't look back.

There in the bright sunshine at The Blue Fin, the present and the past clashed. They were adult Edie and adult Graham, both far from that long-ago day, and yet it felt as real—as tangible—as the wood under her feet, the scents of fried seafood and briny bay water mingling in the air.

Everything she had said to him on the phone from New York City—her truth, her divided heart—and his confusing, almost mocking reply. Then the end of the summer and the beginning of their senior year, Mac pulling her toward him, kissing her like he'd never let her go, and Graham just as smoothly backing off, pulling away. Mac almost frantic in his devotion to her. Graham's energy and light dulled. Gone. She should have questioned it more, should have demanded an answer. Better late than never though, and here she was, all these years later, figuring it out.

"You knew, didn't you?"

"Knew what?" His eyebrows rose behind his sunglasses and he gave his head a little shake.

"About Mac's child."

At her words—"Mac's child"—Graham stilled, all movement suspended. The tapping at the glass in her mind grew louder. Mac told her he didn't know. He said Kat never told him. The letter even said as much, but at the moment, she didn't know who or what to trust.

"You were his best friend too. You had to know. At least about Kat. The girl from the boat?"

Graham just stared at her, mystified. Relief flooded her chest, roared in her ears. *He didn't know. At least Graham didn't lie to me too.*

Then he reached up slowly and pulled off his sunglasses. He wasn't confused, he wasn't unsure—he was incredulous. "Kat was pregnant?"

"Graham." It came out as an exhale of disbelief. "You knew about her?" She imagined the butterfly escaping the jar as the truth flew free.

"It's like you said. He was my best friend too." He paused. "He told me some things. Obviously not everything."

"So you didn't know she was pregnant?"

"No. I didn't know that."

She sat there for a long moment, frozen, trying to form any word or coherent thought. Finally she pushed away from the table.

"Edie." He reached out his hand but she jerked her arm back. One of the women at the table behind them glanced her way, then quickly turned back to her dainty salad. Edie didn't care. She snatched her bag from the ground and turned, knocking over the stack of drawings.

"Edie, let me explain."

She whirled around and flung her words at him, deathly quiet and full of barbs. "I don't need your explanation. I don't need anything."

As she strode back through the restaurant and out to her car parked in the front, she knew she was being childish. She should have listened to him, given him a chance to offer his side. And though she didn't want to admit it, she also knew her anger was misplaced. The root of her anger was embedded in her husband, not Graham. Graham had no commitment to her—not back then, despite what they'd said to each other on the phone on her twenty-first birthday, and definitely not today. But she and Mac had been married for seventeen years. If anyone could expect the truth from her husband, it should have been Edie.

As she walked away from lunch, it felt like everyone had known about Kat but her. She was the one in the dark, skittering around searching for purchase, for something solid to grab on to.

CHAPTER 28

MAC

Present Day

When Mac arrived home after work, Thomas sat at the kitchen table, his head hung low, as Edie stomped around the kitchen, slamming cabinet doors and flinging Italian seasoning in her attempt to get chicken in the oven. Riley and Avery were nowhere to be seen.

"Hello?" He glanced between Thomas and Edie. "All okay in here?"

"Not exactly." Edie's hands stilled as her eyebrows rose practically to her hairline. "Why don't you ask your son where he's been all afternoon?"

Thomas rolled his eyes.

"Tell him." Edie crossed her arms and popped her hip out, her classic "I'm mad and totally in the right" stance. Anytime he saw that particular body position, Mac generally backed down from whatever it was he'd been so sure about, because Edie usually won the argument. But Thomas wasn't giving up.

"I wasn't doing anything."

"Where were you?" Mac tried to imagine where his son possibly could have gone that would have so riled Edie. A crack house? Adult bookstore? Jail? None of those were logical or even possible in Oak Hill, and considering the fact that Thomas was only eleven, he couldn't have gone anywhere else. Not easily anyway.

"I was out walking."

"Walking?" Confused, he turned to Edie.

She moved her hands to her hips, her second most intimidating stance. "He didn't come home after school. Didn't stay there to practice, didn't go to Reston's, didn't go to the coffee shop. He just stayed gone. Walking." The way she spit the word out, Thomas might as well have been smoking or stealing. Or kicking puppies.

"You were out walking?" Mac asked quietly. There had to be more to the story. "Like, for exercise?"

Thomas shrugged. "Not really. I just needed to clear my head. I was planning on taking the long way home, but I wasn't ready to come home yet." His thick dark hair fell as unruly as ever, and his blue eyes were wary. "I didn't think it was that big a deal. If I just had a phone . . ." He glanced sideways at Edie, but her cold stare quickly evaporated the beginnings of his grin.

"Not having a phone has nothing to do with this. We live four blocks from school. You could have stuck your head in the door and said, 'Hey, Mom, I'm going to go for a walk.' To which I would have said, 'No problem, Son. Thanks for letting me know.' Instead I had to call everyone I know, drive up and down streets in this whole town, knock on doors, call your name . . ."

"You called my name? Out loud?" Thomas was horrified. "Geez, Mom. I'm not a baby." He rubbed his forehead.

"Then don't act like one, Thomas Swan. Act responsible and I'll treat you like you are."

Her words were harsh—harsher than Mac thought necessary. "Okay. It sounds like he made a bad call. You really should have let your mom know your plan. That's part of our deal with letting you walk home. You can't go anywhere else without telling one of us. You know that."

"I know." He hung his head, a picture of remorse. "I'm sorry, Mom."

"Of course you're sorry now. You sure weren't sorry when you traipsed home at five fifteen like everything was right in the world."

Mac held his hand up. "Let's just—"

"Let's just nothing. Don't come in here and try to smooth it all out like it wasn't a big deal. You weren't here. You weren't driving all over creation, wondering if someone had snatched him, worrying you'd never see him again."

"Edie—"

"You know what?" She left her post at the stove and handed Mac the wooden spoon she'd been gesturing with. "You finish dinner. I need a break." She yanked the dish towel off her shoulder, thrust it at him, and walked out the front door.

He watched through the window as she trotted down the front steps. She paused at the bottom, then strode toward the sidewalk and up the street.

"See? She's stressed so she's going for a walk." Thomas stood abruptly, his chair squeaking on the hardwood floor. "Why's it the end of the world if I do the same thing?" He stomped up the stairs. When he got to the top, he stomped into his room, slammed the door, and stomped to his bed, his footsteps like bricks on the creaky old floor.

"Can y'all please be quiet?" Avery shouted from her room. "I'm trying to study!"

Silence rang out in the house as the echo of Thomas's door slam still reverberated. Mac remained completely still in the middle of the kitchen where he'd paused when he first walked in. Finally he rubbed a hand over his scratchy cheek, kicked off his shoes at the back door, and took over dinner preparations.

A few minutes later, after setting the timer on the oven, he fought the urge to slump down in a kitchen chair. Instead he headed upstairs. Thomas's door was still closed, and Mac gave it a wide berth. He understood the need to cool off. When he got to Avery's door, he tapped on it.

"I'm busy," came her response.

He opened the door and pressed his face to the open few inches. "Hey, sweetie" was on his lips, but the words froze when he saw Riley sitting on Avery's bed, her back propped up on a pile of pillows. Avery sat at her desk, books spread out on the surface, a pen stuck through her knot of dark hair.

"Oh. Hey," he stammered. "Sorry. You working in here?"

"Yeah. Riley's helping me study."

"Yeah? That's great. What's the subject?"

"Sexual and asexual reproduction."

He must have made a sound, because Avery blew her hair out of her eyes, then rolled them. "It's biology, Dad."

"I know, I know. I remember ninth-grade biology."

It was true, he did. But it still didn't keep him from breaking out in a sweat when he heard the word *sexual* come from his child's mouth. His mind spun back to the long-ago day when she asked him what sexual relations were. She was eight years old, and she'd been flipping through the Bible.

He glanced at Riley, who shrugged. "I didn't pick the topic. But I was good at science."

"Are," he managed. "Not was."

"She is," Avery added. "I told her she'd make a better teacher for our science league than Mr. Connors. He should have stuck to PE."

"Okay, well, let me know if y'all need anything," he said.

"'Kay."

He closed the door partway behind him, then stopped. "Sorry about all the commotion downstairs earlier."

"What got them all riled up?" Avery's gaze was back on her books, but Riley was watching him.

He slid his hands into his pockets and shrugged. "It was just a disagreement. I think they both needed to blow off a little steam."

He glanced at Riley. She shrugged. "You're a family. Families argue sometimes."

Avery turned around in her chair and peered at Riley, then pulled the pen from her hair and went back to her books.

He closed Avery's door and headed into his bedroom, nudged the door closed with his foot, and pulled off his shirt. Unbuckled his belt and unzipped his pants. Clad only in his boxers, he sat on the chair in the corner and raked his hands through his hair.

This too shall pass. The words were a breeze of memory, a phrase his grandmother used to say when someone she loved was facing a difficult time. Would she still say those words to him now though, when he was the cause of his own problem? His family was smack in the middle of a "difficult time" all because of decisions he made long ago.

After a moment he stood to put on some clothes. When he passed Edie's side of the bed on his way to the closet, his gaze was pulled, inexplicably, to the floor by her bed. There, next to the fuzzy slippers she wore all the time, no matter the season or temperature, was a single sheet of paper, yellowed at the edges, and a small photo.

He froze, as if thick sludge had filled every cell of his body. He felt much like he had the moment Riley first handed him the letter, sitting in his car outside Fitz's house, but this time it wasn't a fear of what he would see . . . It was the fear of what Edie had already seen.

———

For the rest of the evening, Edie found a reason to be as far away from him as possible. On the opposite side of the room, in another part of the house, outside while he was inside, upstairs while he was down.

At one point he stood next to her while she washed up at the kitchen sink. With her hands sudsy and dripping, she was a captive audience. "She never sent me the letter," he whispered.

"What?"

"Riley gave it to me the day she got here. Kat never mailed it."

"I'm supposed to believe that?" Shock and confusion filled her eyes, but then Thomas walked in and the chance for explanation was over.

Finally after the three kids were tucked away in their rooms and the house was quiet, she stopped running. He found her at the wrought-iron table in their backyard. It was set up on a little patio under a huge magnolia with thick, low-hanging limbs. When they'd first bought the house, it was all dirt under the tree, and when the kids were young they spent hours, whole afternoons, up in that tree. When their tree-climbing days had passed, Mac spread pea gravel under the limbs—grass didn't grow there anyway—strung those big twinkle lights along the lowest limbs, and moved the table and chairs that had previously been shoved into the back corner of the garage. Now it was an oasis that all of them frequently escaped to when they needed a little peace or privacy. He'd even spotted Riley sitting out here occasionally.

Edie sat with her back to the house, her legs pulled up in front of her, and her chin on her knees. He almost didn't want to disturb her, but they had to talk. It was the last thing he wanted to do, but it was also the only thing he wanted to do.

He didn't notice the letter and photo lying on the table until he reached it. Edie was gazing upward at the magnolia limbs that curved and bent in graceful curves, her face bathed in the warm glow of the lights. She didn't move when he sat down. He leaned forward and rested his elbows on the table. Riley's pink baby face peered up at him from the photo. Kat's freckled cheeks and radiant grin. The words in the letter flashed back to him.

"When I came to see you in Birmingham . . . I fell for you just as hard as you fell for me . . . Look at the photo. We're just fine."

He rubbed the side of his face and pressed his chin into his hand. He pulled the photo toward him. "Edie—"

"She really didn't send you the letter? Is that the truth?"

"Yes," he breathed. "I had no idea about Riley. I told you that."

"Yes, but you also told me you didn't see Kat again." Her voice was weighted with fatigue. "That you hadn't seen her since the end of the summer. But that part was a lie."

"It wasn't—"

"It wasn't a lie? She didn't come to see you at school?" She looked at him for the first time, waiting, as if a part of her hoped the words in the letter really were wrong. That it was Kat who was the liar and not her husband.

"No. I mean, yes. She did come see me." He sucked in a short breath, all he could manage around the fear constricting his chest. "And I did lie to you."

Pain crossed her face. "Mac, your lies are getting hard to keep up with. You've lied our entire marriage by not telling me about Kat, but then you lied to my face and told me you hadn't seen her again. It was all out in the open at that point. Why'd you lie again?"

"Because I didn't think it mattered. Nothing happened when she came.

We talked, said good-bye, and she left. After that, I truly did not see her again. Ever. She wrote me the letter, and I'll never know why she didn't mail it, but the point is, she didn't. I did not know she was pregnant, just like I didn't know . . ."

"You didn't know she'd fallen in love with you." Her voice was still quiet, but it had a hard edge. "But you'd fallen in love with her. You knew that part."

"That was Kat's estimation of the situation. I never said that. I never told her that."

"But was it true?"

His mind swam and he focused on the table, the gravel under his feet, the light breeze rustling the leaves overhead. "I was twenty years old, Edie. My head was a mess. I don't know what I thought back then."

"Did you love her?" she pressed, each word carefully enunciated and sharp. "Simple question."

Simple? Not quite. As they stared at each other—measuring, evaluating, circling—he felt like he was on the slimmest of tightropes, trying to balance between loving and cherishing his wife and not dragging Kat through the mud. It would be easy, of course, to chalk what he had with Kat up to nothing more than primal urges and lust—it'd be untrue, but it would be easy to say.

But how would that feel to Edie? To think the man she married was so low as to have slept with a woman only to satisfy some carnal demand? It was better to go with the truth, as hard as it might be for her to hear.

Edie was watching him, waiting for an answer. So he gave it to her. "Yes. I loved her. But I loved you more."

Her chin dropped just a little, parting her lips, but then she clamped her mouth shut. Somewhere in the trees above them an owl hooted. They both raised their heads, as if to search for the source of the sound. Another hoot and a rustle of a limb, then quiet. Even the insects in the trees had stilled their nightly song.

He slowly extended his arm, tried to touch hers, but she just as slowly pulled her arm away. Then she stood, pushed her chair neatly back under the table, and walked inside. She did not invite him to follow.

CHAPTER 29

MAC

Summer 2000

As the remaining weeks of summer ticked down, Mac found himself sneaking away with Kat as often as they both could. Sometimes it was out to Johnson Beach again, with only a sliver of moon to light their way, but often it was as simple as punching out at night only to turn around and go back to sit at the end of the dock, their legs dangling over the water, the sky velvety and studded with stars. No matter where they went or what they did, their times together were deliciously inadequate, each moment serving to remind Mac that his time with her was limited and every day moved them closer to their end.

At the back of his mind, he knew he was playing with fire, but there was that voice, the one inside that reminded him how good it felt to throw caution to the wind for once in his life. To disregard all the rules that had been built up around him and do what felt good and right and natural. Eventually that voice became louder than the other smaller, quieter one telling him to watch it, to back off, to *remember*.

Late one afternoon, during the last full week of Mac's employment at Sunset Marina, he and Kat stood together by the ice machine at the back of the dock store where they'd first met. Mac should have been ferrying Mr. Ruiz's cigarette boat back to the boat barn, and Kat should have been hauling the day's allotment of red snapper off *Alabama Reds*, but it was the first time they'd seen each other all day, and like magnets they'd found their way to each other as soon as Kat's boat had idled into the marina.

"I'm leaving on Saturday," Mac said quietly. He leaned his hip against the side of the ice machine, the cold seeping through his shorts, cooling his hot skin. "I have to go back to school."

"I know." Kat stood in front of him with her back to the wall. She touched his wrist with one cool finger. "Back where you belong."

He took her hand in his and squeezed gently. "Don't say that. As if I don't belong here."

"You don't belong here. You have a life somewhere else. You have your classes and grades and your future." She slid her hand away from his and crossed her arms over her chest. "You have *people* there."

He understood what she meant by "people." *Who* she meant. His heart did a funny little flip at the thought of Edie, whom he'd spent his summer alternately thinking about and purposefully trying to forget. It hadn't worked—the forgetting part, at least. But now there was Kat, the one thing he did not expect when he made his summer plans. Kat had swooped in and waylaid everything he thought he knew and desired, and his mind and heart were caught up in a whirlwind he didn't know how to get out of.

He gently reached out and tilted her chin so he could see her face. He leaned his head down closer to hers. "I don't want to think about school or grades or anyone else right now. Because I have someone here. *You're* here."

Mac heard a car pull up behind him, but he ignored it. Kat's face was so close to his, the skin of her cheek so soft, her hair tickling his neck where the breeze caught strands and lifted them.

She was just parting her lips to speak when someone called his name. The voice was one he knew better than almost anyone else's. Mac took an automatic step back from Kat. Then another one.

"Hey." Graham strolled toward them from the parking lot.

"Hey, what's up?" Mac kept his gaze on Graham, so he felt rather than saw Kat's nervous shift.

Graham stepped up on the curb and paused a few steps away. He glanced toward the marina where a ragtag group of teenagers on WaveRunners laughed and jeered at each other as they idled away from the dock. "I had to make a run to the foreman's office and passed right by here. Thought I'd stop in and say hey." His eyes skimmed over Kat, then he turned back to Mac. "I wanted to see what you've been up to all summer."

It could have been an offhand comment, but considering Graham had caught Mac and Kat standing much closer than mere coworkers, it felt more like an indictment.

Mac held his arms out to the side. "Well, this is it. I've been washing boats all afternoon, and I'm about to mow the grass out by the road. Just taking a break here." He glanced behind him to where Kat stood. "This is Kat. She's . . . she works on one of the charter boats."

Graham extended his hand, and after a blink of hesitation, Kat took it. "Hey," she muttered.

"Good to meet you, Kat."

Kat nodded and slid her sunglasses from the top of her head down to her eyes. "I gotta get the rest of the fish to the cleaning table. I'll see y'all around." Without looking at Mac she turned and headed off toward the boats. Mac's insides jittered as he watched her leave.

Graham stayed only a few minutes more, making Mac wonder if he'd somehow known Mac was involved with someone and wanted to check up on him. As soon as he left, Mac went to find Kat, but Carla told him she was gone.

"She told Reggie she wasn't feeling good and needed to get out of the sun. That girl works herself to the bone." Carla pulled a cigarette out of the pocket of her sleeveless denim shirt. "Works harder than anyone else around here, to be honest."

She took a long drag and stared at Mac through the smoke. "You two sure have been friendly this summer." When Mac didn't respond, Carla shook her head. "You got it bad."

"I don't have anything bad. I have three days left. Then I'm gone."

"You haven't been too bad a worker yourself. If you find yourself needing a job again in the future, gimme a call."

In the future. For the last handful of years, he'd been constantly focused on what was coming up next—the next test, the next final exam, the next semester. Medical school, residency, his career taking off. Marriage, family. A happy, successful life. At the moment though, all that was cloudy. The only clear thing he knew was that he couldn't leave without seeing Kat again.

Mac dipped his hand into the live bait well and grabbed a wiggling shrimp. With it firmly in place on his hook, he cast it out into Old River and settled back into his folding chair. Lightning flashed to the north, illuminating the clouds that blotted out the moon. Mac waited to hear the thunder that followed, but the only sounds were a heron squawking on a neighboring dock and faint strains of music floating down the river from an idling pontoon boat.

"Heat lightning," Mac murmured.

"No such thing," Graham answered.

Mac turned to peer at Graham. "What?"

"No such thing as heat lightning."

"Sure there is."

Graham's cheeks lifted in a smile. "Nope. It's regular old lightning from a regular old thunderstorm. It's just too far away for us to hear the thunder."

Mac leaned his head against the back of the chair. "I'll give you that one. Mainly because I'm too tired to argue."

"I'll take it."

They fished in silence for several more minutes. Mac felt the change in their friendship like a bruise on his heel. He could go for hours without thinking about it, but as soon as he tested it—as soon as he and Graham were alone together—he was jolted back to reality, faced with the alterations to a friendship that had spanned so many years. Was the change irreparable?

He thought of Edie's letter he'd seen on the couch earlier in the summer—her words addressed to Graham alone. "How's Edie?" Mac asked before he could stop himself.

Graham pulled back on his fishing pole, nudging the bobber closer to the light clipped to the end of the dock. "Edie?"

"Yeah. How are things with her?"

"Pretty good, I'd imagine." Graham leaned forward onto his elbows. "I haven't talked to her in a little while."

"But you have been talking?"

"I don't know, man. I guess. A little." He looked at Mac. "What's going on with you and that girl from the marina? Kate?"

"Kat."

"Kat." Graham studied the end of the fishing pole in his hands. "Y'all seemed close."

Mac was silent a moment. He meant to steer the conversation to Edie, but he couldn't think of what to say to prove or disprove the statement.

Lightning flashed again, and in the space that followed, thunder rolled, long and low.

"There it is," Graham said quietly.

Mac stared at the sky. "You win."

On Friday Mac found Kat on the boat, a large cast net filling the back of the hull, part of it thrown over her shoulder. She glanced up when she heard his feet on the dock. "Idiot college boys got my net all tangled up. One of them forgot to hold the rope in his teeth like I showed him, and he threw the whole thing off the back of the boat. I had to jump in and pull it out."

"College boys," Mac said, in an attempt to get her to smile.

When his words elicited no visible response, he hopped down into the boat and took a tentative step toward her, watching carefully where he put his feet so he didn't step on the net. She kept working her fingers through snarls in the delicate lines.

"You okay?" he asked.

"I'm just annoyed, I told you."

"Right. Everything else okay though?"

She yanked at a cord, then winced and stuck the tip of her finger in her mouth.

He stepped toward her and took her hands, stilled them, and tugged her gently toward him. "Kat, look at me."

She refused. She was standing right in front of him, yet he felt her slipping away. Just like Graham was slipping away. And Edie too. And there was nothing he could do about any of them.

Mac felt pressure on his fingers and focused on Kat. She leaned toward him, so slightly he almost missed it, and squeezed his hands again. "You were ashamed of me. When your friend came."

"Kat—no. No, I wasn't ashamed." A sharp ache knifed through his heart and remorse heated his cheeks. "I just . . . He didn't . . ."

"I get it," she said, her voice still lowered. "I'm not your kind of girl."

"Yes, you—"

"No, Mac. Listen to me. You think we fit. We feel good. Maybe even right. But as far as the rest of your life goes, I'm not her."

Mac thought of his parents—his studious, deliberate, brilliant parents who'd hardly made a misstep in their lives, except for when it came to matters of the heart. His dad would frown and his mother would avert her gaze if they saw Mac with Kat. If they knew what simmered in his heart when he was with her. If they knew all he'd considered, all he'd done, since he met her.

"I've been thinking a lot about the rest of my life lately."

"Don't do that, Mac."

"Don't do what?"

"Don't get my—"

They both turned their heads when heavy footsteps thumped on the dock. Kat's boss, Reggie, strode toward the boat, two large tackle boxes in his hands.

She pulled her hands away. "I have to get back to work."

"Wait." Mac dragged his hands through his hair and groaned. Everything was slipping too fast. "I have to see you again."

"I'm off the next few days. I need the break."

"You'll get your break. But I just need—I've got to see you tomorrow. Carla's out today, so I have to come back here early to pick up my last paycheck before I leave. Will you meet me here?"

She didn't respond, just lifted her eyes to Reggie as he stepped onto the boat.

"Move it or lose it, kid," he grumbled. "Or I can put you to work if you want."

"I'll be gone in just a minute." Mac squatted next to Kat and spoke quietly. "Please. Just say you'll meet me here. Please let me see you one more time before I leave."

She remained quiet a moment, her arms strong as she lifted the now-untangled net to the dock and laid it out straight. Finally she stuck her hands on her hips. "Fine. I'll meet you."

Mac exhaled. "Okay then. Tomorrow morning."

CHAPTER 30

EDIE

Summer 2000

"Of all the places in New York City, you decided to celebrate my birthday here?" Edie laughed and held her arms out to take in the entire unbelievable scene. They were in some kind of warehouse, darkened except for green bulbs emitting a pulsing light that ricocheted off the disco balls hung from the ceiling. All around them were men and women in long, shiny black coats, black sunglasses, and scowls. Here and there, small groups of people maneuvered around, their feet on the ground but their bodies contorting into seemingly impossible stretches, as if they were dodging bullets only they could see.

"Care to tell me what in the world is going on?" Edie had to practically shout to be heard over the pounding music.

Judith grinned. "Isn't it crazy?" she yelled. "It's all run by this acting coach from Brooklyn. Every month he invites a select group of people to come to this party. He features a different movie each time, and everyone is given a part to play. This month is *The Matrix*."

"Yeah, I picked up on that. If we made it into that select group of people, why didn't we dress up?"

Judith held up a hand. "Do you have much black leather in your closet?"

Edie hesitated. "Well, no."

"I didn't think so. Anyway, the coach is a friend of mine from the theater district. He said we could come just to see what it's all about." Judith steered her farther into the crowd. "C'mon, it's your birthday. Don't ask questions."

As they moved deeper into the throng, a man holding a tray of martini glasses walked up and paused next to them. Edie glanced at him warily, but Judith clapped her hands. "I've heard about these."

The man, wearing dark round sunglasses and black leather, leaned toward them. "Red or blue pill?" He nodded to the glasses on the tray. Half the glasses held blue liquid, the other half cherry red.

"What?"

"You have to pick one," Judith said. "They're the signature drinks."

"What's the difference?" Edie asked the man.

"Red for truth," he intoned, his voice crater-deep. "Blue for ignorance."

Edie waited, but the man didn't elaborate. She turned to Judith. "Jude, this is nuts. I'm not taking a drink from this guy."

At that the man lifted his sunglasses. "It's fine," he said, his voice higher than before. "The red is a strawberry Bellini and the blue is just a margarita with blue curaçao." He nodded between them. "I'm supposed to say they represent truth or ignorance. Just pick one."

Judith grinned at Edie. "What's it gonna be?"

Edie glanced back at the tray. "I don't know."

Judith swiped a glass of blue. "I'll take ignorance, thanks." She winked at Edie. "The truth can be hard to handle sometimes."

"Wise words." Edie reached for the blue but at the last second changed her mind and grabbed the red Bellini.

The man sauntered away and Judith clinked her glass carefully to Edie's. "Cheers to you on your twenty-first."

"Cheers," Edie echoed. The red drink was sweet and tangy at the same time, and deliciously cold in the overwarm warehouse. It wasn't the first drink she'd had, but something about it being her actual twenty-first birth-day made this specific drink—this truth serum, if the man in the sunglasses was right—feel and taste significant.

After the second Bellini, time loosened, and Edie and Judith spent the next hour, or maybe hours, dancing with a variety of Neos and Morpheuses. At some point Edie saw a group of girls dressed as the characters from *Clueless*—complete with plaid skirts, feather boas, and cell phones.

"They must have missed the memo about *The Matrix*." Edie giggled.

When the DJ took a break, Edie grabbed her friend's hand. "It's so hot in here. Can we get some fresh air?"

"Sure thing, birthday girl."

Edie and Judith made it through the maze of dancing party guests and stumbled out the door onto a side street. The air outside was still warm but blessedly free from the thump and throb of music in the warehouse. Edie drew in a lungful of night air just as Judith snaked her arm through Edie's elbow.

"Where to now?" Judith asked.

"Now?" Edie glanced at her watch. "It's eleven o'clock."

"Exactly! The night is young and there's no stopping us. You pick—food or drink?"

"Mmm." Edie closed her eyes a moment. "Can I pick both?"

"Yes. Perfect. I know just the place."

A few minutes later the cab deposited them outside a café with neon letters over the door and cozy windows framed by window boxes. "This is one of my favorite places." Judith pulled Edie inside.

At a booth in the back, the girls ordered croque monsieur sandwiches, french fries, and two glasses of red wine.

"Need to see your ID," the waiter said, his eye on Edie.

As Edie pulled her driver's license from her wallet and handed it to the man, Judith squealed, "It's her birthday—she's twenty-one today!"

The man stared back and forth between the license and Edie a few times, then grinned. "Drinks are on the house, ladies."

"So what's going on with your men?" Judith sat back in her seat.

Their sandwiches were gone, as were all but the soggiest of the french fries. They were nursing a second glass of wine, though the headache lodged somewhere in the back of Edie's head told her she should probably stick to just a single drink in the future.

"My men?" Edie passed a hand over her face. "Who are they again?"

"I'm not going to remember names at this point in the evening, but one was your ex and the other was a *friend*." Judith did the air quotes again, making Edie giggle. "Remind me of their names?"

"Mac was my boyfriend, and my friend . . ." Edie paused. "His name is Graham."

Judith leaned forward. "Did you hear how you said his name?"

"Um, no. What did I sound like?"

"It was so wistful. If you were playing a part in a movie, you'd totally be star-crossed lovers, separated by distance—ooh, or maybe even by time too. I've always wanted to get a part in a story about time travel. It's so romantic."

Judith gazed off into the distance so long Edie laughed. "You're the one who sounds wistful. I'm just being honest. His name is Graham and I don't know what's going on with him. Or with Mac and me. With any of us."

"But don't you *want* to know?"

"Sure, but how am I supposed to do that? Mac and I haven't talked all summer. Not a single time. And Graham . . ." She trailed off as she thought of their letters and postcards that had flown north and south all summer.

"Ah, Graham." Judith's smile lifted her round cheeks. "The two of you have talked. You've been pen pals, haven't you?"

Edie smiled. "Yeah, I guess we have."

"A single phone call could clear it all up, you know."

"What?" The word came out as a screech, prompting the people at the next table to glance at them. Edie lowered her voice. "No. I'm not calling him. He wanted to call me, but . . ."

"But what? Why didn't you let him?"

"I don't know. Why should we talk in person when it's all so easy on paper?"

Judith spread her hands out on the table. "Edie. Talking to Graham—in person, on the phone, without three days of lag time between your words—would at least let you know where you stand with him. That way you won't be heading back to school in the dark."

Edie shook her head slowly. "I don't know."

"Do you know his phone number?"

CHAPTER 31

EDIE

Present Day

Edie was at her desk working on sketches for a new client's foyer when someone tapped on her door. Her mind was on the sketches, but it was also tied up with Mac, the kids, and Riley's interview later that afternoon with Cynthia. Expecting it to be Laura Lou at the door, she called out a distracted, "Come on in," without lifting her pencil from the page.

At the silence Edie glanced up and saw it wasn't Laura Lou.

"Do you have a minute?" Graham asked, a drawing tube under one arm.

She closed her notebook and gestured to the chair across from her desk. "I'm surprised you'd want anything to do with me after my meltdown the last time I saw you."

"Are you kidding?" He sat down and set the tube on the floor by his feet. "I wasn't sure you'd even want to talk to me today. I half expected to get a phone call from Turner saying I was off the project."

"I'm sorry. I was mad, but not at you. At least not entirely."

He offered a smile. "Okay. But what happened? Did you just find out? What—?"

"She came to his office."

"Kat?"

"No, Riley. His daughter. His and Kat's daughter. Kat passed away last year sometime."

"Oh, wow. Okay. So tell me about Riley."

Edie took a deep breath and gave him the ten-cent tour, filling in some details and leaving others out. But she told him the main things. The important ones.

"She's living at your house? For how long?"

"I don't know. We'll wait until she has the baby, then just sort of . . . see."

The way he looked at her—with such pity and sadness—almost broke her. "You know, you can talk to me about anything. You also don't have to if you don't want to. But I can be a listening ear if you need it."

"Thank you." She moved her coffee cup a few inches to the right. "Nothing's fixed yet. Or decided. So there's really not much to say."

He was quiet for a beat, then nodded. "Okay."

Edie cleared her throat and sat forward in her chair. "So you brought some drawings?"

When he didn't respond, she lifted her eyebrows and nodded toward the tube on the floor. "Are you going to show them to me or what?"

He eyed her. "Do you promise to say more than just, 'They're great'?"

She smiled. "Sorry about that. Yes, if you let me see them again, I promise to give you a detailed analysis."

"Well, I don't know if I want that." He stood and opened the end of the tube. When he had all the drawings out and in his hands, he glanced down at her desk. Aside from her lamp, she had four stacks of notebooks and papers, two coffee cups, numerous pencils, and a Farrow & Ball fan deck.

"Want to try the floor?" he asked.

She laughed. "Probably a good idea."

He knelt on the gray rug and spread the drawings out, anchoring each one with an array of round glass paperweights. She sat next to him, angling her legs under her, and lifted one of them. It was small—quarter-size—and sat in the center of her palm like a warm pebble. "I like these."

"They were my dad's. Look." He took the glass from her, his fingertips rough against her palm. When he set it on top of the drawing, the words and lines underneath were enlarged. "He used them as magnifying glasses. He always hated reading glasses, so he kept these all over his house. I like them. Thought they'd make good paperweights." He tossed it lightly in the air and caught it, then placed it on the drawing and sat back. "Go easy on me."

"I don't need to go easy." Edie took in each drawing spread across her rug. "I've seen houses you've designed, but seeing your plans . . ." She tilted her head as she stared at one of the drawings, trying to imagine the actual structure built and sitting on Turner's property. "These are works of art. Do you ever give them to your clients once their houses are finished?"

He nodded. "Usually as a gift at the end."

"Unbelievable. These are gorgeous. Turner and Marigold will love it. *I* love it."

"I'm really glad."

"Can I give you a few suggestions?"

He laughed. "I knew that was too easy." He crossed his legs and propped his arms behind him. "Fire away."

For the next two hours, they went over each page of the plans and deliberated over every detail—ceiling treatments, placement of built-ins, window measurements, kitchen layout, sizes of bathrooms and closets. Where he felt strongly about something he'd included, he pushed back at her and she generally let it go. And when she was right about a needed change, he acknowledged it and backed off.

She talked fabrics, finishes, counter surfaces, and flooring options. Artwork, rugs, texture, and balance. She pulled samples from her desk drawers and spread them out so he could touch them. He asked questions, made suggestions, and when it was out of his league, he completely deferred to her.

It felt so good—the rapid-fire conversation, bouncing ideas off each other—that she almost forgot the rest of her life was falling apart.

A little while later a knock sounded at her door, and Laura Lou stuck her head in the doorway. "Look at all this." She entered the office and leaned down to peer at the drawings. "Is this the Kennedy house?" Her voice was a mix of awe and irritation that they'd left her out.

"It is," Graham replied. "Edie's letting me know what I missed."

"Not exactly." She reached over and poked his shoulder. "He didn't miss anything. I'm just adding some details."

"Well, I like what I see here." Laura Lou straightened up and turned back to them. "I like seeing the two of you working together too. I'd like to see more of it, in fact."

Graham smiled at Edie. "I wouldn't say no to that."

"Hmm," Laura Lou mused as she headed back toward the door. "Keep that in the back of your mind, Graham. And Edie, I'd like to see the final plans before you present them to the Kennedys."

"Yes, ma'am."

When she closed the door softly behind her, Graham stood and reached down to pull Edie up. "I think we're done here. I think we've gotten it as good as it's going to get."

"You're right. It's going to be a winner."

"You want to call Turner and set up a time for the presentation?"

"Sure. I'll let you know what he says."

They gathered the drawings and Graham rolled them and slid them back into the tube. At her door he stopped. "This was fun. Working with you."

"You sound surprised that I could be fun."

"Not what I mean. It's just . . ." He gestured between them. "All these ideas. The back-and-forth. Give-and-take. I wasn't sure how it would go, having someone critique my drawings."

"Your clients don't do that?"

"Oh sure. Well, they make changes. We alter details according to what they want. But it's different having a professional do it."

"I actually wondered if you'd hate working with someone else."

Working with me specifically. That's what she was thinking. Honestly, she still wondered why he'd agreed to take on the project, knowing she would be the designer.

"I've been on my own for a long time. I've been told I don't always 'play well with others.'" He chuckled. "It feels pretty good though, being on a team. Having a partner." He held her gaze a moment, then reached for the doorknob. "I'll talk to you soon."

A few hours later Edie was driving down Camellia Avenue with Riley in the passenger seat next to her. Riley sat straight as an arrow, legs crossed, one hand nervously spinning a silver ring on her thumb. "I hope I don't bomb this interview."

Edie's mind was still wrapped up in her morning with Graham, but she tried to focus on the reason they were headed to the Gulf Coast Women's Center again. Aside from what they'd decided would be a regular weekly counseling session, Riley was interviewing for the office assistant job this afternoon.

"I'm sure you won't bomb it," Edie said, "but whatever happens, it'll be a good experience for you to know what a job interview is like. She'll probably want to hear why you want to work there, why you think you'd be a good fit."

"I've had a job interview before." Riley reached into her bag. "I brought a copy of my résumé. I used your printer. Hope that's okay."

"Sure. It's fine. I didn't know you . . ."

"You didn't know I had a résumé? Didn't know I'd ever had an interview?" She blew her hair out of her face. "I grew up a long time ago."

What a contradiction this girl was. *Woman. She's not a girl.* Riley still had her attitude, but it was softening, bit by slow bit. She was so young, still so raw, but her body was blooming before their eyes. She'd had years of hard-earned lessons and wisdom, yet to hear her giggle—on the rare occasions it happened—you'd be forgiven for thinking she was a typical teenager.

Her hair had grown since she'd been with them, and today it fell over her shoulders in a messy blonde waterfall. She rested her hands on top of her belly, making the bump even more pronounced.

"Dex called this morning." Her voice was quiet.

Edie measured her words as she did sometimes with Avery when she mentioned Alex. "Did you talk to him?"

"Yeah, for a minute. He's been calling a lot lately. He wants to 'talk about the future.'" She rolled her eyes. "I wish he didn't have my number."

It made her stomach turn, but Edie couldn't help but think of Mac. If his situation with Kat had been different, if he'd known she was pregnant, would he have done the same thing? Would he have called her, again and again, to talk about the future?

"*. . . somehow make a life for us. For the three of us.*"

She shelved the words in her mind—the words from Kat's letter—but they felt embedded in the very folds of her brain.

After the allotted half-hour counseling session plus an extra twenty or so minutes for the interview, Cynthia's door opened and Riley walked out first. When she spotted Edie, her wide, genuine smile was startling. Of course, Riley bit it back, but in that blink of time, Edie felt like she had seen something real, some piece of the authentic Riley she usually kept hidden.

Cynthia followed Riley out and put her hand on Riley's shoulder. "Say hello to our new office assistant." She didn't even try to hide the pride in her smile. "She made quite a case for herself in there. She even has some ideas for how to spiff up the waiting room and make the check-in process smoother."

"Really?" Edie tried to hide her surprise and instead grinned at Riley, who glanced down and tucked her hair behind her ears.

"Our office manager's maternity leave goes through the end of the year, right around when you'll be having your little one. With both of you being new mothers, it might actually work out well with both of you working here part time. It'll give you each time at home with your babies, plus give us the full-time coverage we need here."

"That's great," Edie said, her eyes on Riley. End of the year? Time at home with the baby? She'd been thinking of this job as temporary, just a couple months until Riley had the baby and things went back to normal. Then again, she supposed *normal* was no longer part of their vernacular. "Congratulations, Riley."

Her face still held remnants of that wide smile, though she tried hard to keep it under wraps.

Cynthia propped her hands on her hips. "It's a reason to celebrate if I've ever heard one. You two go do something special."

Something special? Edie glanced back at Cynthia and she winked at her.

Following Riley down the hall on the way back to the front door, Edie realized it was up to them. If they didn't mark the occasion—this young woman showing some spunk and ingenuity and getting herself a job—no one else would.

On the way home Edie swung by Target so Riley could pick out some maternity clothes. She said her own clothes were fine, but Edie reminded her that while her belly and chest would continue to grow, her clothes wouldn't. And she couldn't start a new job with clothes that barely fit her.

Riley finally caved just before the turn, and as they browsed the aisles of stretchy shirts and cropped leggings, nursing bras and elastic-waist pants, she ran her hands across the fabrics, scrutinizing everything. Finally she took two shirts and a pair of shorts off the rack.

"You need more than that," Edie said. "If you won't pick it out, I'll grab things for you. I don't know about you, but I know Avery would hate that."

Riley lifted her eyebrows. "Actually I'd love that. I hate shopping."

"Hmm." Edie walked to the opposite side of a rack of long flowy skirts with wide-panel waistbands. "That makes two of us. I don't know where Avery gets her love of shopping." She stopped. "Wait, yes I do. She gets it from my mom."

Riley flipped through another couple of racks, and when she finished, they had four shirts, two pairs of leggings, a skirt, and a couple adjustable size bras. After a detour through the toiletry section and a quick foray into the freezer section when Riley made a stop in the restroom, they were finally on their way home.

When they pulled into the driveway, Edie reached for the door handle, but Riley stayed put. "Why are you being so nice to me?" she asked quietly. "Of all people, you should hate me."

"I don't hate you."

"I know. That's what's so weird. You should." She turned her face toward the window. "My mom didn't always make the best choices. And my dad—Mac—I think he got caught up in it all."

Edie was quiet for a moment, sifting her own heart and waiting to see what remained. "I can't answer that for him. But your mom? She'll always be where you started. She'll always be your home base. I think if looking back hurts, maybe you should try to keep your eyes forward. See what's just around the bend."

"Is that what you're doing? Just waiting to see what's coming?"

Edie breathed in deep. "Yeah. I guess I am."

After their dinner that night, Edie pulled out the small cake she'd picked up from Target when Riley wasn't looking. *Congratulations* swirled across the top in pink icing, and the inside was layered with chocolate and vanilla.

"You didn't have to do this," Riley said quietly as Edie set the cake on the table in front of her.

"I didn't do it because I had to. I did it because a new job is a reason to celebrate. Remember?"

She lifted her gaze to Edie. "Thank you."

"You're welcome." Above Riley's head, Mac caught Edie's gaze and smiled, gratitude and fatigue deepening the lines on his face. She smiled back, content in the moment to bathe in his happiness, but then she remembered. And she hated the pall that hung between them, all around them. She hated the reasons for it—Kat, Mac's choices, his omissions. As for the consequence—Riley—Edie found herself softening to her with each passing moment.

She pulled the plastic covering off the cake while Avery grabbed small plates from the cabinet. Mac leaned in toward Riley. "I'm really proud of you."

The look on Riley's face was the look a daughter only has for her father, one Edie had seen many times between Mac and Avery. And the fact that he'd showered Riley with that same unabashed pride filled Edie's heart with both affection and loss.

Thomas drummed his fingers on the table. "Yep, it's awesome. You'll do great. Now who's gonna cut this cake?"

CHAPTER 32

EDIE

Present Day

Edie knew Graham had arrived in their offices by the sound of Laura Lou's voice. Coated in sugar, her tone wasn't one she'd use to talk to any of the other designers or assistants. Not even Turner would pull this amount of sweetness from her, and the Kennedys weren't scheduled to arrive for another twenty minutes.

When the knock sounded at her door, Edie slid her feet back into her shoes and stood just as Laura Lou opened the door. Graham stood behind her, two drawing tubes under his arm.

"Look who the cat dragged in," Laura Lou cooed.

Graham stepped around her into the room, his face showing equal measures of wariness and humor. Edie held back her smile.

"Graham, Edie's shown me what you've cooked up for the Kennedys," Laura Lou said. "The house is going to be a stunner."

"Thank you. It wasn't just me though. I did the initial structural drawings, but Edie added her own touches. They're what made this whole thing really gel. Without her, it'd just be a big house. She's making it a home."

Edie caught his eye and smiled.

"We're a good team," he said.

"Apparently so." Laura Lou gave Edie a meaningful nod before she excused herself.

Edie and Graham inspected the drawings one more time, double-checking everything. She made sure everything in her binder was in place and ready to go, and just as they finished, the Kennedys arrived. Once the four of them were seated around the coffee table in the corner of Edie's office, Graham pulled out the drawings and spread them on the table one by one. They'd planned beforehand for him to go over most of the details on these drawings, and as he did, he answered all their questions about everything from ceiling height and siding material to outdoor lighting and property lines.

When the Kennedys had taken it all in, Edie pulled out the binder of textures, colors, and finishes she'd compiled to make the presentation come alive. She placed a few small pieces of cedar shake on the roof area, fanned a few paint color chips and small seagrass rug squares in the living areas, and set out samples of unlacquered brass, polished nickel, Carrara marble, and limestone, though not of the fossilized variety.

Marigold crossed her legs and leaned forward, studying the drawings and finishes, one high-heeled foot bopping up and down. Next to her, Turner was her exact opposite. Settled back into his chair, one ankle propped over the other knee exposing another wildly printed sock—this time pink and orange stripes—he was the picture of relaxation.

"I love it," he said with a grin. "Every blasted bit of it. You've outdone yourselves." He set his hand on his wife's back. "Mari? Thoughts?"

Marigold's foot ceased its rapid movement, and she pointed a french-manicured finger toward the marble. "That won't work."

"Okay."

"I drink red wine, and there's no way I'll have marble—white, gray, or otherwise—in my kitchen."

"We can work around that."

She sat back and smiled like a cat basking in the sun. "Then I say, when can we start?"

Edie gave them the names of three contractors she'd worked with and told them the one she'd recommend over the others. "He's pricey, but he'll be worth it."

"Done," Turner said. "Let's get him. Don't worry too much about the number."

Edie glanced at Graham as she jotted down the note in her planner. "Yes, sir."

After shaking hands and promising to call with more information soon, Turner and Marigold walked out, escorted by a chipper Laura Lou.

Graham sat back down and exhaled. "I think congratulations are in order."

"I'd say so. For both of us."

"You know, when I present drawings to clients, I typically don't include drawer pulls and countertop samples in my presentations. I think it adds a little something."

Edie laughed. "Don't make fun, mister. It may have gotten us the job."

"I'm actually not kidding. I loved being able to show them a more complete picture. Not just what the outside will look like but an idea of the inside too. I think it's a much better way to present."

"I agree. I think they would have said yes to your drawings even without the details, but it was fun. Doing all this with you."

Graham held her gaze a moment and her cheeks warmed under his scrutiny. When Laura Lou tapped her nails on the door, Edie was relieved to have something else to focus on.

"So." Her perfectly penciled eyebrows arched up. "How did it go?"

"It was great," Graham said. "They loved it."

"Well, how can they not love it when it comes from you?"

She crossed the room and stood next to Graham, glancing down at him adoringly. Edie looked straight at Graham and made a gagging motion with her finger.

"The two of you obviously work well together," she said. "I saw it the other day when you were both in here poring over the drawings. I know I speak for Edie, too, when I say we'd love to be able to do more work with you, Graham."

"Sounds good to me. As long as I get to work with Edie, I'm in."

Laura Lou laughed and patted his shoulder. "I'll be in touch, okay?"

Finally he focused on Laura Lou. "Yes, ma'am."

When she was gone, Graham leaned forward and braced his elbows against his knees. "Why do you work with her?"

"She's the best designer in town."

"I highly doubt that."

"Graham, she's been designing houses for longer than I've been able to vote. She's really good at what she does. Ask *Traditional Home. Veranda. Southern Living.*"

"She's like every other designer I know. If you put one of her houses up next to a house designed by any other popular designer today, you wouldn't be able to tell them apart. Yours are different. You have your own style, your own look. You don't follow trends; you don't defer to what's hot right now." He stared at Edie, then grinned. "You don't need her."

"What are you talking about?" She gave a small laugh as that now-familiar flutter of nerves rippled again in her stomach.

"Everett and Yeager, remember?"

"I remember," she said quietly.

"It's still on the table. Though your name would be different, of course."

"You're not serious."

"I am. Yeager Swan, Swan Yeager, I don't care. Either way works for me." Edie opened her mouth in a retort, but he cut her off. "Laura Lou is right. We do work well together. And who wouldn't want to hire us? I'm a half-decent architect."

Edie laughed.

"And you're an amazing, in-demand designer. We'd make a heck of a team."

She leveled a stare at him. "What are you really saying to me?"

"I'm saying I want you to leave DDG so you and I can open our own firm. Just like we talked about. I want to do this with you." No smile, no teasing, no sarcasm.

Edie cleared her throat and tucked a lock of hair behind her ear. The image was so powerful, the dream she and Graham had concocted so many years ago. "I'll have to think about it." She could barely get the words out.

"Okay," he said softly. "Think about it. Let me know what you decide."

———

That night, Edie and Mac had an unexpected night alone. Thomas and Avery were spending the night at the hunting camp with Edie's dad, and at the last minute, Cynthia asked if she could take Riley out to dinner to discuss plans for revitalizing the front desk and waiting room areas of the women's center.

Edie was sitting on the back porch with the light off and her legs propped up on the coffee table, the last of the season's fireflies blinking in the darkened yard, when Mac joined her, his feet bare and an inch of whiskey in a glass.

Her mind was still flipping through mental images, random and out of order. She saw herself sitting on the rooftop terrace in New York City, writing letter after letter to Graham. She saw herself and Mac signing their names on the papers to buy their first house. She and Graham sharing a pizza in the bottom of the student union, talking about music and books and all the wild things they hoped for themselves. Mac's face when he told her about Riley.

He settled on the chair across from her, sighing as if breathing out everything he no longer wanted to carry. "I think it's time for us to really talk."

"I agree. And I have something I need to tell you." She hadn't meant to blurt it out, but she couldn't help it. The weight of what Graham had asked her pressed heavily on her shoulders. It burned like fire in her belly.

"Graham and I presented our design package to the Kennedys today."

Mac dragged his hand roughly across his face. "I can't believe we're at a point where you had something this big going on today and I didn't even know." He leaned forward on his elbows. "How'd it go?"

"They loved it."

"Really?"

She nodded.

"Edie, that's great. I'm so happy for you."

"Thanks. But that's not what I needed to tell you. Graham and I . . ." She paused and in the quick silence, she heard his breath catch. "We both really enjoyed working together on this, and he . . . well, he asked me if I wanted to team up with him."

"Team up with him? What does that mean?"

"He wants us to work together. To open our own firm."

"You and Graham."

"Yeah. We'd have more to offer clients with architecture and design services combined. And we work well together. Turner saw it, even Laura Lou saw it."

She glanced at him out of the corner of her eye. He was staring down into his glass, slowly swirling the liquid around.

"Do you think that's a good idea? You and Graham working together?"

There was something about the way he asked it, as if it seemed pre-posterous to him. A small part of her thought it sounded preposterous too, but even still, his tone aggravated her. "Why wouldn't it be a good idea? Graham's an excellent architect."

"But Edie, you've been with DDG for years. You've made a place there. Do you want to throw all that away to go into business with someone you haven't seen in decades?"

She stared at him. "You don't get it."

"What? What don't I get?"

She pressed her palms to the sides of her face as she tried to grasp the right words. "Graham is asking me to do this because he genuinely wants to work with me, but a bigger part of it is that he recognizes how stifled I am with Laura Lou. I complain about it to you, but what do you do? You take her side. Like she has her name dragged through the mud anytime her young, immature designer takes on a project."

"Edie, that's ridiculous. I've never said that. And I don't think that."

The sound of cicadas in the trees flared, all the individual noises mingling into one that drowned out everything. When it subsided, she continued, her voice calm but firm.

"You've never once encouraged me to break away from Laura Lou, and Graham takes one look at me working under her thumb and says I should leave."

"So that's what you've been waiting for—encouragement from Graham?"

"No, it has nothing to do with Graham." She swallowed the hard knot in her throat. "It's me and you and everything that's crept between us. It's me wanting to try something different and you being afraid of it."

"How different are we talking about?" He jutted his chin out. "Are we even talking about your job anymore?" He shifted his feet and gripped the armrests. "Graham Yeager pops back into your life out of nowhere, and all of a sudden you're talking about making big life changes. Seems like strange timing to me."

"I'm the one making huge life changes? You made the life change, Mac, when you decided to sleep with Kat and get her pregnant."

"You're right. I did. I can't go back and change that."

She knew she should back down, offer some grace instead of heaping coals, but she couldn't stop herself. "If you'd known, you would have left."

"If I'd known what?"

It had come to her slowly, but the idea was now a blazing truth in her mind. "If you'd known about Riley . . . if Kat had mailed you that letter . . . I know you, Mac. If you'd known she was pregnant, you would have chosen her. You wouldn't have let her raise your child on her own."

"You don't know that." Anger tinged his words, but so did fear.

"I know it and you do too. I don't know what was supposed to happen between you and Kat at the marina on your last day that summer, but it sounds like if things had worked out the way you'd wanted them to, Kat would have met you there and the two of you . . . you would have had your own family. Instead you came back to me."

He put his balled-up fists to his eyes. "What about you and Graham and the letters you sent him? I had no idea what was happening behind my back between the two of you. And now you want to work with him. As if that could possibly help make anything better between me and you."

"You're worried about Graham because I wrote him some letters?" She took a deep breath but the words kept coming, hot and angry. "Why don't you worry because I wanted to move to New York with him after graduation? Because I wanted to open up a firm with him then? If you're going to worry, worry about that."

His entire body stilled—mouth open, eyes wide, glass in one hand—and she felt her insides screech to a halt as well. She'd been worried Mac had chosen the wrong woman. That he was actually supposed to have been with Kat, marrying her and having a family with her. But what if she'd been looking at it wrong? What if *she* was the one who'd made the wrong choice? Was it possible she was supposed to have been somewhere else all this time? With someone else? Maybe even in New York with Graham, working together and having the life they'd once dreamed of?

It was too much to contemplate, but it was also too much to ignore.

Avery. Thomas. Their life.

Her dreams. Plans. Desires.

Slowly Mac set the glass on the table next to him and sat back in his chair. When he spoke, his words were so low she could barely hear him. "You wanted to go to New York with Graham?"

"Yeah. I considered it. But I didn't, Mac. I made the choice to stay with you. *For* you. But you left out a key piece of the puzzle when you neglected to tell me about Kat. So I made my decision—my choice between the two of you—based on a lie. A lie of omission but still a lie." That other life shone again in her mind, the one she might have had if she'd taken the other path.

"And if I'd told you about Kat, you would have chosen Graham," he said as if realizing the possibility for the first time, just as Edie was. "You would have moved to New York. Everything would be different."

She shrugged. "There's no way to know. No way to know what either of us would have done if we'd known everything. If we'd known the whole truth."

They sat in silence for several long moments. A dog barked next door, an answering bark came from farther down the road, then more silence. What else was there to say? Where did they go from here?

Then Mac stood, crossed the floor of the porch, and sat next to her.

They didn't turn to each other but sat side by side, both staring out into the darkened yard. "You're right, you know. You're absolutely right. I didn't give you all the facts, and because of that, you made your choice based on half-truths." He paused. "So I'm going to tell you everything."

"Mac." Edie sighed. "We broke up, you met a girl, and you slept with her. Then you came back to school and we got back together. I get it."

"No, you don't. Yes, I met someone and yes, I slept with her, which is so hard for me to say to you. But the reason it happened . . . Edie, I was under so much pressure at that point in my life. A lot of it came from my dad, but I see now that I caused a lot of it on my own. I had this need to be perfect in everything—my grades, my reputation with professors, my friendships. My relationship with you."

"Why didn't you tell me any of that? You could have told me. I would have understood."

"You wouldn't have understood. Not really. I know you would have tried to, but I didn't want you to think I was weak. That I couldn't stand up under the pressure."

"I didn't put any of that pressure on you, did I?"

"No, you really didn't. I was just scared I was going to mess it all up. Mess everything up. And being away from all that stress that summer—Edie, it was incredible." He turned to her. "I'm sorry to say that to you, but despite everything that happened, I'm still thankful I had that chance to be on my own. To decide for myself what I really wanted."

"What was that?"

"It was you. This life we have now. Up until then it felt like everyone had told me what my future would look like. I'd go into medicine just like my dad, I'd marry my girlfriend, and we'd have a nice life together. But after those handful of months, I could honestly say that was exactly what I wanted. I wanted you, I wanted to be a doctor, and I wanted a family. With you. It was a relief to know for sure.

"A few weeks after school started—after you and I had come back together—Kat did come to my apartment."

She knew it—Kat's letter had told her as much—but it still hurt to hear him say it.

"We just talked for a few minutes, then she left. I always wondered about that. Why she came, if she'd said what she meant to say. But I was so happy with you. I've thought over the years about how you deserved to know the truth, but I always came back to the fact that it would destroy you, and I never wanted to hurt you. It almost felt like what happened with Kat all those years ago didn't matter anymore. But I know it mattered. It *does* matter. And you deserve to know it all."

He sighed and leaned forward onto his elbows. Looked back at her over his shoulder. "That's it. That's everything. I love you and I don't want anyone else. But you are free to make the decision you need to make. The decision you should have been allowed to make after that summer."

"It's not the same now," she whispered. "We have kids. We have a life."

"You're right. It's different now. And infinitely more complicated. But you do have a choice. And it's yours to make." He reached over and took her hand, and her fingertips curled around his out of habit. He squeezed her hand gently between both of his, the pressure of their fingers on each other's skin timid and warm. "You can take as long as you need."

He stood then, pulled his hand from hers, and left the porch. As he retreated, the cicadas kicked up, their music swelling in the trees, then subsided again, leaving her alone in the silence.

CHAPTER 33

EDIE

Summer 2000

"Do you know his phone number?" Judith asked.

Edie nodded, her head swimming with the movement. "I do."

Judith pointed toward a phone booth in the back of the café. It was bright red and encased in glass walls, like ones on a street corner in England. "I say call him." When Edie didn't answer, Judith pulled quarters out of her wallet and slapped them onto the table.

Edie stared at her friend a long moment, then stood from the table. Judith scrunched her nose and raised her closed fists in a cheer. "Go! Do it!"

Edie turned toward the phone booth, then paused and glanced back at her friend. "What do I say?"

"You're the one who shares a history with him, not me."

Edie stood still, chewing on her bottom lip.

"Truth or ignorance, remember?" Judith held her hands out in front of her. Lifted one up, then the other, as if she were weighing Edie's options. "You either choose to know or you choose to stay in the dark. And honey, if you remember, you already chose truth tonight."

Edie thought of the tart and tangy strawberry Bellini. "But you said the truth can be hard to handle. And anyway, isn't ignorance supposed to be bliss?"

Judith rolled her eyes, then motioned for Edie to turn around. "Go. Now. Before I call us a cab and you lose your chance to do anything."

With an exasperated sigh, Edie strode to the back of the diner, deposited her quarters, punched the numbers, and pulled the glass door closed behind her. The air in the booth smelled faintly of cigarette smoke, and a wad of green gum was stuck to the glass just above the phone.

"Hello?" Graham's voice both ratcheted up the tension she felt and soothed it at the same time.

"Hey. It's me." She swallowed. "It's Edie."

His laugh was quiet. "I know your voice, Edie."

"Sorry to call so late. It's probably, what, close to midnight?" She held her watch in front of her eyes. It was 11:37.

"It's just a little past ten thirty here. And it's fine. I'm awake."

"It's my birthday, you know."

"I do know." She heard the smile in his voice. "Happy birthday."

"It's a big one. I'm twenty-one now."

"It's a big responsibility. Think you're ready for it?"

"I'm ready."

Neither of them spoke for a moment. Despite the fact that Edie had been the one to dial the numbers, she wanted Graham to take charge. To tell her what she needed to know. She thought of his last letter to her, his concern that his words—words about them, words about the future—had made her nervous.

"Have you been having—?" he began, just as she blurted out, "Why have we never dated?"

"What?" he asked. Then said again louder, "What?"

She'd startled him. She'd startled herself. The question had been traveling between her brain and her mouth for a while, much longer in fact than this one New York City night in which she felt both alive and exhilarated. Bold and nervous. She'd wondered about Graham often. Every time they sat on Graham's couch together, listening to Counting Crows or

David Gray or The Cure while Mac studied. Anytime the three of them sat together on Monday nights for pizza in the basement of the student union on campus. At night when she couldn't sleep, she'd toss in her slim dorm room bed, her mind spinning with thoughts of the future. Why had Mac always been the obvious choice and Graham the wrong one?

And now her question was out.

"Edie, what?" Graham reminded her that he hadn't answered the question. "Are you drunk?"

"Why has it always been me and Mac? Why have you never tried anything with me? We're always together. We get along so well. We laugh at the same things." She exhaled and pushed her hair back from her face. "Why have you never asked me out? Did you never feel anything about me? Even at the beginning?"

Edie pinched her lips together to cut off the flow of words. Silence buzzed in the air between them. Across the café, the door opened and a group of women burst in, all laughter and wide smiles. Finally he let out a little groan. "You've been drinking, Edie."

"What does that matter? It doesn't change what I'm thinking."

"Actually, it kind of does. I don't think you mean all this."

"Don't tell me what I mean. I'm saying what I mean. I've wanted to ask you this for a long time." She clamped her eyes closed and forced the words out. "I see you watching me sometimes. It's like you're studying me, but then you look away so quickly, I always think I've imagined it. But it's not my imagination, is it?" She said it so low it was almost a whisper. "You said in your letter you'd build a future with me. You—"

"Edie, stop. Don't do this now." The last three words were slow as syrup.

"Why not?" Her head was pounding now. This was not the way she'd thought the conversation would go. "Judith told me I had to pick truth or ignorance, and I'm picking truth, Graham. I want to know the truth. I want to know if you've ever thought of me as . . . as more than a friend. As more than your best friend's girlfriend."

"You know you're more to me than that. You're *my* friend. Not just Mac's girlfriend."

"I'm not Mac's girlfriend."

He sighed. "I know that. Trust me, I know."

"Just tell me the truth. You've never felt anything real for me. It's fine. I can handle it."

"Edie, it's not that. I just—I can't have this conversation with you right now."

"Fine. Consider it over."

"Edie."

Her name on his lips—a whisper, urgent and anguished—made her eyes fill with tears. She swiped at them, angry that her emotions were betraying her. When she was sure her voice wouldn't tremble, she cleared her throat. "I should go. I need to get to bed anyway."

"Wait, can I—?"

"Bye, Graham."

Back at the table, Judith was paying for their food and drinks. "No, you're not paying for me." Edie stood by the table and willed her voice to sound cheerful.

"Of course I am. It's your birthday." Judith signed the receipt, then stood and took Edie by the shoulders. "Did the red pill work? Did you find out what you needed to know?"

Edie nodded. "I did."

Judith's eyebrows arched up. "Good news or bad?"

Edie shrugged. "Neither. Just the truth."

Judith slung her arm around Edie, and they left the café and found a cab to take them back uptown. Edie watched as the city slid by, the lights and doorways and cars and bars—everyone going about their business in a city that never slept.

Maybe this wasn't the place for her, after all. Maybe she'd overshot, thinking she could stake a claim on this city and call it her own. What gave her the right to claim anything or anyone? She didn't have Mac, she didn't have Graham. All she had was herself and a heart that was torn in two.

"Who's it going to be?" Judith tilted her head back, her voice midnight tired. "Mac or Graham?"

In the darkness of the car, shadows swam over Judith's face and her curly red hair. "Does it have to be either one?"

"Absolutely not."

Edie turned her face back to the window. "Is it wrong to want someone to fight for me? I don't mean *fight* fight. Just to want me—to want *us*—bad enough to do something about it. To be up-front and honest and put it all on the line."

Judith was quiet a long moment. "I don't think it's a bad thing to want that. You just can't lose yourself in it. Don't forget about what *you* want."

"What if I don't know what I want?"

Judith squeezed Edie's arm. "You'll figure it out. Somehow."

Edie rolled her window all the way down and Judith did the same. The two women stuck their arms out the windows, letting in the warm breeze and airing out the New York City night.

CHAPTER 34

EDIE

Present Day

Edie stood outside the little yellow house for what felt like days. She hadn't been there in so long, but she still knew the way by heart: down Scenic Highway 98, past the Grand Hotel, past the turn toward the tennis club. Just beyond the thick pine tree with the knee-high notch was the hand-lettered sign bearing the name Casting Off, though the letters were long faded. The driveway was nearly obscured by overgrowth, but she turned in anyway, sure it was the right place.

For weeks now she'd been mostly going through the motions at home—dropping waffles in the toaster, making sandwiches, browning meat for spaghetti. Wiping counters, checking on homework. Shower, sleep, repeat. She'd been operating at half power since this whole thing started, trying to keep the kids from seeing all that had transpired, or deteriorated, between them. On the outside she probably seemed normal, but inside she was a dry leaf. One more gust and she'd blow away entirely. But she had choices to make—about life, about work, about the future. And she was still working to get all the information she needed to chart her course.

She took the steps two at a time, knocked on the door, and waited to hear footsteps. Instead she heard barking, but it wasn't coming from inside. She peered around the side of the house and there was Graham, down on the sandy shore, tossing a ball to a big yellow Lab who high-stepped through the shallow, sun-dappled water.

She watched them a moment, then opened the door to the screened porch and took a seat in one of the rocking chairs. The arms were worn smooth by time and touch, and the bottom was covered in a flat, flowered cushion. She sat there, slowly rocking back and forth, until Graham sent the ball soaring toward the house and the dog jumped out of the water, shook the droplets from his fur, and raced up the dock.

The dog found her first. With the ball in his mouth, he nosed open the screen door, dropped the ball at her feet, and panted, grinning until she patted his head.

"Simon," Graham called on his way up the wharf. "Where'd you go, boy?" He was brushing sand and dirt off his legs and hadn't noticed her yet. She took him in as much as she could from the privacy of her hidden spot.

Finally he looked up and his gaze met hers. Confusion crossed his face, then a smile. He opened the door and Simon swiveled his head toward Graham.

"You'll be covered in slobber if you're not careful," Graham said. "The happier he gets, the more he slobbers." He picked up the wet ball and tossed it out the door, then wiped his hand back and forth against his shorts. "And visitors make him very happy."

She scratched Simon's ear and a long, gooey string dribbled from his mouth.

"See what I mean?" Graham thumped the dog on the behind. "Simon. Give her some space." Simon stood and backed up, then sat at Graham's feet. Graham reached down and scratched his head, though his eyes were on Edie. "Did I forget about a meeting or something?"

She shook her head. "No meeting."

"Okay." He waited for an explanation, and when she didn't give him one, he scratched Simon again. "Well then." He glanced down at his wet clothes. "If you don't mind, I'm going to get cleaned up. I won't be long. Make yourself at home." He left the door open when he went in.

Through the screen door, she could hear him walking around inside, from the kitchen to the den, then deeper into the house where the two small bedrooms were. Simon stood guard at the door, swiveling his head from the door to Edie, as if unsure who he should keep his eye on.

A few minutes later Graham walked back out onto the porch wearing a clean pair of beaten-up khaki shorts and a short-sleeve button-down shirt. His dark hair was wet and she could see brush marks in it. He sat in the rocking chair next to her and crossed one ankle over his other knee. Simon plopped his chin on Graham's thigh.

She leaned her head against the back of the chair. A moment passed before either of them spoke.

"Are things at home going okay?"

"Kat wrote Mac a letter." She felt him turn and stare at her. "She never mailed it. Riley found it and gave it to Mac the first day she got here."

Graham stood abruptly and walked inside. A moment later he came back out holding two beer bottles. He opened one and handed it to Edie, then opened the second and sat back down.

"We're day drinking?" she asked, one eye on the bottle.

"Thought it might help." He took a long swig, then she did the same. The chill that rushed down her throat made her shiver in the afternoon warmth.

"How'd you find out about the letter?"

"I found it in our bedroom the morning you and I had lunch."

"Ah. That's why you were so distracted. Makes sense. The letter held some surprises?"

"A few. One of them being that she came to see him in Birmingham after that summer. She came in September. Mac and I were back together by then." Graham nodded but didn't speak. She pressed at her eyebrows with her fingers. "If you knew about her, why'd you stay quiet? Why didn't you tell me anything?"

"Mac didn't want to tell you. He said it didn't matter that she'd come and that he'd already made up his mind. He was with you. He wanted to be with you. I thought you needed to know but . . ." He shrugged. "It wasn't my place. And he didn't want to hurt you."

"Yeah. That's what he said."

"For what it's worth, I didn't want to hurt you either. That's why I abandoned ship. Moved out and moved on."

"Because you were mad at him?"

"No—well, yeah, a little. But I knew if I stayed—if our friendship went on as it always had—I would have told you."

"What would have been so bad about that? You said you thought I needed to know."

"It wasn't my story to tell. Plus, it had all gotten tangled up with how I felt and I worried if I told you, it wouldn't be for the right reasons."

"Wait." She held up her hand. "What do you mean, how you felt? And if there were right reasons, what would be the wrong ones?"

Graham stared at her. "Come on, Edie. We're adults; we're long past all that kid stuff. Let's just be honest with each other for once. You can't tell me you didn't know how I felt about you back then."

"How you felt?" That skinny phone booth and Judith waiting for her at the table, her heart throbbing in her chest, her headache the following morning. She swallowed hard. "You laughed at me. On the phone, when I called you from New York."

"On your birthday? That's because you were three sheets to the wind. Maybe more."

"No, I wasn't. I put myself—my heart—on the line for you. I was asking how you felt about me, if you'd ever felt anything for me, and you laughed and told me I didn't mean it."

"What was I supposed to do? Tell you I was in love with you?"

In the stunned silence that followed Graham's words, Simon lifted his head and gave a great big bark, then nosed the screen door open, bounded down the front steps, and charged through the grass toward the water. Two seagulls cackled and flew away at his approach.

Graham stood and walked to the other end of the porch. Edie sat, frozen in place. When she could no longer take the silence, she spoke to his back. "Were you? In love with me?"

He clasped his hands together on top of his head, his gaze out toward the water. The bottom edge of his shirt lifted, revealing a stretch of pale skin. She turned her head away.

"I don't know. Maybe? Does it matter now?"

"Of course it does."

Finally he turned back and paced to the other side of the porch. "Really? All these years later, it matters to you how I felt?"

"Yes. Graham, you were so important to me." Even as she said the words, she realized how paltry they sounded. "When you left us, it hurt for a long time. You told me that day on the quad it was because you couldn't be our third wheel anymore, but part of me wondered if you pulled back because of what I'd said on the phone. If I'd crossed a line I shouldn't have crossed and . . ." She shrugged. "I ruined the friendship."

"It wasn't you."

She leaned her head into her hands. "This is such a mess. The three of us had this great friendship, and it all broke down because we weren't honest with each other." She lifted her head. "Don't you see? I didn't know how you felt about me, Mac didn't know all the things I used to think—or wonder—about me and you and that crazy dream to work in New York together. I never knew about Kat and what happened with them that summer. He never even told me about the pressure he was feeling— from all sides—which is what drove him to Kat in the first place. We all kept our truths from each other and look where it got us. Almost twenty years later and we're only just now realizing how tangled it really was. Still is."

He sat down heavily in the rocking chair next to her, then gently pushed off with his foot, sending his chair back and forth. "You're right. About all of it. Well, except for the New York thing. I don't think that dream was crazy."

She glanced at him, but he kept his gaze out toward the scrubby grass where Simon sat stock-still watching the water lap the shore. "Did you tell Mac about our letters? The ones we wrote back and forth that summer?"

He pulled his gaze toward her. "No. Of course not. Those letters were a treasure." He paused. "Mac did read one though. I left it out by accident and he picked it up. I never would have shared that with him on purpose. Those were between you and me."

Edie nodded.

"Bottom line is, I'm sorry everything has happened the way it has. I'm sorry you're having to deal with the fallout of Kat, and I'm sorry Mac never told you. I'm sorry *I* never told you. I'm sorry I wasn't honest with you about everything."

"I'm sorry too."

In the stillness they rocked.

"Why'd you come here?" The gentleness in his voice eased what could have been a jab. Instead he sounded genuinely curious. As Edie was.

"I'm not sure. I just got in the car and this is where I ended up."

"Does Mac know where you are?"

She hesitated, then shook her head. "He was planning to take the kids out for a late lunch. I said I needed to work."

"So we're working today?"

"I guess so."

The edge of his mouth tweaked up. "How do you feel about a walk? We could head up toward the Kennedys' property. Now that the full plans are in place, we can imagine it in all its glory."

"That sounds great."

They stood and started for the door to the porch, but he stopped and backtracked into the house. He returned a moment later with two more drinks. "One for the road?"

The stretch of coastline from Graham's house all the way up to the Grand Hotel was lined with a wooden walkway that hugged the shore and cruised under tree canopies. And late in the afternoon like this, it was dotted with families, kids on bikes, and couples hand in hand. Simon trotted ahead of them, sniffing everyone and everything.

As they walked they pointed out various houses belonging to people they'd known in high school, now grown with their own families. They ambled easily along memory lane, reaching back in their minds and pulling out only the best memories, the ones that occurred before the three of them split up—she and Mac on one side, Graham alone on the other.

By the time they got to Turner and Marigold's property, Edie felt loose and light. Maybe it was the view of the water, maybe it was the scent—wet sand, pine, fragrant gardenias, and confederate jasmine—or maybe it was Graham. Her friend, her ally. It had been so long since she'd enjoyed him. So long since she'd thought about the fact that they'd once called each other their soul mates. The person who stirred something deep inside that they'd never been able to name. Something that not even Mac had been able to touch.

They stood on the wooden path in front of the Kennedys' stretch of sand and grass littered with faint remains of the house that had stood there long ago—a small pile of bricks here, a few feet of crumbling foundation there. He stood close to her and reached his hand out, and with his finger in the air, he drew the house.

She followed the end of his finger, imagining the house coming to life where he pointed. The modest roofline, the deep porch, the casement windows she'd added during their discussion, copper gutters and flashing, a paver pathway winding through the front lawn and leading out to the wharf.

He dropped his arm and shoved his hands in his pockets. "I like my dad's house and all, but this place is going to be fantastic."

"Sure is." She bumped her shoulder to his arm. "Thanks to us."

He glanced down at her and bumped her back. "Thanks to us."

He held her gaze and she couldn't tear her eyes away. They were so close—too close—but she felt rooted in place. A gleeful shriek from a child down the walkway pulled them back to reality. Edie glanced down and tucked her hair behind her ears as Graham took a step back. Finally he smiled. "Ready to head back?"

On the way to his house, he pointed out toward the water. "Middle Bay Lighthouse is about twenty miles that way. You ever seen it?"

"Just in pictures. Never up close."

"I'll have to take you out there sometime." The comment was casual, as easy as the breeze. He glanced at her quickly as if realizing what he'd said. The absurdity that there'd be a situation where they'd be alone together, where a casual boat ride would be in order.

Though they were alone together now. However it was that they got here.

He cleared his throat. "Kids used to take their boats out there and goad each other into climbing the metal supports and spending the night in the house up top."

"You're kidding. Did you ever do it?"

The corner of his mouth lifted into a half smile—wistful, a little sad. "Just once."

Simon had run ahead during the walk, disappearing around a gentle curve in the path, and as they approached Graham's house, he ran to meet them, panting and barking like they'd been gone for days. Graham ruffled the fur on Simon's head, then knelt to talk quietly to him. Edie took a few steps away and turned to face the sun slowly descending toward the faraway Mobile shore. A few moments later, she sensed his presence next to her.

"I guess you'll be needing to head home soon."

There was no loaded expectation in the comment. No hope or judgment. Just a statement of fact. And he was right. She should have said good-bye, walked to her car, and driven back home. But being away from the epicenter of everything that had happened felt so very good. She felt relaxed and free, and just the thought of pulling up in her driveway, of facing Mac and likely having another lengthy, difficult discussion, sent waves of nerves and dread through her stomach.

She knew she shouldn't stay, but she didn't want to go.

She turned toward him. His dark hair, his eyes that same sparkling blue. One side of his collar had turned up against his neck, and the breeze off the bay fluttered it gently. Edie thought of what he'd said earlier. *What was I supposed to do? Tell you I was in love with you?*

He stuck his hands in his back pockets. "Then again . . ." He paused, as if weighing the wisdom of whatever was about to come out of his mouth. A lazy grin crossed his face. "I did go fishing this morning. I could make you a pretty good dinner."

With the smell of pan-fried trout and roasted asparagus filling the kitchen, Edie walked out the back door into the driveway to call Mac.

This is fine.

This is fine.

She kept repeating it to herself, though she wasn't sure if it was because she fully believed it or because she hoped saying the words would make it so. How was this chaotic time in her life tied so inextricably to that one summer so long ago? She remembered, just before she departed for New York, sitting in the airport telling herself it was fine that she was writing Graham a postcard instead of Mac. And here she was, telling herself it was fine all over again.

Except this time, it wasn't writing a postcard. It was sharing a meal, a slice of time. Maybe she should have been back home with her family, working on untangling the knots, but wrenching herself away from the beauty of this place, the simplicity of these moments, felt like too hard a thing to ask.

The sky was now streaked with rosy pink and shocking orange, and a tall-masted sailboat puttered past the end of Graham's pier. She waited for Mac to answer.

"Edie."

His voice wasn't worried or mad or annoyed. It was soft, a little relieved. A little wary. She could see him in her mind, his green eyes and the freckles on his nose. The blond hair that fuzzed on his arms, his broad shoulders, sturdy and steady.

"Hey," she breathed. "I'm sorry I've been gone so long. How is it there?"

"We're fine. Good, actually. Where are you?"

She paused. She couldn't tell him. She didn't want to lie to him. Stuck in the middle, she avoided the question altogether. "I just need to have a little space right now. I'm fine. Really. I'll talk to you tomorrow." She hadn't meant to say it. It hadn't crossed her mind that she'd actually not return home tonight, but once it was out, she couldn't retract it.

"Wait, you're not—are you coming home?"

What was I thinking? "Mac, I . . . I just need a minute. Okay?"

In the silence that followed, a wave of sadness nearly toppled her. She swallowed hard and tried to withstand its force. "Please kiss the kids for me."

The kids. She didn't specify which ones, but Mac could sort that out. She squeezed her eyes closed against the image of her family turning in for the evening without her.

Inside the house was just as Edie remembered it. Wooden beams crossed the ceiling of the main living area, and one end of the old, scratched-up dining table was covered in a jigsaw puzzle. Any walls not full of windows were lined with shelves or pieces of antique furniture. Books were everywhere—on the shelves, stacked on the floor, covering a bench under a window. Graham's wide drafting table was set up in the corner.

When she walked in the kitchen, Graham was plating the food, the scent rich and savory. He glanced at the phone in her hand, but instead of commenting on her call, he gestured to an iron wine rack against the wall. "I have a good bottle of red over there. You mind pouring us two glasses?"

With the food and wine ready, she followed him out to the porch, where they balanced their plates on their knees and perched their wineglasses on the small table between the two rocking chairs. In front of them the sun sliding into the water cast the bay in brilliant golden orange. Tall pine trees around the house swayed in the breeze, and Simon dozed at Graham's feet.

As they ate they talked about some of Edie's favorite design projects and various houses Graham had built as he moved from place to place.

"You've been all over. You started out in New York, right?"

"Yep. I worked for a firm in Tribeca." He took a bite of fish and chewed slowly. "You know I went up there because of you?"

"What?"

He smiled. "Do you remember all the plans we talked about? The double office, the fancy espresso maker in the back . . ."

"Sure I do. You said we wouldn't need it because we'd have an assistant to get coffee for us."

He laughed. "That's right. We'd be living the high life." His face fell a little and he reached for his wineglass. "It was a crazy dream, just like you said, but I couldn't stop thinking about it. Even after you and Mac were back together. I thought maybe . . . I don't know. That you'd remember those plans. And you'd decide to do it. To move back."

"And that's why you went?"

He rubbed his cheek. "I was going anyway. I'd gotten a job that was too good to pass up. But the off chance you might end up there too, well, it made the decision an easy one."

Graham wiped his mouth with his napkin. "I'd been up there a few weeks when Mac called to tell me he'd proposed and you said yes. We hadn't talked since the day I moved out of the apartment, and at first I thought he was calling to, I don't know, gloat or something. Like, 'I got the girl.' But then he asked me to be his best man."

She tried to imagine what it must have felt like, Graham's feelings caught up in the web the three of them had created, then being asked to stand next to Mac and her while they promised themselves to each other.

"I told Mac he needed to pick someone else."

Her heart broke a little for the young kids they were then, trying to figure out the ways of their hearts.

"Mac told me he'd asked you. He said you couldn't make it because of work. At the time I thought it was a weak excuse."

"It would have been if that was the excuse I'd given him. But I didn't. I just said I couldn't do it. I wanted to. I missed the hell out of both of you. Maybe it was selfish; maybe it was petty. But I couldn't stand and watch it. My heart couldn't take it."

"Because of what you knew about Kat?"

His gaze met hers. "That's some of it."

She didn't ask about the rest. She couldn't.

"But that New York pipe dream. We can still make it happen, you know. And we don't even have to go to New York to do it. We can do it right here."

She pushed back on her foot and rocked gently. "I know we could. I'm still thinking."

"Good."

After dinner they cleaned the kitchen, scraping the pans and filling the tiny dishwasher, then Graham pulled out two chairs at the dining table. He nodded toward the puzzle. "How good are you?"

She lifted a shoulder as she sat. "I don't know. I like them. What's the criteria for being good?"

"Oh, you'll see as soon as I get started. I'm an expert puzzler."

She laughed. "Is that so?"

"Absolutely."

"And just how long has this puzzle been sitting here half finished?"

"I reserve the right not to answer that question." He scooted his chair in and ran his hands over the pieces. "Actually my dad left this here."

Her smile faded. "Really?"

He nodded. Picked up a piece and set it back down.

"You sure you want to put it together? It feels a little sacred or something."

"I'm pretty sure nothing would make him happier than to know Edie Everett was sitting at his table helping to put this puzzle together."

Edie Everett. She'd been thinking a lot about her lately. And it felt good. Like she was getting reacquainted with someone she'd been missing for a long time. Just like Graham.

It was late when they finally set the last piece. Just as they sat back from their masterpiece—a map of Mobile Bay stretching down to the Gulf of Mexico—her phone buzzed with a text. Mac.

Going to sleep. I know you need to work through all this. I'll give you whatever space you need. But please come home soon.

"Mac loves you." Graham's voice was low. On the kitchen counter the pages of a cookbook rustled in the breeze from the open window over the sink.

"How do you know?"

"I just know. Even way back then, even after Kat. Even with everything I felt, I knew Mac's love for you was different. It was all-encompassing."

"It must not have been encompassing him when he was with Kat." She sighed. "Did you ever meet her?"

"Once. And just for a minute."

"It feels weird to talk about her like she's a real person. I'd rather she be this figment. An idea, not an actual person." Edie sniffed. "Her daughter sure is a real person though. *Their* daughter."

She covered her mouth with her hand and yawned. Graham watched her a moment, then stood and walked to the back. He returned and set a pillow and a blanket down on the couch. On top of the blanket was a fresh toothbrush.

She walked over to the couch and picked up the toothbrush.

"Lucky for you I had an extra." He smiled and rubbed the back of his neck. "I'd offer you the spare bedroom, but it doesn't have a bed anymore."

"The couch is perfect. Thanks."

"You're juggling a lot right now. Work, Mac, your kids, Riley—all these pieces of your life. It's a lot. And then all that talk about our old dream, all that New York stuff." He kept his eyes down, not meeting hers. "I'm probably inserting myself where I don't belong, but I just don't want you to forget about *you* in all this. What you want. What you need. Whatever that is."

He was so present, so *there* after so many years of being gone. Memories and decisions swirled in her mind until none of it made sense anymore.

"Graham." Her voice came out in a whisper. "You had so much time. So many years to tell me you . . ."

"I know."

"But you never said anything."

He squeezed his hands into fists, then stuck his hands in his pockets. Shrugged. "I know."

"Why not?"

"Would it have changed anything?" He leaned down until she met his gaze.

"I don't know."

In the silence that followed she heard a creak as the house settled. Crickets outside. The hammering of her own heart.

"I'm sorry," he finally said, before reaching out and touching her wrist. "Good night, Edie."

He turned off the light by his drafting table on his way out of the den, and other than a small lamp on the kitchen counter, the room was dark. She sat on the couch and listened as he went through his nighttime routine behind his closed bedroom door. When he was quiet, she tiptoed into the bathroom, brushed her teeth, sipped some water, and crept back to the couch. Stretching out had never felt so good, and sleep came faster than she'd thought possible.

Hours later she woke to the smell of strong coffee and sizzling bacon. They ate their breakfast on the porch, on the rockers where their time together had begun. They talked while they ate, but it wasn't about her or him. It wasn't about Mac or Kat or Riley. They talked about Simon, who darted back and forth between their legs, hoping they'd drop a tiny morsel. They talked about the bay's most recent jubilee. They talked about the Kennedys' house.

Not long after, they stood in the driveway by her car. The air was a wall of humidity, the morning shrouded in clouds. Graham scuffed his foot across the gravel. "I'm glad you came, Edie. Or I'm glad your car decided to bring you here."

She smiled. "I am too."

"Let me know when you hear from that contractor Turner wants to use." Graham's gaze still avoided her face.

"I will. I'll call you." She paused. There was so much more she could have said to him—more they could have said to each other—but at the same time, there was nothing else. They'd untangled all they could.

When he finally looked backed at her, they reached for each other at the same time. His arms circled her back and she stood on her tiptoes and tucked her chin onto his shoulder. The hug—that connection—felt like a welcome, but it also felt like good-bye.

They stayed that way until Simon pushed between them and nosed around her knees. Graham leaned down and pulled on his collar, and Simon trotted back up to the porch. Edie climbed in her car and cranked the engine, and he waved as she pulled away from the house. Behind him, Simon's tail thumped the old wooden porch.

As she drove away, she thought of all those pieces of her life Graham had mentioned last night: work, Mac, Avery, and Thomas. Riley. In an alternate world, if such things existed, maybe she and Graham would be in New York City, working and living. Maybe even loving.

But *this* was her world now. For better or worse, and regardless of their tangled past, she and Mac had built a life together, brick by brick, and that was no small thing. Graham had filled a hole in her life for a time, it was true. He had met a need she hadn't been able to meet elsewhere. But that time was past. It had to be.

Forty minutes later, Edie opened the front door of her house. Avery jumped up and ran to her, hugged her. Thomas nudged his chin toward her in greeting, as if he were sixteen years old. Riley smiled at her from the couch. And from the kitchen in the back, Mac exhaled, his sigh one of pure relief.

CHAPTER 35

MAC

Summer 2000

On his last morning at the beach, Mac woke before dawn, his stomach in knots. He'd lain in bed last night until late, thinking of all he hadn't yet said to Kat. So many thoughts and ideas had flown around in his head all summer—things he wanted to tell her, thoughts he shouldn't have been thinking, and others he needed to keep inside. He didn't know what he'd say to her today, just that he couldn't stand the thought of not seeing her again.

He was packed and ready to go by eight o'clock. Graham wasn't leaving for another few days, but Mac had scoured his bedroom and bathroom, picked up all his trash, wiped out the sink and tub, even unloaded the dishwasher for Graham, all before his friend woke up. By the time Graham trudged out of his bedroom, Mac was carrying the last of his things out to the car.

"So this is it, then." Graham sat at the kitchen table in his boxers, his hair a rumpled dark mess. Mac was struck by how much had changed over the course of their friendship—and how much had stayed the same.

"Yeah, I guess so."

"When are you heading back up to school?"

"Thursday or Friday, probably. What about you?"

"I may wait 'til Sunday."

"Pushing summer to the bitter end, huh?"

Graham shrugged. "Why not? I have no reason to rush back."

Mac thought again of Edie's letter to Graham. He'd only seen the one, though he suspected it hadn't been the only one. He wanted to ask Graham about it again, to question why his girlfriend—okay, his ex-girlfriend, but still *Edie*—was writing earnest letters to his best friend. But after all that had transpired this summer, Mac didn't have a leg to stand on. Neither one of them had been up front with their thoughts or feelings. No need to start now.

"So I'll see you back at the apartment then." Mac moved toward the door.

"Yeah. Drive safe."

Mac nodded. He paused at the door, wanting to say more to his friend, wanting to hear more. Instead he held up a hand, then closed the door behind him.

He drove the five miles from the little blue house on stilts to Sunset Marina with his foot heavy on the gas. One half of his mind—the rational, steady part—saw Edie. Her dark hair, her laugh, her sweet smile that felt like a gift when it was directed at him. Her face when they'd decided to spend the summer apart, physically and emotionally.

The other half—the part that felt like it had been set ablaze—saw Kat. Her long blonde hair pulled to the side in a thick braid. Her rosy, freckled cheeks. Her back as she stood in the sand, staring out into the calm, luminescent Gulf waters. He'd spent most of the summer thinking of her, but Edie had crept in too. Did he love them both? Was that possible?

He didn't know and at the moment, he didn't care. He just knew he couldn't get to the marina fast enough.

When he pulled into the parking lot, he saw Kat's Jeep up front. His heart leapt, and he pulled into a spot a little too quickly, hitting the brakes and skidding on the sand scattered across the asphalt.

He checked in the dock store, and when he didn't see her there, he trotted down to the dock where *Alabama Reds* sat tied to the pilings. The boat was quiet though. No Reggie, no amateur fishermen. No Kat.

"Yo, Polo Shirt." Dave called to him as he passed the tiki hut on his search. "Up for a Bloody Mary?"

"No thanks, man," Mac said without slowing. "It's a little early for that."

"Nah." Dave's voice was gravelly in the early morning sunlight. "Best way to start the day."

Mac made the rounds of the docks and property, but he saw no hint of Kat.

Finally Carla flagged him down. "Boy, I'm watching you chasing your tail all over this place. What in Sam Hill are you searching for?"

"Kat," he said, breathing hard. "Have you seen her?"

"Kat's gone. You didn't talk to her?"

"Gone? Gone where?"

"She went out with *Gulf Heat*."

Mac swung his head in the direction of the yacht that was always docked in the third slot from the end. It was a charter boat but pricier than the others, usually only booked for upper-crust bachelor parties or businessmen in the area for conferences at the beach resort. The third slot from the end was empty.

"Why would she do that? She was supposed to meet me here."

"The captain called me Friday night, saying he was short a hand. I figured Kat would be up for some extra money, so I gave him her number." Carla shrugged. "They left about an hour ago. You say she was supposed to meet you here? Are you late or something?"

Mac stared at Carla. "I'm not late." He lifted his hat and scratched his head, then set the hat back down. "When are they headed back in?" Surely it was just an oversight. She needed the money so she took the trip, trusting that he'd be here when she got back. No harm in waiting a bit before he headed out.

Carla swiped a hand across her forehead, damp in the morning heat. "It's an overnight trip, Mac. They're fishing for marlin. Won't be back 'til tomorrow evening."

The blow was crushing. Kat knew he was coming, knew he wanted to talk to her, and she left. Without a call, without a word. He took a few steps away from Carla. Clenched his fists so tight his knuckles protested.

"I got a paycheck for you up in the store. Want to grab it before you leave?"

Mac tilted his head to stretch the muscles in his neck. "Yeah."

Inside, the register dinged as the cash drawer opened, and Carla pulled an envelope with Mac's name on it from the bottom of the drawer. He reached to take it from her, but she kept a firm grip. When he met her gaze, her eyes were soft.

"You're not the first kid I've seen with stars in his eyes over that young lady." He reached again for the check, but she didn't let go. "I told you not to get yourself mixed up with her."

"I know you did."

"Sometimes it pays to listen to the old woman behind the counter. I been around a long time, and I know things."

"You're probably right." He was dismayed to feel his eyes burning, moisture threatening to pool in the corners. Mac gazed up at the ceiling, willing the mutinous tears to subside. "Next time I'll listen."

"I bet you won't, either." She held the check out again and this time let him take it. "You're a good kid. Take care of yourself."

"You too, Carla."

A couple hours later, Mac was driving north on I-65 with all his windows down, the wind loud enough to drown out his thoughts, which was exactly what he was hoping for. Humiliation and shame mixed with anger and an embarrassing sense of his own gullibility and inexperience. He'd originally planned to stay in Mobile with his parents for a few days before he headed back to school, but after absorbing the blow from Kat, all he wanted was to be alone. He didn't want to see anyone—his parents, his friends. Graham. Edie. Probably not even Kat if by some miracle she showed up at his door. But he wasn't holding his breath for that.

The only place he could think of to be alone was the apartment. So he'd loaded his belongings he'd left in Mobile after the end of the semester, said hello and good-bye to his parents, and jumped back into his car for the four-hour drive to Birmingham.

Three short months ago, he'd fled school with a single goal: to find his way and to do it before he lost everything. But now he'd lost even more. The girl he'd loved for years. His friend he'd loved for even longer than that. And the new person, the one who'd opened his eyes, who'd changed his life in ways he hadn't expected. He had a vague sense that it would be months, maybe even years, before he realized all the ways Kat had changed him, but he put it all behind him. She was in the rearview, and there was nothing he could do about it.

As for what lay ahead, he had no way of knowing. So for now Mac kept his foot on the pedal and his hands on the wheel, the hot end-of-summer air flowing through his car, washing away the last ninety days and the heavy shroud of regret.

A week later he saw her. She was walking out of Evenson Hall, blue backpack slung over one shoulder, dark hair gathered in a long ponytail, bright flowered skirt grazing the tops of yellow Converse sneakers. His regret—that bitter taste he'd spent the week trying to escape—returned with all its nauseating force. The shock of it almost sent him to his knees.

I can't believe I lost her.

Edie was rummaging in her bag for something, and when she finally unearthed it and her gaze met his, they both froze where they were. She a few steps in front of the dorm door, people swarming all around her, and he several yards away in a patch of sunlight outside. As they stared, their gaze long and unbroken, he tried to decipher the tilt of her head, the angle of her jaw, the trace of something—longing? fury? or worse, apathy?—in her eyes.

Then she smiled.

CHAPTER 36

MAC

Present Day

"How are things with you and Edie?"

The Thursday night game ended fifteen minutes ago, but Mac was still shooting hoops with Fitz under the lights. A gnat buzzed by his ear and he swatted it away. It was warm, but the exertion of the night felt good.

"We're okay." He pivoted and shot. Two points. Fitz scrambled to the back court to grab the ball before it bounced into the grass. "No running, old man," Mac called.

"What my wife doesn't know won't hurt her. And anyway, I'm not running. Just refereeing."

"Not anymore, you're not."

Fitz grinned and threw the ball at Mac hard. He caught it at his chest and shot again. Missed.

"Define 'okay.'" Fitz caught the ball and held it against his hip.

"We're not okay." Mac pushed the damp hair off his forehead. "I think she's barely hanging on."

"What about you?"

"I'm holding on. To this family, to her, as long as she'll let me." Fitz eyed Mac, who exhaled. "I gave her a choice. We sort of had it out, and I told her everything that happened with Kat and me. I didn't leave anything out. I apologized for everything, and I told her she could decide what to do with it. So it's up to her now. I'm just waiting to see if she'll stay or go."

"So you've done all you can do."

"Yeah. I have. Everything blew up, and I've patched and repaired as much as I can. Now I just have to see if it'll hold."

"Sometimes that's what a marriage is, Dr. Swan. We hurt each other and we apologize. And we forgive. Over and over. Eventually, we learn how to hurt each other less and love each other more. And better."

"You telling me you've learned how not to hurt your wife anymore?"

"I don't hurt her much. Now, annoy her? Irritate her? Ruffle her feathers a bit?" He grinned. "I do all that in spades. But I think she secretly likes that about me."

Mac laughed and Fitz tossed the ball to him. They shot and rebounded and dribbled in silence as cars passed on the road nearby and stars popped out overhead. Eventually they packed it in and headed to their cars. On the way Fitz kept looking at him. Mac tossed his ball in the backseat and turned back to Fitz. "There's something else. What is it?"

"It's nothing."

"It's something. It's practically oozing out of your ears. Lemme have it."

"It's just something Cynthia told me today. They need a doctor to work a day or two a week at the women's center. They have a clinic where they care for kids of underprivileged parents. It's mostly routine checkups for the kids when their parents come into the center for counseling or classes. Most of them are uninsured or on Medicaid, and some of the kids don't see the doctor that often."

"The clinic's a good idea then."

"Yeah, it would be if they could keep a doctor there. They've had a few, but they've all had to leave for one reason or another. Now they're on the hunt again. They have a resident, but he's not much good without a doctor to work under."

"Any specific reason you're telling me this?"

Fitz shrugged. "I just thought you might be interested. I seem to remember a young man who, once upon a time, hoped to one day be able to help people who couldn't afford to see fancy doctors."

Mac smiled. "I remember that. But doesn't every young doctor say the same thing? That they want to be the one to help the vulnerable and poor?"

"I'll give you that. But life happens and not many actually do it. They get comfortable. Forget the dreams and plans they had when they first started out."

"I haven't been very comfortable lately, I'll tell you that."

"Why don't you stop by the center? I'll tell Cynthia you just want to see the place."

"You sure are pushing this."

"This is not me pushing, Son. When I push, you'll know it."

Mac jangled his keys in his pocket. "There's been a fair amount of upheaval in my life lately. I'm not sure it's the time to add in something new."

"Or maybe it's the best time. Everything's already blown to pieces, and now those pieces are settling. You can decide how they settle. On your end, at least. And Edie will have to do the same for herself."

The next evening after work, Mac and Riley headed off on their nowregular walk around the neighborhood. The cooler air proved they'd turned a corner into fall, and leaves were scattered across the sidewalk in front of them. Pots of fall flowers dotted neighbors' porches.

As they walked in silence, turning off Linden onto Dogwood Lane, Mac gathered his courage and the words he needed to say to Riley. It had occurred to him after his conversation with Edie on the back porch that not only had he kept Edie from being able to make her own choice, he'd essentially done the same thing to Riley. For Edie, it meant letting her make a decision about her future without all the information she needed, and for Riley, it meant preventing her from making a decision at all.

"Do you remember the day you came to my office?"

She cut her eyes at him. "Um, yes."

"Do you remember what you asked me?"

"I asked you a lot of things."

"True. But you said you needed something from me. You asked for money so you could be on your way."

"Yeah. To which you said no."

"Exactly. And I need to apologize to you for that."

"What?"

"You're an adult—a young one, but technically an adult—and you had a plan. Instead of helping you on your way, I told you what to do. I didn't let you make your own choice about your own life, and I'm sorry for that."

"Are you kidding me?" she blurted. "I didn't have a plan. I have no idea what I would have done if you'd given me money. I had nowhere to go."

"Really? I mean, I know there was no Aunt Mary, but you didn't have any plan?"

"No. And truthfully, I was kind of hoping you'd ask me to stay. At least for a little while." She shrugged. "So there's that."

"Huh." They rounded the corner back onto their street. "Well, Riley, I'm glad you stayed." Even though it had caused all sorts of problems—or rather, uncovered hidden fault lines—he was honestly glad she'd walked into his life. For however long she was here, he was glad she'd come.

Next to him, Riley rubbed her hand along the side of her swollen belly, and her shoulders relaxed. "Me too."

A few minutes later they arrived back at their house to find Thomas sitting on the front porch steps, his soccer ball between his feet.

"Hey, buddy," Mac called. "Want to take the next lap with me?"

Thomas shrugged a shoulder.

"Come on. I'm getting old, remember? I need you kids to keep me moving."

When Riley passed him on the steps, she reached down and ruffled his hair. He batted her hand away, but Mac caught the smile he tried to hide. When she closed the door behind her, Thomas reached down and grabbed the ball. He tossed it to Mac and stood. "Only if you do two blocks with me. You really are getting old."

Mac laughed as Thomas grabbed the ball back and fell into step beside him.

CHAPTER 37

EDIE

Present Day

Laura Lou tapped on Edie's door and entered without waiting for an invitation. "I did it." Her smile was wide, bordering on genuine. "I called Graham this morning."

Edie closed her laptop. "You did?"

"I did. I asked him if he was interested in joining DDG as our in-house architect. I saw how well the two of you worked together and thought it was time to bring him on. We'd all benefit from having a nationally recognized architect under our roof. I think it'd give us an even larger edge. What do you think?"

"I think . . ." The idea of Graham working for Laura Lou was preposterous, but Edie couldn't tell her that. "I think anyone who has a chance to work with him will benefit from it."

"I agree. He said he'd take it into consideration and let me know his answer. Work on him, Edie. I get the feeling that he thinks a lot of you. See if you can bring him around."

"I'll see what I can do."

As soon as she was gone, Edie closed her door and called him. "I hear you're joining the distinguished ranks of Davis Design Group."

He snorted. "I was so shocked, I don't think I gave her an answer."

"You didn't. I'm supposed to convince you to say yes."

"Is that why you called?"

"Maybe."

"Do you think I should say yes?"

"What? No. You'd hate it."

"What about you? You hate it, don't you?"

"I never said that."

"Do you hate it?"

She exhaled. "No, Graham. I don't hate it."

"But could things be better? Can you imagine a better situation for yourself, one where you get to call the shots and make your own decisions?"

"Sure," she said quietly. "I can imagine that."

"I can too."

She closed her eyes and tried to picture what it would be like to work alongside Graham. Maybe at his house over the bay, with those tall windows overlooking the water, the long wooden table, the old pharmacy cabinet full of her vintage drawer pulls and fabric samples. Or maybe it'd be a new office, some cool loft downtown, something airy and light filled. The double desks, chairs and couches for clients, small kitchenette in the back.

Suddenly, with the phone pressed to her cheek and Graham listening on the other end, she realized she did want out. She wanted to leave Laura Lou. Even more, she needed to. She didn't go into this career to be watched over and stifled. She was ready to stretch her wings, to push herself creatively, to grab inspiration wherever she found it and have no one but the client to check her when she went too far. She thought working under Laura Lou had been the perfect setup, and maybe it had been perfect once, but she'd outgrown her shell here. Staying only meant more discomfort, more suffocation.

But was Graham the answer? A Swan-Yeager partnership, twenty years in the making?

"Do something for me." He spoke into the silence. "For just a minute, I want you to think about you. Not Laura Lou, not your family, not me. What do *you* need?" He paused. "You know, it's okay to be a little selfish now and then. Especially if it means taking care of yourself when you need to. I learned that after my dad died. Sometimes you have to do more than just pull back on the reins. Sometimes you have to get off the horse altogether."

She tried to swallow, but her mouth was too dry. "Graham, I . . . I still need some time."

"Take whatever time you need. I'm not going anywhere."

That evening, with Mac and Riley gone on their evening walk, Edie sat with Avery under the lights of the magnolia tree. Thomas was kicking his soccer ball against the side of the garage, and Ramona was feeling frisky in the late-October air, bounding through the monkey grass with wild abandon.

"I haven't heard you mention Alex in a while." Edie tried not to sound too interested. The truth was, Avery had gone from name-dropping Alex all the time to not saying his name in at least two weeks.

Avery shrugged. "He's been hanging out with Jane McKenzie."

"Ah." So the science nerd got the cheerleader. "Are you okay with that?"

"Sure. We were just friends anyway." Her shoulders were slumped, and she propped her chin in her hand, eyes half closed as she turned her focus back to her history notebook.

"How are you doing, Ave? I don't necessarily mean Alex, but with everything. Are you sleeping? I know you've been up studying late a lot."

"I don't have another choice. Colleges look at everything, you know? Even freshman grades."

"Honey, that's a lot of pressure to put on yourself. I don't think colleges are going to look at—"

"Yes, Mom. Yes, they are. The college advisor told us that at the beginning of the year. I'll never be a scientist if I don't get into a good school, and if I want to get into a good school, I have to be perfect. And yes, that means starting now."

"Whoa, who said anything about perfect? Study hard, do as well as you can, but no one needs to be perfect. No one *can* be perfect. You know that."

"What about you?"

"Me? You've got to be kidding."

"I'm serious. You've got a great job, you're doing what you love, and you're really good at it. Everyone likes you and looks up to you. Then there's all this stuff with Dad and Riley and . . . you just keep going. Nothing fazes you, nothing makes you scared or worried. You're a rock. I'm not. I could never be like that. Everything makes me nervous."

"Oh, baby. I am not a rock, and virtually everything makes me scared these days."

"Well, you hide it well."

Edie thought again of that photo Blanche had taken of her and her mother back when Riley had first arrived. How fresh and carefree Edie appeared despite the bomb that had exploded in her life. To think that the brave face she'd tried to put on this whole time had inadvertently made her daughter think she was Superwoman.

"Honey, I've gotten really good at making everyone around me think things are just fine. Your dad and I have tried to shield you and Thomas from everything that's happened lately, but the truth is, it's been hard. Really hard. But we're working on it."

"So you're not getting a divorce?"

Edie took a deep breath and blew it out slowly. "I don't think either one of us wants that. No one wants their marriage to end in divorce." It was a nonanswer, but thankfully she didn't pick up on it.

Avery exhaled and dropped her pen on the table. "Things have been really weird."

"I know. And I'm so sorry for that. But you have to know, there is no other girl in the world more important to me than you."

Avery lifted a corner of her mouth. "Thanks, Mom."

They were quiet a moment, listening to the muted thud of Thomas's ball as it hit the garage every few seconds.

"Riley's kind of cool," Avery said.

"You think so?"

"Yeah." A heavy pause. "Does that bother you?"

Edie smiled at her firstborn. "No, baby. It doesn't bother me."

"Good. It's weird, but I think I like her."

CHAPTER 38

MAC

September 2000

Edie had left the apartment only minutes ago to race across campus to her **art** theory class, so when the soft knock sounded at the door, Mac glanced **around** quickly to see what she could have left behind. The only thing he **saw** was her coffee mug sitting on the kitchen counter, but she wouldn't **have** come back for that. Then he realized she rarely knocked before com-**ing** in.

He opened the door and the face he saw on the other side stilled the **blood** in his veins.

"Hey, new kid."

"Kat."

His mind reeled between the past and the present. The summer and all **its** tension, confusion, cravings, and yes, even passion—and the now. The **steady** thrum of life, of comfort, of assurance. A new kind of passion. Kat **was** then—Kat was everything then. But Edie was now.

"What are you doing here?" It came out sharper than he intended, but . . . Kat was here. At his apartment. His skin crawled with heat, and he thought of Edie across campus.

She lifted a shoulder. "I just wanted to see you."

Her gaze slid past him into the apartment, and he glanced behind him as if to assure himself no one else was there.

"Can I come in?" A crease settled between her eyebrows.

"Oh yeah, sure. Sorry." Mac stepped back and opened the door wider. She walked past him, somehow still smelling of salty air and freedom despite being two hundred and fifty miles from the beach. She was still so beautiful, she made his insides ache. He wanted to reach out and touch her—her face, her neck, her shoulders. He balled his hands into tight fists and crossed his arms over his chest.

Once inside the apartment, Kat glanced around at the navy futon half covered in books, the large bulletin board on the wall in the kitchen with band flyers, reminders of tests and intramural games, and a few phone numbers. Graham's bag was spilled open on the kitchen table where he'd left it when he stopped at the apartment on his way to grab lunch.

Kat inhaled deeply and turned back to him. "It's pretty much how I imagined it."

"The apartment?"

"Yeah." She smiled, the apples of her cheeks round and pink, her freckles even more pronounced under the overhead kitchen light. "How are you doing?"

He scrubbed a hand over his face. Ten minutes ago Edie had been standing in his apartment, her arms around his neck, her lips against his, and now Kat was here. The 180-degree spin had left him scattered and unsteady. "How am I doing? I'm fine, but I'm a little confused, Kat. When you ditched me at the marina, I didn't think I'd see you again. Now I'm back here and . . ."

And Edie, Edie, Edie.

"I'm sorry about the marina. I freaked out." She stared down and studied her hands. "That's why I needed to see you. Just once. I couldn't stand for you to go on and not know . . ."

When her voice trailed off, he clenched his hands. "What is it?" Heat tinged his words. He swallowed down his frustration. "What do I need to know?"

Kat stared at him, her eyes framed by pale lashes, her full lips pressed into a thin line. When he could no longer hold her gaze, all her energy seemed to leak out. She glanced around the room again, her eyes scanning every item and surface, then she nodded. "I'm sorry." Her voice was low. She bit her bottom lip and shoved her hands in her back pockets. Smiled. "I'm sorry for everything."

She moved toward the door, but Mac reached out and stopped her. His fingers on her arm were gentle, her skin warm. She turned back and he opened his mouth, unsure of the words that would come out.

"You changed a part of me last summer. A part that needed to be changed. And I'm grateful." He tipped her chin up so she met his gaze. "I can't . . ." He shook his head.

"I know. You can't."

"But I'm not sorry."

"Then I'm not either."

Mac heard the scrape of a foot on the other side of the front door, and he knew what was about to happen a fraction of a second before it happened. The door opened and Graham appeared in the doorway, a brown bag in one hand, a drink in the other. Mac still had his fingers on Kat's chin, and he lowered his hand quickly, taking one step back, then another.

No one moved for a moment, then Graham closed the door with his foot and set his food on the counter. "Hey."

"Hey," Mac managed. "This is—"

"Kat," Graham said. "I remember."

Mac felt Kat's gaze on his face, and when he turned to her, his heart caved in his chest. Shame burned his cheeks and his ears, though he had the presence of mind to realize it was probably worse for her.

She moved toward the door, and Mac followed her. When he passed Graham, his friend's eyes widened, a huge question mark on his face, but Mac ignored it.

Kat opened the door and sunlight from the other side flooded in around her, outlining her body with a bright glow. Something nudged him inside, some internal voice or push, something he couldn't name. But then she moved and the sunlight dimmed, the glow gone.

"Good-bye, Mac." She reached her hand forward, just a couple inches, and he met it, her hand in his.

He nodded and she pulled away. A few seconds later, she was gone.

CHAPTER 39

MAC

Present Day

It was years before Mac thought to search his memory for the seeds that became his and Graham's hard-and-fast friendship. The one that enveloped Edie, too, wrapping all three of them in the safety and comfort that only a solid, trustworthy friendship could bring. It was so precious, almost sacred, that when it disintegrated after that summer, Mac felt an actual physical ache. A yearning for what had been, even as he anticipated a future he was sure he and Edie would have.

When he told Mrs. Kimble he needed to cancel his afternoon appointments, she moaned with nervousness.

"All those parents," she said, wringing her hands. "Do you know how irate they get when we have to reschedule well visits?"

"I do, and I'm sorry. Please tell them something unavoidable came up, and we'll fit them in as soon as we can."

Mrs. K. continued her protest, but he told her he needed to leave, and she finally backed down and accepted that she'd have to face the parents on her own.

He made the drive over the bay in a little over half an hour, and in another fifteen minutes he pulled up outside the little yellow house by the water. He could still hear Mr. Yeager's deep voice as he regaled Mac and Graham with stories of his fishing escapades over the years. Jubilees where he pulled in eight-pound flounders and buckets of shrimp. The time he caught what he swore was an octopus out in the middle of the bay.

Mac had heard about Mr. Yeager's death, and he still felt bad about not showing up at the funeral. He felt bad about a lot when it came to Graham.

Just as Mac was reaching to knock on the back door, Graham opened it. He didn't try to hide the surprise on his face. "Mac. What are you do-ing here?"

"Are you on your way out?" He glanced back to the driveway, where he'd pulled up next to Graham's car.

"No, I was just going to call Simon. He was running around back here last time I saw him."

"Simon?"

Graham stepped past him onto the porch and whistled through his teeth. A moment later a bush at the side of the house rustled and a yellow Lab came trotting out.

"Simon," Graham said.

Mac reached down and scratched the top of the dog's head.

"Shouldn't you be at the office?" Graham asked after a moment.

Mac shrugged. "Just thought maybe we should talk."

Graham nodded. "Probably a good idea." He turned toward the house and the dog followed him. Mac followed the dog. Inside the house Graham walked to the kitchen and opened the fridge. "Care for a drink?"

"Sure."

He straightened up and handed Mac a bottle of Fat Tire, then gestured with his own bottle toward the back porch overlooking the water.

When they were settled, Graham rocked slowly, his gaze out on the water. "I guess Edie told you about my proposition."

"She did."

"Did you tell her not to do it?"

"No. It's not up to me. I asked her if she thought it was a good idea, but no, I'm not telling her what to do either way."

"Why would it not be a good idea? Architects and designers work together all the time."

Mac rolled his head toward Graham and raised an eyebrow. "Come on, man. I'm not an idiot. It took me a while to see it, but I get it now."

The realization had hit him only days before, when he was thinking back to when Kat had shown up at their apartment. Later that day, long after she'd left, Graham asked him about her. Why she'd come, what she wanted, and most importantly, what he planned to tell Edie.

"I'm not telling Edie anything," Mac said. "There's no need for her to know about Kat. We were broken up. Kat didn't—"

"Don't tell me she didn't mean anything," Graham interrupted. "She wouldn't have driven all the way up here if you two meant nothing to each other. Anyway, I saw the two of you together. You were close. What happened, Mac?"

"We were . . . I don't know. But it doesn't matter anymore. I love Edie. I want to marry her."

"Dude, you have to tell her then. She has a right to know who she's marrying."

"Who she's marrying? What are you talking about? She knows exactly who I am. She knows me. You know me."

Graham's face held a mixture of anger and sadness. "No, man. I'm not sure we do." He left the apartment then and didn't come back until late that night.

Mac heard him in the kitchen when he came in, opening the fridge and setting a glass down on the counter. A few minutes later, he knocked on Mac's bedroom door. His eyes were weary. "Look, I'm not going to beat this into the ground, but I just have to ask. You're sure it's Edie? The one you want? Not Kat?"

At the time Mac thought Graham was just looking out for him. Making sure he was thinking everything through. But now, with years of hindsight and a smidge of wisdom, Mac saw it for what it actually was.

The hope on his face as he'd asked that question. *"You're sure it's Edie?"* The wild possibility that maybe—just maybe—Mac would choose Kat, opening the door for Graham to pursue Edie himself. How could Mac not have seen it then?

When Graham left the apartment that night, Mac barely saw him again. Of course he passed him here and there, but their friendship was done. And Mac was the cause of it. Even as Graham walked out of his room, it felt like a part of his body was being torn away. A sixteen-year friendship gone, like a lightbulb that blinked off.

"You loved Edie, too, didn't you?" As soon as Mac said the words into the quietness of Graham's back porch, Graham's legs stilled and his chair slowed to a stop. It was another moment before he spoke.

"How could I not? She's Edie. She's smart, funny . . ."

"Graham. I mean you loved her back then. Back when I was with Kat that summer."

"Yeah. I did." He looked at Mac and Mac held his gaze, remembering his friend, their friend, but maybe seeing things as they really were for the first time. He thought of how different their lives might be now if Kat hadn't happened. If they'd all made different choices that summer.

Graham went back to rocking and Mac joined him, tapping his foot in time with the chair's forward motion. Time stretched.

"She hasn't given me an answer yet about the job." Graham eyed Mac. "And before you think I have an ulterior motive, I don't. I just know she deserves better than Laura Lou. Edie can stand on her own two feet. She needs to be allowed the space to do that."

"I know my wife. And you're right—she deserves better. She does. I don't know what she's going to do though."

"Since that day in eighth grade when I first saw you with her, I knew the two of you belonged together. For a while I may have thought, maybe even hoped . . ." Graham shook his head. "But it doesn't matter now. It's always been the two of you." Graham looked Mac straight in the eyes. "It still is."

"Well, the decision is up to her." Whether they were still talking about the job or something more, Mac wasn't sure. He didn't even want to think about it. "You and I both know how strong-willed she can be."

"It's part of what makes her Edie though." Graham's mouth tweaked up in a half smile. "I think y'all will be fine. You've come too far." He reached his bottle over to Mac and tapped it to his. They both took a long sip.

"Thanks for not kicking me out when I showed up at your door," Mac said.

"Are you kidding? I thought you were here to whip my tail."

Mac laughed and they rocked, Simon snoring at their feet.

"Have you been out to Middle Bay Light recently?" Mac asked.

"Can't say that I have. Not since you and I spent the night out there."

Mac grinned. "I can't believe we did that. Middle of the night out on the water was terrifying."

Graham laughed through his nose. "We had fun though, didn't we?"

Mac made it home by six and convinced Thomas to shoot some hoops with him in the driveway so he could tell Fitz he'd worked on his jump shots. They'd been playing around for a half hour or so when Avery walked out onto the front porch, a book in her hand. "Am I seeing things, or is that something other than a textbook?" he called.

"You're not seeing things." She glanced at the cover. "It's Agatha Christie. I pulled it off Mom's bookshelf. I'm letting myself read until dinner, then I have to go back to studying."

Mac smiled at her. "Sounds like a good balance to me. And good choice on the book."

As he was talking, Thomas stole the ball right out of his hands and tried to make a shot from the top of the driveway.

"It'll never go in," Mac taunted just before it swished through the net. "Look at you. Soccer star can also play a little ball."

"A little?" Thomas grabbed the rebound and dribbled the ball around his dad's legs.

It felt good, moving around the driveway with Thomas. Running, jumping, talking together. He was such a neat kid—imaginative, fearless, and whip-smart—and Mac made a silent promise to himself never to let him go unnoticed, even if he rarely made as much noise or drama as his sister. Either of them.

Just as Edie called out the front door that dinner was ready, Riley pulled into the driveway, having stayed late helping Cynthia and Dr. Pine reorganize the waiting area at the women's center. Mac carried her bag as they headed into the kitchen.

"They wouldn't let me move anything myself, so all I could do was stand around and point." Riley sat on a stool at the island. "But we made it a little cozier. Then Mrs. Cynthia took me to the dollar store to buy a bunch of coloring books and stickers for the kids while they're waiting for their parents."

Mac smiled at her. "So it's going well, you working there? It seems like you enjoy it."

"I do. I like the women who come in there. Most of them anyway. We talk about guys, pregnancy stuff." She shrugged. "It's like we're on the same team or something. We're all dealing with the same things."

"It makes sense," Edie said, as she leaned down to put a plate in the dishwasher. "It helps to have people you can share things with. Especially when you're pregnant and everything feels out of whack."

"Tell me about it." Riley propped her chin in her hand. "Mrs. Cynthia told me she got her degree in social work. And that there's a community college here that lets you take classes toward your degree while you're working."

Mac nodded. "She's right. You think that's something you'd be interested in?"

Riley raised her shoulders. "I know I said I wanted to be a doctor, but maybe this is a better option. I just like the idea of helping girls like me."

"What would you think about me taking on a side job?" Mac asked Edie later in the comforting darkness of their bedroom. They'd turned off the light, but neither of them had fallen asleep.

"What are you talking about? You have a job."

"I know, and Swan Pediatrics isn't going anywhere. But what if I backed off a bit? Worked three or four days there and had a day or two for something else?"

"What kind of something else?"

"It's at the women's center. In their children's clinic."

Edie shifted and turned her head to face him. "Dr. Pine mentioned that the first day I went with Riley. I totally forgot to tell you."

"It's okay. We've had a lot going on."

She blew a puff of air from her nose. "Yeah." She was quiet a moment. "Do you think your other doctors would be okay if you decided to work less?"

He shrugged. "It's my office. I can pretty much do what I want."

"I think you'd be great for the job."

He faced her in the dark. "Thanks."

She nodded and turned her gaze back toward the ceiling. "I need to tell you something."

"Okay." His stomach clenched. *Here it comes.*

"The other night when we talked on the porch and you told me everything about Kat, I should have done the same. I should have told you all the things you didn't know. The things I kept from you."

"Edie, you don't have to—"

"I do. You said you wanted me to have all the information so I could make a decision, and I need to do that for you. I need to be as honest with you as you were with me."

"Okay. You can tell me whatever you need to tell me."

"Graham and I wrote a lot of letters that summer."

Mac swallowed hard.

"At first we were just checking in with each other, but then somehow we started making these plans to work together in New York." She paused and Mac squeezed his hands into fists as he waited for her to continue.

"They were crazy plans at first, or at least far-fetched. But they were exciting too. The idea of leaving everything familiar behind and starting over fresh." She turned to Mac, her hair falling over her cheek. "I guess that's how you felt that summer too, huh?"

He nodded. "Something like that, yeah."

"It was easy to say things in letters that we probably wouldn't have had the nerve to say to each other in person."

"But they were there," he said. "If the feelings came out in letters, they'd been in your minds whether you were saying them out loud or not."

"That's probably right. I mean, we were all friends, but Graham and I met each other on some levels that . . . well, that you and I didn't connect on."

"That's fair. I know you both had a thing for that disgusting pizza in the student union."

She smiled. "Yeah. We did. Anyway, Mac, I loved you." She rolled onto her side toward him and he did the same. "I loved you, but I loved Graham too. In a very different way."

"I get that," he whispered.

"I called him one night toward the end of that summer, to see if there was something there." She rubbed her thumb back and forth across the edge of the bedsheet. "Something we needed to air out or figure out or try. But the call didn't go so well. We just kept misunderstanding each other. And we didn't write after that. Then when I got back to school, I saw you."

"And here we are."

"Here we are."

He listened to Edie breathe, waiting for her to speak, but it seemed she was finished. Then . . .

"There's one more thing." She closed her eyes. "I stayed at Graham's house. The night I didn't come home."

Mac had suspected as much, but it didn't make it any easier to hear.

"Nothing happened. We talked. We hashed out the past. I slept on the couch."

"Okay." He nodded. "Okay. Is there anything else?"

"No. That's it."

"Do you feel better?"

She hesitated. "Yeah. I think so."

"Good. Now, if you told me all that so I could make a decision, I have no decision to make. I made mine a long time ago and nothing's going to change it."

She held his gaze and he saw boldness there. A maturity that came with years and experience and life. They stayed like that a long minute, bodies turned in toward each other, her head on the pillow facing his. He wanted so badly to reach out and touch her. More than that, he wanted to take her in his arms and prove to her that she was all he wanted, but he was afraid to break the fragile peace between them.

"Have you thought any more about Graham's offer?" he asked instead.

"Thought about it, yes. Made a decision, no."

Above them, the ceiling fan sent wisps of cool air over their faces and arms. "Dayspring Salon closed a few weeks ago," she said a few minutes later. He waited, but she didn't offer any more information.

"Sorry, am I supposed to know the significance of that?"

She chuckled. "I guess not. It's in the same shopping center where Firefly is. Just a few doors down. The space is empty."

"Okay . . . ?"

"I thought I might go check it out tomorrow. See what it looks like inside."

His mouth felt like sandpaper. He tried to swallow, but it stuck somewhere in his throat.

She's doing it. Opening a firm with Graham. Working with him. It's happening.

But he didn't say a word. He knew he had to trust her, whatever she decided, because he was asking her to trust him too. To trust that he loved her, wanted her, cherished her. It had to go both ways.

His mind was still racing when he felt Edie's hand slide into his. Gentle pressure on his palm. He squeezed back.

CHAPTER 40

EDIE

Present Day

Edie turned in a slow circle, taking in every detail of the empty office space. The walls were painted a pastel pink she could easily cover over with a bolder, more saturated hue. The place was big enough for the essentials, and one of the rooms in the back could house the necessary printer, drawing table, and display shelves.

"There are three more rooms that way." The leasing agent gestured toward the slim hallway behind them. "One is outfitted as a kitchen, and there's a powder room too. This main room though, this is the one that shines. Light on three sides, and the casement windows here and at the back crank out so you can catch cross breezes."

"I like it." Edie scuffed her shoe against the hardwood floor. "I really do."

"It's hard to pull the trigger, I know."

"It is. Is anyone else interested in the space?"

The woman tilted her head. "Technically I'm not supposed to tell you that. But I will say it's a prime spot. If you decide you want it, don't put off letting me know. Say the word and I'll have the lease in your hand ready to be signed."

"I appreciate it. And thanks for the discretion too." She glanced out the window and to the left, toward Firefly.

"Of course," the agent said with a wink. "No need to upset things before you decide what you want to do. Although on a personal note, I say you go, girl." She grinned. "I left my corporate job to sell real estate, and I've never been happier."

Edie smiled. All she'd said was that she was considering a new venture and she needed to keep it under wraps, not just from her mother and sister down the way, but from everyone.

The agent's phone buzzed and she checked the screen. "I'm so sorry. If it's okay with you, I'm just going to step outside and take this."

Edie waved toward the door. "It's fine."

"Take your time though. Look around. I'll be outside if you need me."

When she walked out Edie turned back to the small office space and tried to imagine it filled with new things. Tried to imagine herself working here, feeling creatively inspired and driven.

She was opening one of the casement windows when her dad called her name. She thought she'd imagined it, but when she spun around, there he was, standing in the doorway in his carpenter's pants, a hammer dangling from a loop on his thigh, and a smudge of white paint on his cheek.

"Dad, what are you doing here?"

He hooked his thumb back toward Firefly. "Your mom called. They needed to add a new dressing room." He shrugged. "She asked for help."

Her sigh came out a little too forcefully. Of course her mother had asked him for help. Bud Everett rarely said no to anyone, especially not to Edie's mother. But then Edie saw the gentle smile on his face. The hope in his eyes as he glanced again toward the shop.

When he turned back to Edie, he held up a hand. "I know what you're going to say, missy, but you have to understand that love is a choice. I made that choice forty-seven years ago, and I'm making it again. I choose to love your mother regardless of what some paper from the court says. Does she infuriate me sometimes? Yes. Do I always understand her reasoning? Not even close. But I'm not giving up on her or on us. So if she asks me for help, I'm going to give it."

"Bud?"

Dad leaned out the doorway. "I'm down here. Talking to Edie."

Edie heard her mom's heels clicking on the sidewalk. "Edie? What are you doing here?"

"Nothing, just checking out the space for a friend." She didn't see a need to go into the real reason she was there. "And I was asking Dad the same thing. He said he's building you a dressing room."

Mom smoothed her hair behind her ear and propped a hand on her hip, then let it fall again. Her blouse was a demure light pink, and Edie was happy to see it was buttoned to an appropriate level on her chest. "Well, Blanche is bringing in so many customers, we need to be able to accommodate them."

"Lucky for you, Dad's a good builder."

She turned and took him in, head to toe, a little like she was seeing him for the first time. Then an exasperated, "Oh, for Pete's sake, Bud." She reached out and rubbed the smudge of paint on his cheek with her thumb, then sighed. "Yes, I'm the lucky one, aren't I?" It was a decent attempt at sarcasm, but anyone could see the smile she tried to keep hidden. It was there in her voice, unmistakable, and Edie was glad to see it directed toward Dad.

He reached out and hugged Edie, then paused at the doorway. "Things going okay at home?"

"Yeah, Dad. They're going okay."

His smile crinkled the corners of his eyes. "I'm glad to hear it. Give our love to Mac and the kids."

CHAPTER 41

MAC

Present Day

On the first truly chilly evening of the year, Mac told Edie he wanted to take her out to dinner. Just the two of them. When their kids were younger, they had a date night once or twice a month. They'd loved those occasions when they could spend two or three luxurious hours far away from the needs and whims of the small people in their life.

Somewhere along the way, they let those nights alone together fall down the list of priorities until they sat one or two rungs above "get an oil change" and "schedule the kids' haircuts." But Mac was determined to change that. To return to their nights out just like they planned orthodontist appointments, soccer practices, and swim meets.

Not that a date night a couple times a month would fix everything wrong between them, but at least it'd give them a chance to relearn each other. To focus on what they had, and what he didn't want to lose.

At their kids' ages, they were in that strange place where Avery didn't need a babysitter and Thomas hardly did, but if left home together, who knew what catastrophes might occur? So Mac and Edie asked Riley if they could leave her in charge while they went to dinner.

"You want me to babysit?" Riley darted a glance to Avery, who let out an annoyed, "Mom!"

Edie backtracked. "You know what? You're right, that's probably not—"

"No, it's fine. Y'all go to dinner. And I'll make sure, I don't know, they brush their teeth. And don't burn the house down."

Avery pressed her lips together, but her cheeks pulled up. "I'll try not to play with any matches."

Riley had been living in their house for almost three months, but that didn't keep Edie from going over every possible danger in the house and showing her the location of every fire extinguisher and the sharpest knife in the kitchen in case of a burglary.

"Geez," Riley groaned. "Do you always worry this much?"

"Let me know if there are any problems," Edie said just before they walked out. "I mean it. We'll have our phones with us, so don't hesitate."

"Go." Riley rolled her eyes. "We'll be fine. Seriously. Have fun."

"Might as well do what she says." Mac held out his hand to Edie. "You ready?"

Their first stop was at Uncorked for a glass of wine and a cheese plate. Before they'd even been served though, at a small table in the corner of the bar, she leaned toward him. "I have to tell you something."

"You're going to have to quit starting conversations this way." He set his fork down. "Let me have it."

"You know that empty office space I told you about? Near Firefly?"

He remembered. He hadn't thought of much else since she'd brought it up. He didn't trust himself to speak, so he just nodded.

She reached down into her purse and pulled out a thin stack of paper-clipped papers. Set them on the table.

"What's this?" He peered down at the top page. *Commercial Lease Agreement, between The Oak Hill Group and Edie Swan, for the property at 1508 Camellia Avenue.*

"I haven't signed it yet, but it's ready. I wanted to get your go-ahead first."

"My go-ahead? Are you serious?"

She nodded. "I'm leaving DDG. I'll be giving my notice to Laura Lou next week."

He nodded, his jaw set. Under the table he squeezed his hands together, hard.

"I thought a lot about it, and I need the change, Mac. I feel really good about it. What do you think about the name Edie Swan Designs?"

"Wait—what?"

"I'm going to start my own company. My own design shop." A smile tugged up the corners of her mouth.

Adrenaline shot through his body, his heart thundering in his chest and heat pricking his cheeks. "What about Graham?"

Edie pressed her lips together. Mac held his face still. "I've already talked to him about it. He and I still want to work on projects together when we can. But if I want to do things on my own and make solely my own decisions, I have to do it alone. Well, maybe an assistant one day, but for now, just me."

Mac closed his eyes and pressed his fingers to the bridge of his nose. When he opened his eyes, her smile had grown a bit wider. "Edie Swan Designs. It's a great name. The best name."

They'd just gotten their check and were planning to move on to Citron downtown for dinner, thanks to Blanche and her coveted reservations, when Mac's phone rang. He grabbed it as he reached for the pen to sign the check.

"Dad?" Avery's voice was frantic, tearful. "Thomas had an accident."

———

By the time they reached the hospital, Edie was in tears and Mac wasn't far behind. All Avery had been able to tell them was that Thomas had fallen and he was at the hospital.

"She didn't say how he'd fallen?" Edie asked for the tenth time. This time he didn't answer. "What does that even mean? The kid is like a cat. How could a fall hurt him so badly?" Then, "Maybe we shouldn't have left Riley in charge. We didn't even ask her if she'd ever babysat before."

"They're not babies," he said quietly. "And whatever happened, I'm sure it wasn't her fault." Even as he said it though, dread slid through his belly and squeezed his throat.

Please, God. Please, God. He could barely formulate clear thoughts, but those two words just kept coming.

When he pulled into a parking space at the hospital, Edie was out the door before he'd even put the car in park. She ran through the ER's double doors and at the front desk gave the receptionist their name. She directed them down to Thomas's room.

Terror in her eyes, Edie looked back at him before she opened the door. He nodded and they walked in together. Avery and Riley popped up from where they'd been sitting next to the bed. Riley's hands cradled her stomach and Avery's face was red and splotchy. Thomas appeared to be asleep in the bed. One arm was covered in scratches and bruises, and his other was in a white sling. His shoulder was bandaged and a large mottled bruise bloomed over one eye.

Edie rushed to the bed. Her hands hovered over Thomas, finally resting on his chest. She swiveled her head toward Riley. "What in the world, Riley?"

"Mom, it's not—" Avery started, but Edie held up a hand.

"We were barely gone an hour. How could you let this happen?"

"Edie," Mac said quietly, but she didn't hear him as Riley immediately went on the defensive.

"I didn't ask to be your babysitter. You put me in charge and he fell, but it wasn't my fault. I didn't know he was climbing the tree."

"The tree?" Mac asked. "The magnolia?" It had been years since Thomas had climbed that tree.

"Yes, your stupid cat was stuck up at the top." Riley sniffed and her eyes swam with tears. "It wasn't my fault. But I took care of it."

"She's right." Avery wiped her own tears away. "You should have seen her. She ran all through the house looking for your keys, Mom. She told me exactly what to do to keep him from falling asleep in case it was a concussion. She found the keys and we were going to drive him here, but she got scared—"

"I wasn't scared," Riley interrupted. "But he started talking all crazy, then he started falling asleep. Plus his shoulder was already swelling and I didn't want to move him too much in case it was broken. So I called an ambulance and they brought him in. Only one of us could ride in the back, so I drove your car." She nodded toward Edie.

"She kissed my head." Thomas's scratchy words were the most beautiful thing Mac had ever heard. He strode to the bed and took his hand. "She gave me a kiss on the forehead. I could have done without that."

Mac tried to laugh but it came out strangled. He looked at Edie, trying to determine her level of remaining anger, but it had evaporated. She kissed Thomas's cheek, then swiped her own cheeks with her fingers and crossed the room to Avery and hugged her. Then she reached for Riley and pulled her in as close as Riley's eight-month belly would allow.

"I'm sorry," Edie said quietly near Riley's ear. "Thank you for taking care of my baby."

Riley stood stiffly at first, then her shoulders lowered and she reached an arm around Edie's back and the other around Avery.

Thank you. Thank you. Thank you.

CHAPTER 42

EDIE

Fall 2001

Edie hadn't planned to see Mac the day of the wedding, but just before the ceremony, she got nervous. They'd put the past behind them and everything had happened just like she'd always thought it would: She and Mac had graduated last year, he proposed, and she gave him a sure yes. He started medical school, she began working at Teak & Twill, and they'd planned their wedding.

But now that the day was here, something didn't feel right, and Edie couldn't walk down the aisle until she talked to him.

When she sent word to Mac's best man—a position that should have been filled by Graham but instead was filled by a cousin—that she needed to talk to him, everyone balked and reminded her of tradition. She informed them she was pulling the bride card, and would they please send Mac to the bridal suite? Still they cautioned her against it, so she relented and said she didn't need to actually see him, but at the very least, she needed to talk to him.

When Mac tapped on the door, Edie cracked it open a few inches and reached her arm out. He took her hand and they held tight to each other.

"Edie?" he ventured nervously. "What's wrong?"

"I don't know. I just needed to talk to you. To hear your voice."

His fingers tightened around hers. "I'm here. I'm not going anywhere."

"This is going to be good, right? What we're doing? It's the right thing?"

"The right thing? Who decides if it's right or not? Is it what you want? Do you want to marry me?"

She nodded. "I do want to. I guess I just want to make sure it's what you really want."

Their weird, disconnected summer wasn't that long ago, and though they'd moved on together, she still felt vestiges of the uncertainty tugging on her. Telling her Mac was marrying her to forget something else. Or that maybe she was.

"What I really want? Edie, there's nothing I want more than to marry you."

"Really?" she whispered.

"Really." He paused. "Look, last summer . . ."

Her breath caught in her chest at the words. It had been on her mind all day, but here he was about to bring it up, and suddenly it was the last thing she wanted to talk about. They'd buried it, as if they'd both known in their hearts they needed to leave it in the past. That what was in the past couldn't affect their future.

Her heart raced.

"We came so close to losing each other," he said. "But I am not letting go. I want you to know that. You're it for me, Edie. You've always been the one."

She loved Mac. She loved him so much. Maybe a part of her loved Graham too, but that was okay. A heart was a big, wide, high, deep thing, and it could hold a lot. What rose to the top was the best, truest thing, and Mac had always been at the top, even when distance and life and complications had made them fall from each other's grasp.

"I won't let go either," she said, her voice as sure as it had ever been.

With their backs pressed to either side of the door, they laid bare their souls. They pledged to love and cherish each other, always and no matter what. They said their own vows, impulsive and fervent, and made their own promises. No pastor, no witnesses, just their own young, wildly thumping, doors-flung-open hearts.

Just before he walked back to his groomsmen and friends, Edie said his name, then leaned her head around the door. He cupped her face with his hands and his lips met hers before she could even take a breath.

CHAPTER 43

EDIE

Present Day

She didn't realize she'd fallen asleep in the hospital chair until she woke up. She gazed around the room, getting her bearings, remembering all that had happened in the hours before. She didn't know what had woken her until she saw Thomas stirring in his bed. He didn't wake up, but he shifted to take some of the pressure off his shoulder, which the doctor had told them had sustained a closed fracture, but it wasn't a bad break. After a moment, he rested again, head to the side, his mop of dark curls falling carelessly over his forehead.

On the other side of the room, Avery and Riley were both asleep on the small love seat, their bodies slumped against each other. Mac was in the chair next to her, but his eyes were open and focused on her.

"I told you that night on the porch that you could make your choice. That you could decide what you want to do, with all the facts laid out for you. You're opening your own company, without Graham, but what does that mean for us?"

She propped an elbow on the arm of the chair and rested her cheek in her hand. "When I was at Graham's house, he asked me what I needed, separate from everything and everyone else in my life. He told me I should think about me for a change." Laura Lou, Mac, Avery, Thomas, Riley, her parents. They all bloomed in her mind. "And I tried to. I thought about what I wanted my future to look like. Workwise and"—she swallowed hard—"and otherwise. But what I realized is I can't actually separate myself from everyone else. I can't think of my life apart from you and the kids. You *are* my life, and dividing us all out into individual strands would break apart the whole thing."

The vows they'd said to each other around the door of that bridal suite on their wedding day still floated through her mind. And she thought about what her dad had said in the empty office space the other day.

In all the craziness of their seventeen married years—the chaos and joy, the grief and love, the laughter and the mundane—she'd forgotten the choosing part. That the choice wasn't a onetime thing. That marriage consisted of choosing the one you married over and over and over again.

"Do you remember our wedding day?" she asked. "When we met in the bridal suite?"

"You mean in the hall. You were the one in the bridal suite. I was crouched out in the hallway."

"Right." She laid her hand on the arm of his chair and he covered it with his.

"Of course I remember. Talking to you around that door meant more to me than the entire ceremony."

"Because it was just us."

He nodded. "Our promises to each other. Not to let go."

She glanced around the room again. At the people who filled it. "This is our family," she whispered.

"Looks a little different these days," he said.

"It does, but this is who we are. And I'm choosing you, Mac. I'm choosing us. Again and again."

He sighed and tilted his head up a moment, then leveled his gaze at her. "I choose you, Edie Swan. There's no other for me."

She looked at the man sitting next to her—really took him in. The years had deepened the lines on his face and grayed his hair, just as they had done to her. They'd shown them both heights and depths. They'd brought them children, and then added to their number again when they never could have expected it. And in mere weeks yet another one would be added.

What the years hadn't done was break them apart. Their marriage was work and it was hard. It might always be. But when she looked at Mac, she saw everything she loved. The life they'd built. The truths they'd hidden and then told, the wounds they'd given and received. The forgiveness and grace they'd offered.

She didn't know what would happen when they left the hospital. What changes they'd make, yet again, to accommodate the curveballs life would throw at them. But she knew they'd be okay. They'd take the hurts with the same hands that took the joys, and they'd take them together. The laughter and the pain, the salty and the sweet.

CHAPTER 44

EDIE

Three Months Later

Edie was at the counter jotting down ideas for a client's new master bathroom when Avery entered the kitchen, her hands on her hips. "They're not here yet? It's six thirty."

"She texted a little while ago and said she was running late." Edie set her pencil on top of her sheet of graph paper. "They should be here any minute. Could you fill the glasses with ice for me?"

As Avery pulled glasses from the cabinet and began filling them, Edie gathered her scattered papers and shoved them into the gigantic color-coded binder she was using to keep herself organized as she brought her new business to life. Edie Swan Designs officially opened its doors three weeks ago, but she was still figuring out the business side of operating her own company. It was much more tedious than she'd imagined.

The front door opened and slammed shut, rattling the plates hanging on the dining room wall. Edie called out, "Thomas, don't slam the door!"

"Sorry, Mom," Thomas said when he made it to the kitchen, a streak of dirt on his cheek and his hair in more disarray than usual. "They're late." He plopped down on a stool at the island. "Where are they?"

"On their way. Did you and Reston decide on a science fair project?"

"Yup. We're testing the effects of music on plant growth."

"Really?" Avery asked from the fridge. "That's kind of fun."

"Yeah," Thomas said. "Reston thinks classical music will work best, but I'm going with Johnny Cash."

Avery laughed. "Seriously?"

"Sure. Why not?"

Just as the timer on the oven beeped, Mac opened the back door, letting in a rush of chilly air. Edie jammed the binder back into her tote bag, but before she could move toward the oven, he held up a hand to stop her.

"I'm on it." He dodged Avery as she set an ice-filled glass on the counter, sheathed his hand in an oven mitt, and pulled the pork tenderloin from the oven. The scents of honey and spices poured from the open door.

Mac groaned as he set the baking sheet down on the stovetop. "Babe, it smells delicious. I've been looking forward to this all day." He returned to the oven and pulled out the second pan of roasted vegetables.

"Does Riley like pork tenderloin?" Thomas leaned over the meat and sniffed. Avery sat next to him.

"She'll love it," Mac said. "She told me anything would be better than the cereal she'd most likely be having on her own."

Edie hung her bag on the pantry door. "Do you remember when we used to have cereal for dinner?"

"Of course I do." Mac grinned. "That was back in the good old days. You, me, a box of Cheerios, a little candlelight. No kids, no responsibilities . . ." He turned and grabbed her by the waist, pulling her in tight.

"Well, except for your patients." She took the mitt out of his hand and swatted his rear with it. "Your burgeoning medical career. My few-and-far-between clients at Teak & Twill."

"Those were the days, weren't they?" He leaned down, slowly enough to make her stomach clench in anticipation, and softly pressed his lips to hers. Behind him, Avery put her head in her hands. "Oh my gosh," she muttered. On the stool next to her, Thomas made gagging noises.

"Oh, please forgive me," Mac said to them with faux politeness. "I forgot you were here. I was lost in rapturous thought over the days when you two were barely a speck in our imaginations."

"Dad!" Avery spouted, aghast.

"Kidding." He grabbed the mitt back from Edie and swatted her leg. "We're kidding, right?"

"Yes. We had a wonderful life before the two of you came along, but we just didn't know what we were missing. Once we had you, that's when the real fun began."

"I thought Thomas had colic when he was a baby." Avery poked her brother in the side.

"Oh, he did. I averaged about twelve hours of sleep a week for his first year." Edie walked around the island and wrapped her arms around Thomas. He squirmed but she held tight. "I was an exhausted shell of a human, but we were a little family." When she straightened, Mac was watching her, one cheek lifted up into a lopsided smile.

Finally Thomas wriggled out of her arms and stood. "I'm going to wait up front." He snagged a stalk of asparagus off the baking sheet and darted toward the front door.

"Thomas," Avery groaned. "He's going to make Riley feel bad for being late."

"I think she'll be okay. He just can't wait to hold the baby."

"I can't either." Avery hesitated, then stood. "Okay, I'm going to wait with him."

Mac tucked aluminum foil over the meat and vegetables, then sat next to Edie, angling his stool so he faced her. "Hi."

"Hi, yourself."

Their knees bumped together as he took her hands and wrapped them in both of his. Warmth from his skin seeped into her. "How was your day?"

"It was good. Marigold sent another friend to me."

"Fantastic. What does this one need? A new walk-in closet? A she-shed?"

Edie laughed. Marigold had directed a handful of girlfriends to her, all with pressing house reno projects. All with seemingly endless budgets. "No, nothing like that. This one is a whole kitchen. Emerald-green cabinets. It's going to be a lot of fun."

"Your first kitchen. That's a big deal."

"I've done dozens of kitchens. You know that."

"Yeah, but it'll be the first with your name on it. Yours alone."

"I guess it is a pretty big deal." She smiled. "What about your day? How was the clinic?"

"It was long but good. I had a ton of patients. These kids are just . . ."

"What?"

"It just feels different, you know? I love my practice and I love my regular patients, but it's humbling to be able to provide a service for kids who otherwise might not be seeing a doctor." He kneaded his knuckles on the top of her thigh. "I'm just thankful Cynthia thought to ask me about it."

"What does Mrs. Kimble think?"

"She's worried, of course. Worried I'll stop coming into the office and see patients solely at the clinic. I told her if I did that, I'd take her with me."

"Is that something you'd ever consider? Working at the clinic full time?"

"I don't know. For now, the Tuesdays and Fridays are working pretty well."

"I'm glad the change has been good. It's been good for both of us. Who knew last summer that we'd be here now, with our jobs looking so different?"

"Not just the jobs. Everything."

She nodded. "You're right. Everything."

He leaned toward her. "The work is fine, but I'm happy because of you."

She met him in the space between and kissed him.

Just then a clamor came from the foyer. "She's here!" Thomas yelled as he threw open the front door.

"Thomas, you'll scare the baby!" Avery screeched, following Thomas out the door.

Edie laughed and leaned her forehead against Mac's.

"Let's go," he whispered before he stood and pulled her up next to him. "Let's get the kids in here."

A moment later the kitchen was full of life and movement. Thomas lumbered under the weight of Riley's massive diaper bag, and Avery carried the pumpkin seat on her arm like a pro. Riley held her two-month-old in her arms, a bundle of pink and white on her shoulder.

"Can I hold her?" Thomas dropped the bag on the floor and peeked around Riley's elbow.

"You got her first last time," Avery countered.

"All right, everyone back off a bit." Edie reached into the huddle and gave Riley a hug. "Are you hungry?"

"Starving." She smiled, her face awash in the typical new-mom flush of exhaustion and happiness. "Sorry I'm late. We had a diaper situation just as I was leaving work. Both Cynthia and Charlie had to help me. I needed all the hands to get her cleaned up."

"Gross." Thomas shuddered.

"It's just part of having a baby." Mac gently took the baby from Riley's arms. "Hello, little Katherine," he whispered. He reached back and grabbed a glass of tea and handed it to Riley. "Thomas, you once filled your car seat with so much yuck, I almost cried. Your mom was out of town."

"I remember that," Edie said. "You called me in such a panic."

"What'd you tell him?" Riley asked her as she eased down into a kitchen chair.

"There wasn't much I could do over the phone. I gave him a few pointers on how to clean the seat, but instead he went out and bought a new one."

"Seriously?" Thomas asked. "You couldn't just clean it up?"

Mac propped Katherine expertly on his shoulder and began setting glasses on the table with the other. "I tell you what, kiddo. Next time Katherine has a dirty diaper, we'll let you take care of it."

"Oh no," Thomas said. "I'm too young for that."

"Riley, how's the house?" Edie asked. "Did your landlord fix the windows?"

Cynthia and Fitz had set Riley up in a duplex not far from their home in Oakleigh. The house was owned by a doctor Fitz used to work with. He'd offered to let Riley stay there free of charge for the first month to help her get on her feet. Now she was paying the rent with her income from working at the women's center plus grocery shopping and running errands for the doctor's elderly aunt who lived in the other half of the duplex.

"Yes, finally. A guy came a couple days ago and put up new wood around them. I said I'd take care of painting the trim though."

"By yourself?" Mac asked. "Those are tall windows. I'd be happy to come do it for you. Or at least help."

"It's okay," Riley said. "Charlie said—I mean, Dr. Pine said he'd come help me next weekend."

"I bet Dr. Pine would be more than happy to help you paint your window trim," Mac said with a smile. "I'll be sure to have a little chat with him about it on Tuesday."

"He's just a friend," Riley said. "He loves babies and he loves a house project." Her words were firm, but when Edie glanced at her, the flush on her cheeks was obvious.

As Edie filled plates and handed them out, Riley set the pitcher of tea on the table and handed a bottle and burp cloth to Mac. "Do you mind?"

"I thought you'd never ask." Mac took the bottle, cloth, and baby to the chair in the corner of the dining room. Once settled, he crossed his legs and propped Katherine into the crook of his knee. "It's you and me, little girl," he said quietly.

After dinner, Thomas and Avery helped Mac clean up the kitchen while Edie and Riley sat on the back porch. Edie held a dozing Katherine in her arms, breathing in her delicious baby scent. "Poor thing doesn't get much rest while she's at our house. She just gets passed from one set of arms to another."

Riley leaned her head back on the couch cushion and closed her eyes. "She loves it."

"Are you doing okay?" Edie asked. "You seem pretty tired."

"I'm always tired." Riley gave a half smile. "They tell me it's normal."

"Oh, it is. I think we're tired until our kids leave the house. Then we'll probably just want them safe under our roof again." Edie reached for the blanket on the back of her chair and draped it over her legs. March had so far refused to give much in the way of spring. "Things are okay otherwise though?"

Riley lifted her head from the cushion. "I guess so. I mean, it's hard. Having a baby is really hard. But it's kind of good too. You know?"

Edie nodded. "I do. Have you heard from Dex lately?"

"Yeah. He wants to see Katherine, but he doesn't want to do the dad thing. I knew he wouldn't. He just wants to see her." She passed a hand over her face. "And he said he'd send me some money."

"Well, that's good news. If you don't want to meet him alone, one of us can go with you."

"Thanks. I'll let you know."

Edie couldn't deny there had been some growing pains in the process of bringing Riley into the fold of their lives. Introducing her to their parents had been interesting, especially with Mac's hard, stoic father. And they'd had to learn when they could give Riley a firm suggestion and when they needed to step back and let her make her own decisions. But overall, the process had been peaceful. Riley and Katherine came over for dinner most Friday nights, Edie checked in with her during the week, and Mac saw her at the clinic every Tuesday and Friday. Mac was still just Mac to her though. She referred to him as her father, but she hadn't called him Dad. And that was okay.

Edie and Riley had developed an interesting relationship. It definitely wasn't a mother-daughter dynamic, but it was much more than a simple friendship. They were caught somewhere between friends, sisters, and strangers, entangled in a web of mutual love, affection, and the particular kind of heartache only mothers could feel.

The two women sat on the darkened porch, the only illumination coming from the light spilling out of the kitchen window. Their conversation was slow and easy, unhurried and comfortable, and inside Edie marveled at how change could feel as jarring as a lightning bolt yet as natural as breathing.

When it was time for Riley and Katherine to leave, the four of them gathered in the driveway to see them off. Mac kissed and nuzzled Katherine's soft head before he settled her into her seat. She only stirred when Thomas leaned in and kissed her plump cheek.

Mac put his arm around Edie, and as they waited for Riley to back out of the driveway, their cat sauntered over and wound around their legs. When Riley pulled onto the street, they waved until she turned off Linden Avenue and toward the direction of her own home.

Edie and Mac trailed back toward their house behind Thomas and Avery, who were talking, their heads uncommonly close in conversation. A moment later Thomas said something that pulled a burst of laughter from Avery. She reached over and pinched his shoulder, and of course, he pushed her hand away, the moment gone.

As they flung open the front door and tromped toward the kitchen, probably in search of more dessert, Edie paused on the porch. A cold wind blew down their street, rustling the leaves in the trees and the hem of her shirt. Mac turned back in the doorway, the warm glow from inside coating his head and shoulders, his brow quirked up in question.

She tucked her hair behind her ear. "Everything's just stretched to fit, hasn't it? Our life. It stretched open."

Mac glanced over his shoulder toward the kids making a racket in the kitchen, then back at Edie. "It has. We've gone from four to six. And quickly." He shrugged, a half smile on his face. "It's not perfect but . . . it kind of is."

Kind of perfect. It sounded a lot like them.

She smiled back at him and he held his hand out. She took it and he kissed her, then pulled her inside.

ACKNOWLEDGMENTS

To my brilliant editor Kimberly Carlton, thank you for asking me so many questions about this story, which in turn made me dig much deeper into my characters and pushed me to go further than I thought I could. That's the sign of a great editor, and I'm so glad you're mine! Thank you to my whole publishing family at Thomas Nelson, including Amanda Bostic, Matt Bray, Jodi Hughes, Margaret Kercher, Becky Monds, Kerri Potts, Nekasha Pratt, Savannah Summers, Marcee Wardell, and Laura Wheeler. Thank you to Julee Schwarzburg for your sharp line-editing skills and for helping me fine-tune my writing every time we work together. Thank you to the sales team for your efforts to get our books into the hands of readers everywhere!

Thank you to my agent, Karen Solem, for always being up for a brainstorming session, for helping me work through plot holes and character wrinkles, and for being a calm, honest, wise voice when I need it. Thank you to my friends Anna Gresham, Holly Mackle, and Lindsey Brackett for the Voxer chats, life coaching, and beta reading. You all helped make this story (and me) better, and I'm so thankful for our friendships. Thank you to the ladies of Tea & Empathy for the support and camaraderie. Thanks to our pediatrician Dr. Jennifer McCain for answering questions about a pediatric practice and to Michael Daniell for information about working at a beachside marina.

Acknowledgments

Thank you to Matt, Kate, and Sela for putting up with me doing this writing thing and sometimes shutting myself away with the computer. I love the three of you so very much, and I'm thankful I can share this with you. Thank you to my parents, Randy and Kaye Koffler, for your constant love and support, and to Joe and Charlotte Denton for loving me like I'm your own.

Thank you to all the book people out there who tell others about what you read, whether through plain old conversation, social media, or a book blog. We authors appreciate your work so very much. One of the best parts of this "job" is hearing when a new reader discovers my books. So thank you to everyone who helps spread the word! And for my loyal (and new!) readers, my constant prayer is that my books can be a source of comfort, hope, humor, and encouragement. I'm already working on my next one for you!

Discussion Questions

1. Did you have a favorite character in the story? One who lit up the page or who you empathized with the most? Was there a character you didn't like?

2. In her opening chapter, Edie ponders the different path her life could have taken if she'd gone to design school in New Orleans instead of attending Southern College with Mac. Has there been a time when you've looked back at a pivotal decision and wondered what life could have looked like if you'd made a different choice?

3. When Edie's sister Blanche takes a photo with Edie and their mom, Edie wonders about the falsehood of social media—the difference between a polished life online and reality. Have you had a situation where you've assumed one thing based on what you saw on social media only to find out the truth was very different?

4. Dr. Abraham Fitzgerald is Mac's mentor, for both his personal and professional life. Have you had someone like that in your life?

5. Have you ever had to take a leap of faith—in your job, in a relationship, or something else—in the hopes of finding more freedom or opportunity?

6. What did you think about how Mac, Edie, and Graham each handled the shock and stress of all the new revelations in their

lives? Have you ever had to deal with a secret from the past that was kept from you, either on purpose or by accident?

7. What did you think about Graham? Did you think he had an ulterior motive for asking Edie to go into business with him? And do you think there's truth to Edie's friend Judith's comment about it being hard to remain "just friends" with someone after a certain age?

8. After learning about Riley, Edie wonders if she'd rather have remained blissfully ignorant of Mac's secret, or if she would rather know the truth, even though it changed everything. If you were in a similar position, do you think you'd rather know the truth, no matter how ugly, or remain happily in the dark?

9. What do you think of the title in regard to what happens in the story? Can you think of another title that would have worked well?

10. Where do you see life taking each of the characters after the book ends? Do you like endings that tell you how everything works out, or do you like open endings?

Neither Lily nor Rose is where she expected
to be, but the summer makes them both
wonder if there's more to life and love
than what they've experienced so far.

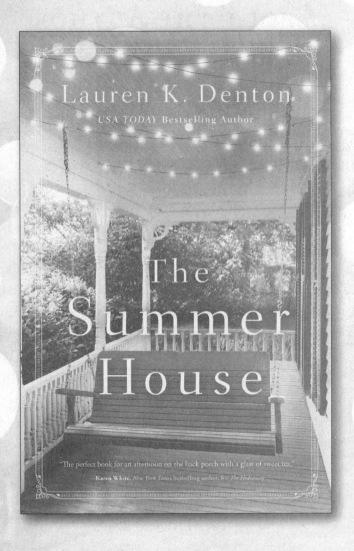

About the Author

Photo by Angie Davis

Lauren K. Denton is the author of the *USA TODAY* bestselling novels *The Hideaway* and *Hurricane Season*. She was born and raised in Mobile, Alabama, and now lives with her husband and two daughters in Homewood, just outside Birmingham. Though her husband tries valiantly to turn her into a mountain girl, she'd still rather be at the beach.

LaurenKDenton.com
Instagram: @LaurenKDentonBooks
Facebook: @LaurenKDentonAuthor
Twitter: @LaurenKDenton
Pinterest: @LKDentonBooks